Andrew McCoy was born  the University of Steller business he embarked on then he has been a croco industrial intelligence con in South America, a transatlantic racing yachtsman and a political organizer.

By the same author

ANDREW McCOY

Lance of God

GRAFTON BOOKS

A Division of the Collins Publishing Group

LONDON GLASGOW
TORONTO SYDNEY AUCKLAND

Grafton Books
A Division of the Collins Publishing Group
8 Grafton Street, London W1X 3LA

Published by Grafton Books 1989

First published in Great Britain by
Martin Secker & Warburg Ltd 1987

ISBN 0-586-20357-5

Printed and bound in Great Britain by
Collins, Glasgow

Set in Ehrhardt

The Good and
the Hungry

Any sky could be that innocently blue only over a desert.

'Where?' She stooped between the pilots to see more of the sky through the windshield and screwed up her eyes but saw nothing except azure so pure it pained her even through photosensitive glass turned almost chocolate by the blue brilliance.

'There.' Tanner pointed.

The two specks jumped out of the horizon at her. She shivered in the hot air rushing through the open window beside her head.

'Libyan MiGs.'

'How do you know?' She regretted snapping at him but she couldn't help it. Even twenty-twenty vision could not distinguish insignia on two pinheads in the sky.

'Who else flies jet fighters here?'

'Perhaps they have other business.'

Tanner merely shook his head. She noticed his hands were perfectly steady on the controls. Perhaps it mattered. The co-pilot, Paul, a boy hardly into his twenties, giggled nervously.

'Belt yourself into the navigator's seat,' Tanner told her.

The jets swooped to buzz the lumbering transport from straight ahead until they could see the flame within driving the MiGs' jets, peeling off left and right only feet from impact. Tanner held the transport steady. 'I'm not playing chicken with you hotshots,' he said conversationally.

The co-pilot giggled again. 'Did you see the corrosion pits in the ali? Buggers don't look after their planes.'

'That's the stuff, Paul. Check the radio.'

'Shall I tell them you notched up eleven Arab MiGs?'

'I hope you're joking, pal. Just find their channel.'

'You reckon, if they find out you're an Israeli ace, they're more likely to shoot us down?'

'I know it.' Tanner looked at the co-pilot. He was thirty-three, only ten years older than the co-pilot, but he could not even pretend to understand the younger man. Enough that the giggle wasn't fear. 'Are you belted up, Christine?' He couldn't look back because the two MiGs were heading at him again, wingtips less than ten feet apart.

'Yes.'

'They are either bloody brilliant or incredibly stupid,' Paul said. 'That's them.' He fine-tuned the radio.

The two Libyan pilots laughed like children on a switch-back.

Paul offered the microphone but Tanner said, 'Not now. They're not listening yet.' The young co-pilot watched with interest as Tanner's hands made small, slow corrections on the controls; now he would see the stuffing inside an ace. He was not disappointed that Tanner did not start sweating, but he was entitled at least to a whitening of the knuckles and felt cheated when the chief pilot's grip remained loose and confident as he righted the big plane in the bucketing wake of the two MiGs scraping by on either side of the transport's nose and then close over the wings, turning laminar airflow into tornados of turbulence.

'Relax, Junior, I'm not going to do anything dumb like throwing an Immelmann,' Tanner said drily. Young Paul would make a fine pilot: he understood he could do nothing about the Libyans – that his fate now rested in the hands of the pilot-in-command – and he concentrated his attention at the point where he could learn most. 'Give me the mike. They've had their fun.'

The Libyans flew at the transport's wingtips. One still giggled, the other snapped their orders. 'Down.'

'They're high on something!' Paul was more shocked by an unprofessional addiction than the attack.

'On Islam,' Christine said. 'Fanatics.'

'You're way out of your playpen,' Tanner said into the mike, turning his head to watch the MiGs at his wingtips. 'This is Chad airspace.'

'Down.'

'This is a British-registered plane. We filed a flight plan at – '

'Down.'

'We are carrying grain for the hungry. The International Red – '

'*Down!*'

'Those boyos aren't laughing any more,' Paul said judiciously.

'Listen, you're pilots. You must speak more English than "Down", hmm?'

'Down.'

'Down!'

'They both speak,' Paul said.

'Shut up,' Tanner told him. 'Watch that one.'

The two Libyan pilots turned up and away in a tight climbing curve to each side.

'Shall I search for their command channel?'

'No. They either use telepathy or they speak Arabic. Can you see yours?'

'No. Those mothers are armed with rockets.'

'I saw. They won't use them yet.' He wished he could feel as certain as he sounded.

The tracers past the Perspex hardly registered on his mind before the MiGs followed, their tails seeming to slam down

9

on the transport's cockpit. Instinctively, Tanner pushed the column forward to drop the plane's nose.

'Down.'

'Down.'

'Down, down, down, down.'

'Down, down, down, down.'

The Libyans settled at the transport's wingtips again, shepherding the lumbering relief plane down, ever downwards.

'Okay, okay, we're going down,' Tanner said soothingly into the mike. He let the button go. 'They should be on the hit parade.'

'Can you outrun them down near the ground?' Christine asked.

Paul, surprised to hear no fear in her voice, turned around in his seat to look at her. 'They carry heat-seeking missiles.'

Christine held her ground. 'That desert down there is nothing but a large heatsink.'

'It's too flat,' Tanner said, 'and this plane is too big and unwieldy.'

At three hundred feet he levelled out.

'*Down!*' the Libyans screamed at him in unison.

At one hundred feet he levelled out once more.

'*Down!*'

'Don't get hysterical,' Tanner muttered. His hand on the throttles slid them ever so slowly while he tipped the nose slightly, just enough to lose height perceptibly. There was not much left to play with.

'Stall, you bastards,' Paul breathed at the Libyans. He found he was digging his fingernails into his palms and blushed.

But the Libyan pilots, already throttled back nearly to stall-point to keep pace, refused to slow any further. They peeled away again and, almost immediately, the transport shuddered

10

as the two fighters swivelled out of a high-Mach turn and raked its unprotected back with bullets.

'Shit!' said Paul. 'They mean business.'

'Landing gear. Flaps.' Tanner could have been ordering a beer.

'Right.' Paul tried for the same level, unemotional tone.

'You can't land yet.' Christine raised her voice over the increased wind noise. 'My people are at least a hundred miles that way.'

'Landing gear down and locked. Flaps down.'

'People are dying of hunger,' Christine shouted. 'Our grain is their only chance to live!'

'Quiet, please,' Tanner said. 'Hold on now.' He was too experienced to attempt putting an overloaded plane down gently on an unmade surface. What appeared a perfectly flat plateau from three thousand feet, from here looked frighteningly rough, with humps and mounds under the tough-looking grass that stood just tall enough to get tangled in the landing gear and pull the speeding plane over on its nose. He turned his head quickly from side to side. He couldn't see the MiGs. They were on his tail again. But he could hear them.

'Down, down, down, down.'

'Down, down, down, down.'

'When they retire from flying, they can make advertising jingles,' Tanner said but nobody heard him because just then he put her down hard and square – young Paul, his eyes riveted to the airspeed indicator, fearing they would stall and fall those critical feet like a stone, thought Tanner had misjudged, stalled the plane, and was leadenly and awkwardly breaking its back. Before he could react – before he could think anything but a flash of his mother gathering toys on a path with a small patch of manicured lawn on either side – the plane was down and rolling through the grass . . .

'Don't touch the brakes,' Tanner told Paul, fearing the co-pilot would panic.

. . . and Paul grinned at him and gestured at the switches and Tanner nodded and hit the ignition switches himself. With his hands busy, Paul felt better.

The long grass, called elephant grass though no elephant had wandered there for six or seven decades, wound about the whirling wheels and brake discs and was brutally torn off between the stub-axle and the wheelhousing. Fortunately the build-up was equal on both sides, otherwise the plane would have turned to one side or the other and, as aeroplanes have centres of gravity much too elevated for high lateral accelerations on the ground, would have fallen over on its side. When the grass had built up enough to cause a disaster, again, fortunately, equally on both sides, the plane rolled at no more than fifteen knots.

Disasters are relative. If the landing had been forced by malfunction, it need not have been more than an expensive misfortune. The presence of the MiGs made all the difference.

The wheels locked on the accumulated grass and the aircraft, still travelling at fifteen knots, could not stop. It fell on its nose with the characteristic crunch of thin sheets of aluminium crumpling. The deceleration tightened their harnesses bruisingly around them, their bodies jerked with the gravity of the sudden braking; perhaps days or weeks were cut from their lifespans by a few braincells destroyed concussively.

Thank god it's not worse, Tanner thought. The heat of the desert, now no longer fanned by the passage of the plane, struck him and he felt the first sweat form in his armpits. He scanned the switches: Paul had tripped them all.

'Everybody out!' Tanner said, jerking his harness free and levering himself out of his seat against the downward slope of the cockpit. Bracing himself with his knees between the seat and the cockpit side, he folded the map he had been using and stuck it into his belt at the back. From his flight bag he took a compass and a pencil, and shoved them into the pocket of his slacks; he also pulled out the twin of his own long-vizored baseball cap – though a lot more oily – and threw that on Christine's lap. He saw Paul taking his proudest possession, his pilot's logbook. 'By tomorrow night that logbook will weigh a ton. Leave it.'

'But – '

'Leave it! Bring a compass if you got one, a pencil, a map, a pocketknife, any string you find.' Paul stared at him open-mouthed. 'Move!' Tanner turned to Christine, who held the oily cap between two fingertips and stared at it with growing revulsion. 'Are you all right, Christine?' He propelled himself across the crazily tilted cabin by such handholds as he could find. Out of the corner of his eye he saw the MiGs pull out of a dive and burn off into the sky, upwards and to each side. He gripped her shoulder. 'Come on! We have to get out of here!'

'What about the grain for – '

Tanner tightened his fingers cruelly into the tendon of her shoulder. 'Do you want to burn with it?'

'Burn? But we landed! We did exactly what they wanted!'

Tanner unsnapped her harness, took the cap from her fingers and pulled it onto her head, then jerked her erect by her shoulder. He pushed her through the door into the cargo hold, then held onto the door-frame with one hand while with the other he took three of the five water bottles from the hook on the bulkhead. 'Bring the other two,' he told Paul.

'We don't have any food.'

'Those MiGs are coming back, sport.'

Paul cocked his head. His smile seemed to ask, If they're going to shoot us up, why force us down first? Then he heard the airscream of the two jets diving at subsonic speed and scrambled for the bulkhead and its water bottles.

'Don't forget the penknife and the string,' Tanner reminded him and went through the door.

Christine stood contemplating the bags of grain stacked behind nets to leave only a narrow passage down the middle of the transport. In passing, Tanner grabbed an unused eight-foot square of the lightweight netting: it would be useful for trapping animals, though they would die of thirst before hunger disabled them. He swung the lever and kicked the door open and looked thirty feet down to the grass. It was the angle of the plane . . .

'Soft landings,' he said, and pushed Christine out. Without waiting to see if she fell neatly, he flung the water bottles as far as he could. He could see the MiGs now.

The two Libyans no longer flew side by side, as if at some air show-off, but one behind the other, so that each would in turn be able to line up his weapons on the stricken transport.

Bastards! 'Paul!' He turned to hurry the co-pilot and bumped into him.

'I got the – '

Tanner threw him physically through the hatch, then jumped himself. Even as he fell, he could hear the MiGs closing: for them, lazily; for him, much too fast.

The sand, held together by the roots of the elephant grass, was harder than any sand had a right to be. The concussion rammed right through him, jarring his teeth, even though he had timed the flexure of his knees to coincide perfectly with his landing. He rolled, over and up, in the same motion and second as he landed.

Christine shouted at the diving MiGs, her words drowned in their malicious, closing, proximity. So was Tanner's 'Run!' Paul had fallen on the two water bottles around his neck and winded himself. Tanner scooped the co-pilot up on the run and flung him over his shoulder, ignoring the 'oomph' transmitted from body to body as the rough handling blew the precious newly regained breath from Paul's body. He also shoved Christine with Paul's body, merely because Paul was on the shoulder most convenient for the job – there was no time for tender courtesies to the wounded and the walking shell-shocked. In one enraged bull-rush, he shoved her as far as the water bottles he had thrown, scooped up the bottles and grabbed her elbow to drag her away with him. Over the scream of aircraft diving – a distinct, much more terrifying sound than their jets working – he distinguished the release of the rockets, a soft *whoosh* of awesome finality. Heat-seeking rockets fired at this range could not fail to annihilate a stationary target.

His breath cut through him like a red-hot chainsaw but there was nowhere to run to, nothing to shelter behind on that featureless plateau except the plane and that was the target. But still, the organism would not admit defeat and he stumbled on – and over an anthill no higher than his knees, bringing Christine, whom he still dragged along by the elbow, down with him and Paul just as the first two rockets struck the grounded plane. Tanner had no energy to cover his ears. He just lay there, on top of Paul and half on top of Christine, trying to breathe, seeing the anthill in front of them quiver with the outrage of the desecrated desert. The second pair of rockets struck as true as the first but Tanner, as a professional ex-fighter pilot in a force that had to count its pennies, felt nothing but contempt for a pilot who would use half a million dollarsworth of armament on an already destroyed target merely to gain a shared kill.

Christine pushed him off and, instead of brushing the bits of burning metal from her, danced around, shaking her fist at the circling MiGs. Tanner's ears were in no state to hear what she shouted but he was in no doubt she was putting God's curse on them. He groaned and rolled off the heaving Paul to lie on his back and stare at that guilty sky. He had hoped the Libyan pilots, their eyes riveted to the target, would not see them make their escape, would assume they were killed in the destroyed plane. But, he now realized, if the Libyans intended to kill them, why first force the plane to land? It didn't make sense. The only sense was that the Libyans wanted them alive.

Oh, shit!

The Hunger had already reduced them to father, mother, daughter and baby. There had been three other children between the eldest and the youngest but two died of the Hunger before they left the village of the famished and the famishing to walk to where the rumours said good people were giving grain to hungry people; another brother they had buried this morning after he died in the night of an empty stomach. They had no energy for sorrow; they had seen too much death in the years since the first drought forced them to eat the seedcorn. Not that they were dulled by a surfeit of death, rather that each plodding, painful step towards food, each day survived, each fieldmouse caught and shared with the family after the baby was fed the hot liver, was a triumphant monument to the dead. Also, in their religion, the dead joined the ancestors to live in a paradise without hunger. Yet they did not want to die. They wanted desperately to live.

When the father saw the column of smoke, he did not speak or point. These things took energy and he had learned under the hardest taskmaster of all, Hunger, to conserve his strength. He stopped and stood looking and the daughter and the mother with the baby at her hip also stopped and turned their eyes and then, hope dawning, their whole heads to the

16

column of smoke rising still and straight in that motionless desert heat.

Smoke. People.

People would, in these parts, very likely kill them quickly. Or people would feed them without asking any questions. It had never occurred to the father, who could write his name and was therefore a man of relative education, that people should not reflect the harshness of a cruel habitat: the very possibility was outside his experience, even his dreams. He did not completely believe that white people would be at their destination, giving away grain so that others could live, and what little faith he had in this proposition derived from the general knowledge, current even in his village of dead and dying souls, that lightskinned people behaved strangely, but they were here mostly because of his wife's faith that it was true – she had spent three years in the Christian mission school before the imam had found out and told her parents they were committing a sin; she *knew* how very strangely such people behave. On that slender hope they had set out: walking to a destination, even a false rumour, was better than sitting fatalistically awaiting death. *That* was not his ancestors' way, nor his.

(Neither he nor his wife nor his daughter had ever even *thought* of eating the dead. That too was not in their lexicon.)

He stood before the column of smoke a long time, not thinking, just standing, hardly seeing it. Behind him his family stood equally still. The numbness of hunger knows the patience of perpetuity; forever is not timebound. When the head of their house turned slightly from the course they had trudged, one step at a time, since before dawn, they followed him without question. Whoever was at the fire would feed them or kill them. In an hour, not hurrying because they no longer had the strength of urgency, they reached the crushed, still smouldering plane.

They met no one there. They had heard or seen no other people but grass flattened by the rotors of a helicopter was still straightening with the infinite slowness of interval photography: they were not curious about this never-before-seen phenomenon, and did not speculate about what wondrous, never-before machine could have created it. Nor did they speculate about the footsteps and sign on the ground. Even the shattered yet still huge aeroplane close by failed to evoke wonder in people who had until then seen aircraft only over-flying their village at 5000 feet.

They were hungry. In their world there was nothing except Hunger. And lying on the ground among the wreckage of the plane was grain. God was merciful.

They had the rags they stood up in, their ruined lives, and the small black cast-iron pot the mother carried on her head. The father started a fire with a glowing piece of metal as its first coal, the mother put the baby down gently on a space she cleared with her hands, and then picked up grain for their first meal in three days. The baby seemed to sense that satiation was near and stopped crying, the daughter in an hour caught seven of the grassmice gathering grains of wheat from the heaps lying in still-smouldering shreds of hessian. Towards evening the father tied a piece of metal to each end of a section of thin copper wire salvaged from the plane and threw it to decapitate an impertinent crow. They held the bleeding neckstump over the baby's mouth; the baby gurgled and giggled and laughed. After dark, when it was cooler, they dug for water and found a trickle in the bottom of the hole. They feasted there for nine days, until the water stopped trickling, then filled the black pot for the last time and continued their odyssey to where rumour had the strangers giving away grain.

(It never occurred to them that they had been partaking of the grain from foreign lands the rumour spoke of, that others, responding to the same rumour, who had arrived at the distribution point before them, would die of hunger because the Libyans had destroyed the relief plane. Better that way for their consciences. Or perhaps any connection between their good luck and the hungry despairing deaths of the other refugees is entirely artificial.)

They were the only refugees to eat of the grain Christine Rawls brought on that first test-flight into Chad. After they left, the birds and small animals which abound almost invisibly in the desert had a field day, which might have consoled her a little, had she known: Christine had once, before the famine, been a campaigner for wildlife conservation. But again, so many human lives wasted for so many animal lives saved? No, even Christine, who had been fanatical to save the animals, would not consider that a fair exchange – most of us would shudder at the very idea: at best, bad taste.

Anywhere else, I would not mention this, but in Africa life is a relative matter and this is a story of relativity, though perhaps not all the characters understood that at the time and, of those who survived, at least one would never accept it. That too is human: it is a rare man who, with a rifle in his hand, heeds the warning that a bullet can kill him as easily as anyone else; a Harley Street cancer specialist told me that, of all those he informs they are terminally ill, physicians take the news least stoically.

After this I will not again intrude the person of the narrator. But it is important that you know I put this story together from what participants told me and from what I could guess; I know the area and the people a little. This isn't a god-view: I don't know everything. For instance, who the devil knows what motivates Muamur Qaddaffi? On second thoughts, considering that example, *I don't want to know everything.* I already have my own visions of hell.

On the eighteenth day after the relief plane was forced down and destroyed, the Libyans released Christine into the care of the Italian diplomat who looked after the affairs of Britons in Qaddaffi's Islamic paradise, the British having broken off diplomatic relations after the Libyans murdered WPC Yvonne Fletcher at the siege of the Libyan Embassy in London.

Christine had been captured, with Tanner and Paul, on the second day after the incident, when they walked into the middle of strategic exercises by troops the Libyans were training for Goukouni Queddei, who occupies northern Chad, with the support of Libyan forces, in defiance of Hissein Habre's Transitional Government of National Unity.

Tanner and Paul were beaten and Christine was raped.

Worst of all for Christine, she saw the camps in which the refugees were starving, she saw the gaunt men and women, she saw the distended bellies of the children and the dull acceptance of death already in their eyes, she saw the ever-growing heaps of dead with the gorged vultures stolidly picking and choosing among the new arrivals, but there was nothing she could do. The grain she wanted to feed them was scattered among the ruins of Tanner's plane. Queddei's army and his Libyan cohorts ate well enough and ill-treatment of their white prisoners did not include withholding food from them but Christine refused to eat and, after Queddei handed the prisoners over to the Libyans and they reached Tripoli, they force-fed Christine.

The Libyans let Christine go 'as a goodwill gesture and because she's just a woman' and, Tanner quipped when she was allowed to see him for fifteen minutes before being given over to the Italians, 'because they don't want the emissaries back'. They kept Tanner and Paul because they were 'terror-fliers in the pay of the CIA' whom they intended to return to Chad for a 'people's trial' at some unspecified time. This last Christine heard from the Italian, after she told him and his wife and their two maids to stop fussing so: she had been raped and that was that and all the fuss in the world would not undo the damage.

In Rome, at the British Embassy, she blew up when they insisted on a medical examination. She walked out into the street, took a taxi to Fiumicino and a plane to London. At Heathrow she made no effort to avoid the press; they had always been her best allies in the fight against hunger. Even so, she was surprised at the swarm of shouting journalists who pressed close around her, jostling to put their microphones near her face. She felt a moment of claustrophobic fear and froze stock-still. The sound level did not fall but the journalists, like some insensate mass organism, somehow divined that she would not run or clam up, that she would give them the sensation they craved. They still jostled each other frantically for advantage but left around Christine a full six inches of space. Luxury, no, power, she thought. Please god, let me use it right, to help the hungry ones most effectively.

'It was horrible,' Christine said in her normal speaking voice. Instantly the hubbub died down, then started again as they shouted at her to speak up, to repeat herself. 'It was horrible,' she said again in the same tone. This time they understood the message and shut up. She knew they would tape her answers and dub in their own questions later. She said, pausing a half-second between sentences, 'We were flying grain to starving people in northern Chad. We had no other purpose than to feed the starving; the Matthew Ellimore Foundation of London W1 is a non-political charity. Our grain-laden transport was shot down in the middle of the

21

desert in Chad by two Russian MiG fighters flown by pilots of Colonel Qaddaffi's Libyan Air Force. We were not armed, we were on a humanitarian mission. The two pilots, Tanner Chapman and Paul Hasluck, and I were then captured by Libyan-supported rebels. The two pilots were beaten. I was raped. I don't want to say anything more about that horrible episode, except that, to feed the millions of starving people isolated from the relief agencies by the Libyans and their evil allies for purely political and ideological reasons, I would gladly go through it again. I shall now work to raise more money for the starving people of Chad, I shall work to move the food to the starving as quickly as possible, and I shall work for the release of two brave and compassionate pilots from that cruel Libyan gaol.'

'You're going *back*?' a woman at her elbow asked incredulously.

'Damn right I'm going back. Didn't you *hear* what I just said? I saw hundreds of thousands of people starving. How can I not go back to feed them as long as I breathe?'

'But the Lib – '

'I don't blame the Libyan people. But I will not be deterred from my sacred duty, from everyone's sacred duty, by that insane gangster Qaddaffi.'

'But Colonel Qaddaffi has arranged for the Russians to give thirty thousand tons of wheat for famine relief in Chad, wheat which is even now on the dock in Odessa,' said a man in an *Economist*-type thornproof suit.

'Look at the map,' Christine told him. 'There are no roads from Benghazi and Tripoli to Chad. And nobody has explained where Qaddaffi will suddenly find the trucks to move thirty thousand tons of grain more than a thousand miles through the desert. And – *and* he has to do it before the rainy season starts and the roads at the Chad end become impassable. Do I need to remind you that the Ethiopian government, with much more experience of this work and all the help the international relief agencies can give them, have so far failed to deliver more than a thousand tons a week?' Christine paused a moment to let the magnitudes of weight and distance sink in, then made her final point. 'Grain on the dock at Odessa is at least sixteen weeks from delivery to Chad. The rains will fall before then. My grain was right there, an hour from the refugee camp. Yet Qaddaffi had my plane shot down. He would deliberately let hundreds of thousands of children starve to death rather than allow Western compassion to feed them.'

'I say, isn't that a bit strong?' a male voice interrupted her. Christine tagged him as a *Times* accent.

'Our plane had red crosses on every available flat surface,' she told him. 'The Libyans knew we were coming with grain.'

'They claim you were carrying arms and ammunition for anti-Queddei rebels.'

Christine looked the reporter steadily in the eye until he dropped his gaze to his notebook. 'I won't dignify such a ludicrous fabrication with an answer.'

'But they did warn you off. Libya is a sovereign state – '

'We were over Chad, not Libya. A hungry stomach doesn't care which country it dies in. Hundreds of thousands, the majority of them children, will die in northern Chad unless we help them. I'm launching a public appeal on behalf of the Matthew Ellimore Foundation for the people of Great Britain to take the starving of Chad to their hearts and to give generously. I pledge that the food will reach the hungry people of Chad. I pledge to see to it myself.'

On the morning of the third day after her return to Britain, the Foundation accountant told her they had cash or promises amounting to six million pounds and that more was rolling in. Roger expected they would end up with double that. He was a little butterball of a man with thinning ginger hair and an unexpectedly sonorous voice; she had never seen him wear anything but a three-piece suit.

'You can't spend it all in Chad,' he now said.

She had not thought on it. In essence, Christine Rawls *was* the Matthew Ellimore Foundation: she had brought in the money to start it, decided what its aims should be, and was its chief executive officer. She had chosen and hired all the staff – eight people in all, not counting the part-time cleaner. Unlike other charities, who made do with volunteers of questionable calibre, compensating for lack of quality by sheer quantity, Christine hired away the best people from the toughest industries by the time-honoured expedient of paying them more money. Then she worked them very hard indeed. The net result was that the Ellimore Foundation spent 4% of its income on salaries, rent, overheads, and perks for executives comparable to what they would get in industry – and 96% on the people for whom they had collected the money. There was no superfluous fat or bureaucracy, as at, to name only one example from many, UNICEF, which spends over 80% of its income on its headquarters in Paris.

Christine had for two days been hustled from interview to interview; almost no one in the nation had not by now heard of the plight of the Chaddi and her ordeal in trying to bring relief to them and her determination still to do so despite anything Qaddaffi's minions could do to stop her. Christine was unstoppable – twelve million pounds was forty per cent of the sum the British government had voted for hunger relief in Ethiopia and Sudan and the problem in Chad was on a much smaller scale.

'Maybe we don't need twelve million to feed the Chaddi. With the remainder we have two choices: help the Chaddi avoid another famine by committing ourselves to long-term

24

agrarian reform programmes, or feed the starving elsewhere that the big guns are ignoring, say Moçambique.'

'You can forget long-term agrarian programmes in Chad while their civil war continues. Actually, the feeling in the office is that you should forget about Chad altogether. We'd hate to lose you.'

'Then we've been gathering money under false pretences.'

'Be your age, Christine. Everybody knows we're the good guys, we feed the starving. But nobody wants you killed because of some hyperbole you use in publicity to raise funds.'

Christine walked around her desk to sit on the edge of the desk in front of him. 'Chad. I'm committed to it. No,' she held up her hand, 'I don't want to hear any more. Spread the word, okay? All I want to hear is the best way of doing it.' She leaned forward to rub the back of her hand against his cheek; because of the lightness of his beard, he shaved only every second day. 'I know you all mean well, Roger, and you think I'm reacting to . . . to being treated like a *thing*. But it's not that. It's those starving people. Qaddaffi has everyone so shit-scared, nobody will help them if we don't. Without us, they will die.'

He looked up at her for a long moment. Then he said, 'All right. I asked a friend at Lloyd's to check on the shipping of that Russian grain and, as far as he can find out, no ships have yet been scheduled to transport it. But I can tell you right now there are no planes for hire to you, no pilots who want to fly to Chad for any money. Even that fellow who did . . .'

'Tanner Chapman.'

'. . . Chapman, did it only because he knew you from way back.'

'He lost his plane. It wasn't insured.'

'We won't have to give him a new one. Friend of mine at

25

the Foreign Office says the Libyans intend shooting him or, more precisely, to give him to their tame Chaddi to shoot.'

Christine sighed. Roger could be nice and he could be nasty; she had hired him for his ruthlessness. 'Tanner will make out. He's a survivor. And I wasn't suggesting we buy him another plane. But we can speak to people who can do him some good once he returns, whoever lends money for planes.'

'If he lives, I'll fix him a sweetheart deal somewhere.'

For the nth time she wondered if Roger ever woke up in the morning hating himself.

In the dawn, Christine stood in the bay window of her living-room and looked out on the Embankment without seeing it. The glass in her hand held water, once ice, melted and now at room temperature. The problem exercising her mind was still the same: no planes, no pilots, then how does one move food and medicine to the hungry and the sick in a landlocked country?

She turned when she sensed another presence in the room.

'Haven't you been to bed at all?' Ruby asked. She carried her suitcase.

Christine shook her head. 'You have your own problems with Tanner in the hands of the Libyans.' She had not told Ruby what Roger had reported from the Foreign Office. Yesterday, when she had taken Ruby around to the Foreign Office, they had told Ruby they were doing their best for Tanner via the Italians. But, to Christine, there was an ominously defeatist tone to their advice that Ruby would do better to return to Rome and do what she could for her husband through the Italians.

Ruby was her friend in a way that Tanner could never be. But Ruby said that, without Tanner, she would die; Christine believed her, in part because Ruby was Chinese. (It was a

26

reason that made Christine uncomfortable, like being in company where racist jokes were told.)

Ruby went into the kitchen to make coffee. When Christine came to the door, Ruby said, 'Tell me anyway. Anything to take my mind off Tanner for a few minutes.'

'All right. It's a simple problem, except there's no solution. I have money to buy grain and medicine but I can't find pilots and planes to deliver it to Chad. The country is landlocked, so there is no access by sea. Overland – well, the place is in the goddamn middle of Africa and Qaddaffi's soldier-fanatics will be shooting at the convoy a lot of those miles. I don't have the expertise to handle that and I don't know anyone who does.'

Ruby looked Christine up and down. She had first known Christine as a foolish, impulsive girl who attracted disaster and even tragedy as honey calls to bees. Christine was still dangerous to know but she had matured at least to the extent of admitting there were things she could not do.

'You're right to blame me for the trouble Tanner's in,' Christine continued in the pause.

'I don't,' Ruby said shortly. 'It was in a good cause, we needed the money and you paid well. No, please don't mention it again. I was about to say, you know . . .' Ruby busied herself with the filter.

It was uncharacteristic of Ruby not to speak in full sentences. 'I know who?'

'You know Lance Weber. He could do it.'

Christine smiled. 'I thought of him. Every day since I returned. But he hates me, he's tungsten steel right through so he wouldn't do this for compassion, and he doesn't need the money. That's three reasons not to humiliate myself by asking him.'

Ruby handed her a cup of coffee. 'Breakfast?'

'Not for me, thanks. But you make whatever you can find.'

27

'Not for me either,' Ruby said. It was typical of Christine that, in her own home, her guests should make the morning coffee and offer to prepare meals. Christine was a monomaniac and had in any event been spoiled by servants in her childhood.

'I don't mean that,' Christine said, blowing on her coffee and sipping at it. 'Humiliation is nothing. Lives are important. But I know tracking down Lance and going to see him is a waste of time.'

Ruby nodded thoughtfully but Christine didn't think it was agreement. Ruby went to brush her teeth and then they drank another cup of coffee while they waited for the taxi which would take Ruby to Victoria where she would catch the tube to Heathrow. Christine had offered the night before to drive her but Ruby had driven with Christine before and her nerves were already on edge from having Tanner in custody to the Libyans, so she declined.

From the window, Ruby said, 'It's only a couple of hours to Brussels and back. Jimmy used to be in love with you.'

'My god, yes! And what Lance Weber can do, Jimmy and his brothers can most certainly do too.'

'That's my taxi.'

They cried on each other's shoulder briefly before Ruby left.

Christine went directly from the door to the phone. At Heathrow her plane for Brussels took off right after Ruby's delayed flight for Rome, though they didn't see each other again.

The maid said Jimmy was at the office and, when she asked the address, shut the door in her face. Christine stood on the porch and surveyed the rich garden and the glassed-in swimming pool, considered the child's tricycle and the doll's pram, complete with doll. Ruby had sent her into enemy country: just as well Jimmy's wife wasn't at home. She was halfway down the steps towards the taxi she had prudently kept when the door opened again behind her and she had, reluctantly, to turn.

For a moment she thought it was Jimmy, grown fat and greyhaired, but it was not. This was another man, a man she knew though she had never met him. The new Christine merely flinched before his reputation; the old Christine, before witnessing so much suffering had metamorphosed her into the new, might have shuddered in revulsion. This was Jimmy's elder brother, Sambo, the head of the tribe. She had been only a schoolgirl but the photograph on the front page of every newspaper in the world was unforgettable: a scene of indescribable carnage during the troubles in the Congo, in the midst of which stood a black man and a white man in battle-dress, cradling FN machine pistols with the loving care not only of long familiarity but of recently having entrusted their lives to their weapons; they were neither smiling nor grimacing, triumphant nor sorrowful, they merely were *there*, survivors. Others had not been so fortunate. Rebels had raped and tortured the nuns of a hospital mission; these men had come to rescue them and, arriving too late to save the nuns, fought the rebels to the end, neither side taking a single prisoner. Christine remembered as if it were yesterday. The white man was Major Ewart Weber, elder brother of Lance Weber. The black man was a younger, slimmer version of the man now before her, Sergeant Sambo. He smiled pleasantly at her.

'I'm Christine Rawls. I'd like to speak to Jimmy.' She felt like that gawky adolescent who had once reported for tennis at the home of the dreamboat already gone up to Cambridge.

'My brother is at the office. Come in, wait. We will bring him to you.'

'I can go there, if you'll give me the address.'

29

He smiled pleasantly. 'You do not come on a social visit, Miss Rawls. I have heard of your attempts to hire mercenary pilots. I can guess what you want with Jimmy. But Jimmy will almost certainly consult me, so you may as well tell your proposal once only to both of us, eh?'

She turned to pay off the taxi but Sambo took her arm and led her through the door. 'I will send somebody to pay him.'

To her surprise, he led her not into a study or an office but a drawing-room where a statuesque blonde woman perhaps a couple of years short of forty was introduced as his wife, Monique. She too insisted on addressing Christine in near-perfect English, certainly superior to Christine's Roedean-and-skiing French. A servant was called to remove the baby crawling around and the toddler playing with varnished wooden bricks. A black man, who was not introduced and seemed to Christine to occupy a position somewhere between a friend and a high-level retainer, was sent to pay the taxi. When he returned and helped Monique clear the table for the tray, Christine struck the right word: courtier. Sambo was a king, or would have been if his tribe had not been destroyed, and his brothers princes. Monique poured coffee.

'I'm grateful – the Foundation is grateful for your annual cheque,' Christine said to break the silence only she seemed to find disturbing.

'Jimmy showed us your letters of thanks,' Sambo said. 'It is a small thing. You do good work.'

The cheques had each year been for a hundred thousand American dollars. A few corporations gave that much annually but no other individuals. To Monique, Christine said, 'My Foundation was started with money your husband's family gave me.'

Monique looked uncomprehendingly at Sambo. Christine thought, I'll bet my Foundation gets their total charitable budget.

Sambo said to his wife, 'That time Jimmy and Pierre and Boo went with Mr Lance to fetch the Ellimore ivory from Lake Kivu,[1] Miss Rawls was with them. Afterwards, on behalf of the family, they gave her money for a charitable foundation. But she flatters us. I always understood the major part of her foundation was funded by Mrs Ellimore and Mr Lance.'

'Ah,' said Monique, apparently perfectly satisfied with this explanation, six years after the event.

My god, thought Christine, this isn't just a court, it is a feudal court.

But when Jimmy arrived fifteen minutes later, he caught Christine in the act of reciting from memory her mother's recipe for making rather delicious cookies in about twenty minutes from packet oatmeal.

'Try it with small proportions first,' Jimmy told Monique in French, too quickly for Christine to follow. 'This one doesn't cook.' He shook Christine's hand formally and bent for her to kiss him. 'Christine. What do you want?'

He had filled out but he was the same Jimmy, big, smiling, a man who reassured the shy and the timid merely by his presence.

'Jimmy.' Warningly from Sambo, an objection to ill manners.

Jimmy snapped his fingers at his brother. 'I told you she would come. We didn't expect you so soon,' he said to Christine.

'Will you excuse us if we go to the study?' Sambo asked his wife.

Once she was seated in the study, which in another house would probably be called the library – it was thirty by eighteen and three of the walls were covered with books which seemed

---

[1] See *Blood Ivory*, Secker & Warburg, 1983; Granada, 1985.

to have been selected for their content rather than their ability to blend with the rest of the decor – Christine said bluntly, 'You know why I'm here. I want to move a cargo of grain and medical supplies into Chad against resistance.'

'Against armed resistance,' Jimmy said casually.

There was a very long silence. Then Sambo spread his forearms and let them fall on the arms of his chesterfield. 'Why come to us? We're no longer soldiers.'

'You can help me if you want to,' Christine said obstinately.

After another long silence, Jimmy sighed. 'Look at the map under the glass on Sambo's desk, Christine.' She rose and the other two followed her to the desk. 'Chad,' Jimmy said, tapping it with his finger. 'You already proved you can't fly in. No sea-coast. Surrounded by enemies, civil wars, countries so corrupt not even gold speaks louder than guns. But, most of all, thousands of kilometres from anywhere. A thousand kilometres of adverse travel, fine. But several thousand?'

'Miss Rawls, these are no longer days when one can hire a mercenary army even for possible dreams.' Sambo traced lines from this port and that to Chad and each time said 'Tch!' when his finger reached a certain point, then started at a new port of origin.

'I doubt even Lance would attempt it,' Jimmy said.

'I'm sorry, Miss Rawls,' Sambo said gently. He pulled a tray with glasses and bottles across the desk. 'Whisky or gin? I can call for sherry or vermouth or – '

'Whisky, thank you.' She was not offered soda or water and would have refused it; she had a taste for malt and Sambo served Glenfiddich. 'Is there any amount of money – '

'If you're in need, just ask and we can let you have any reasonable amount,' Jimmy said.

He had deliberately misunderstood her! Bastard!

Christine knew when she was temporarily checked. But she didn't believe you were beaten until you gave up. 'You say Lance Weber can do it.'

'If anybody can, he can,' Sambo said in the flat voice of absolute certainty.

'All right. You know him better than anybody. How do I persuade him?'

Jimmy grinned in genuine enjoyment. 'Why not just ask him?'

Christine scowled at him. 'People are starving. Let's save the jokes for better times.'

Jimmy snorted. 'The same old Christine. You haven't asked the man to sacrifice his life for your cockeyed ideals but you stand ready to damn him for a refusal he hasn't made.'

Christine bit back a sharp retort and sipped her whisky. 'Is he my last chance?'

'He is your only chance and always was,' Sambo said and that seemed to close the conversation.

'Come,' said Jimmy. 'I'll take you to him.'

'He's in Brussels?'

'No. Vienna.' To Sambo, 'I'll be back tomorrow lunchtime.'

'Sort of the family man's Ferrari,' Christine said, glancing around the expanse of leather inside the four-seater, front-engined 412i. 'Are you married yet?'

'No. The mid-engined jobs are faster but the seats are too small for me. You?'

'No. Thanks, Jimmy.'

'For taking you to Lance? He'll only tell you what you've already heard everywhere else. Don't get your hopes up, Christine.'

'You understand I have to try?'

Jimmy nodded but kept his eyes on the road. The Ferrari

33

touched two hundred and forty kilometres per hour on the German autobahn.

'Does Lance have a key?'

'Certainly. His wife and his daughter.'

'Right. Of course. And all I have to do is abduct them and hold them hostage until he delivers my grain to Chad!'

Jimmy chuckled broadly and refused to be ruffled by her sarcasm.

Christine curled up in her seat and wondered how they had ever become lovers. But that had been six years ago. He was now a very different man, rich, cynical, supercilious, smug even. Then he redeemed himself totally. 'Of course,' he continued equably, 'you could just try offering Lance the obvious temptation, money.'

Christine groaned. 'He doesn't need any. Tanner told me he and Lance lost their ranch in the Argentine during the Falklands war, but Esmeralda is filthy rich in her own right.'

'Do you really see Lance Weber living off his wife?'

She sat up straight and snapped the safety belt decisively around her. 'Can't you go any faster?'

'In English, we're doing a hundred and fifty miles an hour.'

'My Jag can do that,' Christine said dismissively. 'I checked it on the M1. Surely a Ferrari ought to be faster than a Jag?'

'You have a V12 Jaguar?'

'My father gave it to me for my birthday a couple of years ago.'

'Bit flashy for an ascetic do-gooder.'

'I'd forgotten you went to Marlborough. I'd collect a lot less money for those who really need it if I dress in rags, travel on the bus, smell like I keep coal in the bathtub. What should I offer Lance, ten thousand, twenty?'

Jimmy took his eyes from the road for a second to look at her full in the face. 'Half a million. I should think.'

'For maybe six weeks' work?!'

34

'For doing a job nobody else can do.'

'Why not a million?'

'You want to dish out the loaves and the fishes or you want to be sarcastic?'

'Were we always like this?'

Jimmy shrugged irritably. 'Lance borrowed quite a bit of money for his and Tanner's ranch. That's – '

'But he had millions! Why should he borrow?'

'They bought land by the square kilometre and Pierre offered them a good rate on big loans to buy more.'

Pierre was Jimmy's investment-banker brother.

'Who could have foreseen the Argentinians actually declaring war on the British?'

'Exactly. Well, Lance and Tanner being British subjects, and forcibly resisting internment and their women being turned into concubines for the soldiery – sorry! – they lost their land and had to fight their way out.'

'I can just imagine.' On the expedition to Lake Kivu Christine had seen Lance Weber traverse a hostile landscape like a mobile smallscale war; the violence of that journey was not something people who live in cities could believe or even comprehend.

'Uh-huh. So the Argies confiscated all the land. The thing is, Pierre and I were there too, just visiting, and we lent Lance a hand. You know how it is. Now the Argies keep losing Pierre's claims for compensation.'

'I see.'

'Lance then cashed in all his assets elsewhere and paid off all his creditors except for half a million he still owes Pierre.'

'But Pierre can recover that from the Argentinians!'

'So could the other creditors. None of them were pressing Lance. Pierre isn't pressing Lance. He was acutely embarrassed when Lance forced payment of the first instalment on him. You know my whole tribe, what's left of it, owes its very

35

existence to Lance's brother, the Major and our comforts to Lance.'

'You contributed lives and talent to both.'

Jimmy sighed. 'You will never understand. Anyway, Lance needs a half a mill to pay debts that exist only in his own mind, before he can start square again with himself. I'll probably burn in your hell for giving you so much leverage on my friend.'

'Leverage,' she muttered.

'What have we come to?' He crashed his hand on the horn to warn a big Opel a kilometre ahead to vacate the fast lane.

Later, when they reached the outskirts of Vienna, she said, 'A double room, I think.'

'You don't have to.'

'I want to.'

'Isn't . . . aren't you . . .'

'My misfortunes in Chad? Does that put you off?'

'No. I meant, you aren't sore or . . .'

'No. I told you, I want to. Why do men always spoil the romantic moment with rationalization? If you don't want me, say so.'

'I'll use my influence to get us the presidential honeymoon suite.'

The receptionist told them to follow the Number 71 tram and explained, in pleasantly accented English:

'Here in Wien, when somebody dies, we say he's gone away on the Number Seventy-One. The Number Seventy-One tram goes to the Field of Graves, yes. You will find Mr and Mrs Weber at the Field of Graves. So sad.'

Lance of God

Lance Weber was burying his only child. He shook his head at the undertaker's assistants and, after a moment of confusion, they climbed back into the front of the hearse. Lance slid the small coffin out on the rollers. He held a handle on one side and Mwanzo took the other. The coffin weighed very little but they walked slowly down the pathway. Lance looked at Esmeralda, walking beside him, but her puffed eyes were hidden behind a heavy black veil. There was no earthly consolation he could offer her and the helplessness hurt. He turned his head back towards the open grave, their destination, Emmy's final destination. He was in no hurry to reach it: he still carried the irrational belief that, until they buried her, Emmy was not really dead, could still rise again; he *knew* it was not so, but could not believe in, and knew Esmeralda too had difficulty accepting, the finality of the loss. All too soon they reached the gaping grave. The sling and ropes were laid out; he and Mwanzo gently put the coffin down on the canvas sling. Lance and Esmeralda stood on one side of the grave, Mwanzo on the other. Lance reached blindly for Esmeralda's hand and felt it cold even through her glove. He wished they had decided on a religious ceremony, anything to delay lowering the casket into the grave. 'Goodbye, Emmy, my darling,' Esmeralda whispered and stifled a sob. Lance bent to pick up the ropes. He rose and caught Mwanzo's eye. Mwanzo's face gleamed ebony with tears. Lance wiped his own cheeks on the shoulder of his coat. Mwanzo was ready, he was ready, Esmeralda had said her goodbyes. 'Farewell, Emmy,' Lance breathed and let the ropes slide through his hands. When the ropes ran slackly, he leaned over the grave to drop the ends into the gap between the coffin and the cleaved earth, not wanting to drop them on top of the coffin. Mwanzo followed suit. Esmeralda, sobbing continuously, leaned over the grave. Mwanzo cleared his throat behind them. Lance took the spade loaded with earth from him, held it out to Esmeralda, who shook her head firmly. Lance hesitated for another moment. 'Go to the grass and the rivers and the trees and the sky, Emmy. They will welcome your spirit,' he said clearly and slid the soil gently into the grave. It made no sound on the coffin. Lance turned, dug more soil from the heap behind him, threw that into the grave, and again and again. Emmy was dead, a sprite that had graced his and Esmeralda's lives and gone. *Let not her memory be leaden grief.* He straightened with the spade and, turning, through his tears hazily saw Mwanzo with his face collapsed. Lance stopped. The grave was half full; Mwanzo had been Emmy's best friend. He gave the spade to the other man, then shook his head when Mwanzo offered it to him again after shovelling earth for a minute. Mwanzo filled the grave and tamped the earth into a neat mound. One of the undertakers came from the hearse with an ornate flower arrangement but Esmeralda shook her head and he carried the ostentatious wreath back to the hearse. They stood for perhaps a minute, Lance and Esmeralda close together by the grave, Mwanzo a few paces behind them, then, without another word, turned and walked slowly towards the gate.

Lance saw Jimmy and Christine standing by Mozart's tomb but they did not approach; Lance did not expect them to. Turning on the rear seat of the undertaker's limousine to hug Esmeralda to him to give her such comfort as he could, out of the corner of his eye he saw Jimmy's car behind them.

40

'Jimmy and Christine are here,' Lance told her but she did not answer.

At the Bristol, they stood indecisively in the foyer; for weeks now their lives had been regulated by hospital time, their days divided between visiting hours and consultations. Now, with purpose gone, they were at a loose end. Jimmy and Christine came in. Christine embraced Esmeralda, Jimmy hugged Lance. Nobody said anything. Then Christine led Esmeralda away to the lift. Lance turned to follow but Jimmy caught his arm and held up the flat of his hand. Lance nodded his understanding: women always coped better with the grief of others than men. He did not resist when Jimmy took him and Mwanzo by their elbows and led them towards the bar. Getting drunk was something to do, perhaps better than what he really wanted, which was to smash the world for being so unfair to Emmy, who had never harmed anyone.

With his second drink, Lance said to Jimmy, who hadn't asked. 'Leukemia. Mercifully, it was very quick.' Then he lapsed into silence again, not hearing Jimmy and Mwanzo's conversation. When Esmeralda and Christine came down, they moved to a booth. 'You remember Mwanzo the sharp-shooter?' Jimmy asked Christine, who said she did though it was untrue. She observed the cut of Mwanzo's suit and compared it to Lance's and thought, Only Lance Weber takes his servants to his own tailor. Sometimes she was ashamed of her involuntary snobbery but it *was* involuntary: she was the product of her background and education.

'Do you want to eat in the suite tonight?' Lance asked Esmeralda.

'I don't want any food.'

'You must eat. You've eaten nothing for days.'

'And you. I'll do something if I'm cooped up. I want to . . . I want to leave Vienna. I want to leave now.' Esmeralda threw back her veil. She was a strikingly handsome woman but grief

41

takes its toll and Christine, who had long envied Esmeralda her figure and her face and her skin and her poise, felt a thrust of compassion for her as another woman who could never recall time.

'Please ask the kitchen to pack us some sandwiches and the desk to make up our bill,' Lance told Mwanzo. 'We will leave in an hour.'

'Yes, Master.'

'I'm sorry to be rude after you came so far . . .'

'Not at all. We understand, don't we, Christine?'

'Of course we do. You want to be alone.' Graciousness too came naturally with the upbringing.

'Not alone, just not here,' Esmeralda said.

'Then why don't you come to Brussels? That is a formal invitation on behalf of Sambo and the tribe,' Jimmy suggested.

'I'd like that, to see familiar, friendly faces for a while, if you don't mind that we won't be very good company. Unless you'd rather we went to your people,' Lance added to Esmeralda.

She shook her head. 'No, Emmy wouldn't have wanted an interminable Spanish wake.'

And, as she mentioned her dead daughter's name, it came to her that the world rolling on was a *necessary* cliché.

Christine chose to make her pitch in the hour before dawn as they crossed from Germany into Belgium. It was something she had learnt from Lance on that bloody journey across half of Africa and back to fetch Esmeralda's ivory: just before dawn the human metabolism is at its lowest ebb, the exact moment when an attacker disposes of the greatest advantage.

'Lance,' Christine said brightly. 'I understand you're looking for work. I can offer you a job.'

Jimmy groaned at her timing, hit the horn and squeezed

the big Ferrari doing a hundred and sixty kilometres between two semi-trailer trucks travelling at less than half that rate at a lane closure on a sweeping left-hander.

Lance looked around from the front seat at Christine. 'I'm touched. But now's hardly the time nor the place.'

'I'm paying half a million American dollars. I'm sorry if it's bad taste to – '

Lance sighed. 'No. If you want to speak to me, speak to me tonight.'

'People are dying while we wait on good manners!'

'Right now, I'm not likely to agree to anything you want. You're as responsible for Tanner's death as if you pulled the trigger yourself.'

Christine gasped. When she recovered her breath, she said, knowing it was a weak argument, 'He's still alive.'

'For how long?'

'Please, Lance, just – '

'I'll listen to you this afternoon when I've rested and can think straight.'

'You're already thinking too straight for her,' Jimmy said before Christine could continue. 'We're almost home. Pack it in till this evening, Christine.'

At Sambo's home, Lance stood in the uncertain light and looked at the gate as if Mwanzo would drive his car through it any moment, though Jimmy had left Mwanzo several hours behind. 'I *will* listen, Christine,' he said. 'Four o'clock, unless our hosts have other plans. Now I shall sleep and sleep. Goodnight.' He bent into the car to pick up Esmeralda, who was asleep courtesy of four pills Christine had given her, and carried her into the house.

Lance made a small gesture with the glass of Glenfiddich in his hand. 'Your brains are addled, Christine. What do you think I am, some kind of mercenary who clicks his fingers and up rises a legion clutching assault rifles to tackle the forces of evil? You're confusing me with my brother and he's twelve years in his grave. Perhaps *he* could have done what you want.'

'You had no trouble raising, arming and training twenty Swahili to fetch the Ellimore ivory when it suited your pocket,' Christine snapped. She resented making her pitch to Lance in the presence of Sambo and Jimmy, who had already prejudged her case. But it was their house and, without them, Lance would never have heard her out.

'Certainly,' Lance said equably. 'But then I was going up against a few disorganized bandits. This – Are you all right?'

Jimmy's ham hand caught Christine squarely in the middle of her back but that only made the choking worse. When she stopped spluttering, she raged, 'Your audacity astounds me. The Tanzanian Army and Navy, the Rwandan and Burundi armies and police, the Organization for African Unity, a disorganized rabble?'

Lance smiled gently. 'You were there. Now we're all here and alive. Esmeralda recovered her ivory. Twenty Swahili warriors were sufficient.' The gentle smile hardened and Christine flinched visibly when she looked into his chill blue eyes. 'Your memory is selective. I went up that road only to bait a trap for a maniac who had butchered my parents and friends. If there had been any other way to catch Bruun, I would have let that ivory lie forever at the bottom of Lake Kivu.'

The other two men turned involuntarily to look at Christine at the mention of Bruun's name, then looked quickly away as her face distorted with revulsion and her whole body was racked with an uncontrollable shiver. She had herself been in Bruun's hands. But Lance held her eyes.

Christine wondered if cobras have blue eyes.

'Okay, I'm talking to the world's leading experts, all

together in one room. Send me a bill for consultation fees. What do I need?'

Suddenly Lance's smile was friendly again. 'You know, I admire what you do, Christine. But I admire your tenacity even more.' He glanced at Sambo and Jimmy but they were obviously waiting for him to speak. 'I'd say an armoured column with air cover. Sambo?'

'I couldn't say fairer myself, Mr Lance.'

'Jimmy?'

'She knows what we think, Lance.'

'I'll give you some numbers. How much grain do you want to move?'

'A hundred tons, minimum.'

'That's seventeen trucks for grain, three trucks for spares and equipment, four or five more trucks for camping gear and food, maybe a refrigerated truck too, three, maybe four fuel tankers, a couple of command Range Rovers.'

'Who will rent you thirty vehicles once they know where you intend taking them, Miss Christine?' Sambo asked.

'I wish you would just call me Christine.'

'I like the old ways,' Sambo said. 'Without transport . . .'

'I don't need to rent trucks, I can buy them.'

'You're talking about maybe two million dollars,' Lance said judiciously.

'Money is the least of my problems.' Christine flicked the middle finger of her right hand against the thumb as if brushing off something distasteful.

'Okay. Next, you need drivers, and not just the first Watusi who apply for the job but men who will stick to those trucks once the shooting starts.'

'By then they'll be in Chad and too far in to turn back.'

'That kind of cynicism can kill you,' Lance said evenly. 'Do you want me to continue?'

'I apologize. Please go on.'

45

'Chad's in the wrong place for a relief operation, not like the Sudan and Ethiopia which are easy to reach over roads through generally law-abiding countries. To reach Chad, you have to pass through too many places with no law but gun law. So the shooting starts long before you get to Chad, whenever somebody tries to take the grain from you, probably just outside the port where you land it.

'That's my next point, the port. It's a fixed place for the Libyans to find you and you already know they're not too fastidious about borders.'

'What if I buy grain some place that isn't a port?'

'You mean in South Africa?'

It was a mistake to think that on matters African you could ever out-think Lance Weber. She nodded.

'Fine,' Lance said, 'because General Motors or Ford at Port Elizabeth is also the only place to go for so many new vehicles. But then you have to move your convoy up the whole length of Africa. It's a novel way of committing suicide, I'll say that for it. Sambo?'

Sambo nodded gravely and poured more whisky. Christine waited impatiently for the end of the civilities.

Lance savoured a mouthful of Sambo's Scotch. 'I'd almost give up bourbon for this . . . But starting some place that isn't a port does give you an edge, Christine. If you can then move fast and quietly, you could with luck be far enough into Chad to do your refugees some good before anyone even noticed you were underway.'

'Bingo.'

'Too many ifs there,' Sambo said in the small silence. 'You can't put together enough fighting men to protect such a big convoy through Zaire without the news spreading.'

Christine made a moue of distaste. 'Exactly how many "fighting men" are we talking about?'

Lance looked first at Sambo, who tactfully busied himself

with opening another bottle, and then at Jimmy, who said, 'You're elected to tell the lady the good news.'

Lance shrugged. 'Forty, if the drivers can handle firearms as well, say seventy altogether.'

'Listen, I don't want to *start* any wars, I want to save lives!'

'Exactly. That's what we've been telling you. In nine-tenths of Africa, your convoy will provoke an armed takeover bid, long before you get to Chad. People will die moving your grain into position, regardless of resistance from the Libyans in Chad itself.'

Christine looked each of the three men in the eye for several seconds. This was it. She had to commit now or let the famished Chaddi die. She had to faith in the Russian wheat arriving within three months – or at all. Even if it arrived as promised in three months, too many would die of hunger before then.

'Fine,' she said calmly. 'They choose for their own gain to stand in our way with force. The starving people did not choose their predicament.' Again Christine paused to look from face to face. Sambo looked grim, Jimmy smiled broadly, encouragingly, Lance stared at her with the horror of recognition.

'You're a genuinely ruthless bitch,' Lance said conversationally. Sambo drew in a sharp breath. 'Sorry,' Lance said to him. 'This has gone far enough, Christine. The job could barely be done without Libyan resistance. With it, it's impossible. Let's stop this nonsense right here.'

'How long will it take from today until we deliver the grain or perish in the attempt?'

'Or die trying is what you mean,' Lance said shortly. 'Six weeks from when you find somebody to die with you.'

'One million dollars, half now, half on delivery.'

'No.' Lance rose.

'Is the great Lance Weber frightened?'

'Damn right I'm frightened! And if you had any sense, you'd be scared out of your pants too.'

'Who else can do it? Goddammit, you *must* know of *somebody*!'

'Miss Christine,' Sambo said firmly, 'Lance is the best there is. If he says it can't be done, it can't be done.'

'Then I'll go with second-best! People are starving, don't you understand?'

Sambo nodded. Jimmy said, 'In this business there is no second-best. There's the best and the dead. And Sambo told you before we went to Vienna, the choice isn't large, the best being mostly grey and overweight from riding chauffeur-driven cars to plush offices. You're on a hiding to nothing, Christine.'

Lance sat down again. He picked up the bottle and looked at Sambo, who nodded permission. Lance poured. 'Let her talk to Lestronge in Hong Kong, Sambo.'

Sambo checked his watch. 'He's always waking me up.' He walked behind his desk and consulted a small notebook before dialling.

'He's an ex-mercenary, now director of security for an oil company,' Jimmy told Christine. 'He keeps a computer record of all the world's . . . uh . . .'

'"Dangerous men", that's what he calls them,' Lance supplied the phrase. Christine had an impression he found this hugely amusing.

'He owes us favours,' Jimmy continued. 'He'll have his computer sort out a few candidates for you.'

Sambo spoke a few French words into the phone and then held it out to Christine. 'He speaks English.'

She explained her problem in a few clear sentences. When she stopped, there was a brief pause.

Lestronge had a deep voice; his accent was somewhere

between German and French: she tagged him correctly as a native of Alsace. 'Miss Rawls, for this I need not consult my records. I know the man you want. I'm surprised Prince Knékwassé didn't put you directly onto him. His name is Lance Weber and you can find him care of Barclays Bank in Nairobi.'

'I'm looking at him now. He won't do it. He suggested you would know someone else.'

'I see.' There was a long pause. 'I understand, ah, his financial position is delicate.'

'I'm offering whatever it takes. I offered him one million dollars.'

There was a respectful pause. 'If Lance won't do it for so much, Miss Rawls, I suspect the job cannot be done and would advise you to forget it.'

'No. I'm told you have a list of men – '

'Toughs, thugs and hired killers, Miss Rawls. They would as soon slice your throat as deliver food to the hungry. They will take your money, certainly, but if Lance won't undertake your mission, they will fail. I'm sorry, Miss Rawls. I will send a cheque to your foundation. Now I must return to my sleep.'

Christine put the dead phone down and glared contemptuously across the desk at the three men. Then she rose and walked out of the room without another word. She walked into the furthest corner of the garden and beat her fists against the wall and screamed and screamed until she was hoarse. People were dying and nobody cared but her.

'What did Christine want?'

'For me to jockey a hundred tons of grain all the way up Africa and into Chad.'

'She's going back?'

'No. She can't find anybody to lead the expedition. Even Lestronge said it couldn't be done.'

'That's not right. Lestronge said, if *you* won't do it, it probably can't be done.' They turned to look at Christine in the open door of their bedroom. 'Can I come in.'

'Of course,' Lance said. 'It's the same thing.'

'No, it isn't. It's like ... It's like show-jumping. If the champion says a fence can be jumped, then it can be jumped, even if nobody but the champion can jump it. See?'

Lance just looked at Christine. It was typical of the bloody woman to choose exactly that example. He had no interest in horses himself though he could ride well enough to earn a six handicap at polo, but Esmeralda was a champion jumper.

'No,' said Esmeralda, 'I don't see.'

'Well, Lance did say my grain can be delivered to the starving people in time. "Quick in and out," he said, "before anybody finds out what's happening." Everybody tells me he's the champ. And the champ says the job can be done. But he won't do it.'

Esmeralda looked at Lance, who shook his head. 'She's trying to raise fighting men to take on the Libyan Army. You remember what it was like fetching your ivory. This would be a hundred times worse. Jimmy told her it can't be done. Sambo told her it can't be done. We even got Lestronge out of bed in Hong Kong to tell her it can't be done. *You* reason with her.'

'Again, what they all said was that only Lance can do it,' Christine told Esmeralda. 'Children will die because he *won't* do it.'

'That's below the belt even for you, Christine.' Lance undid the double-knotted laces of his shoes, kicked the shoes off and lay back on the bed. To Esmeralda: 'She's offering a million dollars for six weeks' work. That tells you how desperate she is. And it tells you she knows the danger.'

'Hundreds of thousands of children starving to death.'

'Oh Christine, go home, find a new cause,' Lance said wearily.

'Can what she wants be done?'

Lance looked up at his wife. 'Anything can be done if you're willing to pay the price.'

'So?'

'You know the scum who lurk in dongas to feed off the desperate needs of Africa. We would have to kill many of them. Our own people will die in the process. There is every likelihood we'll have to fight the Libyan Army if we run into them.'

'For starving children,' Christine said again.

Esmeralda ignored her. She knew her husband had not finished. 'So?'

'So our very own little Miss Do-Gooder here is setting herself up to judge so many of Them dead, so many of Us dead on the road to salvation for her refugees. In her mind it's a neat little sum. Ten of my Swahili dead defending her grain equals a hundred famished children saved.'

'A thousand children. More,' Christine said fervently. ' "Ten of *my* Swahili . . ." You *have* been thinking about it!'

Lance sighed and sat up. 'Sure. I'm no more taken than you with the idea of children starving so Qaddaffi and his Russian pals can score points.'

'How possible is it to do like you said quick and about?' Esmeralda asked quietly.

'Quick in and out.' Lance's mind was calculating while he automatically corrected his wife's quaint English idiom. 'With a lot of luck and the best equipment and men and an absolutely ruthless commitment to speed above all, it is possible.'

'How much so?' Esmeralda persisted.

Lance saw Christine's classically narrow face illuminated with her wish for him to say yes. He told her, 'Your delusion that you can do something monumentally meaningful is contagious.' And your sainthood will be bought by dragging down many others into the valley of martyrdom, he thought. To Esmeralda, he said, 'Not very probable, darling. But yes, possible and probable.'

Christine had the good sense to keep quiet.

'All those children saved,' Esmeralda said. 'It would be a fine monument for our Emmy.'

Lance put his arm around her shoulders and hugged her tight to him. What the name must have cost her, so soon afterwards! 'Yes, wouldn't it. Leave us, Christine. I'll speak to you later.'

When Lance and Esmeralda came down the next morning, Christine was gone on the first plane to London. Pierre and Boo sat at the breakfast table. They were Jimmy and Sambo's brothers and had their own establishments. Lance listened to their commiserations and noted their lightweight suits, too light for a European spring that had arrived nowhere but on the calendar.

'You know, Sambo, your tribe's debt to my brothers has been repaid many times over to me. You don't have to send anyone with me this time.' He did not need to tell Sambo many, perhaps all, would not return.

Sambo finished boning his kipper before he answered. 'For such a large body of men you will need lieutenants. Where did you intend finding them, Mr Lance?'

Lance nodded thoughtfully. He had yet given it no thought.

'Pierre can handle business affairs, Boo can select your fighting men and drivers, Jimmy can help with the training. You're looking much better this morning, Esmeralda.' Sambo touched the bags under his own eyes to indicate that Esmeralda's eyes were no longer puffed from crying. For Sambo the other subject was closed.

Lance was overjoyed. He could never have asked for help, because he saw himself as indebted to these men and had indeed never accepted their view that they owed his late brother such a debt of honour that they could never repay it. But, when he had first gone into the bush on that crocodile hunt of Ewart's,[1] Jimmy had been there to guide him; in every hazardous venture since, Jimmy had been at his shoulder with advice and assistance when required. Lance Weber saw himself as a man who had fallen into trouble gambling and had to be rescued by his elder brother; he had been there to inherit his brother's crocodile skins and from there luck and a certain inborn skill with a rifle had made him rich, until he lost his wealth the same way he made it. Lance did not think himself very clever and often woke in the mornings amazed at his good fortune in having a wife like Esmeralda, a child like Emmy, friends like Jimmy and his brothers and Tanner. Now Emmy was dead and Tanner about to be shot . . .

Yes, he had decided right. A monument to Emmy, saving those children from certain starvation. And a monument to Tanner, defying the Libyans to do it.

There was nothing he wanted to do more. Everything is possible, he again heard himself telling Esmeralda yesterday, if you're willing to pay the price.

And no, there was no point in arguing with Sambo. The big black man would listen respectfully and then do whatever he had already decided to do.

'Pierre and Boo are both divorced,' Sambo said. 'And Jimmy not yet married. All my other brothers and tribesmen are happily married with large families.'

'Our sister-in-law is a lot more shocked than Sambo about divorces in the family,' Pierre said, pointing with his fork

[1] See *African Revenge*, Secker & Warburg, 1980; Granada, 1985.

towards the kitchen, where Monique had gone for more coffee. 'Sambo's just toeing the party line.'

'I'm a good Catholic,' Sambo said with dignity.

'Maybe,' Boo said, and addressed his sausages, kidneys, eggs, grilled tomatoes and toast.

'You got religion since we last met?' Pierre asked Lance.

'Pierre!' Sambo protested sharply.

Lance held up his hand. 'No. There will be shooting. He's right to ask. The answer is no, I'm the same man I was before my daughter died.'

Boo grunted his approval.

Pierre grinned an apology. He was a sleek man of about forty who looked more like the banker he now was than the famed close-quarters fighter he had once been. Boo, who was equally famed as a scout, on the other hand, looked like a punchdrunk prizefighter which, he said, was useful in the real-estate business since so many fools took him at face value.

Boo turned his palm up. 'I'm sweating to return to Africa. An American told me, "Once a nigger, always a nigger". I'm sorry I wasn't kinder to him, now I realize how very right he was.'

'You don't have to be black to pine for Africa,' Esmeralda said. 'You can tell how long Lance has been away by just looking at him.'

'I want twenty short-wheelbase three-axle trucks and ten long-wheelbase three-axle trucks,' Lance said the next morning and twelve thousand miles away in Port Elizabeth. 'All with all-wheel drive, all with heavy-duty chassis strengthening and transfer boxes with extra-low gear ranges, all with the fattest tyres you can fit. Three of the short trucks will be fuel tankers, the other seventeen must carry a minimum of six tons of grain each plus the weight of a bulk skip. One of the long trucks will be refrigerated but the rest won't be heavily loaded. All the same, all trucks should have the biggest standard diesel engine you normally fit. I'll want a good quantity of spares to take away with me too.'

The GM sales director looked up from his notes. 'I still have the list you used the last time you bought trucks from us. We kept it on file as a model of forethought.'

'Excellent. It'll save us a lot of time if I just check that and update it as required,' Lance said. 'We'd like you to arrange for building the tankers and the skips and the refrigerator truck and flatbeds on the rest. Don't worry about getting quotes. Just give the job to people who'll do it right first time, no excuses.'

'Right.'

'I'll be back in two weeks with my drivers,' Lance said.

Pierre had his chequebook open. 'I'll give you half as a deposit, hmm?'

The sales director tore his eyes away from the chequebook. 'Two weeks, did I hear you right?'

Lance nodded.

'I can maybe squeeze you out six trucks, Mr Weber. But thirty? You're joking.'

'I'm not. What if I give you another week?'

'You don't understand. The class of truck you want we make to order. I'm offering you six trucks ordered by somebody else. I need three, perhaps four months to deliver thirty trucks.'

'But last time I bought trucks from you – '

'You gave me three months warning.'

'We want those trucks for famine relief,' Lance said. 'Three months from now those people will be dead.'

'Oh, Christ! All the same – '

'What about your competitors? Sorry to have to ask but . . .'

'Sure, I understand. Some of the importers – Volvo, Mercedes, maybe Fiat – might have three or even four suitable trucks they could put off delivering – '

Lance was already shaking his head.

' – but you can't carry spare parts for five or six makes. That leaves the fellows across the road. But I know they're hard up against delivery schedules too. I can call my opposite number at Ford and try to shame him into doing something for you, if you like.'

'We'd appreciate it.'

The man left his office to make the call. He was away for ten minutes. 'Like I said, he's up against delivery schedules but he'll match my six trucks and lay on some overtime out of his public relations budget.'

'Hey, we'll pay for overtime here too. Does that – '

'Sorry. We're into overtime already. Listen, these are all twelve-tonners. Why load them only six tons?'

Lance said, 'We're going to Chad, probably through Zaire, but any way you go the roads are terrible.'

'Yeah. Better to arrive with a half-loaded truck than not at all.'

'Look, can you hold the offer open till tomorrow? I have to ask the people financing this if they still want to proceed.'

'Of course. Take your time.'

In the outer office, Pierre said, 'Even two makes of truck is a recipe for hold-ups and mistakes.'

Lance nodded. Then he turned, knocked once on the door he had just closed behind him and opened it to put his head around. 'Sorry to bother you again. It must be a pretty big order you can squeeze six trucks out of without losing the customer.'

'Yeah, right. He buys a hundred and twenty a year.'

'In quarterly instalments of thirty trucks each?'

'Yes. How did you – ?'

56

'Fate, I guess. Would you mind if I go see him?'

The sales director thought for only a moment. 'You mention the General's trucks in your publicity?'

Lance nodded and thought, *Afterwards!* He didn't intend advertising his coming to Qaddaffi.

'Okay. He's a good guy. He lives in Cape Town. I'll call him and just tell him you're coming, okay? You make your own pitch. It'll come better from you than from a guy trying to give his order to someone else.'

'You're a prince,' Lance took the proffered sheet of paper, looked at the address, and put it in his pocket. 'I'll try not to lose your customer.'

'I grew up in Cape Town but actually I felt a lot more at home in Port Elizabeth this morning, maybe because it's so grimy. Cape Town used to be like that when I was a boy, or at least Maitland was.' Lance gestured at the expansive, expensively kept gardens to indicate he did not mean to include his host's home among the grimy. Five hours later and three hundred miles south, they were in Cape Town. 'Now Cape Town has all these freeways and it's so clean . . . it has a hard sparkle. I suppose I've been away too long.'

Hans Tullius had received Lance and Pierre courteously and listened to their request in silence. Then he asked where they came from and so on, Pierre first, then Lance. Both answered patiently: Tullius was a good listener and both his visitors were mature enough to know when they were being tested for their mettle as good old boys.

'Poor boy made good?' Tullius said approvingly.

'Once,' Lance said. 'Lost it all in Argentina. I'm doing this trip to Chad for pay.'

'You're not finished till you stop fighting. I grew up in Goodwood, just down the road from you. Used think the park next to the Maitland town hall was jungle.' Tullius

57

waved his hand across the lush acreage in Hout Bay and the sea far below them, indicating how far he had come. 'Ewart Weber was your brother then?'

Lance nodded.

'I met him once on the Roux farm at Paarl. Didn't know who he was until afterwards but he made a big impression on everyone who met him. It can't be easy to live up to a brother like that.'

'You're so right! Pierre fought beside him for several years.'

'Aaah!' Tullius was delighted. 'Listen, I'll make my old trucks last another three months. You boys – no offence, Pierre – you boys can have the new trucks. I'll arrange for you to get them at my discount price as a regular big customer. But in return, you'll stay for dinner and tell an old man a tale or two, what?'

Later, while his guests sipped twenty-five-year-old KWV Directors' Reserve brandy and puffed illegally-imported Havana cigars after an excellent dinner, Tullius stroked his white Vandyke and asked, 'You given any thought to where you'll buy your grain?'

Lance shook his head. 'No. We know we don't want maize. We must have grain, preferably wheat.'

'Buggers won't eat anything else?'

'Yes. I saw it in Kenya, the Masai starving rather than eat maize. Pitiful.'

'Which ones are they?'

'Liquid diet. Blood and sour milk.'

Tullius nodded. 'We have a drought too, you know.'

Pierre said, 'If a short harvest has driven up the price, we'll just have to pay. Money isn't the problem, time is.'

Both Tullius and Lance laughed aloud.

Tullius explained, chuckling, 'No, no, no. It just means our farmers produce less of a surplus and the government throws less subsidized food in the sea at the taxpayers' expense.'

'Like the EEC?'

'Much worse. The farmers are the single most important political constituency in this country. What I was thinking was, I could speak to some people in the government and probably get you your grain free of charge out of the surplus.'

If Lance had known which 'people in government' this request would reach, he would never have agreed so gratefully and readily. Perhaps, if he had been less lulled with fine food and wine and good companions, he might have taken a moment to consider what a small place South Africa really is and how infinitely smaller the circle of people who take decisions.

The next day Tullius drove his Mercedes into Cape Town. He couldn't find any parking nearer than up the side of Stuttaford's department store, so he drove to the front door of his club and let his driver, brought along for exactly this contingency, drive the car around the block while he went in to lunch. He'd walk for exercise after lunch. He stood beside the bar watching the men who ran the country come in, nodding to most and speaking to a few. If you counted, you belonged to the RSA; if you didn't count, you weren't invited to join. At quarter to one the man he wanted to speak to came in. Tullius crooked a finger at him.

'Jansman, how are you?' He spoke Afrikaans; Jansman translates rather roughly as John-boy. Tullius gestured at the barman to give the minister a drink; the barman would not need to ask what.

'Hello Hans. How's gravel?' It was an old joke: Tullius was the largest gravel supplier in a country with more miles of blacktop per car than any other.

'Fair. You have a luncheon appointment?'

'Yes, unfortunately. You want to speak to me?'

'It won't take long. I'd like for you to give a hundred tons of the surplus wheat to the Matthew Ellimore Foundation.'

'That rings a bell.'

'The woman whose plane – '

' – was shot down by the Libyans and she got raped. Rawls. Something Rawls.'

'Christine Rawls.'

'Know her, do you?'

'No. But I know people connected with her, people you'll probably want to meet.'

'Who's she picked on this time?'

'The grain's going to Chad.'

Jansman Roux shook his distinguished head. 'Foreign Affairs won't like that. Qaddaffi warned her off.'

'I should think Foreign Affairs would be *very* happy to see Qaddaffi dealt a slap in the face, as long as you didn't tell them any too precisely in advance what's going on.'

'Naaw, Hans, she'll bomb again and then it's our grain involved in a provocation.'

'She won't bomb. She's hired Lance Weber and those black Belgian Congolese fighters of his late brother to ride shotgun on the grain. Qaddaffi will get his nose twisted.'

The minister whistled. The barman came at a trot, saw the two glasses hardly touched but set up fresh drinks all the same. Neither man noticed him.

'Lance Weber, eh? You know he killed the man who murdered my brother Jacques' widow, an absolute sadist called Bruun. I've been meaning to shake his hand for a long time.'

'He told me a little something about that last night. Can he have the grain?'

'Yes, yes of course. Tell him to drop into my office and I'll make the arrangements. After all, we only throw it in the sea; it's our Christian duty to give a little to charity, eh?'

'Precisely.'

Tullius selected cold cuts and salads from the long buffet and sat down at the big table where members without guests or private business usually lunched. He closed his eyes to say a quick prayer for the meal, as did many other men. With his coffee, he shifted two seats from which men had hurried away to urgent business to place him next to the Foreign Minister. He told him the delicious joke he and Jansman Roux were preparing to play on Qaddaffi; the politician too thought it a good one. 'Hans,' he said, still chuckling, 'you and Jansman both know he doesn't need to ask my permission for what he does in his own department.' It was a polite reminder not to inform him officially.

Four days later, the Foreign Minister mentioned the Chad expedition to his regular golfing partner and son-in-law, who was a senior officer of the National Intelligence Service, which used to be BOSS and was still the same secret police under a different name. 'We know. Burger mentioned it yesterday.'

It was typical of Rocco Burger that he should come alone, driving himself in a plain police car, rather than in a limousine with outriders or in the helicopter he undoubtedly commanded; any other secret police chief would probably not have come at all but had Lance brought to him instead. It was absolutely characteristic of Burger that none of the workmen thought him worth a second glance as he walked between the rows of trucks on the coachworks floor.

But Lance had sensed him before he could see him. It was like walking in the tall grass and suddenly knowing a predator was stalking you. Lance whirled and watched the sliding doors a full three seconds before Burger walked through the

61

gap. The secret policeman was older, only the vestiges of ginger remaining in his hair, but weighed not a pound more than when Lance had first met him twelve years before and, as always, he was an autumnal symphony: highly polished brown shoes, salt-and-pepper brown suit, cream silk shirt, a tie that was olive or chocolate depending on how the light caught it, brown-tinted photosensitive lenses to his glasses. He looked like a clerk who spent too much of his salary on his wardrobe. He was the most dangerous dandy in the world. Lance did not once take his eyes off him until Burger stopped in front of him, half a foot shorter but as slim and straight as Lance, who was two decades younger.

'What's it now? General?'

'Lieutenant-General. And you're alive and causing trouble. You muddied our relations with our friends the Argentinians by conducting a diversionary war in their interior during the Falklands conflict.'

'Come now, sir. I defend myself and mine and that's the end of it.'

Burger smiled thinly.

That smile enraged Lance unreasonably. 'I really don't care whether you believe me or the Argentinians. But since you're such bosom buddies with them, you might ask them who started shooting. It wasn't me.'

'Oh, I believe you. And I know you're now a Kenyan citizen and a British subject. But the problem was convincing the Argentinians that the man tying up two thousand troops in the hinterland – and killing more of them than was fair – was not one of ours.'

'They were *shooting* at us!' Lance heard his voice become thin and unattractive but his outrage was such that he couldn't control it. 'They sent a whole bloody army after the nine of us, six men, two women and a child. Fair?'

Burger nodded understandingly. 'Please. I've said I believe

you. The Argentinians started it and foolishly escalated every time they lost a few men. But that's the enigma of the Webers, my Lance. They don't have to look for trouble, it finds them.'

'I'm glad you realize that, General. Because I'm on a humanitarian mission –'

'For which you need no fewer than three of your brother's Baluba Butchers, each of whom by himself is an incitement to violence anywhere in Africa – and just accidentally the three who helped you cause an international incident in the Argentine, plus seventy Swahili warriors?'

'General, you're out of practice at sarcasm. You know where I'm heading and you know I can't go there naked.'

'Your very passage will provoke violence and you know it.' Burger did not raise his voice but his tongue lashed.

'That's their choice, not mine. I'm feeding the hungry, nothing else, nothing more, nothing less.'

'There are hungry in Botswana, Lesotho, Maputo, Zimbabwe, Angola, to mention only those immediately beyond our borders. Why look for trouble so far away?'

Lance grinned. 'But, General, I'm only an employee. I go where I'm told.'

Burger waited three seconds before he answered. 'Without you there will be no expedition to Chad. Did you really think I couldn't work that out for myself?' Burger was genuinely curious.

Lance chose to duck the question; there was no point to admitting he'd made a foolish mistake. 'I have the support of your government.'

'Of a minister or two. That's the only reason I don't have you and Pierre in the cells awaiting deportation right now. But, let me warn you, those ministers' writ does not run beyond the borders of this country. Mine does. Once you cross the Beit Bridge, they can't protect you.'

'And you're offering me protection? General, how gracious of you!' Lance just couldn't help himself.

Burger laughed pleasantly. 'I can't think of anyone who needs protection less than you, my boy. No, I'm warning you. One small whiff of an incident that can embarrass South Africa and my Special Security Police will deal with you. I'm putting them on instant alert until you return.'

Lance shivered. Burger's Special Security Police was a paramilitary force that dealt extralegally with extraterritorial threats to South African security. South African security, in Burger's view (and the President was the only one who could overrule him) was threatened as much by scandal as by terrorists.

'People think of you as Weber, the notorious South African mercenary,' Burger rammed his message home. 'The public don't know your brother is long dead and the journalists are too ignorant or venal to expose a favourite violent myth as merely the little brother. That's your misfortune. Your good fortune – and all that has kept you alive, given the challenges such a reputation provokes – is that you are quite as lethal as Ewart ever was.'

Lance was uncomfortably aware that he was blushing. Nor could he think of anything scathing to say.

'But reflect, my Lance. Your utterly competent and hugely experienced brother died all the same, almost accidentally, in the final moments of a battle already won.'

Lance again saw Ewart rolling under the tanker to aid Lance, the tanker exploding from bullets he and Jimmy had just fired at Bruun, Ewart burning, bone almost immediately showing through the flesh, Sambo shouting at him to put Ewart out of his misery and then doing it himself when Lance stood shocked into immobility. Lance had been twenty years old.

Burger couldn't know!

No, not the details, but the generality of it: Burger had been there that day at Lobengula's kraal in northwestern Zaire, arriving while Ewart's embers still glowed brightly.

For the merest moment Lance was tempted to tell Burger he was bringing succour to starving Chaddi children as a monument to his own dead daughter. But only for a moment. Such an appeal would demean him and cut no ice with Burger.

'I hear you, General.'

'I'd rather you believe me.'

'I do, General.'

To Lance's utter amazement, Burger clapped him on the arm.

'I don't want an impasse, understand?'

'General, I'd rather run than fight, now more so than ever.'

Burger stared into Lance's face for another few seconds, then nodded thoughtfully and, without another word, turned on his heel and walked away. Through the open doors, Lance saw him climb into his cheap-model police car and drive off.

'That man turns my blood into icicles,' Pierre said behind Lance, startling him, 'especially when he comes all the way to Port Elizabeth from Pretoria to warn us off.'

'No. The police killed twenty or so blacks up the road at Uitenhage. PE has the nearest airport. Burger's probably the power behind the enquiry that's bound to follow. We're a sideshow.'

'A pretty important sideshow if he comes himself while the main event is the twenty-fifth anniversary of Sharpeville featuring riots and killings in every city and town.'

Time pinched off whole days. In Port Elizabeth, Lance and Pierre were minutely inspecting the workmanship of their trucks and being threatened by General Rocco Burger of BOSS; in Mombasa, Jimmy, Boo and Mwanzo selected the

65

last of their seventy Swahili warriors and Jimmy left to buy arms in Dar-es-Salaam while Boo and Mwanzo started training the men; in Johannesburg, Esmeralda bought equipment, camping gear and food by the ton from a list she had taken five days to complete; in Pretoria, Christine harried officials for permits to bring the Swahili into the country, to let them drive on South African roads, to let them drive heavy goods vehicles, to load and export the grain, to buy and export medicines, to import and re-export other medicines – the list of required permits went on and on and on. Even so, Christine had time to fret over delays. She and Esmeralda stayed at the Hilton in Johannesburg, an hour's drive from Pretoria, and Esmeralda told Lance in one of their daily telephone conversations that Christine was hugely depressed when he put back their departure by three days because two of the three fuel tanks had shown stress concentrations under magnafluxing that on bad roads would soon develop into splits and cracks; the tanks had to be remade from scratch. Lance was unsympathetic. 'Tell her we'll do the job right or not at all. If she bitches to you, tell her to call me instead.' In the end, it was Christine's part of the work that held them up for an additional day, four in total past the target departure date. Officials in several ministries were delaying paperwork for essential anti-diarrhoea drugs. Lance called Tullius for advice and the old man found him a young MP who, for a 'consultation fee', called on the recalcitrant officials' superiors, presented his visiting card, and explained he would wait until he could take the completed paperwork away with him: nowhere did he have to wait for more than an hour. On the morning of the fifth day after the original target date, they left the Hilton at three-thirty in the morning to drive south to Vereeniging, where Esmeralda had borrowed a dormitory from a mining company to put up the Swahili.

Jimmy, Boo and Mwanzo introduced Pierre and Lance to

each and every man. Lance made a point of knowing each man's name, his father's name and the name of his eldest son, if any. He was delighted to recognize five men who had gone to Lake Kivu with him six years ago; these he hugged cheek to cheek. All of this took over an hour. Christine fidgeted impatiently until Esmeralda told her to get to know the kitchen staff of nine.

After greeting the men, Lance spent another hour personally checking every load and its fastenings. The trucks had been driven up from PE two days ago and the several tons of equipment and provisions had arrived by chartered carrier yesterday. Then Lance inspected the dormitory and toilets and showers to confirm his men had left them in good order; he expected to find them spotless and he did, but he was demonstrating to the men that he attended to detail, in itself an important consideration to men who knew their lives could soon depend on him. By now Christine was dancing from foot to foot.

She asked Esmeralda, 'How'd you persuade Lance to let you come?'

'Actually, he was surprisingly reasonable. I just told him Emmy was *our* child and I should be allowed to help build a monument for her.'

'If you two are ready,' Lance called, 'we can leave.'

They drove still further south, away from Chad, to Potchefstroom, where government silos towered. Lance led the convoy in his Range Rover, carrying as passengers Esmeralda, Mwanzo and Nasheer, the young Arab Jimmy had hired in Nairobi to negotiate and pay the multitudinous bribes that would smoothe their way up the length of Africa; Nasheer too had been a member of the Lake Kivu expedition. Jimmy, in another Range Rover, brought up the rear with Christine and two of the Swahili warriors as his passengers. Boo, who was baggage-master, had decided to space his tankers at

67

intervals through the convoy; he himself rode in the refrigerated truck which he intended to use as a shield for the middle
tanker in case of attack. Pierre elected to ride in a truck near
the middle, among the men he would command. Nobody
handed out assignments; they had all worked together before
and knew how their skills slotted together.

At the silo near the railway yards at Potchefstroom, the
trucks pulled up one by one under the spout, a workman
pulled a lever, eight tons of best-quality wheat dropped into
the skip in less than a minute, and the lever-man slapped the
roof of the cab to move the driver on. In under an hour they
loaded one hundred and fifty-six tons of grain. Christine,
impressed by how smoothly things now progressed after the
days and weeks of frantic preparation and frustrating delays,
said wistfully, 'We should have tried for twice as many trucks.'

They turned north for Beit Bridge and Zimbabwe five
hundred miles away – and Chad four thousand miles beyond
that.

They made camp in the dark twelve hours later just short of
Beit Bridge and left South Africa by crossing the Limpopo at
dawn the next morning after a snack of coffee and rusks or
putu, a cold, stiffened maize porridge Esmeralda had prepared the night before with their evening meal. At ten or
eleven they would break for an hour to prepare and eat
brunch, and then, by the accepted usages of African travel,
they should drive on till four or four-thirty at the latest before
stopping for the evening meal and the night. Lance, walking
about on his usual keen inspection to ensure they were
leaving the campsite a great deal cleaner than they found it,
raised his voice to tell them they would not camp until an
hour before sunset. That would keep them on the road for
fourteen hours. The fat cook shook his head incredulously.

He had heard Lance Weber was a hard man but this was insanity!

When they broke for brunch, Lance and Jimmy walked to the road and stood looking at the sky. Christine joined them. 'What are we waiting for?'

'Our arms,' Jimmy told her. 'Coming by plane.'

Christine looked around the featureless landscape, or rather, not featureless, just the same grass and trees and occasional huts she had seen for mile upon mile for five hours. 'How does the pilot know where to find us?'

'Think of the obvious.'

'You mean he flies up the road until he sees our convoy?'

'Right. He knows we're about five hours from Beit Bridge. That gives him his fix.'

'You can't just arm seventy men right here on the public highway!'

Lance turned to look at her curiously. 'Why not?'

She had no answer. He was utterly at home here whereas she felt vaguely uneasy in the rolling open savannah of expansive, unprotected space.

The plane, heard before they could see it, skimmed across the stunted trees and plopped down on the road between the eight-foot-deep storm drains with a precision that belied its ungainly fat-bellied appearance. It rolled briefly and stopped ten feet from Jimmy's Range Rover at the back of the convoy.

'Knows his stuff,' Lance said admiringly of the pilot.

'Old pal of Tanner's,' Jimmy told him. 'Doesn't usually get involved in this kind of thing but . . .'

The pilot climbed out. He was about thirty, lean and dark and tanned. He pulled open the cargo door. 'Everything in there comes out,' he said in Swahili to Mwanzo, who stood by with a gang. He turned to shake hands with Jimmy and was introduced to Christine and Lance.

'Christine Rawls, eh? You're the one that dropped Tanner in it.' It was an accusation.

'Unfortunately.'

The pilot stared at her for a moment, then relented. 'It's the luck of the draw. I'm sorry for Ruby, though.'

'We're still hoping to get Tanner out. The Italian Foreign –'

'Diplomats!' The pilot flicked them away contemptuously. 'Don't forget to call me if the hat has to go round for Ruby.'

'Thank you, I'll remember,' Christine said.

The crates were unloaded. The pilot raised a hand and climbed into his plane. Lance told the Swahili to turn it around. The pilot waved at them, ran up the engines and took off, heading low over the trees to the east.

'Did you pay him up front?' Lance asked Jimmy.

'No. He refused pay. He's doing it for Tanner.'

The Swahili whooped for joy as they broke open the crates and distributed the firearms.

'Mwanzo!'

The Swahili caught Lance's eye and threw him a sample. Lance gave it a single glance. 'Christ,' he said to Jimmy, 'what the hell did you want to spend all this money for on FNs? Couldn't you get Kalashnikovs?'

'Plenty of Kalashnikovs about. But your brother preferred these and they're a goddam sight better made than the AK47s.'

'What's this?' Christine wanted to know.

'Jimmy's been splashing out your money for Rolls-Royces when all we needed were Volkswagens at a quarter the price.'

Christine looked up at Jimmy, who was not disconcerted at all. 'The best tools for the job. Our Swahili will fight so much harder because we give them each a precision-made FN rather than a piece of Czech crud. Even Lance will admit that.'

Lance walked away without answering.

'Odd,' Christine said. 'I always assumed that Lance is one of those who love firearms better than people.'

'Are you crazy? He hates guns.'

'And you?'

'They're tools, Christine. You use them to do a job. The problem with Lance is that he's a closet Christian. He thinks killing's bad, regardless of who he has to kill. But he's not just a Christian, he's a Calvinist, so he does the job that needs to be done and agonizes over it later.'

'And you don't?'

'I see no moral problem about killing a bad man. Or a good man who happens to be shooting at me. Those Swahili see no problem about killing anyone who isn't a Swahili. You used to be soft about killing animals for food. It's rubbish to pretend it's a moral question − respect for life is relative and a consequence of environment and upbringing.'

In its basic form, the FN is a short-barrel semi-automatic machine pistol. Jimmy had also bought, for each one, a long barrel and a stock to turn it into an assault rifle. In addition, there were half a dozen extra-long barrels with sniperscopes and two nightlight intensifier scopes. Each firearm was further provided with a dozen ammunition clips, cleaning tools and materials, two thousand rounds of ammunition, and a mini-rack with self-tapping screws. Lance inspected the fitting of the racks in the truck cabs, and had two that could bruise shins moved to safer locations.

Lance watched the Swahili stripping and cleaning and loading their weapons. Jimmy and Mwanzo had trained them well. They were like children with new toys, teeth gleaming everywhere. A car appeared on the road, slowed, and drove on in a hurry after the driver saw all the armed men. Pierre, who had taken charge of camp security, helped Boo distribute the ammunition between the trucks.

Mwanzo unlooped the chain from the trigger guard of Lance's custom Mannlicher in the gun rack in the back of the Range Rover. Then he racked up his own FN and a couple of spares.

Pierre appeared with two pistols. 'Christine?'

'No thanks.'

'I insist,' Lance said.

'I couldn't kill anyone.'

'Fine. But a time could come when you might want to kill yourself.'

'What a Neanderthal you are. One does recover from a "fate worse than death", you know.'

'I wasn't thinking of rape, Christine. But we'll be crossing the tribal lands of people who as a matter of course skin strangers alive.'

'Take the pistol, Christine.' Jimmy still smiled but there was a steely note in his voice.

'Listen, I don't – '

'No, you'd rather hire your killing done,' Jimmy snapped. 'Does that make you less guilty?'

Christine took the pistol and its holster from Pierre.

'Wear it in good health,' Pierre said. 'But all the time, eh? Here, Esmeralda. I'll arrange for someone to give you some instruction no later than tomorrow. Until then, keep the safety on.'

'Let's eat and move on.' Lance headed for the jug and washbasin set up on a folding table as a field bathroom. 'We've already lost an hour.'

'Every passing year you become more like your brother,' Boo told him.

'I feel his spirit moving in me.' Lance, who knew full well that Boo had a tendency to superstition, watched with interest as Boo rolled his eyes in awe that was only half mocking.

Once they were seated, Jimmy said, 'Christine thinks you're maligning the nice black people up the road.'

Lance snorted. He wasn't about to argue with Christine.

'But do you remember,' Jimmy insisted, 'you thought we were having you on when we told you what it would be like the first time you went up this road.'

Lance smiled. 'Yes! I told you it was unkind to make fun of strangers. How wonderfully innocent we all were then.'

'Ha! You were merely ignorant.'

'Ignorance too is a state of grace.' Lance noticed the sharp glance Christine cast him. And wilful blindness? he wondered but kept his peace.

A pickup stopped on the road and nine men in battledress with gold leopard insignia on their wine-red berets, cradling machine pistols, sauntered across the pierced steel plank Lance's party had laid to bridge the storm drain. They stopped in formation almost on the fire. The cook scuttled away fearfully. Lance rose from his table.

'And good morning to you too.'

The leader didn't return the greeting. 'I'm commandeering your grain for the hungry people.'

Lance nodded as if agreeing. But the nod was intended for Mwanzo, who walked casually to the rear of the Range Rover.

'And the women will come with us. Their papers aren't in order.'

Again Lance nodded. He didn't bother to state the obvious, that papers not examined could equally well be in order. Out of the corner of his eye, Lance saw Christine shiver. The man did indeed brag an evil appearance, with bloodshot eyes, a much-broken nose and several large ragged scars disfiguring his face. Nor were his companions paragons of beauty. 'And who are you?'

'Fifth Parachute Brigade.'

73

'Mmm. I've heard about you. Nasheer.'

Nasheer carried a gold rod in one hand and a pair of wire-cutters in the other. He walked right up to the soldier, passed the rod around the back of the man's neck, bent it into a circle, and twisted the ends into a knot in front. He snipped the ends off with his wire-cutters and dropped them into his shirt pocket.

'Soft,' Nasheer said. 'One hundred per cent gold.'

'Okay. We take two trucks and the women come with us.'

'That is three ounces of gold. A thousand dollars,' Nasheer said. He took the ends out of his shirt pocket and dropped them in the black soldier's pocket. 'We have paid you for your protection. We do not want trouble. But, if you make trouble, aah!'

'Okay. No grain. You, women, you come with us.' He gestured with his machine pistol.

'Mwanzo!'

Mwanzo cocked the Mannlicher and flung it across the donga. Lance caught it without taking his eyes from the soldiers and stuck the barrel into the leader's stomach while Nasheer was still stepping aside and before any of the Fifth Parachute Brigade's finest realized resistance had erupted. By the time they turned their arms on Lance, all around them they could hear safety catches flicking off.

'Don't shoot,' Lance said in Swahili. 'You'll soon have plenty of use for your fine new weapons. Lie flat on the ground Esmeralda, Christine,' he added in English. He did not raise his voice; in that sudden hush, his normal speaking voice could be heard a hundred feet away.

Esmeralda promptly rolled off her chair and stretched out full length on the earth. Christine sat rooted, staring at the scarred black man, until Esmeralda tugged at her ankle.

For another ten seconds – an eternity to stand with a cocked rifle pushed into your stomach – Lance waited.

'You're poor specimens,' he finally said sternly. 'You didn't even notice we were armed. Lay down your weapons.'

Their leader's eyes burned hatred into Lance's face.

Lance gave him another three seconds, then reached a long arm past his own rifle to grab the front of the other man's blouse and jerk him forwards. He let go, used the same hand to smash the soldier through the face so hard that yellow snot flew from the man's nose, while his other hand reversed his rifle and smacked the butt hard on the man's wrist. The man staggered back from the blow and his weapon dropped. Lance caught the Chinese machine pistol before it touched ground. He put his foot on the barrel and pulled. The barrel bent. Lance flung the useless weapon from him and smiled slightly as the soldier rose from the ground with a huge flickknife in his hand. Lance's heavy boot caught him over the ear, then in the stomach as he staggered backwards, then under the chin as he jerked forwards. The man fell and lay still.

There was another silence. Then one of the Swahili spat in disgust: it hadn't been much of a fight.

'Exactly,' said Jimmy. 'Now see what happens when you send a boy to do a man's work.'

Lance gestured a millimetre with the barrel of his rifle. The soldiers hurriedly put their firearms on the ground. One threw down a knife and the others followed suit. Then they raised their arms high in the air.

Jimmy put his own FN flat on the ground and rose. He picked up one of the Zimbabweans' machine pistols. 'Tch! Filthy. And even worse made than the Kalashnikov. And the safety's off.' He clicked the safety back on and threw the weapon to Boo, who bent the barrel between his two huge hands. Muscles rippled in his bare forearms but his face remained impassive. Jimmy leaned close to one of the soldiers. 'And you're the famous North Korean-trained Fifth

Parachute Brigade? The ones widely feared for the beatings and murders and rapes they've been perpetrating on the Matabele? Amazing.'

The soldier flinched and tensed himself for the blow. But Jimmy returned to the table, sat down and continued his meal.

'Mwendli and Mpengo, pick up their arms,' Lance told two Swahili. When the armament had been removed, he washed his hands, pulled Esmeralda up and sat down to his food again.

Christine sat up and started screaming.

'Oh shit!' Lance leaned over to press the nerve above her elbow until she stopped. Esmeralda led her away.

'Any time you feel you can't cope, Lance, just send for us,' Pierre said. His brothers chuckled at his wit but Lance's mind was elsewhere.

'They certainly put the fear of god into Christine,' Lance said reflectively. 'What kind of world do we live in when such ... such *failures* can terrorize a whole nation?' He paused with his fork halfway to his mouth to consider the men with their hands still in the air as if trying to find some quality he had missed. Finding nothing, he returned to his food. When the steward came to the table, he said, 'Please take a tray to my wife and Miss Christine. Plenty of liquid, hmm, orange juice, tea, coffee. And stop shaking, man. There were only nine of them.'

'They get away with it because they're officially protected by Robert Mugabe's government,' Jimmy said. 'Joshua Nkomo and his Matabele are all that stand between Mugabe and the one-party state he wants.'

Lance pushed his chair back and rose. 'We leave as soon as we clear up here. Mwanzo.' The sharpshooter rose among the Swahili, his bowl in his hand. 'When you finish eating,

76

strip this scum naked. Bring their clothes with us. Also the wheels of their truck.'

'I think you should execute them, Mr Weber,' Nasheer said. 'If you pay too much in a hurry, people think you're frightened and try to take everything, just like these men did. But news of an execution will travel ahead and grease our way.'

'Certainly,' Lance said patiently, knowing Nasheer was in absolute earnest, 'but it will also travel in the other direction.'

'I beg your pardon, sir?'

'Which way do you face when you say your prayers, Nasheer?'

Nasheer was bewildered. 'Towards Mecca. You know that, Mr Weber.'

'Uh-huh. Well, every morning and evening I face Pretoria and pray with all my heart that General Burger never hears my name again and consequently doesn't send his Special Security Police to drop on us out of that innocent sky and kill me and everybody in my party.' Lance paused to watch Nasheer's growing comprehension. 'Exactly. Who do you think the government here will call first if they find nine of their pet thugs dead in a storm drain right after we pass?'

'Pretoria.'

Lance clapped Nasheer on the shoulder and walked with him down the line of trucks. 'I'm glad you understand, Nasheer. I'm not especially tender about such murderous scum, but I must look out for our own welfare. I want you to show the women how to use their firearms.' Nasheer was an excellent shot.

'Of course. It will be a pleasure.'

'You'll have fifteen minutes. Just give me a minute with them first.'

Nasheer tactfully wandered away. Lance climbed into the front seat of Jimmy's Range Rover and turned to study

77

Esmeralda and Christine in the back seat. Both women showed the strain of the last twenty minutes and both had beads of sweat on their upper lips.

'Those specimens were so poor,' Lance said conversationally, 'nobody even thought to offer me assistance in dealing with them. Of course, ten minutes earlier we would have been unarmed and then it could have been a different story . . . But I didn't bring seventy men to handle trash. I brought seventy men because from now on it gets worse.'

It was the closest Esmeralda ever came to hating him. He had given a virtuoso display of coordination and determination and power but one slip, one hesitation and he would have died in the crossfire. There was a madness in her Lance that was new, that she recognized only because she had her own share. Only later would it occur to her that she too had been sitting at the congruence of all firing lines.

'Christine, go home. You have no purpose on this journey. You can't fire a rifle, you can't drive a truck, there is nothing more you can do. Go raise money for the next cause.'

'No.' Christine took her pistol out of its holder and stared uncomprehendingly at it. Lance took it gently from her and put it on the front passenger seat. 'I promised to deliver the food personally to Chad.'

'Please don't be obtuse, Christine. Your presence makes it less likely that we will actually deliver the food.'

Christine shook her head. She reached over the seat for the pistol. Lance took the magazine out, checked there was nothing in the breach and gave it to her.

'You're five hours out of South Africa and already you can't take the pace. How do you think you will survive three, maybe four weeks of increasing pressure?'

Christine would not answer. She looked into all the orifices of the pistol as if to divine its secrets.

'Esmeralda, can you reason with her?'

'She won't listen, Lance.'

'Then will *you* go back before it is too late? Please.'

'Will you come with me and leave this doomed expedition to its fate?'

'I can't. You know that.'

'Then you know I can't either.'

Lance sighed. 'Nasheer will instruct you in the use of your pistols, starting immediately. Don't leave her alone with a loaded pistol.' Lance gestured at Christine.

'I'm frightened and angry, not suicidal,' Christine said. 'What's the point of having a pistol if it isn't loaded?'

'You must not point a gun unless you are prepared to use it.'

'I am.'

'All right. Nasheer!'

Nearly seven hours later, Christine asked Jimmy, 'Do you think people like those really would have given our grain to the hungry?'

Jimmy laughed so hard he had to stop the Range Rover and wait until he could see again through the tears in his eyes before he drove on. 'Sure,' he said once they were underway again. 'And this year we'll see them in the Christmas panto. Oh, Christine, you're priceless!'

For the rest of the day Christine said not a word.

Later that day Lance made his first mistake when he decided that, since they were past Salisbury, the capital, they could camp reasonably safe from retaliation by the authorities for nine naked paratroopers wandering the highway. He should have kept them on the road through the night and across the Zambian border. But that was another two hundred and fifty miles – over six hours – and a sleepy driver could lose them a truck and eight tons of grain with it.

They drove on at dawn but within the hour official wrath caught up with them.

The helicopter came out of nowhere and buzzed Lance's Range Rover and then the whole mile-long column.

Beethoven's Sixth Symphony, the Pastoral, in the tape player clicked off as Jimmy cut in on the transceiver. 'That's not a friendly.'

Lance took the mike from its hook.

'Is he still there?'

'He's turning for a strafing run. We're five hours from the border.'

'Nobody's asked us to stop.'

Jimmy chuckled. 'Right. Did you see his spotter friend?'

'No.'

'Light plane hanging around in the sun for about ten minutes until he came, then disappeared.'

'We'll carry on, wait and see.' Lance pushed the von Karajan/Berlin interpretation back into the tape deck. 'Nasheer, what do you know about baksheesh here?'

'They shoot people who take bribes.'

Lance groaned.

'They started doing that when they found out how bad the corruption was,' Nasheer added.

Esmeralda opened the map on her lap. 'There's a marginally shorter road that'll take us into Moçambique.'

The tape clicked off again. Jimmy, not quite suppressing a chuckle, said, 'Christine thinks that, since we've done nothing wrong, we should stop and explain to the relevant authorities.'

'I'm not volunteering to become an Amnesty International statistic.' Lance clicked the music back on.

'On the other hand,' Nasheer continued, 'you can still buy the whole firing squad for less than a hundred dollars American or five cartons of Texan.' Texan was the local

Zimbabwean brand of cigarette, unfiltered and fiercely strong.

'Your sense of humour will land you in trouble yet,' Lance warned Nasheer.

'Sorry, Mr Weber.' He didn't sound very contrite.

'Are you certain you can buy these people before a bigger trouble catches up with us?'

'Upon my mother's virtue, sir.'

Lance watched as the helicopter settled on the road half a mile from them. He picked up the mike. When he pressed the button, the music cut out. 'Jimmy, we're stopping. Nasheer says he can do business.'

'But quickly, eh. The back of my neck feels freshly shaven. Those boyos we left in their birthday suits are not only favourite sons but standard-bearers for a certain image we've damaged. Like the Roman eagles the Germanic tribes took and the Romans spent a century recovering.'

'On his mother's virtue, he says.'

'That's good enough for me.'

Lance slowed and stopped the Range Rover and sat for a moment watching the mirror as the truck behind him pulled up ten feet away. 'Pass me my rifle, if you please, Mwanzo. Do you want Mwanzo as well, Nasheer?'

'No sir. Just you and me. Mrs Weber, please don't get out.'

Lance and Nasheer approached the helicopter but stopped at the tip of the rotor. Lance carried his rifle loosely in his hand, the barrel pointing at the road. The two men in the small bubble carried sidearms in buttoned holsters. One was obviously the pilot; the man who climbed out wore a gorgeous uniform, with eggstains on the lapels.

'I have reports that you refused to show your papers yesterday in the land of the rebel Matabele,' he said before he reached them.

Lance knew it would be all right. The man even *looked*

venal. Nasheer could deal with this on his own. Lance threw a brisk salute more in honour of the Hungarian Hussar's uniform than its occupant and returned to the Range Rover.

It took Nasheer ten minutes. The helicopter left immediately. Lance drove on. 'I didn't see any money change hands.'

'No, Mr Weber. We won't pay until we're free. Don't stop before the border. The Army have orders to shoot us on sight.'

'Ouch!'

'He will try to arrange that they don't sight us.'

'That sounds very expensive.'

'Not unreasonably so. A middle-size Mercedes for him, a Volkswagen Golf for the pilot.'

'He's trusting us?'

'My family is not unknown here. And your name also carries a certain weight.'

'I see. Well done, Nasheer.'

But they still had to reach and cross the border.

'Can't we go any faster?' Christine demanded of Jimmy.

'Lance is leading us at the fastest possible pace.'

'Seventy miles an hour, pfft!'

'For us in the Range Rover, maybe. But any faster and we could lose a truck full of grain.' Jimmy picked up the mike and offered it to her. 'I'm sure Lance itches to go faster. It's your grain – ask him to step on it.'

Christine took the mike, considered for a moment, then returned it to its hook. 'Forget it.'

She fell to studying her map again. Africa is a monstrously large place but not at all heavily populated. In consequence, there is nowhere a great choice of roads to any destination. In particular, on this road, with the Zambezi River and Lake Kariba and the Kariba Dam between them and safety in

Zambia, they had no choice at all. They had to go down to the Kariba Gorge and cross the single bridge.

'It's that or turn back and meet them head-on,' Jimmy said without removing his eyes from the road.

'Did you know we would run into trouble in Rhod – I mean Zimbabwe?' Otherwise, why would he have the map imprinted on his mind?

'Not *know*, perhaps. Strongly suspected it though.'

'Why?'

'Well, the place was recently liberated from colonial rule by guerrilla fighters and outright terrorists, so a lot of these fellows not yet weaned of their old habits will be in the army and police. Secondly, they're fighting among themselves for supremacy – there's something very little short of a civil war in progress here and that always brings out the worst in people. Mugabe's Shona are hyping themselves up for geno-cide on the Matabele, so why not include a few foreigners in the head-count?'

'But not all nations born in brutality end up bad. Look at Kenya.'

'Every time you pick the exception that proves the rule. You make it impossible to have a reasoned discussion.'

After a while, she said, 'I didn't mean to. What makes Kenya different?'

'Kenyatta embraced terror as a *means* and discarded it once he had achieved his ends. That's because he was his own man and an intellectual giant in his own right. But Mugabe is a Marxist or, more precisely, a Leninist-Stalinist: he does not have to choose terror, it is a permanent part of his ideology. He does not even conceive of the possibility of rejecting force once it has achieved his ends. What's more, if perpetual revolution is part of your ideology, once in power you have by definition to be paranoid – and paranoia breeds violence like nothing else. No, you can't get to Kenya from Moscow.'

Unexpectedly, Christine laughed. 'And I suppose you'll say all those fascist South American regimes and Israel are the same thing seen from the other side.'

'Sure. If you're under perpetual threat, whether real as in the case of Israel or imaginary like some of those Latin-American generals, it's only human to react with escalating force. It's a cycle that's almost impossible to stop.'

'God, you're a pessimist.'

'No, I'm an African and a realist. Look at your map. Check the countries where power was handed over peacefully when the colonial powers left. They are the ones most likely still to retain a measure of democracy. Like Zambia, up the road. But where power was wrested by force, the rulers soon turn on those in whose interest they claim to act.'

'What about places like Uganda?'

'Uganda just proves my point. There was, anyhow by African standards, tranquillity and security under Obote, even if he was, by your lights, a tyrant and an asshole. But then Amin took power by force and things got so bad that the Tanzanians had to depose him by force and now Obote's back and running an oppressive regime because he doesn't want another Amin to oust him. It's a vicious circle. Name me one African country that, once fallen into violence, has ever recovered permanently.'

'Yes, but it's not their fault if the imperialists imposed alien concepts of democracy on them and lumped together ancient tribal enemies in artificial geographic constructs.'

'Oh shit! "Artificial geographic constructs"! If it's all right for a black man to be a mad butcher because of some historic wrong done to his people, then Hitler must have been right to start his war because of the injustices of the Treaty of Versailles. Making allowances for black people just because they are black is a particularly destructive form of racism.'

Christine said nothing for several minutes until Jimmy spoke again.

'It's that sort of reverse discrimination that's responsible for people dying of hunger.'

'How?' Christine snapped.

'The Africans were doing everything wrong but nobody told them for two decades because every criticism, however constructive, was immediately damned as the outgrowth of a racist mind-set. They broke up the huge, profitable colonial estates – '

'The profits of slavery!'

'Of course. But they could have paid decent wages and still have contributed hugely to export earnings to keep the debt spiral down. Before independence, virtually every African country not only fed itself but was a food exporter. Until they collectivized the land in spite of the history of failure of Russian and Chinese communal agriculture. Let's skip lightly over the competent and efficient European technocrats pushed out in Africanization programmes and – '

'There are a lot of efficient Africans around,' Christine protested.

'And mostly under thirty-five?' Jimmy glanced at her.

Christine nodded. It was true.

'A new generation. They'd have to be superhuman to save anything out of the mess they inherited. Never mind the disasters with nationalized industry: every socialist country had those. Let's just stick to agriculture. Next, they made laws to keep farm produce prices down simply to keep themselves in power. This was another vicious circle. Because the farm prices were low, there was no new investment in agriculture. People deserted the land to migrate to the cities. The cities grew and, because they would riot and perhaps topple the leaders every time food prices rose – over seventy coups in Africa in twenty-five years, food was the one thing

85

never allowed a realistic price increase. So, in the end, countries that had once produced mountainous food surpluses starved at the first drought.'

'Come on, Jimmy, three years of drought – '

'I'm talking about the drought of 1972. Three hundred thousand dead of starvation in the Sahel alone and nobody learned any lessons. As late as 1980, several African leaders damned the Berg report as mere racist propaganda.'

'The West hasn't helped by insisting on cash crops and prestige projects.'

'It's not "the West", Christine. These were individuals hired by the African governments to advise them. Will you excuse Nixon because he listened to bad advice?'

'No. But – '

'Then you can't make bad advice an extenuating circumstance for another leader just because he's black. In any event, they were given a good deal of advice that, even in retrospect, was of the highest calibre but which failed because of endemic incompetence and the corruption of greed or ideology.'

'You're pretty hard on your own people.'

'It's pretty hard to die of hunger.'

'I didn't know you cared so much.'

'I wouldn't if it was unavoidable. I would see the dying and consider it their natural fate. But this, millions dead or dying because of stupidity, it angers me unreasonably.'

'No, very reasonably,' Christine said. 'There's a tank on that hill and it's pointing its thing at us.'

Jimmy said, 'Lance saw it minutes ago. He's been speeding up ever since.'

Lance reached over the drive tunnel to jerk the fire-extinguisher free from its spring clips. It rolled on the floor at

Esmeralda's feet as he dropped it to grab at the wheel to correct a swerve caused by a pothole in the road.

Esmeralda bent to pick up the extinguisher and cradled it on her lap. It was the biggest that would fit in the Range Rover and weighed twenty-one pounds.

'Get the spare from the back, Mwanzo,' Lance shouted when the Range Rover stopped swinging this way and that across the road. 'Esmeralda, tell Jimmy to point his fire-extinguishers out of the windows and follow me.'

Esmeralda picked up the mike. Lance watched the tank's barrel elevate. The tank commander intended to knock his Range Rover out and perhaps one or two of the leading trucks if the road wasn't completely blocked by the Range Rover's wreckage. He didn't know what range the man would start firing at – already they were within a thousand yards of the tank. Of course, the tank commander need be in no hurry: there was nowhere for the convoy to escape except down the narrow road. They couldn't even go bush because the storm drains on each side of the road were twelve feet wide and eight deep.

'We're a dream target,' Jimmy told Lance on the radio.

Esmeralda held the mike before Lance's mouth. 'Only while he sits on that little knoll,' Lance said.

It was time. Lance wished he had radio contact with the trucks but there had been no time to install a complete net. And he had not seen the need for such extravagance . . . He could only hope the truck drivers would not try to follow him. He stuck his arm out of the window and made scooping motions with his hand: Please pass!

'Hang on, everybody,' Lance said. He put his foot in the corner and listened to the V8 scream until he was certain there was no more speed to be had. Then he set the Range Rover at an angle to the storm drain. The moment he felt the right front wheel drop, he flicked the steering-wheel right then left and prayed they were travelling fast enough for centrifugal force to keep the heavy vehicle from dropping on its side into the bottom of the storm drain. He closed his eyes as he saw the stones set in concrete rush to the side of his face. When he opened his eyes again, the stones were twelve inches from his temples. They were riding along the wall of death. To make a smooth transition onto the bottom of the storm drain without crashing, he wanted to run up to just under the rim of the side wall which would give him space to angle onto the floor. Lance tried to put his foot through the floor but the rev counter was well into the red and there was no more power to be had. He jiggled the wheel gently and gained perhaps six inches. In the mirror he saw Jimmy's Range Rover ricochet off the lefthand wall, shoot across the floor of the storm drain and bounce off the righthand wall. Lance leaned away from the lethal floor of the drain and flicked the wheel. There was an anguished tearing of metal as the front corner of the wing dug in. Then Esmeralda crashed against him as they bounced off the far wall. He had lost no speed and immediately set the Range Rover at the right-hand wall at so steep an angle that it shot to the top and over. They landed forty feet from the storm drain, so hard that Lance's head dented the roof of the Range Rover before his safety belt could restrain him. Esmeralda swore in Spanish as the heavy fire-extinguisher broke free of her hold, fell into the footwell and promptly cracked her across the shins. She caught it and hauled it back onto her lap while Lance fought to straighten the Range Rover and slow it to some manageable speed. Out of the corner of his eye, Lance saw Jimmy's Range Rover bounce once, twice, three times, then spin round and round and round to a complete standstill. They were less than three hundred yards from the tank and the turret was turning to line them up. Jimmy was pointed left, so Lance went right.

'Just the tips of those fire-extinguishers out of the windows,' Lance shouted.

He hauled the Range Rover up short a hundred yards from the tank. He jumped out, grabbed the rifle Nasheer passed through the window, and clanged two shots off the lower parts of the tank as the commander, thinking he was under fire, hurriedly popped down his hole and pulled the lid to. The tank fired once but the barrel was already pointing at the air as the driver reversed frantically off the knoll to put it between him and the anti-tank rockets the commander was shouting dementedly about. A stutter of heavy-calibre machine-gun bullets also spent their rage at the sky.

The last truck of the convoy passed on the road below.

Lance jumped into the driving seat, the rifle leading to be stuffed in the passenger footwell next to Esmeralda's feet, vanity case, thermos, and the extinguisher.

'Get the hell out, Lance!' Jimmy said over the radio. 'He's coming round your side.'

Lance raised his foot fractionally and dipped the clutch to slip it so the wheels could bite instead of spinning off torque on the flattened grass. Then the Range Rover rocketed forward and he sighed. In the mirror he saw the turret of the tank appear cautiously over the top of the knoll. Jimmy drove parallel to him, forty feet away. Lance jerked his head backwards. Before Jimmy could respond, a shell exploded a hundred and fifty yards ahead of them.

'Premature ejaculation,' Esmeralda said.

Lance laughed. The tail end of the convoy was a mile down the road, the head of the mile-long snake already on the damwall which was also the bridge. He flung the Range Rover over the side of the storm drain too fast to try for a respite on the side wall before attempting the transition from side to floor. They heard and felt more rending of metal and a wheezing thud which Lance knew was a suspension damper valve collapsing. In the mirror he saw Jimmy's Range Rover slide into the storm drain even more precipitately than his own entry. Over his shoulder, he could see the tank again standing proud on the knoll.

'If we can see him . . .' Esmeralda shouted.

Lance fought the juddering wheel. At over ninety miles per hour he didn't want to brush that wall. The lack of a damper on one side threw the Range Rover from side to side along the rough bottom of the storm drain.

'The sides of the storm drain will protect us against anything but a direct hit,' he said calmly.

The next shell fell right on the edge of the storm drain only twenty yards ahead. The concussion rocked the Range Rover and the falling rubble crashed against it and flew through the open window, blinding Lance momentarily. The sound he heard was the left front mudguard being torn off and scraping along between the wall of the storm drain and the vehicle.

'Lance, back on the road,' Esmeralda shouted just as his eyes cleared and he saw blue sky straight ahead as the storm drain fell away to the Zambesi River. He flicked the wheel, flicked it again to hold momentarily on the side wall, then again to slide the crippled Range Rover onto the road as gently as he could. He connected Esmeralda's door solidly with the cornerpost of the bridge on the far side of the road, saw Jimmy's mount sliding very quickly towards him and accelerated away just as Jimmy in turn hit the cornerpost ringingly. A shell whizzed by and exploded in the water below, splashing the windshield with water and creating a mudbath that blacked out the windshield completely. Lance stuck his head out of the window to see. He wasn't stopping. From behind him came small-arms fire: no doubt the border-post soldiers, though he had not even seen them. Before him was another border post, with armed men scrambling into a jeep and others waving their arms and shouting. Lance didn't stop there either; it was obvious his Swahili and the grain trucks had driven straight through – pieces of the striped pole were still falling to the ground.

Lance accelerated until he came to the rearmost truck, then passed the trucks one by one as fast as he could. At the head of the column, he put his hand out of the window and waved it up and down to slow the convoy. Finally they stopped.

The jeep he had seen back at the border post roared up and stopped on the other side of the road. Lance climbed out, carrying his rifle but with the barrel pointing to the road. Nasheer joined him. Mwanzo too climbed out and went to stand at the front of the Range Rover, cradling his FN.

'Sorry about the unceremonious arrival,' Lance said to the officer sitting in the passenger seat of the jeep. 'They were shooting at us.'

'They're ruining the whole region's tourist trade,' the officer said. He swung his legs out of the jeep and stretched. Then he considered Lance and Mwanzo's arms, and the arms Pierre and several of the Swahili were carefully pointing at the ground about twenty feet away.

'Were you shooting back?'

Lance put his rifle back in the Range Rover, fetched a fire-extinguisher and gave it a squirt. 'They thought these were anti-tank rockets.'

The Zambian threw back his head and roared with laughter.

Pierre nodded to the Swahili and led them back to their trucks. Mwanzo started racking the firearms in the back of the Range Rover and Nasheer took the fire-extinguisher from Lance and stowed it.

'I don't suppose you have Zambian permits for so many rifles?'

'There wasn't time,' Lance said. 'We're carrying grain for famine relief in Chad.'

'Ah. Well, I obviously haven't the manpower to confiscate your weapons but you'd better stop off at the ministry in Lusaka and please – explain.' He took an envelope from his pocket and wrote on it. 'See this man. He's reasonable.' He looked at Nasheer. 'And don't try to bribe him, eh?'

'Thanks,' Lance said, taking the envelope.

'Any time. Tell your friends we welcome tourists.'

The next day, as they ate their brunch beside the Kafue before crossing the border into Zaire, Christine spread her maps beside her plate and, measuring with spread fingers, said, 'In four days we've covered more than a third of the distance from the silos in Potchefstroom to the hungry people of northern Chad.'

Lance nodded. He knew what was coming.

'Can we deliver the food in eight days?'

'No. We'll be very lucky to be there in eighteen days. Three weeks is more likely.'

'Why?'

'Because the roads get worse and the people more hostile,' Lance said bluntly.

'You told me this morning,' Jimmy said to Christine, 'that the roads are excellent in South Africa, worse to very bad in Zimbabwe, and terrifying in Zambia. Extrapolate to no roads at all and worse and you've got the general idea.'

'Still – '

'Some days we won't make fifty miles,' Lance said. 'Three hundred miles in a day from here to the Mediterranean is good going, I assure you. If the rains come early, even fifty miles a day will soon seem a momentous achievement.'

A black Peugeot with a pennant on the fender drove into

92

their camp. A grey-haired man climbed from the back seat and put on his suit jacket. Lance went forward to meet him.

'I'm looking for Miss Rawls.'

It turned out he was the Minister of Agriculture.

'Miss Rawls,' he said, 'my colleague at Interior told me you are in our country. It really is remiss of you to pass through Lusaka and not call so that we can express our gratitude.'

For a moment, Christine merely nodded uncomprehendingly. Then she said brightly, 'Ah, yes, the hydroponics institute my Foundation finances. I trust it goes well.'

'Indeed. We are now tomato-exporters. I could not let pass this opportunity to convey personally the gratitude of my government and our people.'

'You've come to the right place,' Christine said. 'Mrs Weber is our chief financial benefactress and the widow of Matthew Ellimore, did you know that? And Mr Weber and the Princes Knékwassé – ' she gestured at Pierre, Boo and Jimmy – 'were the other original benefactors. You are now looking at all the founders of the Matthew Ellimore Foundation.'

To everyone's embarrassment except Christine's, the minister insisted on rising and shaking hands with them once more.

Before the Minister went, he told Christine, 'Your office wrote asking if we could send four men for two years to a similar project in Moçambique. We should be very happy to do that.'

They stood watching the dust of his car as he headed back to Lusaka.

'The Foundation spent a hundred and eighty thousand pounds on that project,' Christine said. 'Now they're exporting tomatoes and can send four men to a country where two hundred thousand have already died of hunger.' She crashed –

her fist on the table. 'So little, after so much time and effort. If we had time, I would get drunk.'

None of them had any consolation to offer Christine. They were all uncomfortably aware that feeding the starving in Chad, or anywhere else, was a temporary expedient rather than a solution to the problem.

But, while Lance inspected the campsite before they set off, Esmeralda told Christine, 'Perhaps you're looking in the wrong end of the telescope. Maybe, without your hydroponics institute, these people too would have starved or suffered vitamin-deficiency diseases. That they can spare even four trained experts to help someone else speaks books for the success of your scheme.'

'Speaks *volumes* for,' Christine said.

'And people here look better to me than in Zimbabwe.'

Christine nodded. It was true. In Zimbabwe they had seen evidence of very severe malnutrition in the people beside the road. Here, in Zambia, there were some grey-tinged skins and a few knobble-kneed pot-bellied children but, to Christine's experienced eye, there were the signs of severe poverty and great shortage, even undernourishment – a gulf away from starvation. If her Foundation had contributed by its action to that difference, then the project had indeed been the unqualified success the minister thought it.

'Relief workers are like the Dutch boy with his finger in the dike. Just to avert disaster for a while starts looking like an achievement. It becomes impossible to believe in permanent success.'

While they hobnobbed with the minister, Nasheer arranged for them to cross into Zaire without customs inspection. 'Three cases of Scotch. It is an extortion,' Nasheer told Lance when he returned to the Zambian side of the Kafue.

'Sounds all right to me,' Lance said mildly. 'And if that's

94

the prologue to another lecture on how you need either more time or a show of force to do the job right, forget it. I'm satisfied. Miss Rawls, whose money you're spending, is more than satisfied.'

'There is craftsmanship even in corruption, Mr Weber. If I had a few more hours – '

'Hey, you have a sense of humour!' Christine said.

'A sealed bottle of Scotch is worth hundred-seventy-five dollars in Lubumbashi,' Nasheer told her severely.

'But we paid only nine dollars a bottle in South Africa,' Esmeralda interposed mildly.

'Right,' Christine said gleefully. 'We paid three hundred and twenty-four dollars to a man not to delay us what? – a day? – two days? So what if he sells our bribe for six and a half thousand dollars?'

'A day,' Nasheer said aggressively. 'He could not delay us more than a day. But it is the principle that matters, Miss Rawls. We are inviting trouble for later.'

'Principle? Are you the same man who yesterday gave away two motorcars to licensed gangsters who is now lecturing me on principle?' Christine's face flushed with sudden anger.

'That was different. That was a shooting matter,' Nasheer said firmly. 'Is my judgement in question here?'

'No!' Lance said hastily. 'Christine, you will apologize immediately. Nasheer knows exactly what he is doing.'

Christine inclined her head abruptly towards Nasheer and stalked away to Jimmy's Range Rover.

'And you,' Lance said to Nasheer, 'for god's sake get off our nerves. We have money, we haven't got time. Get that through your head, will you.'

Nasheer flushed, turned around, climbed into Lance's Range Rover and slammed the door.

'His people were buying slaves here while yours still ran around the Scottish highlands in animal skins,' Jimmy said.

'He's right, you know. There's a proper way and a wrong way to do things. We're buying trouble.'

Lance glanced at Pierre and Boo but it was obvious they agreed with Jimmy. 'What do you think, Esmeralda?'

'Well, Nasheer is undoubtedly right. But darling, aren't we addressing the wrong question, the price of whisky? Shouldn't we ask instead how many people will starve to death while we dawdle on the road negotiating according to the local custom?'

An hour up the road, at Lubumbashi, Lance declared a half-holiday.

'You're *what*!' Christine demanded, her voice rising uncontrollably.

'Declaring a halfday of rest. The men have now worked six days straight and this is the last place they can have a little fun.'

'You're stopping so your Swahili can go brothel-creeping?' Christine could not believe her ears.

Nasheer stood nearby, a slight smile on his face.

Lance looked down at Christine's upturned face. 'Perhaps you would like to command this convoy.'

The silence stretched.

'Well?' Lance demanded.

'No. But it is hardly fair to dump on Nasheer for wanting an extra hour to do his work better and then to give your men half a day in the bars and brothels.'

Nasheer did not nod or say anything but Lance thought, Good for you, Christine. You've made a friend for life. 'Just this once, I'll explain.'

Christine nodded and sat down at the table the kitchen staff had already set up.

Lance popped ice into a glass and poured bourbon from

96

the bottle on the tray. 'Christine?' She shook her head. 'Nasheer?'

Nasheer took the glass and sat down. At home, as a Muslim, he would not touch alcohol but elsewhere he was a chameleon, utterly adaptable.

'It's simple,' Lance said. 'First, the men deserve some time off. They know it and they know I know it. If I don't give it to them, we'll have a morale problem which will cause delays that soon will add up to days rather than a mere half day. Second, I don't know when I will next be able to give them a break. Say they have to work for the next three weeks straight – I'd rather start such a stint through dangerous country with fresh men. Third, seventy of my Swahili beating up these bars and brothels of Lubumbashi serves as a warning to those even now contemplating taking your trucks and grain and perhaps even you from us. It undoes some of the harm you and I are doing by rushing Nasheer's work unreasonably. Fair enough?'

'Like it or lump it?'

'Yes. Did you ever captain a sports team at school?'

'No.'

'That explains everything.'

'It does?'

'Sure. You assume I lead these men.'

Lance was pushing her into a trap but there was no way to avoid it. She said, 'Exactly.'

'Wrong. I don't lead them, they follow me.'

'You're splitting hairs. You give them their orders and they execute them. The result's the same.'

'No. Do you know what we pay our men, Christine?'

Christine looked after the last of the Swahili wandering down the road to the town, singing. 'No.'

'Thousand dollars a month if they make it back, ten thousand to their families if they don't.'

97

'That doesn't seem very much, considering the risks.'

Lance wasn't interested in pursuing that line of her argument. 'It's four times the going rate and they're happy to have it. But, regardless of the amount, these men are not in the Foreign Legion. I have no sanction for disobedience except to withhold their pay. They won't fight for any amount of money unless they are convinced I have their best interests at heart.'

'You mean they obey out of respect for you?'

'The alternative is fear. There are few of us and seventy of them, so what do they have to fear?'

'Then aren't *you* frightened of a rebellion?'

Lance shook his head.

'And your leadership qualities consist of giving them time off to visit the brothels?'

Lance was tired of explaining to her. She would never understand. 'For the last time, do you want to take over?'

Christine shook her head. 'I'll have a drink now.' Nasheer poured it for her.

Lance rose and stretched. He listened for a moment to the burbling of the stream, a few bird-calls, the rustle of leaves and grass. The world was at peace. He sniffed. It smelt green. This was his Africa.

'What do you smell?' Christine asked.

'Africa. South Africa smells sterile, from there through Zimbabwe and Zambia smells of red dust, but here the real rich African smells start.'

To Christine the air was slightly decayed, a mite morbid.

'City people often find that at first,' Nasheer said, 'but they soon realize nothing new can grow until something old has died. It's what ecologists call a zero-sum cycle.'

'You read minds, do you?'

'No, Miss Rawls, others have mentioned the smell to me.'

'Well, I happen to think Rome literally stinks of putrefaction,' Lance said.

Christine nodded. 'On that at least we can agree. It's a filthy place. Poor Ruby.'

Lance spent the afternoon greasing truck axles with the help of Jimmy, Pierre and Boo. Nasheer cut gold rod into small nuggets with a pair of pliers. In the dusk, the men rubbed their chests and arms with Swarfega to remove the grease and washed it away in the stream. Then they stood with their backs to the stream while the two women bathed.

'You want to go into town?' Lance asked Pierre, Boo and Nasheer. 'Jimmy and I can manage here.'

Pierre shook his head. 'Things aren't as well regulated as they used to be.'

'Yes,' Lance said, 'I remember, the first time I came through here, Rosie telling Jacques and Ewart she was getting out, going back to Hong Kong, because standards were falling under Mobutu.'

'Ah, Rosie,' Boo sighed.

'I saw the sign, *Rosie's*,' Esmeralda said behind them. Lance started.

'Friend of yours, this Rosie?' Christine asked Jimmy as they walked back to camp.

'If only she were. She was a Eurasian with legs up to here and her skin was as smooth and creamy as Esmeralda's. But, *hélas!* I was a humble footsoldier and she was the friend of statesmen and field-grade officers.'

Everyone laughed, except Christine who was conventionally blonde and beautiful but neither tall nor exotic.

'Actually, the one time I saw her,' Lance volunteered, 'I never got a chance to speak to her but I'm sure I would've stammered myself into incoherence.'

'I'm glad to hear that,' Esmeralda said gravely.

With their cold meal, which the kitchen servants had laid

out before going into Lubumbashi, Lance opened two bottles of Piesporter Goldtropchen and later another two and yet another two while they watched a film on video. When it was time to fetch the men, they were all pleasantly stewed.

Lance shone a torch around the perimeter of their camp. Eyes glinted everywhere but none of them belonged to animals: these were human scavengers waiting to steal something; in the morning Esmeralda would leave a hundred pounds of cooked porridge for them, as she had at all their other camps. 'Nasheer, I'm taking the women into town with me. Do you need help to guard the camp?'

'No thank you, Mr Weber. I'll put all the lights on instead,' Nasheer said carefully.

Lance considered the young Arab for a moment but Nasheer, given that he hardly ever drank, had a good head. Having offered help and been declined, he could not now offend Nasheer by insisting that someone stay with him.

All six of them piled into one Range Rover. In town, they stopped in front of Rosie's.

Esmeralda peered intently at the building through the darkness – there was not a single working streetlight. 'You can see it once had a certain grandeur.'

Lance listened for a moment to the sounds of revelry: mainly shouts, off-key music, female screams, and the tinkle of broken glass. 'You two stay in the car,' he told Esmeralda and Christine. Esmeralda sighed. 'The inside is even more dilapidated than the outside,' he added, though he had not been there for over twelve years. But taking women like Esmeralda and Christine into a brothel in Lubumbashi would be equivalent to a declaration of war; not that Lance would have taken a woman into a brothel anyway, though he was aware that sophisticates did do such things. Rosie's was the only brothel he had ever entered, and then only to do what he did tonight, to fetch his men from their revels.

Inside really was worse than outside. Far worse. 'This place hasn't been painted since we were here twelve years ago,' Pierre said.

Lance looked with distaste at the dangerously littered floor. 'It hasn't even been swept since then,' he said. A woman with a running sore on her cheek headed for them but caught Lance's eye and veered off. 'Let's get it over with.' He switched to Swahili and raised his voice. 'All my Swahili, it is time to leave.'

A small hush fell. Faces turned to them, counted them, measured them, turned away. The hubbub rose again. The kitchen staff and Mwanzo joined Lance.

Lance raised his voice higher. 'All my Swahili, it is time to leave.'

This time the intrusion could not be overlooked. The very tidiness and relative sobriety of Lance and his three black officers – and, not to put too fine a point on it, Lance's white skin – were a reproach and a provocation to men who could rut in such a pigsty. Three of the Swahili joined them but more looked into their bottles or ordered new drinks.

A huge black man rose from his table and swaggered up to them.

'The local tough guy,' Jimmy said.

'Shall I?' Pierre asked sotto voce.

'Thanks but no. I'll only have to deal with the next one,' Lance replied in the same low tone.

The man stopped in front of Lance, shuffled his feet square, and demanded, 'Who do you think you are?'

'I know who I am. Lance Weber.'

'Weber, eh? Wasn't there a Weber before? My cousin Lobengula ate his liver.'

Lance nodded pleasantly. Out of the corner of his eye he saw Jimmy's smile building. 'Why yes, that was my brother Ewart. But you are mistaken about your history. First he

101

levelled Lobengula's kraal, then he died in an accident with a truck. I was there when a woman made fat Lobengula beg for his life. I remember, he tried to hide behind his wives.'

'It is true,' Jimmy and Pierre and Boo chorused.

The big man ignored them and swung at Lance, who swayed slightly, grabbed the man's arm, pulled him close enough to be revolted by his breath and kneed him in the groin at the same time as he forearmed him under the chin. The whole building shook as he fell. Lance kicked him in the temple to be quite certain he stayed down.

'No more use than his cousin Lobengula,' Pierre said loudly. The whole room laughed. A few more Swahili joined them but several still sat at their tables, glowering red-eyed defiance.

'Pierre, Boo, you take upstairs. Jimmy and I will finish down here.' He watched Pierre and Boo go upstairs. 'Take this lot outside and wait at the jeep,' he told Mwanzo. 'Take your rifle from the jeep but don't arm anyone else.' He didn't want a bunch of drunken Swahili shooting up the town.

Lance moved to the first of his Swahili he could see, took the bottle from the man, poured the contents on the floor and jerked the man erect by his shoulder while saying pleasantly, 'Here, let me help you, brother.'

The Swahili stared at him, confused by the pleasant tone, then chuckled and walked outside. Lance sighed in relief. The first one was always the hardest. If this one had started a fight, the others would have joined in. It didn't bear thinking about. The second and third and fourth Swahili rose, downed their drinks and staggered out, then there was a mass movement of Swahili for the door.

Upstairs there was a commotion, then Pierre waltzed down the stairs with two of the men each held by an arm turned up behind his back. He was pursued by a naked woman who beat him about the head with a greasy bedroom slipper. Boo, behind him with an unconscious man over his shoulder, laughed so much he dropped the man and had to pick him up again, at which the enraged prostitute transferred her attentions to him. Boo stiff-armed her and trotted down the stairs in a hurry.

'That's all from upstairs,' he told Lance as he passed. 'Had to knock this one out.' The unconscious man wore socks and a shirt but nothing else.

By now the whole house was laughing; the tension was gone.

Outside, Pierre said, 'If only it's as easy at the other place.'

'How many missing?' Lance asked Mwanzo.

'Only fourteen, Massa. They go Lubumbashi Grand maybe one hour.'

'All right. You men, march back to camp with Mwanzo and go to bed in orderly fashion. We leave at dawn.' Lance stood for a moment but there was no protest. 'Any man who returns to the town will not be allowed to go with us tomorrow. You two, pick up that man and carry him. Now, I know the Swahili are clean-living but you are too drunk to bathe tonight. I don't want anyone to drown – all right? Go in peace.'

At the Grand they ran into trouble. There was a roaring fight in progress, in the middle of which a naked girl of perhaps twelve or thirteen danced in drug-induced unconcern on a table, miraculously never stepping on the multitude of glasses littering it. It was the only upright table in the room.

The fourteen Swahili had their backs to the wall and before them stood a solid wall of enraged Baluba.

'Oh shit!' said Lance with feeling, taking in the situation at a glance.

'Your Swahili?' The man looked like an ebony ballbearing: shaven head, muscled shoulders, bare muscled legs in cut-off trousers, not much over five feet tall. He carried a double-barrelled sawn-off shotgun and promptly pointed it at Lance's stomach.

'Point that shotgun elsewhere,' Lance said shortly.

'You must pay – '

'Before I stuff it down your throat,' Lance added.

The shotgun wavered slightly.

Lance smiled and nodded at Pierre, who pulled a thick roll of notes from his hip pocket and offered the man a handful without counting the notes. The man took the notes and, without looking at the denominations, stuffed them down the front of his shorts. 'More.'

'You won't be satisfied until you take the lot,' Pierre said and threw the roll at the man. Jimmy caught the roll in midair. Lance, watching the man's eyes, saw them flick into the air with the money, then widen with anger as Jimmy caught the roll. The shotgun started turning on Jimmy. When it pointed exactly midway between himself and Jimmy, Lance put his thumb into the striker mechanism. Boo, who was left-handed, stepped up from his right and hit the man a short blow that cracked his jaw. The man staggered back against the deserted bar and slid down it, his eyes glazing. Lance handed the shotgun to Jimmy to free his other hand to clutch the excruciating pain in his thumb. When that didn't help, he sucked it. That didn't help much either. He inspected the thumb. The hole in the web between the thumb and palm bled freely and didn't hurt so much; it was the other hole, right through the nail and into the flesh below, that hurt like lucifer – blood was already spreading under the nail and he knew he would lose it. 'What?' he said to Jimmy.

'I said: Like it was choreographed. But next time, arrange for the barrels to point at someone else's balls when you do your party trick.'

Lance turned towards the brawl on the far side of the

barnlike room. Beside him Jimmy fired one barrel at the roof. Lance was deafened but at the other end of the room the fight continued unabated. Jimmy grunted and fired the other barrel. Suddenly the fighting stopped. Those facing the Swahili turned, stared at the one white and three black men in their spotless safari suits: the image of despised authority.

One of them said, 'He fired twice. The gun is empty. The Swahili can wait while we deal with their masters.'

The rabble advanced on Lance's small party. The door was behind Lance but he had come for his Swahili and he had no intention of leaving without them. There was an unnatural silence. None of them were armed, except Jimmy, who could use the empty shotgun as a club.

'Swahili!' Jimmy shouted. 'Scrum! Scrum! Scrum!'

It was like a signal to the Baluba: they broke into a rush to reach Lance, Jimmy, Pierre and Boo.

'Out of the door and into the jeep!' Jimmy shouted.

Beyond the Baluba, Lance saw the Swahili throw their arms around each others' shoulders and hunker down and –

A fist caught him in the eye and he struck out blindly, feeling the blow land by the jarring of his wrist and arm up to the shoulder. Then the apex of the Swahili triangle scythed through the Baluba and carried Lance out of the door and onto the porch and over the side – what the hell had happened to the steps? – and into the street. Lance tripped a Baluba and grabbed Jimmy's shoulder to steady him as he stumbled. The Baluba paused as they saw the white women in the Range Rover; they emitted a low, keening growl. Lance saw Esmeralda shiver convulsively, pull herself together and slide over into the driver's seat. He stepped on the back of the rising Baluba, collected another blow high up on the cheek and swung up the tailgate of the Range Rover and jerked his rifle free from the clips and stepped aside as the Swahili slid in an injured comrade they carried shoulder-high, feet first the better to batter the Baluba. Lance cocked the rifle, felt a blow to the stomach, fired into the air, looked into the face of the man who had hit him, reversed the rifle and hit his assailant in the stomach with the butt.

The rifleshot stopped everything dead. Lance reached in to the gun rack again and flung an FN to Jimmy, who fired a short burst into the air. There was a pause of perhaps three seconds while the Swahili piled into the Range Rover and clung to the sides. Then a low growl rose from the Baluba as they realized they were many and the guns were few. They promptly advanced again. Lance hit the flat of his hand on the roof of the Range Rover. 'Go, Esmeralda! Go!' The Range Rover jerked into motion while Lance stood firing single shots at the feet of the most aggressive of the Baluba. Pierre jerked him along by his collar but, since Pierre himself was hanging onto the open tailgate with one hand, Lance's air was cut off by his bunched-up shirt. His feet scrabbled for purchase to take the pressure off his neck but found nothing. He clicked the safety off and shoved the rifle behind him into the Range Rover and heard a Swahili curse. One hand found purchase on someone's leg, the other on metal and he was able to help Pierre haul in his own 205 pounds until his feet found purchase – more Swahili curses from the men he stepped on – and Pierre could let go. When Lance stopped heaving and the red cleared from his eyes, the Range Rover had stopped and Jimmy was saying to Christine, 'Fucking lot of help you were, freezing up like that. Everybody out so I can count you. Move, you hyenas' arses!'

'Where's Boo?' Lance asked.

Two Swahili were thrown bodily from the rear of the Range Rover, taking Lance with them, as Boo rose; they had been on top of him.

'You looking for me?' He picked up Lance's rifle and checked quickly that nothing was broken, then racked it.

Jimmy clicked the safety on his FN and threw it to Boo who racked that as well.

'Fourteen Swahili and one drunken Baluba that somebody loaded by mistake,' Jimmy said. He pointed to the snoring outsider.

'Leave him beside the road,' Lance ordered. He walked around the side of the Range Rover. 'Good work,' he said as he opened the door. Esmeralda was shaking uncontrollably, the depressive aftereffects of adrenalin catching up. Lance hugged her tightly, then lifted her out of the driver's seat and carried her around to the passenger side. 'The wounded can ride inside, the rest of you cling on.'

At the camp there was more trouble. A couple of tables were smashed and two dead men lay on the ground. Nasheer sat in the shadow of the refrigerator truck, his rifle across his knees. Mwanzo stood nearby, cradling his own rifle. He had also armed two of the more sober Swahili, who were strategically disposed.

'Those goddam Swahili of yours have caused more trouble,' Christine said through clenched teeth.

But to Lance the scene told a different story: the men were all facing the darkness outside the light the lamps cast. He did not bother to answer Christine but climbed out and asked Nasheer, 'When did it happen?'

'The local scavengers tried to rush me right after you left. They didn't think I would shoot at them. I fired all but two shots over their heads. Still they came. What was I to do?'

'You did exactly right.' Thank god it had happened before the Swahili returned or they would have massacred the retreating attackers. 'Are they still there?'

'A few, sir. The more timid ones have gone.'

'Well done, Nasheer. Mwanzo, bury them right here dead centre in the lights so anybody watching can see.'

'Look here,' Christine said hotly, 'you can't just – '

'I can. I will. I am,' Lance said firmly. 'If you want to wait here three weeks while the police hold an inquest at their own pace – '

'But burying them in plain sight of their friends will – '

'Will tell the police clear as a neon sign that my contempt for them is backed by seventy Swahili warriors. Now, if you don't mind, I have work to do. Please bring the medicine chest. Pierre, just sit still while I look at this man first.'

Christine hesitated. Esmeralda bent into the Range Rover to pull out the medicine chest.

'Snap to it!' Jimmy snarled at Christine. 'Try to be useful, will you?'

She helped Esmeralda with the chest.

'Bring a light up close,' Lance said and Christine brought the Coleman from the drinks table. The Swahili had pink foam at his lips. Lance took some on his finger and tasted it. He ripped the man's shirt and, seeing no wound on his front, rolled him over briskly. The wound at the edge of his back and quite high up was foaming pinkly rather than bleeding. Esmeralda offered a steripad but Lance shook his head. 'He's suffocating in his own blood, not bleeding to death on the outside.' He picked up the Swahili and put him in the back of the Range Rover. 'Anybody else for the hospital?'

'My arm needs stitches,' Pierre said. 'I'll have that pad, Esmeralda.'

'Any of those, Jimmy?' Lance called to where Jimmy was inspecting the Swahili from the Grand.

Jimmy bent and flung a Swahili who was staggering on his feet over his shoulder and laid him into the back of the Range Rover beside the one with the knife wound in the lung. 'Stitches for a scalp wound.'

'Bring the hospital a gift of medicines,' Lance told Esmeralda.

'No, I'll do that,' Christine said.

108

'No more fuck-ups and no more arguments or you go back tomorrow, understand?'

Christine ran to the fridge truck and grabbed two boxes of assorted medicines. Lance already had the Range Rover moving when she clambered in beside Pierre in the back seat. Jimmy, in the front beside Lance, slotted a fresh clip into an FN, then checked Lance's rifle and put it in the footwell. Christine shivered but said nothing. The ferocious efficiency of Lance Weber acted as a magnet to trouble but that was the choice she had made.

Lance hit the main street of Lubumbashi at over sixty miles an hour but nobody shot at them and they saw no one on the street except a few drunks who shouted friendly greetings.

'I'd feel a lot happier if those Baluba had stayed in town to lay ambush for us here when we came through to the hospital with the wounded,' Pierre said.

Lance grunted and Jimmy sighed.

'What do you mean?' Christine asked, unable to restrain her curiosity.

'They've gone home to plot something,' Pierre said.

'What?'

'An ambush tomorrow on the road, most likely,' Lance said. 'A nuisance, if they delay us long, nothing more. Don't worry about it.'

Christine gritted her teeth and shut up. One day, soon, she was going to murder Lance Weber. It would be the first time a man's unshakable calm competence supplied the motive. She ripped off Pierre's sleeve and used it to tie a tourniquet around his arm. 'How'd this happen?'

Pierre shrugged. 'Don't really know. When I got back to camp, I was bleeding.'

Christine shivered in the warm, humid night. A few inches this way or that and he would have been dead – and he had not even seen his attacker. It could have happened to any one of them, perhaps Jimmy.

At the hospital, Lance carried the lung-wounded man into the building in his arms while Jimmy again flung the unconscious man with the scalp wound over his shoulder. Pierre walked in unassisted, hitting a bell on a desk with the flat of his hand as he passed. Christine, who had already passed the bell, was again reminded of her helpless ignorance.

A nun fluttered out of a side door, pulling at her habit. The moment she saw the wounded men, she turned utterly professional. A doctor and several more nurses appeared as if magically. The lung-wounded man was whisked away to the operating theatre, the man with the scalp wound came to and was found to be slightly concussed. He and Pierre were sewn up. Pierre could return to the camp with them immediately; the hospital would keep the concussed man until morning when they would probably be able to take him with them.

Christine and Esmeralda came down to the stream with their washbags to find nearly eighty naked black men, including the kitchen staff, bent over with their rumps in the air and Jimmy, Boo and Lance working their way down the line with disposable syringes from the tray Nasheer carried. 'That'll keep your willie from dropping off,' they heard Jimmy say each time he jabbed in another needle. Tactfully, the women returned to camp until the short-arm inspection was over.

At the end of the line, Lance straightened and pressed his hands into the small of his back. His left eye, which had been hit twice, throbbed ferociously. He was desperately tired. In the night Esmeralda had made love to him fiercely, three times. He caught Jimmy's eye: his friend too looked slightly grey under his skin. Christine too had reacted like Esmeralda to the threats and the fears of the evening before: a tearingly urgent need to reaffirm the continuity of life.

Jimmy grinned weakly. 'They feel worse than we do,' he said, looking at the red-eyed, hungover Swahili and kitchen staff straightening up and dressing with muttered curses at the sting of the hypodermics.

'That'll be small consolation if the Baluba are lying in wait for us up the road.'

Later, while they stood dunking rusks in mugs of coffee, Lance suddenly lunged at the radio, spilling coffee, to turn the volume up.

'. . . stopped off in Lusaka to confer with ministry officials about the assistance the Foundation-funded hydroponics institute is sending to famine-struck Moçambique. The Minister said Miss Rawls is on her way via Zambia and Zaire to Chad with thirty truckloads of food and medicines. The relief convoy is said to be led by Mr Lance Weber and protected by a large contingent of armed men. If this is true, it is a deliberately provocative response to Miss Rawls' maltreatment at the hands of the Libyans in February. This is Mike Robinson in Lusaka.' Another voice said, 'The two pilots who flew Miss Rawls on her first relief mission, when their plane was shot down by Libyan jets, are still held in Tripoli but the Foreign Office say that Italian diplomats in Tripoli, who are looking after British interests there, expect the Libyans to hand them over soon to General Goukouni Queddei, who occupies northern Chad with Libyan backing. A spokesman for Queddei's headquarters has already said the two men, Tanner Chapman and Paul Hasluck, will be tried as spies and shot. Now to Delhi, where Mark Tully – '

Lance snapped the radio off. He held out his mug to Esmeralda, who had the coffeepot in her hands. Their eyes met. She raised an eyebrow. Lance shrugged.

'We should have told the man to keep his mouth shut,' Christine said.

'You can bet they listen to the BBC World Service in Tripoli,' Pierre said. 'There goes our advantage, Lance.'

Lance pressed the flat of his hand against his bruised cheekbone and closed left eye to still the throbbing for a moment so that he could think without distraction. He drank his coffee and threw the grounds on the earth. They were all looking at him. He looked from face to face. 'I'm going on,' he said mildly. 'But there's no shame for anyone who wants to leave the party now. In fact, it is the only sensible thing to do. Now that the Libyans have been forewarned, it's odds-on we won't be coming back.'

Boo yawned. Mwanzo, standing nearby, rubbing the residual sting of the hypodermic on his buttock. Jimmy picked up the coffeepot, found it empty, gestured with it at the steward. Christine looked at the ground. Pierre whistled a few bars nobody recognized. Esmeralda turned away to check the food they would leave for the hungry people watching from the fringes of the camp.

'Your brother would never have said anything quite as dumb as that,' Pierre said finally.

'I'm really godawfully tired of being compared to my brother,' Lance said tightly. 'He wouldn't have started this in the first instance. But I did, and intend to finish it.'

'Fine,' Jimmy said. 'But calm determination is one thing, hot fanaticism another.'

'I'd be happy to take orders from any of you.'

Pierre nodded. 'Of course. Nobody doubts that.'

'Tell the Swahili this is their last chance to back out,' Lance ordered. Pierre took Mwanzo by the elbow and they went towards the Swahili, who stood at a respectful distance observing the tension among the convoy's leaders.

Christine felt like an other-caste: she had missed a signal. 'They're coming with us then?' she asked Lance.

Lance nodded and walked away towards Esmeralda.

Christine looked appealingly at Jimmy.

'If he becomes too emotionally involved, we can't trust him to make rational decisions,' Jimmy told her.

Boo chuckled. 'Actually, his brother would have said *exactly* that.' He too headed for the Swahili and Jimmy followed him.

Lance took Esmeralda's elbow. 'I have never ordered you to do anything,' he began, 'but – '

'Don't start now, Lance. It's still the same monument we are building for our daughter, still the same price to pay if things go wrong. That one vain man has made it a little more certain we will have to pay the price makes no difference.'

'It makes a very great difference.'

'Not to the principle.'

'Esmeralda – '

'No. Please don't ask me any more.'

He stared at her intently for a few moments, as if willing her to comply with his wish. Then he said, 'I must speak to the Swahili.'

When he was a few paces away, she called, 'We will succeed. I know it. As a wife and mother, I know it.'

He stood there, looking thoughtfully at her for a long time. Finally he nodded and turned towards the Swahili again. He had faith in Esmeralda's intuition but here he was in his element and, no matter how well she had adapted to Africa, she was not a native as he was.

To Christine, he said, 'I can spare some men to escort you as far as Lusaka.' He walked by without waiting for an answer.

'To hell with you,' Christine said clearly.

Lance laughed aloud. 'No,' he told her over his shoulder, 'to Chad.'

When he reached the Swahili, he was smiling. They were talking in small clumps. Lance walked among them. 'Men,' he said in his normal voice and waited for them to be quiet. 'Men. There is now a greater danger ahead than we expected when we engaged you. I know you're brave men, but many of you have families and other responsibilities. I will not think less of any man who decides he does not wish to continue.' Lance looked around the red, hungover eyes. 'Talk about it among yourselves.'

'We have already talked, Master.' The one who spoke was a few years older than the rest. 'We will all continue.'

'Perhaps the married men would like to reconsider,' Lance insisted.

The induna looked around but the Swahili merely grinned at him. He returned his eyes to Lance but said nothing more.

'Beyond this, there will be no opportunity to change your minds,' Lance said once more.

The induna frowned.

Behind Lance, Mwanzo said softly, 'Not again, Master.'

Lance nodded. He was in danger of offending these men. He could not remember Mwanzo ever before volunteering advice or instruction.

'You are truly the sons of your fathers,' Lance told the Swahili.

'Hau!' they saluted this fine compliment. 'Hau! Hau!'

'Let's roll,' Lance told Boo. He didn't have to say that speed was now more important than ever.

But, to prove to the others no less than to himself that he was strictly in control, he made his usual inspection of the campsite even more meticulous.

When they were on the road, Jimmy activated the radio. 'Guess what?'

'What?'

114

'Just as I drove out of camp behind the last truck, guess who drove into camp?'

'The local police. Are they following us?'

'Naw, they've returned to base. They obviously decided we got clean away.'

'Sensible.' Lance put the mike back on the hook.

In the back of the Range Rover, Nasheer sighed relievedly. 'I didn't much look forward to being questioned by the local police. Thank you, Mr Weber.'

Lance understood. The brutality of the police and Army in Zaire is a byword in Africa; only Uganda under Amin had been worse. Interrogation would routinely be prefaced by a beating. And in this case, where there was no case to answer, where Nasheer had clearly been defending himself, the beating would be so much worse because it would be the prelude to a bargaining session. It was an admission of their corruption that the police should ostentatiously arrive too late to question Nasheer: men who routinely resort to unnecessary force rather than legal argument would treat greater force circumspectly regardless of the rights or wrongs of particular circumstances.

Lance kept his eyes on the hills to the left of the road. Anyone in them would have the early morning sun in his eyes but there was no shelter to the right of the road.

'I always thought the Congo was all tropical forest,' Esmeralda said, studying the grasslands stretching in all directions, broken by low stunted trees, perhaps greener than those they had seen to the south but certainly no forest.

'At the end of the savannah, up there,' Lance gestured, 'it changes. Actually, it's not quite tropical then but sub-tropical – you have to be a botanist to know the difference. You'll see, one minute we'll be out in the open among scrub, the next inside the forest. It's a magic moment.'

'What are you looking for in those hills?'

115

'The glint of sunlight on a rifle barrel or binoculars.'

'You expect an attack?'

'Yes.'

'Those people from the Grand?'

'Yes. And bandits from Angola.' Lance pointed over his left shoulder. 'This, if I remember correctly, is the last good place to mount an ambush until well past Likasi – and there the road splits, so it's here or nowhere.'

Mwanzo passed Lance's rifle and Esmeralda put it in the footwell. But nothing happened. They passed the hills and drove on, a Haydn symphony filling the Range Rover. Once Lance said to Esmeralda, 'You know, German music is really Austrian music? Look at Beethoven and Mozart and Schubert. Even Haydn did his best work in London. The only German composer of really large stature who worked solely in Germany was Wagner and see what it did to his music.'

But Esmeralda, who by education knew more about music than Lance though she did not love it half as well as his self-tutored ear, had her nose in her daybook, a ring-bound scratchpad in which each day's tasks and menus were inscribed chronologically; feeding and clothing a convoy of eighty-five people is not a task to be left to *ad hoc* measures. The raw materials for each meal had been weighed and labelled in advance and loaded in reverse order. Every morning each person was given a parcel containing clean underwear, every second day a clean shirt and trousers. Soiled clothing was neatly parcelled up and left for the scavengers; the convoy had no laundry facilities. There was also a large cake of red Sunlight soap and a new toothbrush and a tube of toothpaste for each person once a week, again in separate parcels. Sanitary napkins for the women. The Swahili were entitled to a ration of cane spirit once a day and as much 'native' beer – a milky substance in a carton, rated at six per cent alcohol content by volume – as they wanted.

(Christine had been horrified at the pure bulk of this 'beer' carried by the expedition but without it, Jimmy had told her, the Swahili would go nowhere.) Liquor for the rest of the party was no problem but that carried for Nasheer to use as bribes consumed much space. By now Esmeralda had the kitchen staff dragooned into a brisk routine: she could serve a hot meal forty-five minutes after Lance signalled a halt. It was a major organizational triumph. Of course, it was not her first expedition, but the expedition to Kivu had been less than half the size of the present one.

'Those chemical toilets are working well,' she told Lance.

'They make me vaguely uncomfortable.'

'Why?'

'I keep expecting them to explode under me.'

'Nonsense. They're perfectly safe.'

'I still prefer to dig a hole in the ground and hang my arse over it.'

'Don't be vulgar.'

'Well, I feel like a berk going bush with my own portapotty. Don't you, Nasheer?'

'No sir. I find Mrs Weber's toilet arrangements a great deal more comfortable than the last time I travelled with you.'

'What about you, Mwanzo?'

'Hau, Master!' It was wonder and enthusiasm all at once, Mwanzo's tactful manner of not taking sides.

Lance snorted in disgust.

'That looks like a good stream,' Esmeralda said.

Lance glanced at the dash clock. 'Right. Brunch.' He stuck his hand out of the window to slow the trucks behind him.

'The roads are worse again,' Christine said to Lance as they met at the washtable.

Lance nodded. 'Relatively. But we're still covering forty-five or fifty miles in every hour. They will become very much worse.'

117

'Why don't these people look after their roads? I mean, without proper roads, how can their economies ever recover?'

'Yes, I know. But the mineral companies do what they can for these roads because it's in their own interest. And there are the railways, too. This is what you might call the developed part of Zaire. The infrastructure here is fantastic compared to the hinterland.'

'Infrastructure, huh?'

Lance grinned. 'When I was at Stellenbosch University on a rugger scholarship, I had to choose some filler subjects besides Phys. Ed. Some joker told me Economics was a soft option.'

Christine was amazed; she had always, without giving it any conscious thought, assumed that Lance Weber had somehow sprung to life full-blown and violent from one of the scummier parts of the world. 'How'd you score?'

'As well as could be expected from a *jokkel*. I scraped by. Thanks.' He took the towel from her. 'I spent more time at Coetzenberg training than in class.'

Muamur Qaddaffi does not live in a tent in the middle of desert because, as has often been said, that makes it easier to protect him from the regular assassination attempts. In fact, a tent in the middle of a desert is a security man's nightmare: any really determined assassin, and especially the fanatic who glories in dying in the attempt which is exactly the kind of assailant Qaddaffi attracts, can arrive by helicopter or parachute or hang-glider and then there is no second line of defence because a tent is vulnerable from all sides, unlike a walled building, and no reserves to call on as there would be in a city. It is merely part of the Libyan leader's image of himself as the lean desert-Arab messiah that he lives unencumbered by luxury in a tent; he is a genuine ascetic. They make great visionaries and the worst fanatics. Even when in

Tripoli, Qaddaffi pitches a tent on the lawn of a government building in preference to living inside. Perhaps sometimes, in the hour before dawn, Qaddaffi shivers, in the way of tyrants who stole power by force, when he remembers what he and his cohorts did to King Idris in his palace; perhaps that is why Qaddaffi prefers the tent in the desert to the tent on the lawn in front of the edifice of power. Wherever Qaddaffi is, there lies the real power in Libya.

The tent was furnished with only two articles: a mat, on which Qaddaffi sat cross-legged, and a small trunk, which held a yellow Bic government-issue ballpoint and his seal together with a wax taper and a box of matches to melt the wax; the matches had never been used because a candle-lamp was always brought instantly from another tent whenever he produced the seal; his coffee tray, when it came, would rest on top of the trunk. The mat was a valuable Kashmiri given to him by Zia ul-Haq of Pakistan, the chest, of plain solid oak, was scarred by time and travel and had once been government-issue to Cadet Qaddaffi and was still government property both in the quartermaster sense and as an historical artifact. From the edge of the Kashmiri, through the open flap of the tent, to the horizon, stretched the blinding white sands Qaddaffi loved with the unreasoning intensity of the true patriot; for him, these sands were Libya: all else – the cities and, especially, the oil derricks – were spoiling afterthoughts of a careless designer. He looked straight south, towards Chad, where he would soon mount a relief operation in cooperation with his friends the Russians to prove to the world that, despite the bungling of the Ethiopians, democratic Islamic socialism too has compassion for the weak and the hungry. And beyond Chad, to the madwoman Rawls, whom he should never have released as a goodwill gesture to the treacherous British, and her hired mercenary scum Weber, who were interfering with his plans

119

and making triumphant semi-state visits on the way. Nothing showed on his face: emotion had long since burned him out: everything was trapped inside, like an imploding sun, only infrequently breaking through, when his eyes appeared even more like black holes to mystic inner space.

'Ali,' Qaddaffi said in his normal voice to the unlimited desert before him.

A man stepped around the edge of the canvas and the illusion of the single tent in the middle of the vast eternity of blinding white light was shattered: Qaddaffi still, after all these years, died the small death of reality at the knowledge that there were more men waiting out of sight and, around the back of the tent, more tents, vehicles, men – hundreds of them.

'My friend,' Qaddaffi said to the man before him, who wore the sky-blue dress uniform of a major in the air force pursuit fighter squadron but who had not flown a plane in over a year, his present duties being intelligence-liaison. The major saluted briskly and stood at attention on the white sand in front of the mat (no one was allowed onto the mat). 'My friend,' Qaddaffi said again. This was the man who had brought him the news of the Rawls woman's new convoy and her incredible stupidity in broadcasting its existence and purpose and whereabouts to the world. 'Send enough good men to stop them. Allah speed your feet.'

The officer saluted again. He asked no questions. He knew where to find 'good men' and he knew what 'stop' meant. Qaddaffi spoke in absolutes and the officer was a careerist who executed his orders.

As the man reached the flap, Qaddaffi added, 'And hand the terror-fliers over to our colleague Queddei. He'll know what to do with them. Announce their extradition to the scene of their crimes in accordance with international law. Allah have mercy on their souls.'

The major performed his salaams and left. When the racket of the helicopter returning him to Tripoli rent the still desert air, Qaddaffi winced at the intrusion.

Less than an hour after brunch, a spring on one of the trucks broke in a pothole. Christine, walking down the convoy after sitting in the Range Rover for fifteen minutes, found Lance and a row of Swahili bent under the truck, literally lifting it on their backs while Boo positioned a jack under the spring.

'Listen, Lance, can't the rest of the trucks go on and this one catch up?'

Lance put one hand on the road and wiped sweat from his eyes with the other. 'No.'

'Why not?'

'Because we would lose it.'

'Oh, come on! There's nobody here.'

'Turn around and see for yourself.'

Under a tree twenty yards away she saw three men with rifles over their shoulders. They stared at her. One made a rude gesture, the tip of his thumb between the fore and middle fingers.

'Get back in the Range Rover, Christine,' Jimmy told her.

For the first time she noticed him leaning against the front of the truck, an FN casually in his hands, pointed nowhere in particular. Beyond him she could see Pierre, also armed, and several of the Swahili facing both sides of the road.

Christine returned to the Range Rover. She noticed that the two Swahili who drove with her and Jimmy followed her and climbed into the back to wait with her. There was a sense of menace in the air. After a while, Jimmy came and slammed the door, startling her.

'Who're they?'

'Government soldiers.'

Christine nearly said, Then we're safe, but she remembered

the Zimbabwean Fifth Parachute Brigade, who were very much government soldiers . . .

To one side of the road, she could see Nasheer talking to a man with bars on his shoulders. 'Is Nasheer paying him off?'

'Perhaps,' Jimmy replied. 'I hope so.'

Christine saw Lance walk into the grass, his rifle in his hand. 'Lance is becoming impatient.'

Just then Nasheer saw Lance and said something quick to the army commander. The almost tangible tension intensified for a moment, then the man laughed and Nasheer clapped him on the shoulder and they walked together to the truck where Nasheer kept his liquor store. Lance turned back to his Range Rover and three minutes later they drove off. Christine felt limp with perspiration. The Range Rovers were not air-conditioned because Lance maintained that air-conditioning causes chills.

'Where did they come from?' Christine asked.

'Oh, they were there all the time,' Jimmy said.

'Does every encounter with people here have to become a confrontation?'

'The mining company exploiters and imperialists would be happy to see us,' Jimmy said.

'Give me a break, eh?'

'Okay. But, apart from the mining companies, I can't think of anybody who doesn't want our trucks and our women.'

'That's pretty basic.'

'A real tourist attraction.'

At Likasi, which they reached an hour before nightfall, Lance called a council while the trucks were being refuelled from their own tankers. 'Boo, come here for a moment.' Esmeralda's kitchen staff had put up a folding table and Lance spread his map on it. He waited for Boo to wipe his hands on disposable waste and join the others around the table. 'We're here.' Lance put his finger on Likasi. 'Now we can go three ways. We can go west towards Kinshasa and then north. We can go east to Lake Tanganyika and then north and then head west across northern Zaire until we can enter the Central African Republic. Or we can head straight north.'

'Roads to Kinshasa are good,' Pierre said, 'but from there north, that's a bad choice. Besides, I don't fancy tangling with the Kinshasa politicians.'

Lance nodded.

Christine traced a line east from Likasi, up the side of Lake Tanganyika, Burundi and Rwanda, then west across northern Zaire. 'That's the long way round.'

'But on better roads than the short option,' Boo said.

'Would the longer road be faster?'

'Depends on when the rains fall,' Jimmy said.

'But the drought – '

'We'll be crossing the equator,' Lance cut in. 'It always rains where we're going. The long road up the side here is possible, if a mite difficult, even in the rainy season. On this middle road here, the section from Kibombo to Kisangani straddling the equator is passable only in the dry season. If the rain doesn't catch us on it we can save five or six or seven days.'

'Off the eighteen you were talking about?' Christine asked enthusiastically.

'No. If we take the longer, surer route, the extra days are just that, extra,' Lance replied.

'Then let's – '

'Not so fast,' Jimmy cut in. 'Lance and Pierre and Boo and I, we went up that road twelve years ago in the rainy season. We were eight days between Kibombo and Kisangani even with Mercedes Unimogs and we weren't carrying any hundred-fifty-plus tons of wheat.'

123

'How long does it take in the dry?' Esmeralda asked.

'Three, perhaps four days,' Pierre said. 'Depends on whether you're lucky with breakages. Even in the dry season, it's no pleasure trip.'

'So, if the rain catches us on that stretch, we perhaps add five days to our journey, but if we choose the long way we certainly add five days,' Esmeralda said.

Pierre told Esmeralda, 'When you're covered in foul-smelling mud from head to toe, I'll remind you of your implacable logic.'

'I too vote for the short way,' Christine said.

'Lance isn't taking a vote,' Jimmy admonished her gently.

Lance looked at Boo. 'How are our tankers holding out?'

'We have fuel either way.'

Lance looked at the sinking sun. 'There's a fourth way which leaves our options open. We'll drive north to Kibombo. If the rains have started when we reach there, we'll take the long way round via Bukavu, if not, we'll head straight for Kisangani.'

'Spoken like Solomon,' Jimmy said. 'Are we driving on or camping?'

'We'll stay on the road another two hours,' Lance decided.

'Right. I'll catch up. I saw some sweet potatoes and fresh cucumber for sale back there.'

'Yes please,' Esmeralda said promptly. 'You mind if I go with Jimmy, Christine?'

'Why not bump one of the Swahili?'

'No,' Lance said. 'You can ride with me, Christine. Mwanzo!'

Without further instruction, Mwanzo fetched his FN from the gun rack and climbed into the back of Jimmy's Range Rover.

Christine decided it would not only be petty to pick an argument over who rode where, but a little ludicrous to insist on her right as a woman to be allowed on a market shopping expedition. The role suited Esmeralda, who was unobtrusively competent at so many other things small and large, and actually enjoyed being a *Hausfrau*, glowing at any task well done no matter how humble its position in the lexicon of female politics. But Christine thought of her position in a male-dominated world as hard-won and under constant threat; she knew she lacked Esmeralda's radiant confidence, so why should she give anyone an edge by insisting on a subordinate role?

Once underway, Lance said to her, 'I wanted to speak to you.'

'You are speaking to me.'

'Yes. How much money does this Foundation of yours have left?'

'I don't know.'

'But you're its director.'

'Yes. But money comes in and goes out. Like a game reserve or a ranch.'

'I see. It's a business.'

'Right. You want to be paid more?'

'No. I want to spend more.'

'That's no problem. We spent only part of what I raised for relief in Chad.'

Lance was respectfully silent for a moment.

'And I can always raise more,' Christine added.

Lance glanced at her in the last of the natural light.

'You sound bloody confident.'

'You know what you do best. So do I.'

'Okay. I want to buy some inflatable rafts and charter planes to drop them. We might never use them, though.'

'How can you do that from here?'

'Stop off at one of the Belgian mining companies and ask.'

'They have inflatable rafts?'

'No. Sorry. They have radios with satellite links. They can speak to anyone anywhere in the world. Is there somebody at your Foundation you can trust to organize buying the rafts and hiring the planes?'

'There's a highly competent professional staff of eight.'

'No bleeding hearts or ego-tripping debs?'

'Only me and I'm in the field a lot of the time or out raising funds. Put me in touch with London and you can consider whatever you need as delivered.'

'Excellent.'

They drove in silence for several minutes before Christine asked, 'Whatever do you want inflatable rafts for? There are ferries at all the river crossings, aren't there?'

'Actually, that's debatable. But no, we can rig our pierced steel planks into a makeshift bridge over anything but a major river. Look at the map in the door pocket.' Lance angled the red maplight on its gooseneck and tapped the map on her lap without taking his eyes from the road. 'See that river?'

'The Lualaba?'

'Just above Kibombo, where the Elila runs into it.' Again Lance tapped the map without looking at it. Again his finger hit the spot unerringly. 'That's the real start of the great River Congo, the Zaire.'

'But I thought – '

' – the Congo runs west and south? It does, but the lesser rivers that make it don't.'

'You want to ride this river on rafts? Is the river big enough?'

'Once the rains come, it's as big as any river in England and, by the time it reaches Kisangani, much bigger. In the rainy season it flows six to ten knots every hour, day and night, say at least 150 miles every day. On the road, in the mud, we'll slow down to as little as fifty miles per day.'

'And the reason you didn't think of it before is that it has never been done before?'

'Congratulations. If it's dry at Kibombo, the rafts are a waste of money. If it rains, you then have the choice of deciding to risk your Foundation's grain – '

'It's your Foundation as much as mine, Lance.'

He glanced at her again.

'I just realized you're on my side,' Christine said impulsively.

'Right. Now, if it rains at Kibombo, you then have two choices: do you want to take the long road and add five or six days to the trip, or do you want to risk your grain on the river which might even save two or three days – if it works.'

'And if it doesn't?'

'Your grain and your trucks end up on the bottom of the river.'

They settled into that routine of a hard-driven convoy that turns the most alert into zombies and, even in the fittest of men, fatigues every muscle into dull, throbbing pain. Lance raced the rain for Kibombo and Kisangani beyond: two days running he kept the convoy, slowed by worsening roads and the breakages they caused to an average speed of just over twenty miles per hour, on the road for sixteen hours. No one had energy to argue with him; they were too bone-weary and they all knew that if they beat the rains to Kibombo they could cut five or even seven days from the time before they could deliver the food to the starving refugees in Chad. Christine had mentioned the rafts to Jimmy, who had been appalled at the very idea. By now everyone accepted that, if the rafts arrived and the rain too, Lance would scorn the long way round and use the rafts. Lance had not said so, but not even Christine, whom he had told unequivocally that it would be her choice, considered the possibility that Lance would travel the long road. In a way it was a relief to her not to be forced to make a decision so fraught with lives. Lance heard Christine tell Boo, 'The majority don't die from starvation, not in the medical sense as written on the death certificate. They die of associated or consequential diseases, mainly pneumonia and diarrhoea. And they die in forced migrations like that in Ethiopia. Mass transports in Ethiopia have arrived with over fifty per cent dead. That's worse than in Kampuchea under the Khmer Rouge.' All of this she related in the matter-of-fact voice of a fundraiser who had long ago learnt that too much emotion collects less money, but her eyes burned in outrage. Lance, who had not known any of this even though he had seen the famine in Kenya before they had to take their daughter to the specialists in Vienna, was embarrassed by his ignorance and in his embarrassment lashed out by later telling Esmeralda, 'Christine would love people loved she not humanity more.' Esmeralda said, 'We're all becoming a little like that.' It was true, all of them were infected with relief fever, so that even Esmeralda, who best knew her husband's strength and reserves, wondered if he was not driving himself too hard. But, sensibly, she said nothing: there was great love between them, but they had lost their daughter and she had asserted herself to accompany this expedition and she felt she should tread carefully with Lance in his present single-minded ruthlessness or their marriage could be damaged. She refused to admit even to herself that it didn't matter, that, with Qaddaffi forewarned, none of them would return to resume their lives and marriages. Then, on the morning of the third day, Lance declared that they would camp at Kibombo that night, if nothing went wrong. Nobody made any reply but Boo put his coffee mug on the table and trotted away to see to his trucks and Esmeralda hurried the kitchen servants about packing up. Lance even cut his campsite inspection short: the minute Boo had the truck engines warmed through, he climbed into his

128

Range Rover and drove on. But, beyond Kongolo and across the Lualaba for the first time, the Libyans lay in ambush for them.

Just after they took to the road that morning, two Hercules transports flew over at about two thousand feet and Christine recognized their colour scheme as that of a charter company the Foundation had used before. She studied the planes through Jimmy's binoculars until they could no longer be seen. 'Those are our rafts,' she told Lance on the radio. Lance and Jimmy both tuned to the prearranged signal frequency and heard: 'Matthew Ellimore Foundation rafts flying over.' They could not transmit on that waveband but Lance fired a green flare out of the window and the transmission stopped. Christine studied the Lualaba doubtfully the first time they crossed it. It was not exactly a mean trickle but it would be dwarfed by the size of raft necessary to float a truck which, with its grain, would weigh twelve tons. 'Nearly four hundred miles up there,' Lance pointed north, 'it's a real river. You'll see.' Once they were on the move again, Jimmy said to her, 'It's not the size of water that worries me but the speed, once the rains start falling. Have you ever seen an African river in torrent?' She shook her head. 'It's a fearsome sight,' Jimmy said. 'Enough to turn strong men to religion.' Christine did not answer and he let it drop. She rather received the impression his heart wasn't in the argument, that he was making it for the sake of form, that he too had been infected with relief fever.

In the leading Range Rover, Lance was looking out for a place to break for brunch when the first Libyan shot clanged off the bullbars and the second burst the left front tyre of his Range Rover. As he fought to straighten the bucking vehicle, he heard Mwanzo return fire out of the window behind him. And, further back, Pierre and the Swahili opening fire. The fusillade, he saw as he braked gently, came from a kopje on the left and slightly ahead of the Range Rover. He slid the gearlever into neutral and jerked the handbrake on with one hand while with the other he swung his door open. Then he grabbed Esmeralda in the armpits and dragged her physically across the drive tunnel and rolled with her out of the Range Rover and over the edge of the gravel bed on which the road was built. The moment she was in shelter, he rose, his hands ready to catch the Mannlicher as Nasheer threw it to him. Lance cocked the rifle and fired spaced shots at the top of the hill, not trying to find and hit anyone, just shooting to keep their heads down. Nasheer and Mwanzo rolled over the side of the road and to his feet. They rose and started firing too. Mwanzo had the top corner of his right ear missing. To his left, Lance sensed trucks pulling up and men piling out. With his clip empty, he sank to the ground behind the two-foot-high shelter of the gravel bed and looked left. Boo and Mwanzo had trained the Swahili well: the trucks were pulled up in two staggered rows so that men could shelter behind them and so that the tyres of half the trucks were protected. Lance looked over his shoulder. Rolling grass, then scrub, a few stunted trees. It was satisfactory if not ideal.

Pierre arrived running, crouched low even though he was sheltered by the double row of trucks. Behind him were about twenty of the Swahili. But for the moment the shooting from the hill had stopped and Lance held up the flat of his hand. Pierre and his men halted behind the last of the trucks. Lance crooked his finger at Pierre, who wriggled towards him on his belly, his FN at the ready before him, his elbows apparently immune to pain from the sharp-edged flints. 'I want the medicine chest and some ammo for my rifle from the Range Rover,' Lance said. 'Bring up a few men with long barrels and lay down cover for me. Does Jimmy have the extra-long barrels and the sniperscopes?'

'I've sent for them already.'

'Good. We'll wait till they come, then.'

Esmeralda inspected the abrasions on her elbows. She wore a short-sleeved blouse but sleeves would not have saved her: her trouser-knees too were ragged and bloody. Mwanzo sat down next to her and she pressed her handkerchief to his ear.

'Maybe four, five men,' Nasheer said. There was a lull in the firing.

'I think five,' Lance said. 'Thanks, Nasheer. You move back now and take Esmeralda with you.'

'I'm – '

'No! I hired you for your brains, not your bravery. I need you alive and well.'

'I'll go when I've seen to Mwanzo's ear,' Esmeralda said.

'Let me see.'

She took the handkerchief away. The wound started bleeding immediately.

'All right. You go along, Mwanzo. Don't give him anything to dull his senses, Esmeralda. I'll want him alert. Are you all right yourself?'

'Bruises and scratches. You fell on me twice.'

'Sorry. Off you go. I'll send the medicine chest down as soon as I have it.'

'There are medicines further back.'

Lance nodded. 'Sure. But getting this one serves the double purpose of winkling them out.'

Nasheer, Esmeralda and Mwanzo crept away. Jimmy arrived with the sniper barrels and the scopes. He gave Pierre one set, attached the other set to his own rifle.

'Fit your long barrels, check your magazines,' Pierre told the Swahili waiting behind the first trucks. He called out ten names. 'You ten come up here.'

Lance saw one of the men not named slide over the edge of the road and slither around behind a truck wheel.

131

'Boo! Get that man back! And explain to the others an exploding truck tyre will kill them as effectively as a bullet.'

The Swahili Pierre had named arrived on their knees and elbows. 'I hope Esmeralda packed lots of elastoplast,' Jimmy said. He offered his scoped rifle to Lance. 'You're the best shot here.'

Lance shook his head. 'You and Pierre get my vote.'

A single shot rang out and they heard a truck tyre bursting. Then a volley of shots and tyres bursting.

Lance sighed, said, 'Now,' conversationally in Swahili and counted to five to give the covering fusillade time to put the attackers' heads down. Then he rose, jumped up onto the road and ran to the Range Rover, jerked the lid open, grabbed the medicine chest and slid it along the road and over the edge, where Boo gathered it up in his arms and dashed off behind the trucks. Lance found a box of ammunition and flung that over the edge of the road as well and then rolled over himself. Once sheltered again, he sourly inspected his elbows and knees.

'You could've walked upright like a man,' Jimmy told him. 'The only firing came from our side. They don't exactly have an army up there. I saw only five flashes.'

'That's what I saw too. Did we lose anybody?'

'The driver of the rearmost truck, at the same time as they shot you up. His passenger reacted quickly and pulled the body away and took over. Mpengo.'

Lance nodded. 'You and Pierre hold the fort here.' He crawled away, rising only when he was well into the shelter of the trucks. He found Christine sitting on the side of the road, staring blankly ahead. He knew what was ailing her. 'They wouldn't shoot the driver of the Range Rover,' he told her. 'They wanted to block our retreat and it's too easy to push a Range Rover out of the way with a truck.'

Christine nodded. 'I was thinking about that poor man.

What did he ever do to those people on the hill that they should kill him without any warning?'

Lance shook his head. He didn't know. 'Let's have lunch.'

'Lunch? You're going to eat while we're under attack?'

'Not just me, everybody.' Lance gestured to where Esmeralda already had her kitchen paraphernalia set up in a long row under the shelter of the trucks with the kitchen staff busy preparing the meal. 'You're in charge of the medicine cabinet, remember? We're going to have a lot of skinned elbows and knees.'

'I'm not a child!'

'Exactly.'

'Won't they creep up on us from this side?' Christine pointed at the grass, scrub and occasional tree in front of her.

Lance picked up a piece of road-gravel and showed her it was no larger than his thumbnail. He flung it twenty paces into the grass. Immediately a set of concentric circles spread from the small impact. 'Only if they're suicidal.'

'I'd better start with your elbows and knees.'

After lunch, Lance sat at the table with Boo, Jimmy, Pierre and Mwanzo. 'It's obvious they're trying to hold us down until a superior force arrives. Now, as you all know, normally I would wait until they came to me. But today I'm in a hurry and we're already twenty minutes behind.'

'Effectively the rest of the day is lost unless their reinforcements come before sunset,' Pierre said. 'We can't creep up on them for the same reason they can't creep up on us.'

They all studied the grass. 'If only there was a breeze,' Boo said.

Lance nodded thoughtfully. 'Maybe we can make our own. There are only five of them up there.'

'They're sheltered,' Jimmy said. 'A frontal attack isn't – '

'I wasn't thinking so much of a frontal attack,' Lance interrupted, 'as an all-points-of-the-compass attack.' He

133

scanned the grim faces at the table. 'What I have in mind is sending five of the grain lorries out there with a couple of Swahili lying on top of the grain to shoot them up from behind. Those bulk tips are of inch-thick high-tensile alloy, they're like natural armourplate.'

'But the drivers won't be protected,' Boo said.

'True. That's why I suggest we do the driving ourselves.'

The three brothers looked at each other. Then Jimmy said, speaking for all of them, 'You're quite mad, you know.' He put his hands on the table and pushed himself erect. 'If we're doing it, let's do it now before we change our minds.'

As he rose, Lance caught Esmeralda's eyes and tried to read something – anything – in her face but she was neutral; he knew that face, she was frightened for him. That hurt, but there was nothing he could do about it, not until after the food was delivered to Chad. Christine, he noticed, was dripping tears into the medicine chest. Only days ago she would have tried to stop him . . .

So that the surprise could be total, the Swahili left behind under Mpengo were told to hold their fire until the trucks were well under way. Lance hoped they would not be overcome by the excitement of the moment, or the trucks would be caught in a crossfire between their enemies and their own side.

He lay across the seat of the truck he would drive and listened to the two Swahili in the tip above him laughing softly with the excitement of fighting at last in prospect: they had not been overly impressed with their leaders' tendency thus far to hog all the action. When he had counted to one hundred, he pressed the starter button and let it go. The never-still bush air was horrifically rent with the scream of diesels. He heard firing from the small hill, then Mpengo's men answering, but did not look up. When he had counted to twenty again, he sat up, engaged all-wheel drive and let the clutch in. The heavy truck lurched off the drop from the road to the veld and he bumped his forehead against the windshield but didn't fasten the safety belt; instead he felt to make sure his rifle was still on the seat beside him. He changed gear and looked left and right. The other trucks raced parallel with his. The sun was at high noon and directly ahead of them. The windshield in front of him starred in two places but he kept driving: they couldn't see him behind the huge sheet of reflection. Over his head he heard shots as the Swahili returned fire. On the kopje he saw a man rear up, jerk as another shot hit him, then fall over backwards. For the moment there was only the scream of tortured diesel engines. He changed gear again and raised his foot marginally on the accelerator. He followed Jimmy's and Mwanzo's trucks to the right of the kopje and saw in his mirrors that Pierre and Boo were splitting off to the left. Immediately they had a clear field, the Swahili at the road laid down a barrage on every hiding-place on the kopje. Lance braked and stopped his truck on the rear slope of the little hill. He could see a man not forty yards from him turning, fitting a fresh clip to a rifle. A fusillade of shots tore the man from the earth and his life as the Swahili on three trucks simultaneously fired at him. The ambushers were now besieged, totally surrounded. Lance patted his pockets to check the whereabouts of his spare clips, took his rifle, stepped out on the running board and rolled over the top of the skip. He stretched out next to the Swahili on the grain and looked over the edge of the skip but saw only two dead men, one half over a rock, one still twitching despite the many bullets in him. He heard two single shots from the trucks to his right but couldn't see what they were shooting at. Sun flashed on metal on top of the hill and he fired. There was a scream and a fusillade of shots from his own side. Lance didn't fire again. A shot clanged off his own truck but he couldn't see instantly who had fired it and put his head down promptly so as not to offer a target.

'He's behind the rock with the red glint, Master,' Mwanzo called.

'Thanks!' Still Lance kept his head down.

When next the metal of his own truck clanged, he raised his head two inches and looked the man in the eyes and then shot him between them. Only then did it strike him – Arabs!

Lance turned to lie on his back in the grain and stare at the sky as he shouted to Jimmy. 'Bloody Libyans.'

'Looks like it, doesn't it,' Jimmy shouted back. 'How many do you reckon are left?'

'One?'

'Two, I think.'

'Mwanzo?'

'Two, Master.'

Lance took his hat by the brim and raised the crown slowly over the edge of the tip, with his other hand holding down the two Swahili. There were a great many good marksmen in the other grain trucks and he didn't want these two to get in the way of misaimed shots. The two shots that made the holes in his hat were almost immediately drowned by the barrage from elsewhere. When there was only silence, Lance called, 'You get them both?'

'I think so,' Jimmy called. He shouted to the other side and waited for a reply. 'Pierre says one of his Swahili scored one dead to rights. I got one in the shoulder myself but nobody seems to have hit him as well.'

Lance groaned. 'I don't fancy winkling out a wounded man.'

'I wounded him. I'll winkle him out.'

'No, it's all right. Cover me. Now!'

As the first shots rang out, Lance rolled over the edge of the skip and flexed his knees as he landed. There was no

136

point in rolling: the grass would signal his whereabouts. He just ran for the nearest cover, a small smooth rock about halfway up the little hill. He fell behind it, heaving for breath. He had been born fit and practised as a professional athlete for nearly a quarter of his thirty-two years, but the temperature was 112 degrees in the shade and the humidity in the high nineties. Killing weather.

'Your arse is showing,' Jimmy shouted at him. 'But nobody's shooting at it.'

Lance scrunched himself up smaller. It was not a very large rock and he was a very large man. He waited until his breathing steadied, then raised his hand, paused until firing picked up, and made a dash for the top of the hill, his rifle leading. Just before the top, he checked, not wanting to be shot by his own Swahili down at the trucks. That was when an Arab rose from behind a rock. Part of his scalp hung loose and blood flowed freely across his face. But he grinned triumphantly at Lance over his sights. Lance shot him twice in the chest as the man pulled the trigger but the Arab was held upright by the fusillade to his back from down by the road. Lance did not tarry to see him fall. He flattened himself on the ground to present the smallest possible head-on target and tried to watch everywhere but the place where the dead man was held erect by lead. Two wounded men. One with an empty rifle. Lance had heard the hollow click quite clearly above all the other noise: the mind being self-protectively selective. After five minutes, the cicadas resumed their interrupted singing. He raised his arm at his own people behind him, then ran over the last little crest in one concerted rush, bent double so as not to rise over the horizon of the Swahili at the trucks. At his feet lay a man with blood audibly gurgling through the hole in his neck where his jugular had been. Lance spun around in a full circle like a cornered animal. In the little hollow nothing lived except himself and a

137

crow pecking impertinently at the eyes of a dead man while regarding Lance askance. As a reflex, without raising his rifle from his hip, just pointing it and squeezing the trigger, he shot the crow; he was a keen conservationist but crows were a pest: if the insects do not inherit the earth after Man destroys himself, the crows will. Then he sat down to rest for a moment. If bloody Jimmy had looked more carefully where he had shot the Arab, still gurgling in his own blood, he could have avoided all this strenuous tension.

'Lance!'

He roused himself and fired another shot to put the throatless Arab out of his misery. 'I'm alright. It's over.'

After a while Jimmy and Mwanzo joined him and went through the pockets of the dead Arabs. They all carried Libyan passports and three had addresses in Tripoli; the other two appeared to live in Beirut. 'Professional trouble-makers,' Jimmy said.

Down at the road, Esmeralda flung herself at Lance and hugged him tightly. It was not glee for victory but joy that he was alive. He swung her around so fast her feet flew from the ground. The Swahili cheered loudly: he was very much man and it was fitting that he should have so very much woman.

The engagement cost them all the hours until four o'clock to make the trucks roadworthy again and, with the normal accidents of the road, held them up crucially, though they did not yet know it. At midnight they reached Kasongo, sixty miles short of Kibombo. Even Lance was weaving on his feet. Here he called a halt. While the tents were being set, he and Pierre and Boo and Jimmy and Nasheer and Mwanzo stood in a line facing east, sniff, sniff, sniffing. 'Are they praying?' Christine asked Esmeralda, who replied, 'No, they're smelling rain in the air.' In bed, holding Esmeralda tightly, Lance

138

said, 'It isn't like Qaddaffi to send only five men.' He fell asleep without hearing her answer.

At breakfast, with the red edge of light just rising in the east, Lance said, 'The rains will come this afternoon.'

'How do you know?' Christine demanded. Her eyes were red-rimmed; she had cried through the night. She was not used to killing done inescapably on her behalf, at her implicit instruction. However good the cause.

'Black man's magic,' Lance said, tapping the belt of black treesnake skin he always wore.

'You can smell it, Miss Rawls,' Nasheer said when Lance went back to his coffee and rusk. 'Lake Tanganyika is only two hundred miles away.' He pointed towards the edge of light on the horizon.

Christine sniffed but found nothing different, merely the slightly morbid smell of Africa that always revolted her. She imagined that this was what pregnant women must feel like in the morning, nauseated by small clinging odours, unrested, irritable.

'Look, Christine, dik-dik,' Jimmy said and put his mug down to turn her head between his hands. 'Concentrate on the pattern of the leaves and the grass and you'll see it just behind the first screen. No, down, down, it's only about a third of a metre, uh, a foot high.'

She saw the little doe, standing quite still in the low foliage and looking calmly at them.

A Swahili reached for his rifle and Lance said something to him. The man grinned defensively and put his rifle down.

The little antelope wandered away.

It was a magical moment.

'What did you say to him?' Christine asked.

'We have enough meat,' Lance replied.

But that hadn't been his tone. 'No, really.'

Jimmy growled, 'He said he'd cut him.'

139

'Cut – ? Oh, I see, yes.'

Boo laughed aloud.

Before the disc of the sun was fully over the horizon, the convoy arrived at the junction of the Kibombo/Bukavu road. Lance slowed the Range Rover when he saw the junction.

'The rains will start this afternoon,' he said to Esmeralda.

'You want to take to the rafts.'

She hadn't asked a question but he said, 'Yes. Every day we spend on the road, many more people die. Should I ask Christine?'

'Does she know the risk?'

'I'll tell her again.' He signalled a halt, then drove down the length of the convoy until he reached Jimmy's Range Rover. He wound his window down and called across Jimmy to Christine in the passenger seat of the other vehicle: 'This is where the road forks. To the left the rafts and the unknown river. To the right the certain, long way.'

Christine looked at the sky, which was just turning from purple to blue. There was not a single cloud in sight.

'The rains will start this afternoon,' Jimmy told her with absolute certainty.

Still Christine hesitated.

'Flip a coin,' Jimmy suggested. 'Sorry,' he added to Lance who, as a reformed gambler, was virulently opposed to all games of chance.

'Not for people's lives,' Christine said firmly. To Lance, 'How many days difference?'

'Five days to a week.'

'Do you know how many people can die in five days?'

Lance shook his head.

'Then what do you want to do?'

'Don't snarl at me, Christine. We're on the same side. It's simple: the long way I can virtually guarantee not to lose your

140

grain but will need another five to seven days to deliver it. The short way I can guarantee nothing except speed.'

'All right, I'm sorry. What's your inclination then?'

The temptation was a red-hot poker through Lance's intestines: born a gambler, always a gambler. But more was at stake here than his skill and luck at the highest stakes of all. 'Do you want to take a vote?'

'No,' Christine said firmly, 'you lead this expedition. You must decide.'

Lance slapped the side of the Range Rover ringingly with the flat of his hand. 'Of course,' Christine added, 'you can take a vote if you wish.'

Lance put the Range Rover in gear and turned it around and drove to the head of the column again. There he stopped momentarily.

At the back of the column, Jimmy told Christine, 'That was cruel.'

'I couldn't, Jimmy. I just couldn't decide.'

At the head of the column, Lance turned in his seat to face Esmeralda. 'The whole stack on number thirteen,' he said.

'Tomorrow is your birthday,' she said, not inconsequentially at all.

The cheerful building on Schoemanstraat in Pretoria is quite out of kilter with its sinister inhabitants: it is a metal and glass structure, the glass plain and clear, not mirrored or smoked, and the metal panels gaily coloured in multi-pastels. It is the home of one of the more efficient secret police services in the world; the only other contestants for the top spot, the Israelis, consider the South Africans their equals and training exchanges are common. But Rocco Burger took no special credit for this, merely pointing out mildly that one would expect his small department (less than a thousand souls including clerks and temporary training attachments from

141

other and foreign services) to operate more efficiently than, say, the monstrous KGB, which has more than a thousand generals among its nearly half a million staff. Burger was not above conducting staff raids in colleagues' offices but he was always willing to give back a man of lesser quality in return for the exceptional man stolen; he was not building an empire but a machine, and he was too secure to need numbers to prove his importance. Besides, tangling with Burger in the bureaucratic wars was no small thing. Only an innocent would take for gospel his official place in the hierarchy as depicted on the Police Minister's organization chart; insiders knew that the Justice and Interior Ministries had more influence with Burger, and those who had taken Burger this far found only the President could countermand the secret service chief and was not likely to do so, for the simple reason that it is the one post in the land whose incumbent must command 100 per cent of the President's personal trust and faith. Burger-the-civil-servant therefore existed only on the hierarchical tree and in the minds of the ignorant or innocent; Burger-the-law-unto-himself operated (with possible but unlikely *post facto* adjustment by the President) from a cheerful five-storey building on a jacaranda-lined street in South Africa's pleasant administrative capital. The department has small offices in other cities, usually shared with the police. At Schoemanstraat there are no detention cells or torture chambers; Burger's detention powers must in fact be backed up by a uniformed policeman. Detention and interrogation is carried out at police stations. (Burger has been heard to say that, if he had his own detention facilities, Steve Biko would still be alive: he does not hold the average redneck constable in high regard.) The department shares training facilities such as the Police Driving School; their helicopters are serviced by the Air Force and flown from Valhalla. Burger's department had never actually spent its entire secret budget. Insofar as he behaved like a civil servant, he was a splendid civil servant, but the politician responsible for him, the President, could not care less: Burger was valued not for staying within his budget but for his quiet efficiency in uncovering and eliminating threats to the well-being of the volk and the fatherland. In that inner circle that lunches almost daily at the RSA in Cape Town (where Burger, a connoisseur of fine food which is most emphatically what the RSA does not serve, never went except as a command performance for the President) stories were sometimes told of how Burger mopped up threats to the volk and the fatherland even before they reached the borders, while they still blustered from foreign soil . . .

Today, Burger was considering just such a foreign adventure. Other potentates of police and the armed forces might envy him his power and freedom of initiative but he was well aware that he kept his privileges by using them wisely and, more important to his master, discreetly.

Outside his window, the jacaranda blossoms fell on the parked cars. His predecessor, Lieutenant-General Ernst Freiherr von Hoesch, would swear a continuous stream of German filth every afternoon while he picked the staining flowers from the roof of his beloved white BMW coupé. Von Hoesch had been picking off blossoms when the terrorists stopped next to him and from twelve inches fired twenty-one bullets into him. Burger drove a different car each day and had it brought around to the back door by a driver from the pool at the very last moment. But, except for deadlocks on the front and rear doors of his ninth-floor flat, that was the only security precaution he felt necessary. And who should know better than he? He did not carry a firearm – he never had and he was too old to start now. Besides, it would be an admission of defeat. He fought with his brain, not his hands, and then only when he was forced to fight.

He was still investigating the von Hoesch killing, becoming daily more certain that the conservatives, the right-wing opposition to the government's concessions to the non-whites, were behind the assassination, as they were behind the wave of black unrest, hoping for such police retaliation that the black locations would explode, resulting in turn in a white backlash that would unseat Botha and bring the right wing to power. Lance Weber was a distraction.

Burger turned away from the window and the purple beauty of the jacarandas.

That amateur at Foreign Affairs should have told him.

He read the report again. It was off the SAPA-Reuters ticker and in blunt telegraphese reported that Robert Mugabe's Zimbabwean government were livid because the South African Government had sent a notorious mercenary, Lance Weber, into their country to humiliate them. This humiliation had taken the form of Weber leaving a party of notorious Fifth Parachute Brigade troopers beside the main road in their birthday suits. The South Africans had merely replied that Weber was a Kenyan, not a South African, and that he was escorting a relief convoy for the Matthew Ellimore Foundation; Christine Rawls, Director of the Foundation, was also on the convoy, as was Mr Weber's wife. The Fifth Parachute Brigade had been accused of murders, rapes, abductions, beatings of the Matabele and were widely feared in Zimbabwe. Weber had not only stripped them naked, he had bent the barrels of their rifles . . .

Burger did not have to be a journalist to know that newspapers across the world would treat this item in only one of two ways: they could make a major story of the arrogance of the South Africans, or they could use the story as light relief next to the front-page news of more blacks killed by police in South Africa (nineteen at Langa that day). The second way, ridiculing the Zimbabweans' most feared soldiers, would probably be worse . . . In most papers, the fact that Weber was now a Kenyan citizen would not rate a mention and it would be a rare newspaper or television news bulletin that would find space for it. But, being a thoroughly modest man as well as a thorough one, Burger called the editor of *Die Burger* in Cape Town, a government-oriented paper, to confirm his guess. He had met the man two or three times. When he was put through, he asked, 'Have you seen the Reuters report of Weber and the Fifth Parachute Brigade?'

'Yes. It just came in. I'm about to allocate it.'

'That's what I want to know. How will you treat it?'

'As balance to the Langa tragedy. A bit of humour in these times, even if it is graveyard humour. What's your interest, General?'

'Weber.'

'Oh yes, him. I met his brother once.'

'He's a Kenyan citizen now.'

'Is he really?'

'It's in the piece.'

'Oh.' The rustle of paper travelled clearly over the telephone to Burger. 'You're right. You want me to feature that?'

'Yes, please. Will everybody react like you? I mean internationally.'

'I should think so, General. The Fifth Parachute have generated a lot of adverse publicity and this is a good story in itself, a non-violent, charitable relief column stripping those bullyboys and butchers naked and leaving them beside the road with bent rifles. Hell, there's not a reader that won't understand the symbolism.'

Burger sighed. 'Tell me all the same.'

'Bent cocks. It's a blow to their manhood, wouldn't you say?'

'And if you're insecure in anyway . . .'

145

'Exactly! General, is your interest official?'

'Yes. But confidential.'

'I understand. What do you think the Zimbabweans will do next? Non-attributable.'

'If they have any sense, they'll shut the hell up and let the hullaballoo die of its own accord.'

'If they had any sense, they would've rid themselves of the Fifth Parachute Brigade long ago. I think they should thank Rawls and Weber for doing them a favour. Hey, that's good for my cartoonist.'

Burger thanked the man and rang off. Now he knew. He buzzed for his assistant, a twenty-eight-year-old university-educated captain by the name of Jannie Bosman.

'Jannie,' he said when the young man stuck his head around the door connecting their offices, 'put Peet le Roux and two squads on two-hour readiness alert.'

'Where for, sir?'

'Probably Zaire.'

'Peet's booked his holiday starting next week.'

'He'll be back long before. And get me that colonel who runs the long-range aerial reconnaissance unit.'

Jannie Bosman looked at his watch. 'They shut up shop already at Valhalla, sir.'

Burger glanced at the clock on the wall. Six forty-five. Goddamn that Lance Weber: he had spent most of the afternoon thinking about a sideshow when his country was falling apart around his ears. 'Get his home number. Use my name.'

When his aide had gone, Burger leaned back in his chair and stretched. He didn't want to kill Lance Weber. Though Lance might not believe it, Burger liked him. But, five hours out of South Africa, the boy had, even after Burger had warned him, created an international incident. There was no knowing what international embarrassment he would cause

146

next. He was simply one of those people whom trouble infallibly found.

Nor did Burger want to kill the rest of Lance's party but they would talk and it was the very backbone of his extra-territorial adventures that he left no witnesses who could talk. He had learnt much from the Israelis' mistakes in abducting Nazis from other nations' sovereign soil and then trying them in public: nobody loved them for their adherence to justice. Perhaps he could manage to blame what had to be done on the Libyans . . .

The phone rang and he pulled a map towards him to explain to the reconnaissance expert which roads in Zaire he wanted photographed.

As yet, Burger did not know that Lance had only yesterday buried five Libyans beside the road in Zaire. Or that the main body of the Libyans, unaware of the annihilation of their advance party, still lay in wait for Lance.

'What do you reckon?' Lance asked Jimmy. The question was, would the river below them, the Lualaba, be big enough, come the rains, to carry a raft laden with a truck?

'Let's see your map, Christine.' Jimmy held out his hand without looking away from the river.

Esmeralda leaned into the Range Rover and put a map in his hand.

'Thanks.' Then he saw Christine wading into the water below and did a double-take. He shouted at her: 'Get out of the water, stupid! It's full of crocodiles.'

Lance fetched his rifle from the Range Rover. He twice shot a submerged log floating fast towards Christine but it turned out to be just that, a log. Nobody laughed at his mistake. It had looked like a crocodile to them, too, and all of them had before today seen swimming crocodiles look exactly like submerged floating logs. Christine rushed out of the water at the sound of the shots, then stood glaring furiously at them.

'She thinks we rearrange Africa to inconvenience her,' Jimmy said to Lance.

Lance shrugged. He thought cities were expressly designed to be as dangerous as possible for people, and specifically to him and his family, so why shouldn't Christine be paranoid here? 'Mwanzo!' He pointed to a sandbank. 'Take a couple of your brothers and dig up the crocodile eggs for an omelette.'

'Yes, Master!'

'What do you reckon?' Lance again asked Jimmy.

'What's the alternative?' Jimmy folded the map in his hands and studied a small section. He answered himself. 'Eighty miles to the junction of the Lualaba with the Elila, which is about the same size. No question about it, from there, even before the rains, we'll float.'

They turned to watch the other side of the bridge, where, on a clearing at the riverside, Pierre and Boo directed gangs of Swahili to stack the crates containing their inflatable rafts. The rafts weighed only three tons altogether, including their packing crates, but they were much bulkier in their uninflated state than any of them had expected.

'To the junction of the rivers and back, say four hours, plus an hour to unload the trucks. Then an hour to load the inflatables here and four hours back up to – '

'By which time,' Lance interrupted Jimmy, 'the rains will be on us and that little trip will surely take seven or eight hours.'

'Well.' Jimmy turned back to peer over the bridge. 'If this river won't carry us even after the rains come, we'll just have to do it. Did you ask how often the train runs on this spur up to Kindu?' He showed the map to Lance. 'That's almost the junction of the rivers.'

148

'The train runs next week,' Lance said. 'Maybe.' He had taken Nasheer into Kibombo to pay their respects to the mayor and chief of police and to enquire about obstructions on the river – ferry cables and suchlike. 'The mining company can lend us a diesel loco but they haven't any flatbed trucks. You'd think at the end of a railroad that runs all the way from Cape Town . . .'

'Yeah. How deep is it, Christine?'

'I only reached knee-deep before you started shooting at me.'

'Not me. Lance shot at a crocodile.'

'A log,' retorted Christine scathingly and stalked by.

'They look the same until it's too late,' Lance called after her. 'But just say the word and next time I'll hold fire until it takes a bite out of you and we can all be sure it isn't a log.'

Lance peered through the telescope of the rifle he still held at the stack of crates holding their inflatables. The size, 13m × 4m, was stencilled on each. 'Anything that floats displaces its own weight of water. How much does water weigh per cubic foot?' he asked Jimmy.

'Hell, I don't know.'

'But Esmeralda keeps a sailboat at Mombasa,' Lance said and strode towards his wife, who was supervising the preparation of brunch. When he returned, he had a page torn from her spiral-bound pad in his hand. He paced off the width of the river on the bridge, then did it again, starting several paces in from the edge of the water.

'We're okay for width,' he told Jimmy, 'and Esmeralda reckons the grain, the truck, people and the weight of the raft itself will draw only twenty inches.'

'That river's a lot deeper than twenty inches.'

'Pierre! Boo! Open the crates. We're floating from here.' Lance turned to Jimmy again. 'Next question. How do we put the trucks on the inflatables without any upsets?'

149

That proved to be easy, once they had wasted an hour working it out: spread the uninflated inflatable in the water, drive the truck into the water and onto the uninflated inflatable, then connect the pump and inflate the inflatable. But it was hard work since, even after they had taken their pills and shots, Lance ordered all cuts and abrasions smeared with grease and then tightly bound with waterproof bindings against bilharzia before he would let anyone in the water. Since it is impossible to travel as they had been travelling without collecting a display of cuts and abrasions, they all looked like part-wrapped mummies. The Swahili, who regard bilharzia as an occupational disease, were scornful of Lance's preparations but even so Esmeralda noticed that they were careful to drink only boiled water. It was three-thirty in the afternoon before all the trucks and the two Range Rovers were loaded onto inflatables and all the inflatables pumped up with the compressor that had also been airdropped. Roger had, thoughtfully, included a hundred life jackets in the drop.

Christine looked doubtfully at the pure blue sky and then again at the life jacket in her hand. Esmeralda slipped hers over her head and tied it. Since nobody else seemed to feel ridiculous wearing a life jacket on a bright sunny day beside a dawdling river, Christine too put hers on. Jimmy swung her aboard the inflatable and, before she could tell him she was quite capable of jumping three feet, Lance said to her, 'We should have asked for a dinghy as well, to get around the rafts.' There were men aboard each raft, armed with aluminium poles, but, except for the two inflatables carrying the smaller Range Rovers, the rafts were crowded and dangerous: each one was thirteen feet wide but the weight of the truck distorted it by bending up the sides so that passing from the front to the rear of the raft was difficult and, under adverse circumstances, might be impossible. Out in the middle of the river, Lance told the Swahili to clip their lifelines onto the safety ropes; several looked at him strangely but clipped their lines on all the same. Christine was convinced it was all a bit much: they were not racing a yacht around Cape Horn. In the foremost raft Esmeralda set up a table with a gaily striped Cinzano umbrella over it and soon the steward started serving drinks; in the rear of the raft, the cooks were busy about their kitchen.

They moved excruciatingly slowly by reference to the trees on the riverbank. 'If it doesn't rain this afternoon,' Christine said bitterly to Lance, 'you'll have wasted a whole day to get us on the rafts and perhaps another day to put us back on the road.' She looked up at the clear blue sky – not a cloud – and then back at the sluggish mudbrown river. 'Look, that log is overtaking us.'

'That log's a crocodile,' Lance said without thinking and was immediately sorry.

'Like the one this morning, huh?'

Lance took an aluminium pole from the Swahili next to him and poked at the black mass in the dark brown water. The 'log' turned towards them, broke surface and opened its mouth to snap at them. Christine saw the twin horseshoes of yellowed teeth and an effluvium of carrion struck her in the face. She crashed into the table behind her as she retreated frantically. Lance, laughing, pushed the crocodile away with the pole; it promptly dived and disappeared.

'Crocodiles are basically shy and retiring,' Lance told Christine. 'Have no fear they'll try to share our raft with us. Here, Gatsha, please bring Miss Rawls another drink.' He picked up Christine's glass and put it on the steward's tray. 'What we want to watch out for is hippo. A hippopotamus is as likely to bite a man in two as to retreat.'

Christine thought this another horror story to repay her for pointing up Lance's mistake with the log this morning. She looked at Esmeralda, who could never stop a small smile from creeping onto her lips when Lance made a joke but Esmeralda, stretched out in her folding chair, studied the sky serenely as if from the verandah of the Mombasa Yacht Club. Jimmy too looked serious.

'Nooo,' Pierre said dismissively, 'not many hippopotami left on this river.'

'If there's just one, we're certain to run into it,' Lance said. 'This river isn't big enough for us and a hippo both. And we'll never see it.'

'It's a big animal,' Esmeralda said, 'even half-submerged.'

'It feeds at night,' Lance told her.

'Oh, I didn't know that.'

'Anybody who knew everything about Africa would be as old as Methuselah.'

'And still learning,' Jimmy said. 'Anyhow, I lived seventeen years around here and only once was lucky enough to see a hippo.'

'What happened to them all? Did people eat them?' Esmeralda asked.

'Not in these parts,' Pierre said.

'Hunting hippo is dangerous even with a rifle,' Jimmy said. 'With a spear it's suicide. You know what happened to them, Lance? Did you have any on your game reserve?'

Lance nodded. 'They breed only once every several years. They're nocturnal and they're subaqueous. I reckon they're one of the few animals nothing has actually happened to. Christine used to be a conservationist.'

'It's possible there never were as many hippos as was once thought,' Christine said. 'It's also probable that the encroachment of people onto their breeding grounds slows down their reproduction cycle even more. But nobody knows exactly how many hippo there are or whether they are in fact an endangered species.'

The first drops fell just then and Christine, who had taken

152

a seat under the umbrella, stuck her hand out to feel it wetted almost instantly. Minutes ago the sky had been blue from horizon to horizon, now the sun was invisible and a curtain of rain in waving sheets draped itself across her vision, totally obscuring the next raft.

The rain stopped eighty-five minutes later. 'Keep your oilskins on,' Lance warned them. It was sweltering inside the oilskins. The river now flowed so brown with mud, it was almost black. It had risen at least a foot and flowed twice as fast as before the rain. The sky, again blue from edge to edge, threatened nothing, but Lance and his lieutenants watched the river itself anxiously. When the second rain fell twenty minutes later, the river was still not in flood. Lance and Jimmy laboriously pulled the next raft towards them with its tie-rope, jumped onto it, ascertained that all the Swahili had their safety lines clipped on, then repeated the process until they reached the rearmost raft, carrying Jimmy's Range Rover and a large complement of Swahili under Boo to render assistance to any raft that should float out of line. Boo too was watching the water, though he had not bothered with an oilskin in the warm rain. Many of the Swahili around him were naked. Most watched the river apprehensively: the Swahili are from Zanzibar, an island with no large rivers but smack in the path of the monsoons roaring in off the Indian Ocean; this river in its suddenly aggrandized condition merged the threat of the unfamiliar with the terror only too familiarly feared in the tribal consciousness and the personal memory.

'This is just the normal rise,' Boo said. 'Two feet in two hours. But I'd be happier if it were four feet. Then that other two feet couldn't hit us suddenly.'

'Oh,' said Lance to give himself time to think. He could no longer see the river banks but in the interval between the first and the second rains, he had seen that the river was now

153

twice the width it had been before the rain started. And two feet higher. They had to stay in the middle of the flow; they could not risk the more sheltered sides for fear of tearing a raft on a submerged tree and losing a truck. 'If we're in any part where the river narrows between natural features when that other two feet of water hits us, it could be five or six feet high,' he finally said. 'What then?'

Boo shrugged and Jimmy said, 'Then that's all she wrote. Once a raft capsizes, the truck is gone. At least we won't lose any Swahili, as long as they keep their lines clipped. These inflatables are unsinkable.'

'Is that right?'

'Oh yes, they put a cover over them and use them for lifeboats. It said so in the leaflets.'

'Then we won't lose any trucks either,' Lance said. 'Tie every truck down to its raft and make sure those canvas covers are stretched real tight over the grain skips.'

'Those tarps won't hold eight tons of grain,' Boo said.

'We won't know until we try,' Lance said cheerfully.

'I'm not so sure I wouldn't rather be in the mud,' Boo said.

'Me too,' Jimmy agreed. 'At least we've done that before.'

'It's too slow,' Lance said with finality. 'Let's see to the trucks.' He bent and, with his hand, pushed away a sharp-pointed fresh-torn tree-trunk. 'Can you swim?' he asked the Swahili leaning on his pole next to him.

'No Master.'

'Then you'd better keep sharp things from this crêpe de Chine you're floating on.' He kicked the side of the inflatable.

'A condom, Master?'

'Right. And as easily punctured.'

'Hau!' The Swahili bent to clip on his safety line, then put his aluminium pole over the side and fixed his eyes on his square of water. The others, who listened while politely looking elsewhere, promptly followed suit and a few who had taken off their life jackets put them back on.

Lance pointed to the river. 'A wall of water will come. Be ready.'

'Hau!' they said in unison.

'Like the wind from the sea?' asked the elder, the induna.

'Like the wind from the sea,' Lance agreed. 'More dangerous than all our enemies.'

They nodded thoughtfully. That was very wise. An enemy one could shoot, a wall of water one could do nothing about. This Lance Weber was not only a man of demonstrable juju and a fighter so favoured by the gods that he was never punished with fear, he was as wise as a greybeard. And cunning: leaving those men in Zimbabwe naked and with their rifles bent, that was worse than cutting them! How could men chopped so small ever return to their families and villages? Hau! *Far* worse than cutting them . . .

Lance was tying down a truck in the middle of the row of inflatables when the light plane flew over in another pause in the rain. Lance glanced up at it, then back along the river, whence the sound of big water mounting reached him clearly even over the whining of the plane's engine. He looked from side to side and cursed: here the river had, over a few centuries, cut through the earth to leave walls of red clay bound by tree roots and dead grass to a height of twelve feet even above the present elevated level of the water. There was nowhere to run to.

Juju is anything between extraordinary luck and invincible magic. The leader of the Libyans sent to 'stop' the Matthew Ellimore Foundation relief convoy was convinced he suffered extraordinary bad luck. (Having had a perfectly good education at Moscow's Patrice Lumumba University, he could not believe in invincible magic, though he would, if provoked, offer the patronizing opinion that the savages Weber had hired to protect the convoy were likely to confuse good luck with magic.) His name was Ahmed Ree and he had been ten years a revolutionary about Qaddaffi's business. In cities. He felt more than vaguely ill at ease in what he thought of, in perfect English, as 'the bush'. But he could read a map of a country as well as a street map of a city. He had sent a plane to spot the convoy and then split his force into the main contingent, under his own command, to lay an ambush on the road to Bukavu, and a scout party of five to wait for the convoy on the road from the south and either report back that Weber had taken the left fork to Kibombo, in the stupid belief that he could reach Kisangani before the rains came, or follow and block Weber's retreat when the main party ambushed him. When neither Weber's convoy nor his own scout party turned up a full day after he expected them, Ree went down that road from the south with trepidation in his heart and all his men at his back: he had learnt his lesson, he would not split them again.

He read the sign just as he would in a city after a guerrilla war. His men had become ambitious and started shooting at Weber from the hollow on top of the hill. Weber, with his superior force, had stormed them, surrounded them and, finally, killed them all. Weber must have taken his own dead, of which there would have been many, with him; there were, in the mass grave, only five of his men and one of Weber's Swahili. Ree couldn't understand why Weber had left one of his own dead behind; then it struck him: of course, burying a black savage in the same grave as good Libyans was a calculated insult, exactly the kind one would expect from a racist pig like Weber.

Since Weber had passed here but had not passed him, he must have turned for Kibombo. At Kibombo, he soon heard that a white man answering to Weber's description had liberally greased his questions about the river and that a pair of big planes had dropped rafts, on which Weber was right now attempting the river . . . There was a generally incredulous attitude to this venture.

Fine and well. A convoy on a river would be even more exposed than on the road.

There was a field long and smooth enough for his light support plane. He sat strapped into his seat, tapping his fingers in frustration, until a break in the rain let them into the air. They found the convoy almost immediately.

Back at the landing strip, he told his men to rest well. They would set out at dawn. Even on muddy roads they would make better speed than Weber could on the river. If Weber survived the night . . .

He had seen the wall of water building up downriver but the pilot, fearing the return of the rain and zero visibility, could not be persuaded to wait for Ree to enjoy the sight of Nature doing his work for him.

Lance flew through the air, his feet scrabbled for purchase on the evasive soft rolled edge of the next inflatable, and jack-knifed his body in the air to fling him hard up against the front of the truck, where he grabbed hold of the windshield wiper to steady himself. Immediately he had footing, he was away round the truck and down the side of the inflatable, stepping on Swahili where none of the treacherous sinking footing of the inflatable's rolled edge offered. 'Clip your safety lines on and hold tight,' he shouted at the Swahili who, to a man, faced rearwards. Lance heard the big water racing towards them: it did not roar so much as growl ferociously. It was raining again, making the wet rubber even more treacherous, cutting visibility to less than twenty feet, so that he could not see if they were perhaps out of the cutting and therefore relatively safe. Once he misjudged and fell hipdeep into the churning water, one hand on the safety rope on the next inflatable. The two nearest Swahili hauled him in. He cast aside his oilskins as he ran. He hoped Esmeralda still had her safety line clipped on and would make Christine do likewise; no, Pierre was up there and he had a cool head. Everything would be all right. He, Lance, would be more use at the point of impact. He launched himself from the penultimate raft to the last. From the air, over Jimmy's Range Rover, he could see the four-foot high wave of water Boo had forecast, but that was only the praetorian of a pulse three times as high which followed it close. Lance knew what had happened: the cutting narrowed and his star betrayed him to put him exactly in the neck of disaster when the gathered rivulets, streams, creeks, dongas and minor waterways all joined forces to deliver their mightiest blow to his hubris. He sprawled flat on his face in the bottom of the last raft and, as he was rising, Jimmy crashed into his back and flattened him again. Mwanzo, following Lance, landed on Jimmy. Boo, already there because he had been working further back in the train of rafts, pulled Mwanzo away by his collar, then Jimmy. While Boo was clipping Jimmy, winded by Mwanzo's flying 180 pounds, to the safety rope, Mwanzo, grinning hugely, dragged the heaving Lance to the other side and clipped him on. 'See to your brothers,' Lance gasped at him. Now the big water didn't growl, it roared frighteningly. Lance heaved once more for air. At Jimmy, he shouted, 'Are all the trucks secure?' Jimmy had been working further forward than he. Jimmy, with no breath to speak, nodded. Then the water hit them.

It crashed over the top of the Range Rover, bodily pushing the heavy vehicle sideways in its moorings, ripping mirrors and wipers from the outside. Lance thought, That wave foams at the mouth in its lust to devour us. The poetic image was inspired by fear. He gulped air and a mouthful of the

158

foul thick muddy water before he was engulfed. He saw Jimmy's body fly through the air and thud down under the water as the safety line brought him up short. Poor Jimmy, he thought, he still has no air in his lungs. Something hit Lance in the back of the neck, floating log, catfish, crocodile, he knew not what. The safety line tugging at his middle was cutting him in two. A blow to the back from another hazard hurled forward by the monstrous anger of the water blew all the breath from him and he started drowning. His last thought was that at least Esmeralda stood a better chance on the leading raft, with all the other rafts behind to protect and shelter it; the force of the water would be broken by the time it reached there. He passed out from another blow to the head.

Lance came to just as the water receded, no, he corrected himself, as the inflatable floated to the top of the new water-level. He saw Jimmy face-down in the water at the bottom of the inflatable and rolled him over and raised his head. Lance stood on his knees for almost a minute, head down, heaving up filthy thin mud, trying at the same time to gasp for air while his hands pushed at Jimmy's chest. Then Jimmy spouted runny mud from his mouth and coughed and pushed Lance off and rolled over to retch and heave for his own air. Lance saw Mwanzo hauling Boo over the side and walked on his knees through the water, to help, but Mwanzo was managing. Lance saw a Swahili with a bloody scalp floating in the water and pulled him in by his safety line until he could grab him under the arms and haul him in.

Lance looked over the side but the safety lines had saved everyone. He caught a glimpse of a fast-rising tree through the rain – the river fell as fast as it had risen but now it settled at a much higher level and Lance guessed it flowed at ten or eleven knots, far too fast for the Swahili to control the rafts with their poles. Lance was not at all surprised that so many of the Swahili had held onto their poles: that was what he had hired them for, in preference to the Watusi who were better drivers but no bloody good in a crisis; at a pinch Lance would choose, above all others, Jimmy's people or the Swahili or the Zulu as his comrades in arms.

Their raft bumped into the one in front. Lance hauled Jimmy up by his collar. Jimmy shook his head. 'I thought you were going to give me the kiss of life,' he shouted. Lance grinned at him and pointed at the jam in front of them. Jimmy nodded and unclipped his safety line. He bent over Boo, who lay on his back, heaving for air and rolling his eyes, winded but unharmed.

Lance led the way. The rafts were locked together but moving twice as fast as before and a man falling between them would be drowned before they could part the jam and pull him up. Lance moved with care from handhold to handhold on the trucks, placing his leading foot firmly on the rolled edge of the raft before moving the other one. He was impatient to see if Esmeralda was all right but willed himself to move with forethought.

They had lost two men: one with a branch driven through his chest, the other unaccounted for, presumably swept away and drowned.

The third raft from the front had capsized. The rolled buoyant sides had popped the other way and floated half submerged; the truck could every now and then be seen hanging upside down by its lashings underneath. It brought home to them awesomely the growth of a river which only hours ago they were happy to find exceeded twenty inches in depth. The drag of the truck slowed down the whole train of rafts, including the two in front. Lance gained the foremost raft by pulling in the ropes and jumping. The awning over the kitchen had gone and the gay umbrella, table and chairs, but everyone was safe. Esmeralda had already combed some of the mud out of her hair and was busy repacking the medicine chest. Lance kissed her from behind in the junction of her neck and shoulder.

'It wasn't as bad as I expected,' she said. She turned to kiss his lips. 'You're pale.'

'And I smell. It was worse back there. We lost two men. We'll bring the casualties to you, okay? I don't want you getting in the way of the men on the rafts.'

Christine, sleekly wet, seemed calm. 'What about that truck?'

'We'll leave it upside down,' Lance said.

'It's eight tonnes of food,' Christine said evenly.

'I know. But it's wet now. It'll rot before we can deliver it. And the truck slows us down. If we right it and speed up, we could lose everything.'

Jimmy arrived and Christine started attending to a cut across his shoulder that Lance had not noticed before. Jimmy pushed her away. 'It's a scratch. There are men hurt worse back there. They're being brought.'

'Then I'll just have to finish with you before they come,' Christine said firmly. Over her bent head, Jimmy raised an eyebrow at Lance.

Mwanzo, carrying over his shoulder the Swahili who needed stitches in his scalp, reported that one raft was leaking air. Lance went to look but the thing was floating, if a little lopsided, and he couldn't find the hole; the water flowed too fast for bubbles to rise to the top. Jimmy, with an outsize strip of Elastoplast across his chest, came and said the insides of the rafts were lined with a self-sealing compound: he had read that too in the leaflets – they could actually have to be torn or have a good-sized hole in them, rather than just a small puncture, before they would lose air seriously enough to sink.

It was fearsomely hard work keeping the rafts behind the

161

overturned truck from piling into each other and then sliding away towards the dangerous submerged stumps and whole trees at the sides of the river. If they wanted to arrive at Kisangani with their convoy intact, they must stay in the middle of the river. A floating pointed stick could puncture an inflatable but a firmly planted tree-trunk split to a wicked sickle by lightning would rip the bottom out of it far beyond the capabilities of the wonderful self-sealing butyl vinyl lining. A truck dragged upside-down underneath an intact inflatable was useful; a truck sunk would be no use at all and would delay them for at least an hour while they cut it free and reformed the convoy.

Pierre wiped the sweat from his face and stood for a moment resting on his pole. 'It'll be dark in an hour,' he told Lance. 'We'll have to stop for the night.'

Lance's reluctance must have shown on his face, for Jimmy said, 'Carrying on like this when we can't see is to invite disaster.'

Lance considered. If only they could stop the rafts bunching up behind the overturned truck and pressing to the sides, most of their problems would evaporate. He studied the rain encircling him. The light was dull grey, the colour of lead; an hour from now it would disappear and a pitch black would fall all over until the rain stopped and the moon cast its light.

'No,' Lance said, 'I'm not stopping for the night. Instead, let's put our sea-anchor at the back to hold the line straight.'

They pursed their lips doubtfully but Lance, mindful of the failing light, was already telling Mwanzo to bring forward every man not vitally necessary to keep the rearmost inflatables from piling up on the riverbank. His plan was simple in conception, exhausting and dangerous in execution.

First he strung a long line from the second raft to the fourth, bypassing the third with its upturned truck. Then he climbed aboard the capsized inflatable with as many Swahili

162

as he could fit. Pierre was stationed in the second raft, Mwanzo in the fourth, Jimmy and Boo in the last one. Lance waved to Esmeralda, who peered anxiously at him through the rain. It struck him that, even when done up in full rig for a formal ball at Government House, she had never looked so beautiful as now, wet but not at all bedraggled; not even the leaden light could dull the vibrant olive glow of her skin. He blew her a kiss, then shouted, 'Mwanzo, on the count of three. Start counting out loud.'

He could barely see Mwanzo through sixty feet of that persistent rain but he heard him as through a heavy drape: 'Yes Master. One!'

Lance poised his knife. 'Two!' he shouted. 'Three!' And he slashed the rope tying the upturned inflatable to the one in front. It swung with a lurch, in the wrong direction, to the right, and for a moment Lance feared Mwanzo had failed to cut the rope to the one behind, but then the Swahili started poling to the left and Lance heard Pierre, whom he could not see at all, spurring the Swahili on to greater efforts in poling the second raft rightwards; then again he heard Mwanzo laugh in the fourth raft as it came by unseen. Lance hoped he would be able to see the last raft before it passed him by. He picked up the coil of rope at his feet and tested the knot attaching it to the hook of the inflatable.

'Lance! Lance, where the hell are you?' he heard Jimmy's voice, *ahead* of him.

Christ, the rearmost raft had passed! 'Here!'

'*Throw that bloody rope, man!*'

Lance had already flung it. He watched anxiously as the coils reeled out. The last coil snaked out, the rope hung slackly in the water and then slowly started bending to one side. Lance wanted to vomit. He had lost his convoy. He stood staring into the rain. *Oh, shit!* Around him the Swahili stopped poling and the smiles of this great adventure fell

163

from their faces as they registered their predicament, unarmed on the bottom of a capsized inflatable on a river in flood in the middle of a violently antipathetic land not their own.

They all staggered as the line snapped taut.

'Hau!' This time their all-purpose exclamation was a sigh of relief. And then, glancing at Lance, 'Hau!', an apology that they could even momentarily have doubted his juju. And, once it was certain, because he looked at no man directly, that he would not direct his juju against *them*, 'Hau!' in admiration of a bold plan audaciously executed.

Lance took hold of the rope and started hauling them up to the next float. A Swahili took the handful of slack that required all Lance's strength, then another Swahili took the handful the two of them released, and so on. Even with nearly thirty men, it took fifteen minutes before they bumped into the raft in front. Lance was drenched in sweat.

Jimmy dried off the last of the Range Rover's plugs and screwed it back in. 'You could've waited to be winched in,' he said, running the winch experimentally. 'Perfect.'

'I didn't think you'd get it working so quickly.' Lance walked to the forward edge of the raft and peered into the rain. As far as he could see, the Swahili rested on their aluminium poles, with nothing to do except push away the odd floating log. The convoy ran straight and fast down the middle of the river.

'Do we have to go through that again tomorrow and every day?' Esmeralda asked at dinner. She had rigged a canopy over 'her' raft and they had all washed and changed in the screened 'bathroom' set up next to the kitchen. ('Black tie or white for dinner?' Jimmy quipped.) Now the snowy dining-table, softly lit by Colemans, floating above a black river in the rain, made a most romantic setting, framed as it was by a

164

double row of Swahili, who had already eaten, poling away logs, and serenaded by the Zulu cooks softly singing *Nkosi sekelele Afrika* in the 'kitchen'. It was a wonderful moment after the tribulations of the day.

Lance raised his glass to Esmeralda in gratitude and admiration. 'No,' he answered her. 'The river will have its ups and downs, certainly, but nothing as violent as on the first day of the rains. That's like all the water locked in the earth is suddenly released. The worst is over.'

'The river's still flowing faster than we are,' Christine said.

'Sure. But not much. And that upturned truck back there causes just enough drag to hold the convoy straight in the middle of the river. I'm not losing that for the doubtful advantage of an extra couple of knots an hour.' To Lance's great relief, Christine did not argue. Lance was at peace with himself and the world.

In the dawn, while Lance and Esmeralda made love in their tent on the raft, Ahmed Ree, who most definitely intended destroying Lance's peace, cursed the rain. It was not raining now, and would not rain until the afternoon, but what had yesterday been dusty dry ruts were now muddy gullies on which in four hours he covered thirty kilometres. It struck him that the river flowed faster and that, when the rain fell in the afternoon, he would slow down even more. He returned to Kibombo, reaching there an exhausted man who fell into his bedroll on the rear seat of a car without bothering to scrape and crack the crusted mud from him; he did not even remove his boots. His men were mutinous and he told them to take the next day off; it was already two in the morning of that day. When he woke, he had himself flown up the river in his plane and late that afternoon, just before the pilot insisted on landing for the last time before the rain, was appalled to find Weber proceeding in apparently good order past Lowa, halfway to Kisangani. For the first time Ree thought of Weber as a man to be reckoned with; he had of course heard the reputation but, while the present Weber had impressive achievements to his credit, he was credited with and feared for much his late brother had done before Weber himself had reached puberty; besides, Ree himself was a man of formidable reputation in his own circles and knew himself to be only human: the only man he had ever met who did not grievously let down his advance billing was Muamur Qaddaffi.

Tomorrow this time, Weber would be at Kisangani.

Ree lay awake all night trying to decide between ambushing the convoy while still on the river or ensuring that he was ahead of it by leaving Kisangani before Weber did. In the end, logistics decided his course. The plane could carry, besides the pilot, only three of his men at a time. He waited all the next day for the pilot to ferry all his men from Kibombo to Kisangani; in the afternoon, he went to the river and sat on a veranda drinking coffee, watching the river appear intermittently through the rain, waiting for Lance Weber to pass.

Lance had his own problems. In the night, on the Equator, just beyond Ubundu (a placename that delighted Esmeralda because it gave her a handle on the colloquial English), they ran across the nuclear family of hippopotami: cow and calf and bull. Quite literally, they ran *across* them.

The cow and the calf were grazing on the newly sodden banks when one of the Swahili on the river called a sharp warning to another about a log that had appeared out of the darkness beyond the range of their lamps. The cow started shepherding the calf towards the dark hiding of the water. The calf obstinately wanted to continue its meal: it was nearly weaned and gloried in its new enjoyment of greens. The bull saw a huge caterpillar of light approaching menacingly and

166

officiously trundled up with apparent clumsiness (only apparent: a hippo on dry land can run much faster than a rhinoceros and also faster than a man) and started bumping cow and calf into the water. The cow, thinking the bull was amorously inclined and would in that state kill the bullcalf, promptly led the frightened calf as far away as possible, towards the middle of the river. The bull, still seeing the monstrous firefly approach, followed to protect them from attack.

The leading inflatable slid over the cow and then the calf. The cow promptly dived and swam under, pushing the calf before her. The calf's thin roar of frustrated rage – *he* wanted to attack, his mother wanted him to hide – woke everyone in the convoy. Their shouted queries only enraged the bull further. By the time the bull reached the convoy in the middle of the wide flattened river, it was almost past, but under the water he came face to face with a worthy opponent whom he promptly attacked.

For a moment the whole convoy jerked to a standstill. And again and again it jerked.

Christine screamed when she heard the fearful bellowing. Jimmy gathered her to him with one arm. She noticed he was not carrying his rifle.

'What is it?'

'We're under attack.'

'I can see that!' The whole of the upturned inflatable was jerked this way and that in the uncertain light of the false dawn. 'By whom?'

'Hippo.'

Lance came jumping from raft to raft. He wore only shorts and his boots but they were meticulously laced and double-knotted. In his hand he carried his rifle. 'Hippo?'

'Libyan submarine,' Jimmy retorted.

Lance laughed. As yet they did not know they had dealt

167

only with a scouting party of the Libyans, that the main force was still extant.

'Won't it attack us next?' Christine asked.

Lance shrugged. 'If it does, jump to the next raft.'

Esmeralda came to the edge of the next raft. 'Is it all right for me to come look, Lance?' she called.

'Sure.' He caught her as she jumped.

'I can't see anything.'

'He's under there all right. He has to come up for air. There's a cow and a calf in the shallow water over there. Here, use the scope of my rifle,' Lance added when she peered in the growing light.

Christine, wondering what would happen if the hippo attacked them while Lance was without his rifle, went to Jimmy's Range Rover and fetched the binoculars, which she offered to Esmeralda, who said, 'No, you use them.' Christine reluctantly used the binoculars to look quickly at the cow and the calf, then concentrated fearfully on the churning water under the upended inflatable.

Esmeralda returned the rifle to Lance. Just then the hippo rose for air and spat out what looked to Christine like a large section of the truck roof. It was a monstrous prehistoric animal, much more frightening for its pure size than any crocodile she had ever seen. Its little eyes stared at her for a moment but she received the distinct impression through her revulsion and fear that it had no interest in her, that she was beneath its contempt. With one part of her mind, she wanted Lance to shoot it, with another she wanted to reach out and pet this relic of a less constricted age. It dived to do battle once more.

After a while, the hippo decided his opponent was dead and stopped fighting. He rose to the surface, trumpeted his triumph to the cow, and stomped back onto his grazing grounds a victor.

There was now nearly full light and what could be seen of the truck under the inflatable was badly mangled: part of the cab had been torn off, and there were two distinct bites out of the inch-thick alloy of the tip, which only three days ago Lance had described as natural armourplate . . .

Christine was now only too happy to believe that a hippo could bite a man in two, and relieved she had escaped witnessing an actual demonstration.

'That must be the most powerful animal on earth,' Esmeralda said. Nobody could think of any more powerful.

'Champagne for breakfast,' Lance said. 'We're just about on the equator. But, considering who else we're sharing the river with, I don't think we'll dunk first-timers.'

After all the wet grain ran out through the holes the hippo had torn in the tip, the drag factor of the truck under water, which depended on its wetted area, was much reduced because it floated higher. As a consequence, the whole convoy floated faster and they had to work that much harder to keep all the rafts straight and in the middle of the river; paradoxically, this slowed them and it was nearly sunset before they arrived at Kisangani, where Lance ran the inflatables aground, deflated them and drove the vehicles through twenty inches of water onto dry land within sight of Ahmed Ree.

By going on the river, they had saved five days.

'In space, we're two-thirds there,' Lance told Christine. 'In time, we're halfway or better, if nothing goes wrong.'

'Excellent!' Her eyes shone now that her dream seemed to be so possible. Lance Weber, who was making it possible, now appeared godlike and unblemished to her. 'What can go wrong?'

Lance didn't answer immediately. He studied the map on the table under the Coleman. They were less than two thousand miles from the starving people of Northern Chad.

It was a heady prospect, being on the verge of doing something significant. But Lance was vaguely dissatisfied. It had all been too easy. True, those who did not know Africa would be appalled at the violence they had already encountered but they had so far not even been attacked by bandits and had lost only two men to the river and one in the Libyan ambush. But that might only mean that the gods of chance, whom he had so publicly deserted, were storing up their three misfortunes to throw all at once into his face when he was least prepared. He studied the map, not because there was a choice of roads north – there was only one road and it was, for the time and the place, reasonably good, far superior to the 'road' from Kibombo to Kisangani he had scorned, to trust his precious cargo to the river instead. No, he wanted to climb inside that map, to find the places where the gods of chance were setting their traps of malice for him. 'We'll cross into the Central African Republic at Bangassou,' he said at last. 'That way we can give Bangui a miss.'

From the ground beside the fire, where he lay with his head in Christine's lap, Jimmy growled, 'Let's get out of the Congo before we start worrying about the rapacity of the bureaucrats in Bangui.'

'What's eating your liver?' Lance asked his friend.

But Pierre answered for the three brothers. 'Doesn't it strike you as odd that Kinshasa hasn't yet sent someone to collect their cut?'

Lance shrugged. 'When they do, Nasheer will pay them.'

'That's it, Mr Weber,' Nasheer said. 'They're leaving it as late as possible so that they can hold us up just before the border for an extra big baksheesh.'

'Then,' Lance said in a voice that even in that warm evening sent a shiver down the spines of the hard men with him, 'there will be shooting, won't there.' It was not a question.

'General Burger,' Pierre said bluntly.

'Pierre, if he intended to act, it would've been over the Fifth Parachute Brigade bullies running around with their cocks flapping in the wind and their rifles bent into alphabet noodles right on South Africa's border. He's not interested in what we do this far away.'

There was a long silence before Jimmy said, 'Lance, think back to the day you first met Burger.'

'I don't want to,' Lance said evenly.

'It was north of here,' Jimmy said obstinately.

'So it was.' But Lance's tone belied the agreeable tenor of the words and sounded a clarion warning.

After a minute or so, Jimmy rose abruptly. 'Since conversation is dead for tonight, I'm for bed.' Everybody else thought it a good idea. Nobody wanted to stay up after that. The river had been a respite, the more precious for its brevity.

In their tent, Esmeralda said mildly, 'We all love you, darling, and none more than I, but we are all frightened of this sudden rage in you.'

'You don't see it in yourself?'

'Yes, and that is how I recognize it in you. Let's not fight.' She put her arms around him.

'I'd rather make love any day,' he said. 'They know it, so they should stop riding me.'

'This business has made you different, darling, more . . . more intense. They don't feel they know you any more, you're so unpredictable.' She started unbuttoning his shirt.

'Do *you* think that?'

'No. You're just the same old Lance, only more so. But to them – '

'Enough, sweetheart. Tomorrow I'll put things to rights.'

'You're a lamb.'

* * *

171

Lance had recovered his cheerful optimism. At breakfast he asked Jimmy, Pierre and Boo if he should send Nasheer down to Kinshasa to pay off the politicians; they took this for the apology it was intended to be. And now they were across the Aruwimi and it appeared they would cross the border into the Central African Republic either later today (if the afternoon rains were both late and light) or before brunch tomorrow unless they ran into very serious trouble. Lance sang along with *The Magic Flute* in his sound but untutored voice and even Esmeralda, whose modest musical training had spoilt her enjoyment to the extent that she would not open her mouth unless she could be note-perfect, joined in. Mwanzo made harmonizing noises and Nasheer, who (unusually for an Arab, Lance thought) could not carry a tune, tapped time against an empty bourbon bottle with a long thin knife he carried in his boot. It was the first time that Lance and Esmeralda even momentarily did not have Emmy somewhere in their minds. They were still singing when Lance pulled into the clearing where they were to break for brunch. It was horseshoe-shaped beside the road, with many trees still left in the middle, made as a passing-place by the heavy trucks that plied the good but often single-lane gravel road between Bangui and Kisangani with almost all of the latter's consumer goods. The horseshoe was too short for Lance's convoy, so he drove the Range Rover around the horseshoe and back on the main road in the direction from which he had just come, pulling once more into the leg of the other horseshoe on the tail of Jimmy's Range Rover. The whole snake went round until his own vehicle was back at the main road once again, then halted. The singing had long since stopped. Tension mounted in the Range Rover. Lance punched the Mozart out of the tape player to listen to the tension. It had nothing to do with so many heavy trucks running nose to tail: the Swahili had turned out to be

172

amazingly good drivers. But Lance and Mwanzo and Nasheer were survivors of Africa and such men develop a sense of approaching danger, which some say resides in the short hairs at the back of the neck; without it – and more, a willingness to heed it without feeling ludicrous – one does not long survive the bush- and grass-stalkers and -creepers. Esmeralda was a quick study and sensitive to the mood of others: the tension was tangible.

'Drive out, Mr Weber!' Nasheer said urgently.

'No The trucks will never make it. We're trapped. My rifle please, Mwanzo. When I say *go*, jump out that side and roll under the Range Rover,' he said to Esmeralda, his eyes on the trees.

Behind him a door slammed and he saw in the nearside mirror that the Swahili were all piling out on the inner protected side of the laager of lorries. The first shot almost coincided with the slam of the door.

The irony is that, in the six hundred or so road miles through the tropical forests between Kisangani and Bangassou just into the Central African Republic, there are very few places to ambush a convoy as big and strong as Lance's relief column. The blissfully ignorant or the careless might look at a map and think any of many river crossings ideal, but they are ideal only for those setting an official ambush: every river crossing has its own town of settlement, even if only fifty souls. Witnesses. News travels in Africa, perhaps faster than in developed countries exactly because its conduits are not formalized. The Westerner who scoffs at tom-toms and the gossip of the village market while himself waiting five or six hours for the next television or radio news bulletin is probably merely ignorant; a soldier about secret business in Africa would be foolish to ignore such considerations. It is of course possible to waylay such a convoy on a narrow piece of road where it cannot turn and where its forces will be spread out,

173

difficult to form into a coherent command unit, and easy targets for hidden snipers – if you have a good man to mark each vehicle or, where vehicles carry more than two men, a man of your own for every two of the opposition. You would have only one chance to kill the opposition in that short time between the moment they realize they are under attack and when they disappear in the trees beside the road. Ahmed Ree didn't have the men to mount such an ambitious trap and he realized that, if any of Weber's trained men escaped into the trees to circle around behind the ambushers, his guerrillas would be at a serious disadvantage because they were street-fighters rather than forest-fighters. As for General Burger, he had the men, both in quality and numbers, but even he considered such an extended front too great a risk. But both men had an alternative: Weber's column had to stop twice a day, once for brunch, once for the night – and there were only so many places he could stop and feed a convoy of that size, probably at any particular moment only one such place. All one had to do was study the map carefully to predict with fair accuracy where next he would stop.

Esmeralda had the door open and was rolling out when Lance pushed her out with his own body, diving over her and rolling upright and firing three shots from the hip and in the same motion bulldozing her forwards and under the Range Rover. Distinctly, over the shots, they heard two bodies fall from some height into the undergrowth.

'Ouch!' said Esmeralda. 'I was doing what you said, you know.'

'But not fast enough,' Lance said. 'You're getting bloody blasé about being shot at. You have no magic immunity from bullets.'

That was unfair, she thought. She had moved as fast as she could, which was very fast indeed because she too was an athlete of some talent. It was only that Lance was so much

174

faster and never for a moment considered that anyone else could not meet his standards.

'What happened to the third one?' Lance asked.

'You missed him, Master,' Mwanzo said.

'Oh.'

'I hit him,' Nasheer said. 'He's in a fork behind the tree with the red streak. You can just see his boot sticking out there. He's still alive.'

'Keep your head down, Nasheer,' Lance said warningly and kept his own down as an example.

'They're Arabs,' Mwanzo said.

There was, for the moment, no firing. Lance had killed two of the Libyans, Nasheer had wounded another one. That was a quarter of Ahmed Ree's men: he had come with seventeen men and had lost five on the scouting mission before Kibombo. Of the rest, even as they piled out of their vehicles and searched for bolt-holes, Weber's Belgian Congolese officers and his Swahili warriors had killed four more and wounded another. Ahmed Ree now had seven men and himself. He hit the tree in front of him with his fist, then licked the blood on his knuckles. His people had been so well hidden! How in Allah's exalted name could such a thing have happened? But he knew: in the streets of Beirut, he would have placed a car bomb and blown Weber to his just deserts from a safe distance; even if there was a shootout in the streets, Weber and his Swahili would not have stood a chance . . . but this was Weber's home ground, and luck had favoured him, in that his convoy was exactly long enough to stand nose to tail around the horseshoe, a movable fort. On the other hand, if he could not destroy Weber's men, he could prevent them from moving on for as long as he pleased and there was nothing they could do about it: Weber might even surrender when thirst and hunger began to bite. Or they could drown in the water running in the tyre-ruts when the rains fell in the afternoon. Altogether, Ree was not displeased with his day's work. He climbed down his tree, careful not to expose any part of himself, and headed into the forest, where he circled around and crept up behind each of his men to give them their instructions. 'Don't expose yourself. Shoot only if they try to come out from under the trucks.' Some of the men wanted to shoot at the tyres but Ree said, 'And while you're shooting the tyres of one truck, the ones under the other trucks will be shooting at you.' Oh, he thought, oh, my left hand for a crate of grenades. Or a few boxes of landmines we could've planted before they arrived.

'The Libyans,' Lance said. He called, 'Jimmy!'

'Here!'

'Call round. The men are not to expose themselves. Are there any wounded? How many opposition did they see?'

'Okay. There's one still alive in that red-streaked tree in front of you, you know.'

'Don't expose yourself. There may be more.'

'I don't think so. There were only three, pretty widely spread out, on this side.'

'All the same, keep your head down.' To the other side, Lance called, 'Who's in that truck?'

'Mpengo, Master.'

Lance repeated his instructions. It took twenty minutes for the men to call from truck to truck and then for the responses to be called back. Two men had been killed, seven wounded, one was in a serious condition, but the wounded were all in shelter. It was thought four of the attackers had been killed and there were altogether not more than a dozen left.

'Now that's starting to look a spot brighter,' Lance said to no one in particular.

'Just so,' Boo said behind him.

Lance started and bumped his head on the still hot exhaust

pipe. He hauled Boo in by his shirt collar. It was uncomfortably crowded under the Range Rover with the five of them.

'Goddammit Boo, I told you to stay put.'

'Did you hear me coming? Did you hear anybody shooting
at me?'

'No but – '

'I was a scout for your brother before you had your first
girl.'

'Second to Kombi,' Lance said. Kombi had died on the
crocodile-hunting expedition.

'Everybody was second to Kombi,' Boo said with dignity.
'Now I'm the best.'

Lance decided not to contest the truth. It was uncanny
how Boo could disappear into the landscape even when you
knew where to look for him. 'How are the wounded men?'

'Most can wait. But one's gutshot. He needs morphine.'

'Jimmy, Mpengo! Cover me,' Lance shouted.

'Yesmassa!'

'Hok-kay!'

'Now!' Lance rolled out before the rear wheel of the Range
Rover on the inside of the circle. Mpengo's truck was almost
touching the rear of the smaller vehicle and it was awkward
opening the hatch. Lance tried only once, then gave up and
ran around to the side door and jerked it open. He didn't
look up at the trees. Others were taking care of that. There
was a lusty amount of shooting but he didn't know if any of it
came his way. There was nothing he could do about it if it
did. He stood on his knees on the seat and hauled the
medicine box over the back of the seat, then cradled it to his
chest and dropped to the ground with it. In his peripheral
vision, through the Range Rover, he saw the wounded Libyan
falling, falling, jerking in midair as the bullets followed him
down. A bullet from behind him somewhere clanged off the
Range Rover and horneted past his head. He winced and

177

crawled hastily under the Range Rover and resisted the temptation to put his hands over his head.

Ahmed Ree cursed terribly. His men, thinking a breakout was attempted, had started shooting, so giving away their positions. He had lost another two men to the devastatingly accurate fire from Weber's party. Ahmed Ree had difficulty grasping this: the street-fighter sprays many bullets from an automatic weapon and hopes to hit something, the hunter uses one bullet carefully aimed at his target; the Swahili were cornered hunters. Once more Ree made the rounds of his remaining men, impressing on them that they must do nothing to give away their positions. They were frightened and mutinous: they were the best and not used to large losses among themselves, the killer elite; the blacks should by now, by all rights, have been cowering in a tight group with their hands on their heads. Instead they could be heard laughing excitedly under their trucks.

'What about the one behind me?' Lance asked when he could again hear himself speak.

'Jimmy got him,' Boo said. 'Jimmy, is it clear on the inside?'

'Sure,' Jimmy shouted back.

Lance reached out for the medicine chest and quickly dragged it towards him. It wouldn't fit under the Range Rover. Lance considered.

'You will not go out there to open it,' Esmeralda said firmly.

Lance chuckled. 'No, I'll just turn it on its side, like this, so I can open the lid. Which is the morphine?'

'The tubes on the left.'

Lance gave Boo a handful plus several disposable syringes. 'Want me to come with you?'

Boo shook his head and bashed it against the transfer gearbox. 'Aargh! No. I'll go faster alone.'

'Okay. Can you come back here afterwards?'

'If it's worth it. You have a plan?'

'Yes. I'll tell you when you return.' Lance raised his voice enough to carry to Mpengo and Jimmy but no further. 'Boo's coming out. Don't shoot unless they start.'

Boo nodded: he didn't want attention drawn to him. He stuffed some dressings inside his shirt, then rolled out from under the Range Rover and crawled quickly away. A moment after he entered the sparse undergrowth, he was gone. Nobody shot at him. Lance, peering out from under the Range Rover, saw none of the opposition. After fifteen minutes, he crawled as far under the Range Rover as the three other bodies would permit, curled up spoon-fashion with Esmeralda, who had lost her resentment at his sharp words, and went to sleep.

Lance would never know what woke him, Esmeralda saying, 'I'm hungry,' or Boo poking him in the small of the back with a forefinger, or the far-off, half-dreamed sound of helicopters that was no longer in the air when he woke. From lying against Esmeralda, he had an erection and from her mischievous smile he knew she had felt it. 'I'm thinking,' he told Boo.

'What with?'

'Your brains.'

'I brought Pierre. He's in with Jimmy. It would've been too crowded here.'

'Excellent.' Lance glanced at the angle of the shadows beyond the edge of the Range Rover. One o'clock. *Shit!* 'I reckon this piece of forest in front of us is clear. I want to enter here, circle round and take them. Can we do it now or do we have to wait for darkness?'

While Boo considered, Lance asked, 'How are the wounded?'

'None serious except one and he'll survive.' Boo held a bloody finger to Lance's nose. 'It's like those miracles

Sambo's wife believes in. I stuck that in the hole. No shit-smell. The intestine isn't broken.'

'So it's no worse than a serious flesh wound?'

Boo nodded. Esmeralda asked, 'Did you check his spine?'

Boo shook his head. 'Bullet came out a good ten centi-metres clear and low down.' To Lance, 'Depends.'

Lance understood. Speed depended, as always, on the price he wanted to pay.

'Dusk would be better,' Boo said. 'How good do you think they are?'

'They're not bush Arabs,' Lance said.

Boo grunted. 'City terrorists, just like the others.'

'All right. We move as soon as I brief Jimmy.'

'You're coming?'

'Yes. How many others?'

'Pierre and Mwanzo and Mpengo.'

Fifteen minutes later they slipped into the underbrush on the outside of the horseshoe, one at a time, five minutes apart. Lance went last. Twenty trees into the forest he rose and waited for his eyes to accommodate to the gloom. After another five minutes, Boo gestured to the right and they moved in single file, about five paces apart. Moving quietly was excruciatingly slow. Lance sighed. They would be here overnight. But there was nothing else for it; Boo was the expert and he was moving as fast as he thought wise.

After more than an hour, Boo stopped and waited patiently for the others to reach him. Then he pointed. The Libyan sat on a branch with his back to them. Boo tapped Pierre on the chest and held up the palm of his hand to the others. Lance sat on a low-flying branch and Mwanzo joined him. Mpengo leaned against a fungus on a dying tree. Boo and Pierre walked upright but very slowly, putting each foot down carefully after studying the spot in advance for anything that would crackle underfoot. After twenty-five minutes they were within ten feet of the man. Lance curled up inside for the Libyan in the tree: could the man not *feel* that he was being stalked?

Like Ahmed Ree, General Rocco Burger too could read a map and calculate time to distance and did so to perfection. His plan was, as all his plans, of deceptive simplicity and underpinned by a sophisticated understanding of human psychology. He too knew there are two points where a convoy is vulnerable: on the road, all strung out, which takes a very large benison of trained manpower if the attack requires a 100 per cent guarantee of success (defined by Burger as no survivors to tell tales); and when it is at a standstill and an enemy can sneak up on it to find it eating or sleeping or about its other bodily functions, but in any event taken by surprise. Burger had discarded the first as too risky and the second as too expensive because Lance Weber was not the kind of leader who would overlook the detail of setting out guards whenever he stopped. That left the third possibility: when the convoy was in transition from standstill to the road, fed and rested and relieved to have completed another phase of the journey successfully but not yet alert to the hazards of the next stage because they were still in an environment already proved secure. Burger's plan was for his two helicopters to arrive just as the convoy prepared to take to the road again and simply to rake the whole column with heavy-calibre machine-gun fire, even rockets if necessary. His men would pick off any survivors trying to escape into the forest. A few Swahili succeeding would not matter much: the local inhabitants would eat their livers. But the Webers, the Rawls woman, and Weber's principal assistants must not be allowed to survive. Above all, the operation must be fast and clean. Burger had asked no one's permission for what he intended, least of all the Kinshasa government, in whose territory he was operating. But Burger's expedition was held up by electronic trouble with one of his helicopters. Burger was in a dilemma. In another day, Weber's convoy would be outside the range of his helicopters from their refuelling stop with the forward units of the South African Army in Angola and then he would have to refuel in either Zaire or the Central African Republic, which would necessitate involving either the Belgians or the French to order their former colonials to pay him courtesy and, in turn, he would then not only owe favours but be inviting at least two other parties into knowledge he did not want to share. Burger decided to mount the more difficult attack with the convoy strung out on the open road. From Kisangani, the place they knew the convoy had left this morning, they flew up the road and across the Aruwimi and . . . Burger could not believe his luck! There was the convoy and he had twenty minutes of fuel in hand, more than enough to do a thorough job. But then he noticed the convoy was pulled into a defensive laager. Aah! Next, it struck him that he could see no one. That was very clever: a convoy drawn up as a laager but the defenders outside in the bush ready to ambush the ambushers. He spoke into his throat mike. 'Forget the trucks. They're in the forest. Concentrate your fire on the forest. Chaka, take the east and north of the rectangle, Dingaan the west and south.'

'Chaka. Confirm east and north.'

'Dingaan. Confirm west and south.'

Burger waited until his helicopters were in position, then said, 'Fire at will.' To himself he kept the thought, May god speed your souls and forgive mine. Ignoring the stutter of machine guns overriding the clacking of the rotors, he opened his briefcase again and continued working through his papers. The top piece of paper was a memorandum from the State President's Office asking if the Lance Weber who had caused

182

the stir in Zimbabwe was employed by Burger's Department . . .

Through the screen of leaves, Lance could barely see the helicopters but he could hear them and he had seen Burger in operation before. The Libyan in the tree had not, and actually fired his machine pistol ineffectually at the helicopter; for his temerity, he was rewarded by being cut in half by .50 bullets. Pierre and Boo, squashed up to the protective trunk of the tree under the Libyan, were liberally doused with his innards. Lance jerked Mwanzo and Mpengo behind a thick tree and roared over the noise at them to *stay*.

For ten minutes the machine guns quartered the forest.

'Sir,' said the pilot in Burger's earphones, 'two men on the road outside the firezone.'

'Take us there.'

The pilot swung the big helicopter over the trees and dropped it onto the road right in front of Ahmed Ree and his one remaining man, who threw away their rifles and put their hands on their heads at first sight of the machine-gun barrels trying to suck them in. At the same moment, Lance stepped out of the forest onto the road. The pilot raised the helicopter a few inches and swivelled it to line up the machine-gun barrels on Lance, who promptly shot the pilot and co-pilot through the bubble. Both died instantly with two bullets each through the heart. The helicopter bumped to the uneven road. Before the men inside the helicopter could line up their weapons on him through the hatch, Lance stepped behind his tree.

'Hold your fire,' Burger said into his throat mike, not raising his voice. 'Switch the engines off.' This was a pickle, in the middle of a foreign state in a helicopter gunship with both pilots dead.

Lance waited until the rotors stopped turning before

stepping out into the road. 'General, we meet again. Only this time it's not you doing the threatening.'

Burger glanced at his men. Several had their lower lips dangling from the uppers. These good farm boys could not credit the impertinence of a man who, with all their rifles pointed at him, still gave cheek to the feared Boss of BOSS. Burger smiled thinly at their naïvety.

'Pierre, ring the bell,' Lance called out.

The shot from the forest was so finely angled it dinged the thin aluminium skin of the helicopter without piercing it. Burger pumped his ears. Lance waited patiently until he was certain those in the chopper could hear him.

'I've more men in the forest. Their next shots will be into the fuel tank. Now pass out your arms.'

'What about them?' asked one fresh-faced farm boy wearing sergeant's stripes and killer's eyes, gesturing with his rifle at the Libyans standing in the middle of the road with their hands on their heads. They were obviously not white and Lance was not only white, he had a recognizably South African accent.

'I want to question them. You can execute them later,' Lance said. 'Now give me your rifle.'

'Do as he says,' Burger ordered.

Lance leaned his own rifle against the helicopter and took the arms handed to him, checked that the safety catches were on, and threw them in a heap beside the road. 'Remember all those rifles aimed at the fuel tank,' he said once.

When he had all the rifles, he said, 'Now the officers' sidearms. And any knives you're carrying. Dying in fire is very unpleasant.'

'Generaal, hy's net een man,' a young lieutenant said plaintively.

Lance picked up his rifle and fired a single shot through the helicopter's floor between the man's feet. 'I understand

Afrikaans, pal, and I'm not just one man, I'm the one man who stands between you and hellfire.'

When all the arms were on the ground, he turned around to look into the machine-gun barrels of the other helicopter, which had come to hover over him.

Lance grinned at Burger. 'Want to bet they kill us all before one of us hits your fuel tank?'

'I thought you renounced gambling.'

'To catch an alcoholic, set a teetotaller. Give them their orders, General.'

Burger spoke once more into his throat mike. Lance looked down the road and saw Jimmy leading a group of Swahili across the road and into the trees on the other side. He tapped Burger on the shoulder and pointed. Burger added to his instructions, 'Don't do anything sudden. We're surrounded and we're dealing with a fanatic who *wants* to become a martyr.'

'Excellent, General. You just remember that.'

Lance, his rifle casually pointed at Burger, watched the other helicopter land. He grinned at the innocent-appearing young sergeant. 'Forget it. I'm not about to turn my back so you can get me with your pocket knife. I too command competent men of initiative.'

He watched Jimmy walk up to the hatch of the other helicopter and start throwing the arms of the men inside down by the road. 'Joseph Rodgers of Sheffield, is it?'

The sergeant, hardly more than a boy, grinned and nodded. 'Sure. Only knife to have.' Very carefully he took the knife out of his pocket, opened it, pared a thick thumbnail, closed it and held it out to Lance.

After admiring it, Lance gave it back. The boy deserved to keep his proudest possession for that fine show of bravado. 'I'm afraid I was a bit of a sissy.'

'Swiss Army knife?'

'Yes.'

'Will you kill us?'

'Are you afraid?'

'No. But I would like to pray first.'

'I won't kill you unless you do something stupid.'

The collective sigh of relief was quite audible.

'Because there are too many of us?' Burger asked.

Lance nodded, bent to pick up the weapons of the Libyans and threw them too on the pile. 'Any of these boys interrogators?'

Burger nodded. 'Peet, Japie.' A major and the lieutenant who had guessed wrong about Lance's command of Afrikaans came to the lip of the hatch. 'What do you want to know?' Burger asked Lance.

'Usual thing. Their orders. How many they were. Are there any more left? Do they have communications? What happens if they don't call in?'

Burger nodded at his two officers, who jumped down and marched briskly to Ree and his remaining man. The lieutenant promptly hit the gibbering man in the stomach with his fist, lifting him a clear three inches off the ground. Then, as the man fell screaming, he kneed him in the face. Lance distinctly heard cartilage crush.

The major stood in front of Ree, who looked at him without a sound but with a twitching face.

The major lit two cigarettes and put one between Ree's lips.

'Libyan?'

Ree puffed at his cigarette and said nothing.

The lieutenant kicked the Libyan on the ground in the kidneys; the man screamed only briefly before becoming unconscious.

'I was trained by the Israelis,' the major said conversationally. 'As a return favour, I trained many of them. I have a reputation, you know. I can't afford to fail.'

The lieutenant took a clasp knife out of his pocket, opened it and bent to the unconscious Libyan. He tipped the man's chin up.

'Don't kill him, Japie,' the major said. 'We'll need him if the electric shocks to the balls kill this one like that Palestinian the Israelis gave us to practise on.' To Ree, he added, 'Lieutenant de Witt is very enthusiastic but these things require experience and finesse, as you know yourself.'

Ahmed Ree did know; he had conducted many interrogations. 'What is it you want to know?' he asked quietly.

When Lance was satisfied that the Libyan threat was for the moment fangless, he thanked the two interrogators politely. After Jimmy supervised the removal of the piles of arms, Lance had the South Africans shepherded away under guard and set their helicopters alight by firing into the fuel tanks. The tanks, he found, were filled with foam that held the fuel in non-explosive suspension. Only when some fuel had run out, and a second shot was fired at least half a minute after the first, did it catch alight. Lance glanced at Burger, who looked thoughtful. Thirty seconds is quite long enough for twenty soldiers to shoot one man blocking the hatch of a helicopter and jump over his body to safety.

Lance shivered. It had been a near thing.

Lance borrowed Esmeralda's instant camera. 'Mingle with the South Africans,' he told Christine and Esmeralda. 'Just on the fringes. You keep close to them, Jimmy, Pierre. We don't want any hostages taken.' He took half a dozen Polaroid shots, then approached Burger and gave him one. 'General, a memento of our meeting. I want to say on behalf of myself and the Matthew Ellimore Foundation that you could not have come at a more opportune moment. From the bottom of my heart I thank you, as we all do.'

'What's this shit?' Christine demanded. 'This paramilitary butcher didn't come to help us. He came to kill us, same as the Libyan filth.' Reaction against the day's adrenalin was catching up on her, as on everyone.

'Uh-huh,' Lance said. 'The alternative is to kill them all, every last one. Mwanzo, kindly provide Miss Rawls with a machine pistol with a full clip.'

'Christ, Lance,' Jimmy said.

Christine looked at the machine pistol in her hands, then clicked the safety off. She pointed it at the South Africans, who stirred uneasily. Several put the palms of their hands together – two kneeled – and started praying. Not one begged for his life, though the fresh-faced sergeant looked resentfully at Lance.

But Lance had his eyes on Christine: wanting to shoot Burger and his licensed thugs was the right instinct, blocked by her conditioned responses, by her very good intentions. For the first time Lance understood the anger and frustration that drove Christine. He glanced at Esmeralda and the same revelation was in the compassion on her face.

Lance took the weapon from Christine. 'Ends and means,' he told her.

'You've already killed the pilots. You do it,' she said.

'No.'

'Why not? What's a few more?'

'That was necessary. This is not.'

'They'll be back and then there will be no food for the starving children in Chad!'

'No, they won't,' Lance said. 'Pierre, make up a firing squad and execute the Libyans. Esmeralda, give him the camera. Be sure to take some clear photographs, Pierre.'

They all turned to watch the screaming Libyans being dragged into the forest. When the shots from the forest died away, they waited in silence, even Christine holding in her

188

sobs, until Pierre gave Lance the photographs. Lance gave one to Burger. 'For the record, General.'

'One day you will be too clever for your own good,' Burger said. But his heart wasn't in it: this was admirably intelligent.

'Just so we have no misunderstanding, General,' Lance said, 'I'll be posting these photographs and a description of what happened here to trustworthy people with instructions to publish should anything happen to this convoy. You can guess what the description will say: you came all the way into Zaire almost to the CAR border to help us wipe out Qaddafi's Libyan terrorists. The photographs are all the proof we need. There are some particularly good likenesses of you, wouldn't you say?'

Burger did not reply.

Boo said, 'I will be happy to shoot them. Christine wasn't behind that tree, being sprayed with blood and shit and seeing the tree grow visibly thinner. I was.'

'I agree with Boo. Let's shoot them,' Pierre said.

Lance shook his head. 'There are too many of them. The South African government couldn't afford to let us pass. They'll send the paracommandos after us.'

Between the Libyans and South Africans the convoy lost the rest of the day. The dead had to be buried, the wounded driven to the nearest suitable hospital at Kisangani, trucks inspected and repaired. By dint of pressing mercilessly once underway the next morning, they were within seventy miles of the CAR border when the rain started later than usual at half-past four the next afternoon. 'We never before used to worry about an hour this way or that,' Esmeralda told Lance ruefully. Lance nodded but pressed on into the rain, ignoring the mutinous mutterings of the Swahili and the curses of his lieutenants. Only Christine said nothing: she stood pale and wan in the rain every time they dug a truck out, underfoot to

189

the Swahili manhandling the heavy pierced steel planks from the rear to the front of the stuck truck until Jimmy told her shortly to stay in the Range Rover before her head was bashed in by a swinging PSP. But, if tempers grew short, and that could be blamed mainly on reaction to the adrenalin-flow of the dangerous immediate past, progress was speedy; seventy miles in under four hours once the rain fell was outstanding. They camped, just as the rain stopped and still in the last dregs of daylight, on the south bank of the Bomu fifty miles upriver from its junction with the massive Oubangi and almost within sight of Bangassou in the CAR. Within fifteen minutes Esmeralda had two showers standing and an hour later dinner was served; even Christine smiled and spoke for the first time since her impulse to shoot Burger and his men, saying what was in all their minds, that there was only one more country to cross and then they would be in Chad, among the needy. It was a heady wine of hope. They were still at table when the helicopter arrived to hover overhead and play its lights, seeking the most advantageous landing-place.

Lance leaned over to shout in Nasheer's ear above the racket the thing made. 'At dawn, we leave. Buy them before then.'

Nasheer nodded. Out of the corner of his eye, Lance saw Mwanzo move to stand at the rear of the Range Rover, near their weapons. Lance rose from the table, stopping halfway out of his chair when he heard Pierre's sharp inhalation.

'That's Mobutu himself,' Pierre said.

'Oh.' Nasheer sounded deflated.

'Sit tight, Nasheer. Pierre will handle this.' Lance put his hand on the young Arab's shoulder for a moment to soften the blow to his pride, but Nasheer looked relieved: he was too sensible not to know when he was out of his league.

The eight soldiers who jumped out of the helicopter were

turned out smartly enough but their coordination was sloppy, Lance thought; he saw Jimmy's lip curl.

'They've been at peace for a very long time,' Boo said softly as the helicopter's rotors wound down.

'What say we give him an honour guard?' Lance suggested. Pierre nodded. 'Mwanzo! Call the Swahili to attention.' Lance watched carefully but the soldiers from the helicopter did not seem to feel themselves threatened by the armed Swahili rising in place; Mwanzo made no attempt to line them up.

The man who came from the helicopter could be any age between thirty and sixty: he was just a man, black, slightly overweight (in fact trim if one knew his age and circumstances), with black horn-rimmed glasses, dressed in black trousers and a shirt-jacket of vaguely Chinese cut but made of a horizontally striped material that Lance knew was native to one of Zaire's two hundred tribes; his shoes were well-polished and he wore only one piece of jewellery, a gold watch on a gold band. All in all he did not look like the ruler of a huge mineral-wealthy country.

Lance nodded at Mwanzo, who threw him his rifle. He raised the rifle in both hands above his head, three times. The Swahili promptly followed suit. 'Hau!' they shouted, and 'Hau!', and again 'Hau!'

Mobutu saluted them smartly. Pierre stepped forward. 'An honour, Your Excellency.'

Mobutu peered at him closely. 'Pierre Knékwassé? You've grown sleek since you fought against me.'

'You were a gracious victor, Excellency.'

Mobutu nodded, accepting his due. Then he nodded to Boo and Jimmy. 'I am not always honoured with a salute by royalty. There will be business with Kinshasa for all of you if you return to Brussels alive.'

Pierre bowed low and, after a second's hesitation, so did

Jimmy and Boo, both baring their teeth at Mobutu, who was already turning to Lance.

'I knew your brother well,' he said, putting out his hand, which Lance shook. 'Both as an enemy to be feared and an associate to be respected. Or perhaps I should say, held in awe. He could truly achieve the impossible.'

Lance, not knowing what to say, nodded.

'I see you have his becoming modesty. Good! You will need it. There are not many men who have bested General Burger.'

'I apologize that such an incident should occur in your country, Excellency, but we honestly did nothing to provoke him.'

Mobutu, still holding Lance's hand, stared up into his eyes for a moment, his eyes clouding in that uncertain artificial light. Lance wished desperately he knew what was going through the man's mind. Pierre said something fast in a local dialect.

'Ah!' exclaimed Mobutu. 'And sly like your brother too! Too damn right. But no, I was not offended. I offered them transport back to their own country. It is always good to have a powerful neighbour in one's debt.'

'And now we are in your debt, Excellency,' Lance said.

Behind Mobutu, Pierre shook his head ever so slightly.

But Lance had no intention of committing a gaffe by offering such a man a bribe. 'My brother always spoke highly of you and of your magnanimity in giving him and Colonel Roux the crocodile-hunting concession.'

Mobutu nodded absently, a man used to flattery.

'Let me introduce the rest of the party,' said Lance. 'My wife, Esmeralda.'

Mobutu bowed. 'The legend of your beauty has preceded you, Madame, and it has spoken only truth.' Esmeralda nodded gravely, and Mobutu, obviously approving of a beautiful, *quiet* woman, smiled at her before turning to Christine.

'Christine Rawls. Miss Rawls is the director of the Matthew Ellimore Foundation, the charitable trust on whose behalf we pass through your country.'

Again Mobutu bowed. 'You are young for so much responsibility.'

Before Christine could snap something awkward, Lance said, 'She makes up for it in fervour for the hungry. As you compensated for youth, Excellency, by fervour for your country.'

Mobutu was delighted. He clapped Lance on the shoulder. 'And that same quick intelligence with which your brother charmed his friends and confounded his enemies.' Over his shoulder, to Christine, 'Kinshasa will contribute to your Foundation. We wish nothing in return but goodwill.' He held Lance firmly by the elbow as he walked back to his helicopter. He made no effort to lower his voice. 'I'm surprised that such people should be sufficiently aware of African realities to understand that good can only be done through strength.'

'Miss Rawls has a great deal of African experience,' Lance said loyally.

'Most of it unfortunate,' Mobutu said dismissively. 'She is lucky to have found you, though I think this Chad venture of yours is suicidal. Qaddaffi is an obsessive madman.'

'You mean, Excellency, that he won't give up?'

'Your brother too was a blunt speaker. If you survive Qaddaffi's legions, you may settle in my country if you wish. There are opportunities for men of initiative. Or I can offer you government service.'

'I am overcome, Excellency.'

Mobutu turned on the step of his helicopter, smiled at the

assembled company, and disappeared into the body of the bladed whale.

When the helicopter had clattered into the night, Lance and Pierre sighed deeply, simultaneously. 'Whew!'

'What was all that about?' Christine wanted to know.

'What he told you,' Jimmy replied. 'Goodwill.'

'Hmm?'

'He's worried about his place in history. He doesn't want to go down as a robber baron and jumped-up thug. So he collects a little credit for smoothing our humanitarian way through his country.'

'But we made it by ourselves!'

Lance shook his head. 'No. He could have held us up for days, for ever. He considers he has been amazingly generous.'

'To you, offering you a home.' Christine was still angry about Mobutu's casual dismissal of her and her achievements; she resented having Lance defend her ability to the likes of Mobutu.

'What was that playby between you and him?' Esmeralda asked Boo, who looked first blank and then appealingly at Lance.

'Byplay,' Lance said. 'Uh, undercurrent. She means all that baring of teeth.'

'My people used to eat the livers of his people,' Boo said. 'Also, we suspect he was behind the massacre of our tribe.'

'But he said you fought on his side,' Christine objected.

'Stranger alliances were made by the white man's colonial boundaries,' Jimmy said in his best Uncle Tom voice. 'But don't feel guilty about it; we don't blame you personally.'

She looked him up and down. 'You want to kill Mobutu, fine. But don't take it out on me, I'm only a woman.'

'Game, set and match to Christine,' Esmeralda said. 'Lance, let's open the brandy Mr Tullius gave you. I'll get coffee.'

* * *

Nasheer put a bottle of Scotch and a gold nugget on the desk in front of the border-post commander. 'Good morning,' he said in French. The man grunted and stared blearily at the bottle and the nugget. In the open neck of his uniform his undershirt, once white, was chocolate brown with dirt.

'With whisky and gold you can do what you did with your grandmother,' the commander said succinctly.

Nasheer smiled serenely. 'Or perhaps what I will do with your wife.'

The man rose behind his desk. He was at least twice Nasheer's weight while not even as tall. Nasheer kept his seat. 'Perhaps you heard that last night Mobutu Sese Seko visited the camp of a certain famous man on the other side of the river.'

The commander slumped into his chair. His red-rimmed eyes turned upwards as he frowned, trying to marshal a hungover mind. 'Weber,' he said at last. 'The Major has returned and Mobutu embraced him because, the day before yesterday, the Major defeated an invasion by the South African Special Security Police.'

Nasheer said nothing to correct this welter of confusion of identity and intent: this was the way history was made, as a conglomeration of legend and half-truths. He took the nugget and returned it to his pocket. 'Weber is a hard man to work for. If I pay too much, he will phone Kinshasa to protest your greed. Kinshasa will phone Bangui and Bangui will relieve you. How will you then keep your expensive young wife with the tight little heaven between her legs?' Nasheer had spent five minutes gossiping with the other ranks while waiting for the commander: time well spent.

The man started once more at the deliberately offensive words but decided discretion was the better part of valour. 'I let you pass cheap. One rotor for General Motors distributor.'

This is a valuable commodity all over Africa. People

routinely prevent theft of trucks by removing the rotor from the distributor; therefore, if one possesses a rotor, one can steal such trucks. And not only the Chevrolet and GMC variety: their Delco distributor-rotors are of a standard type fitted to many other types of trucks. Next best is a rotor for a Bosch distributor; a Lucas rotor one cannot give away because no one is so poor he will steal a British truck.

'No.' Nasheer rose. He flicked the gold nugget across the man's desk. 'A bonus, because it was so quick.' It was another insult: the border commander's stock-in-trade was his capacity for delaying convoys until he had extracted the maximum bribe. Nasheer whistled as he left the man's office. Working for Lance Weber became easier by the day. He returned to camp just as Esmeralda poured their breakfast coffee. 'Mobutu's visit impressed them deeply over there,' he told Lance, gesturing across the river. 'Perhaps we should wait here while the news travels ahead of us.'

Lance was stopped from snarling something rude by the slight smile about Nasheer's lips; the young Arab was making a joke, something Lance had rarely known him to do. Instead, he said, 'I want to be in Chad tomorrow. Let's hope the news of Mobutu's friendship impresses them.'

Up the road, after brunch, on the short stretch of road between Bambari and Grimari, they ran into bandits for the first time on their journey, freelance bandits rather than thieving soldiers licensed by their country's uniform.

They drove over a rise and looked down on a long straight stretch of road. Down below a convoy of trucks stood at the side of the road. In front of the convoy a jeep was drawn across the road, to one side stood a group of people looking ill at ease and uncertain what to do with their hands, nearby scruffy smiling men pointed their rifles carelessly at the unhappy ones. Lance took it all in at a glance. He picked up the mike, cutting off Mendelssohn's Fifth Symphony, the 'Reformation'.

'Angels at six o'clock,' he told Jimmy.

'Sorry, I was too young for that movie.'

'Right. I'll drive down the line so we can mark them truck for truck.'

'Okay. It's probably faster and easier than turning our convoy around.'

Lance hung the mike on its hook. As he approached the jeep across the road, he blew the Range Rover's horn officiously. A gap-toothed man came running, moved the jeep and waved Lance through with an exaggerated bow and sweeping motion of his hand.

'Step into my parlour, said the spider to the fly.'

'My god, Nasheer, that's the second joke you've cracked today.'

'I assume you won't need my special talents to deal with this scum?'

'No, I don't think so. Take a rest. Or lend a hand, if you like.'

'Thank you, sir.'

'That woman's blouse has been ripped,' Esmeralda said as they passed the group of people under the guns of the grinning bandits. 'We came just under the bell.'

No one corrected her weird idiom.

As Lance's Range Rover approached the end of the stopped convoy, another jeep shot out from behind the last truck and blocked the road completely. Lance braked and took his rifle from Esmeralda's lap.

'The one in the tattered green shirt is the leader,' Esmeralda said.

When the Range Rover stopped, the man in the torn green shirt sauntered over, his machine pistol pointing at Lance.

'If you point that thing at me, you'd better be prepared to use it,' Lance said.

The man pushed his dark glasses to his forehead. Then, for a reply, and without raising the machine pistol from his hip, he fired a burst that exploded the spare tyre on the hood of the Range Rover. He kept his finger on the trigger as he traversed the stuttering machine pistol towards the passenger cabin of the Range Rover. Beside Lance the outside mirror shattered. Esmeralda screamed. Lance pointed his rifle over the windowsill and shot the bandit leader through the right eye, the sound of his shot blending with the reverberations from the destroyed tyre. Shots from Mwanzo and Nasheer were only fractionally behind his and struck the man in the mouth and chest. The other bandits were dancing around, pointing at the women, applauding their leader's marksmanship, and didn't notice until it was too late that they were under attack. When they did, nine of their seventeen lay dead on the ground and a seemingly endless horde of Swahili warriors armed with the latest automatic weapons poured out of the trucks, shooting with devastating accuracy at anything that moved. The bandits, unused to victims who shot back, did the sensible thing; they threw their firearms to the ground and raised their hands high in the air. The whole affair was over in seconds.

Lance climbed out, his rifle in his hand. Nasheer said something Arabic that sounded like a curse. 'What was that, Nasheer?'

'It was over too quickly, Mr Weber.'

Suddenly Lance was in excellent spirits. 'Come, let's see if we can find you a spot more excitement.' He walked down the double line of trucks.

At the rear of the side-by-side convoys, a thin woman stood screaming. She had good reason. One of the bandits stood with the barrel of his machine gun pressed to her throat

198

while his other hand roamed over her breasts. Her blouse and bra were ripped. To one side stood Christine, gritting her teeth, to the other Jimmy, his rifle casually in his hand. The tableau was completed by two bandits who stood on either side of a man with straggly red hair and a near-terminal case of sunburn; they each had a rifle stuck in one of his ears. The man's eyes were closed and he was loudly reciting the Lord's Prayer. The two bandits grinned triumphantly at the interlopers.

'Seems to me we've been here before,' Lance said conversationally to Jimmy.

'Indeed,' Jimmy replied. 'When you're ready, say the word.'

Lance looked over his shoulder but Mwanzo had stayed with Esmeralda. He would have to make do with Nasheer.

'Nasheer, I'll do the one with the woman, you do the lefthand one with the man, Jimmy will do the righthand one.' One of the three men holding guns on the hostages said something sharp and urgent in his own dialect. Without further ado, Lance said, 'Now,' and shot the man pawing the woman twice in the head. He staggerd backwards; a burst from his machine pistol spent itself in thin air. Christine rushed to the woman's aid. Lance turned to the male hostage, who still prayed as his captors fell to earth. Lance turned the corpses beside him over with his boot. Both had been shot in the face, one once, the other twice.

'Nasheer, two shots, always two shots,' Lance said tightly. 'A single shot in circumstances like these betrays an excess of pride in your marksmanship.'

Nasheer nodded.

The thin woman clung to Christine's knees; Christine looked less embarrassed than absolutely furious: 'Goddammit, don't you know better than to bring your wife with you,' she said bitterly to the red-haired man who now kneeled between the two dead highwaymen. Christine made the

199

introductions. 'Oliver Exton of Salvation for Sudan. Lance Weber, the leader of our column.'

The red-haired man rose and turned savagely on Lance. 'You murderous bastard! See what you've done. They're dead, do you hear me, dead!'

Lance took his hand back from midair.

'A severe case of sudden self-mortality knowledge,' Jimmy said.

Exton looked at Jimmy, then turned on Lance again. 'We could have talked to them, persuaded them,' he shouted. 'And now you killed them.'

'Notice,' said Jimmy, 'how you are solely to blame, mainly because of your white skin. He worries that, if he criticizes me, I will accuse him of racism.'

Lance turned to Exton. 'Where are the men protecting your convoy?'

'We don't need any. We're on a humanitarian relief mission with grain for the Sudan.'

'You've overshot your target by a thousand-odd miles,' Lance said cheerfully.

'No, no,' Exton snapped irritably. 'From the west. From Douala across the Cameroon and into the CAR and then across northern Zaire and to Sudan.'

Lance gaped at him open-mouthed. Finally, he managed, 'But why?'

'Djibouti's congested and the Ethiopian government uses its trucks to fight in Eritrea and Tigré instead of for famine relief, at Port Sudan they're on strike, from Mombasa through Uganda is too dangerous, so from the west is obvious,' Exton said. 'Besides, there was this ship carrying Argentinian grain in there for repairs and we could get the grain cheap and we already had the trucks, it was only a matter of airlifting them. It's not only Christine who can do things on a big scale. Though,' Exton added nastily, 'we prefer not to kill anyone in the process.'

'No, just get killed yourself.'

'Or worse,' the woman sobbed into Christine's knees.

'They would only have taken two or three trucks of our grain,' Exton said knowingly. 'That's what they take from every convoy passing through Uganda.'

'Because they're certain there will be more convoys to rob,' Lance said cuttingly. 'Here there is no such expectation or convention.'

'I'm starting to be sorry we saved his arse,' Jimmy said succinctly.

Me too, Lance thought. 'I'm surprised you came this far without incident.'

Exton dismissed him with a wave of his hand. 'We would've paid these like we paid the customs officials.'

Christine helped the woman up and tried to pull her torn bra together without success; her blouse was beyond salvage.

Esmeralda arrived, Mwanzo close by. 'Come,' she said, 'we'll find you fresh clothes.'

The woman turned on Exton. 'I want to go home,' she said, hysteria just under the surface, tightly contained.

'It won't happen again,' Exton said airily.

'It will,' Christine said. 'Lance – '

'We can spare an escort for her to Bangui,' Lance said.

Esmeralda led her away.

'Where are your drivers?' Lance asked Exton.

'Ran into the forest. They'll be back after a while.'

Lance looked at the two others in the group, a small, smiling Indonesian with a Red Cross armband and a black man in a safari suit. 'Have either of you passed through here before?'

They both shook their heads. The black man said, in oddly

accented English, 'Those drivers aren't coming back, Exton. You'll have to face it. This convoy is finished.'

'He has spare drivers,' Exton said, looking at Lance.

'My extra men are not drivers but guards,' Lance said calmly, restraining himself from adding, And with your attitude, I wouldn't give you the time of day. 'If you want some guards, I can let you have a few, complete with their armament and enough ammunition to see you to the Sudan.'

Exton stepped up and leaned forward to study Lance closely; he suffered from halitosis as well. 'Are you being sarcastic, Weber? No, I don't suppose you'd stretch to that. I don't want thugs, I want drivers.'

'Not from me you won't get them,' Lance said shortly and turned his back on the man. But after a couple of steps he stopped. He turned again. 'How many trucks of grain, Mr Exton?'

'Thirty.'

Lance looked down the line. He had counted twenty-eight. 'You lost two already?'

Exton nodded reluctantly.

'And spare parts and fuel?'

'We buy as we go.'

Lance smiled agreeably. 'I'll tell you what. We'll buy your trucks and grain for whatever you paid for them.'

'For Chad?'

'Yes. We were limited in the grain we could bring by the number of trucks we could buy immediately.'

'Well, the need in Chad is more urgent, we all know that, and we admire Christine tremendously for trying to do something about it. But you'll never make it.'

'We stand a better chance than you do, I assure you,' Lance said firmly, 'even if only because we are both logistically and psychologically better prepared.'

'Because you have fuel tankers and spare parts and don't

mind killing people who stand in your way,' Exton said offensively.

'Exactly,' Lance agreed cheerfully. 'Don't you distinguish between people who are starving through no fault of their own and scum who want to take their food by force?' He was genuinely curious.

Exton was horrified. 'They're all God's children, even you, Weber.'

'Remember that the next time two fun-loving children stick their rifles in your ear-holes,' Lance said. 'And don't forget to pray in their dialect, to be certain they understand you mean well.'

The black man in the safari suit turned to Jimmy. 'It will happen again?' he asked in French, then repeated himself in his strange English.

'Almost certainly,' Jimmy replied in French. 'This is civilization compared to where you're heading.'

The Indonesian grimaced. 'We're missionary doctors, not soldiers,' he said apologetically, indicating the black man in the safari suit and himself. 'We will not do much good if we never reach our destination.' He too spoke French.

'I think you should be sensible and sell out to us, Ollie,' Christine said. 'I would, in your place.'

'Yes, I'm shaken. And I'm tempted. But what the hell do I tell my Board? I'm not a *Führerprinzip* operator like you, you know that.'

Keep that up and soon we'll believe you're human after all, Lance thought. 'You tell them what you just told us: the need is greater in Chad.'

Exton nodded thoughtfully.

'And you tell them you almost lost the whole caboodle before you got halfway there,' Christine added.

Exton actually wrung his hands while they watched, fascinated. 'All right,' he finally burst out, 'I'll come with you.'

203

Lance shook his head firmly. 'No. Your trucks and your grain we're happy to have. But we're fully serviced in the general do-gooder department.' He gestured at Christine. 'Unless you want to carry and use a machine pistol?'

Exton shook his head. 'I really don't know what my Board will say about getting mixed up with a notorious character like you.'

'Sell us your trucks, give the remaining highwaymen their rifles back,' Lance said shortly, 'and you won't have to worry about your Board ever again.'

'You know, you're not only violent, you're bloody offensive.'

Lance sighed, reflecting that British public schools did nothing for the manners of an English gentleman. 'Your answer please, Mr Exton.'

'You have the money, Christine? Sorry to ask, but your man here did offer.'

'The Foundation has money, Oliver. Talk to Roger when you reach London. We'll pay anything you can show an invoice for. We still haven't spent half of what we raised for Chad.'

Exton nodded abruptly and walked away.

The black doctor stepped forward. 'Perhaps you can use a doctor, Mr Weber.'

The Indonesian held up two fingers, then pointed at himself and nodded his head vigorously: he wanted to be included.

Lance looked at Christine. Starving people suffered all kinds of illnesses and diseases. 'In what condition were those people you saw in the camps?'

'We can use doctors. I tried to find some in London but they wouldn't send any to Chad without the government's consent and they knew from what had happened to me that it was useless to ask.'

'Well, we're here now and without facilities for referring back to London,' the black doctor said.

'You're welcome,' Lance said. 'But understand, your business is the sick, mine is delivering food and you. I'll look after my own soul.'

The doctor grinned and shook Lance's hand. 'That's all right, I'm not religious either. The religious paid for my medical studies, so I offer them service.'

'No offence intended.'

'None taken. My friend is a Buddhist. He can come too?'

Lance nodded.

'Would you like death certificates for the bandits you shot?'

Lance shook his head. 'Just make sure we're not burying any still alive.'

Jimmy said, 'Better have a word with Exton to impress on him that reporting this fracas to the authorities is only likely to get him locked up.'

'You want to handle it, Christine?'

Christine nodded and walked away after Exton, who was wandering down the line of trucks as if saying an individual goodbye to each one.

'She's shaping up well,' Lance said.

Jimmy grinned at him. 'She'd be stupid not to, what we've gone through so far.'

'That's a bit harsh. I mean, Exton didn't.'

'Yeah, but he is stupid. Too stupid to be frightened.'

Pierre arrived. 'You want me to shoot the rest of these bandits des grands chemins?'

'No. Just take all their clothes, bend the barrels of their firearms, put their vehicles permanently out of order. Let the story spread as a warning to protect other relief workers with the same bright idea of moving grain west across Africa to Sudan.'

'West?'

Lance explained about the strike in Sudan.

'People are dying of hunger and the dockworkers go on strike? Are you sure that's right?'

Lance was certain. 'It's called democracy.'

'Makes you wonder whether Mobutu doesn't have the right idea after all.'

'All it proves to me is that coercive force needn't necessarily come out of the barrel of a gun to do its harm,' Lance said. 'Jimmy, take four men and escort Exton to Bangui.'

'Ah, shit, I saved his life already. Saddle somebody else with the chore.'

'Haven't you heard the Chinese fable: if you save a man's life, you're forever responsible for him?'

'Pygmies.'

Boo's voice was low but his single word electrified everyone. Christine, joining them just then, was amazed to see a shiver of revulsion roll down the faces of Lance and each of his lieutenants; it was a moment of real fear, something she had not recognized in them when men shot at them or when they faced the unbridled rage of the river. But the tableau held for only part of a second before they jerked into action and Christine was left wondering if she had really seen such terror so nakedly displayed; had the impact of so much sudden death so close to her toppled her mind into wishful thinking? But the Swahili were still rippling with revulsion and many were purposefully slapping new clips into their machine pistols.

Lance understood how the Swahili felt. There are few in Africa who do not. But uneasiness at the otherness of the pygmies was no reason indiscriminately to open fire on them. He ran down the line of trucks, roaring in Swahili, pushing down the barrels of their FNs.

206

'The wrinkled little men would eat our livers,' Mpengo said, dignity overcoming fear.

'This is their forest, Mpengo. We cannot kill them merely for inhabiting it. Between the trucks, everyone.'

At the end of the line he waited for Pierre and Jimmy; Boo was already there, studying the forest. Christine joined them.

'What now?' Jimmy asked.

'We go about our business,' Lance said. 'They won't attack. We're too many.'

'There are maybe thirty of them,' Boo said.

From the way the eyes of the others flicked across the forest, Christine knew none of them had counted as many. But no one argued with the scout. Christine had not seen even one pygmy and that made her uncomfortable as a pygmy in the flesh would not; but a vague unease was a long way from the attitude of everyone around her.

'What's all this fear and trepidation?' she asked lightly.

'Pygmies,' Pierre told her without looking at her, as if the single word explained everything.

'So?'

That grabbed their attention. Like the stupidest girl in school dropping a choice clanger, Christine thought. Simultaneously they looked away again, as if embarrassed by her ignorance.

'They're not like people,' Jimmy said to Lance. 'They don't think like us. They could attack.'

'I want the dead buried,' Lance said stubbornly. 'The rest of the Swahili can wait in the trucks with the windows closed.'

Exton ambled up to them. 'What's the delay? Why is everyone so tense?'

'Pygmies in the trees,' Christine told him.

He stared and saw nothing.

'Little brown man sitting in the tree fork about eye height

207

ten metres out on a line perpendicular to the road directly in front of you,' Boo said.

After a minute, Christine saw him. He was certainly ugly but, paradoxically, contrary to the almost tangible atmosphere around her, she felt happier for knowing what they looked like and where at least one was right then. The little man stared intrepidly back at her over a hand cupped to his mouth as one would hold a cigarette in a high wind. Christine politely looked away.

'No pygmies here,' Exton said. Then, 'Oh, I see him. Funny little fellow. There aren't *supposed* to be any pygmies here. Maybe a hundred miles that way but not here.'

He pointed southeast. No one corrected him, though all except Christine knew he meant southwest, in the direction beyond Bangui.

'They too are starving,' Pierre said. 'They travel in search of food. They would probably have tried to take one or more of your trucks from the highwaymen after they had taken them from you.'

'Doesn't their government look after them?' Exton was outraged. 'There's no general famine here.'

'Like Hitler looked after the Jews,' Boo told him bluntly. 'They're happy to let the pygmies starve.'

'Then we will feed them,' Exton said and, before anyone could stop him, strode into the forest straight towards the pygmy.

He had taken five paces on his long legs and was halfway to the little man before Lance, Pierre and Boo all reacted at once: in the event they only took one step each after Exton before there was a sound from the forest as if the pygmy had spat out an orange-pip. Exton clutched at his throat and danced around dementedly, screaming. Christine started towards him but Jimmy flung her bodily under the rearmost of Exton's trucks and then opened fire on the forest, quartering the shade, spraying leaves everywhere. Pierre and Boo sank to their knees and started firing blindly into the forest too. Lance rolled over and over and brought Exton down by the simple expedient of rolling into him. He rolled on top of Exton and pinned the man's flailing arms with his knees. He jerked the dart from Exton's throat, flung it from him in revulsion and fear, and brought his pocket knife from his trousers. He opened the largest blade, simply because he could grasp the protruding back edge between his fingers and there was no time for opening one of the smaller blades with his thumbnail. Without attempting delicate aim, he simply cut a deep cross into Exton's neck with the pinprick at the centre. Exton screamed and tried to throw Lance off to grasp at his neck. Lance threw the knife aside in order to use both hands to hold Exton down. He bent forward, sucked a mouthful of blood, spat it out, sucked another mouthful of blood, spat that out, another and another. Then Exton convulsed and sent Lance's 205 pounds flying. Lance lay on the ground, too winded even to roll to the relative safety of the trucks, and watched Exton die; there was nothing he could do once the poison on the pygmy's dart reached the central nervous system. Exton clawed at his throat and made a strange gurgling sound. He was not clutching at the pain of the dart or the cut Lance had made – he was suffocating, trying to tear his own throat out because he believed it constricted. Within twenty seconds he was dead. From the time when the dart struck him until he died less than a minute had elapsed. Lance could not think of a more horrible death. The firing stopped and Pierre helped him up.

Lance still had no breath for speaking but nodded at Boo and then looked into the forest. Boo understood: Lance wanted to know that the pygmies were out of range; he disappeared into the forest.

'My god,' Christine said. 'He wanted to *feed* them. They could see he was unarmed.'

'He's different to them,' Lance told her wearily. 'And could you see the pygmy was armed?'

Christine did not answer but Lance was satisfied that she would never do anything as stupid as Exton had died for.

Christine shivered and turned from Lance's cold blue eyes to the shadows under the trees. For the first time she felt a sense of the menace of the forest and its inhabitants, stood in that same awe of Africa she had observed and silently scoffed at in the men. Perhaps they were not exaggerating the dangers.

Exton's wife could not believe he was dead. 'How could you allow it?' she shouted at Lance. Then she grew hysterical and would let neither of the doctors near her, screaming that they intended to rape her. Christine finally persuaded her to take six Valium.

Boo came out of the forest as suddenly as he had entered it. The pygmies had gone, taking their dead, if any, with them; they had killed all Exton's drivers when they had tried to escape from the highwaymen.

Lance's party had no fatalities and only one flesh wound in the upper inside arm of one of the Swahili from a shot fired by one of the highwaymen. The total delay, from stopping to offer Exton assistance until they took to the road once more, was under two hours.

'That's Chad,' Lance stated the obvious, pointing across the Aouk. He did not expect an answer and received none. Christine, Nasheer and Pierre, who sat with their backs to the river, turned around even though they had seen it before. 'We're still three to five days from the hunger camps,' Jimmy told Christine, 'depending on Lance's plan.'

Pierre poured wine. 'You do have a plan?' he asked Lance.

Lance shook out his map and moved his remaining cutlery away.

'I'll have the table cleared.' Esmeralda gestured at the waiter and the steward in their white jackets. There was a moment's delay: they too were staring across the river into Chad.

'Even the cooks know that tomorrow or the day after we tackle the professional soldiers,' Jimmy said.

'Arm them before we leave tomorrow. That's why we hired Zulu for the kitchen.' Lance opened his map and spread it on the table. 'The camps are here, south of Ellila. Queddei holds the road from north of Abéché.'

'And there's only one road,' Pierre said.

'Except for this road from Largeau in the north on which Queddei will bring reinforcements,' Jimmy said. 'We've bitten off more than we can chew.'

Lance nodded easily. He was enjoying what might be the last days of his life. He had eaten well, drunk good wine, he had loyal friends and a beautiful wife who was also his friend, he was engaged on a worthwhile task, he had a plan to meet the greatest challenge of his life. It was enough. 'Sure. Anybody with a map can see there's only one road through Ellila and it runs from Abéché to Largeau.'

'That doesn't leave too many options, darling,' Esmeralda said. 'We're absolutely swinging on your lips.'

'Hanging,' Lance corrected her.

'That's what I said.'

'But do you see – ' Lance paused, enjoying himself hugely ' – there's this other road here up the west side of Chad from Ndjamena to Largeau.'

'So what?' Boo said. 'Most of that road's held by Queddei too.'

'Ah, true,' Lance agreed expansively. 'But they don't expect *us* on it. Now, if we somehow managed to join this excellent road *behind* Queddei's southernmost front – '

'You mean *cross-country*?' Jimmy demanded incredulously. 'With sixty trucks?'

Lance nodded.

Boo said, 'As an older man, let me give you some advice, Lance. Cross-country is hell on piles.'

'Stand on the running board to take the weight off them.'

'You are an unfeeling lightskinned barbarian.'

Pierre leaned over the map. 'All right, so we're on this fantastic road that leads right into the dragon's lair at Largeau. What do we do when we get there, commit hara-kiri?'

'Well, you see,' Lance said innocuously, 'we don't go there. They will sit there waiting, waiting, thinking we're coming to ask them to dance but we won't, we'll be taking a shortcut to Ellila.'

'Another nearly two hundred kilometres cross-country?'

Lance nodded. 'Why not?'

'Because it's madness,' Pierre said levelly.

'Exactly. It'll be days before anyone even conceives of the possibility that we would try it. By then it will be too late to send planes after us: we'll be at Ellila and the bread baking and the porridge cooking.'

'Well,' Jimmy dragged it out, '*toujours l'audace*.'

'Utter madness,' Boo said. 'And that's my mind speaking, not my piles.'

'And therefore totally unexpected,' Esmeralda said.

'You two want to put in your ha'pen'orth?' Lance asked the two doctors and then had to explain what he meant, after which they shook their heads. 'Nasheer?' The young Arab too shook his head but his eyes and teeth gleamed at the prospect of a fight; for the first time it occurred to Lance that Nasheer might resent his role as briber and corrupter of men.

212

'All right then. Actually it's not much more than a hundred kilometres cross-country. Then we pick up the Largeau-Ellila gravel road and by comparison that will feel like a four-lane highway.'

'Your mind is made up then?' Pierre asked.

'No, I'm open to persuasion. Tell me an alternative short of fighting a pitched battle at Abéché and a rearguard action all the way from there four hundred kilometres to Ellila and then trying to distribute food under fire. I'll be happy to listen to any plan that carries less risk.' Lance turned the map around to Pierre.

Pierre studied the map for a while, then chuckled. 'No, all right, the alternative was not to have started on this expedition. Since we're here already, let's finish the job.'

'Any other offers?'

Jimmy yawned. 'Queddei knows we're here, of course.'

Lance nodded. 'That's all right. We'll give his watchers ample reason to think we're heading for Abéché before we turn west.'

Christine studied the grave faces of the men. Esmeralda wore her inward smile. The two doctors looked attentive but Christine wondered if they truly knew what Lance was planning; she was not certain she knew herself except that it would be strenuous, dangerous and very probably violent. *What else is new?* She would not ask: she admitted to herself she did not really want to know. As long as Lance delivered the food to the hungry, she no longer cared how he did it. No, that was not right. She cared, but not as much as she used to. In the two days since poor Oliver and Madge Exton's experiences on the road, she had several times caught herself thinking that perhaps Mobutu had been right: that only the strong can do good in Africa – and Lance was an African Samson. Each time she pulled her mind up short: that sort of thinking would not do for the director of a charitable

213

institution. Everyone rose. Christine wondered if she had missed something but no, they were just heading for an early night.

In the night, as he reached for Esmeralda, Lance told her, 'This is the first night I have not dreamt of Emmy.'

As he shaved, Jimmy told Christine, 'Go wait for me in Brussels. Please.'

She shook her head. 'I can't, Jimmy. I'm too close now.'

He wiped his face, splashed on a handful of Eau Sauvage and held the tent-flap for her. 'I intend coming out of this alive. I'll stand a better chance if I don't have to look out for you as well.'

'Then don't, dammit. I'm an adult. I can look after myself.'

In that moment Jimmy accepted what he had long known: he and Christine would never make a life together. For her there would always be another cause, another battle to fight. 'I'll see you in Brussels next time you need help.'

She stood on tiptoe to peer into his face in the darkness and to kiss him. 'Don't be bitter, Jimmy. I can't help the way I am.' She passed out of the tent into the pitch dark in which a single Coleman floated over the breakfast table. Like a target, she thought uncharacteristically, shivering even though it was not cold. Then Boo and Pierre materialized out of the dark, startling her.

'Nobody's been sniffing around except the local police,' Boo told Lance as he came from his tent.

'The guards never saw anyone either,' Pierre added.

'That's not surprising. We can't go anywhere but through Sarh. If there are watchers, they'll be waiting for us there.'

'You can bet your last dollar there'll be watchers. Qaddaffi is a belt-and-braces man. He wouldn't just rely on the one lot we disposed of at home.' Pierre meant Zaire.

'I don't gamble,' Lance snapped. He saw Christine staring at him. 'Sorry, Pierre, I know it's just a figure of speech.

Esmeralda, please hurry them in the kitchen. I want to reach the far side of Sarh just after dawn.'

Jimmy waited until he had a mug of coffee and a rusk in his hand before he spoke. Once they crossed that border, there was no turning back. 'Dawn is when people start going about their business in these parts. The morning rush hour.'

'Exactly,' Lance said. 'Pierre knows what I intend.'

'To look like a stupid white foreigner who doesn't know any better?'

'We'll also act as furtively as possible in Sarh,' Lance said.

It was a good road for those parts, the main artery between two capitals, but it wasn't good enough to carry heavy trucks at nearly seventy miles per hour through the dark. 'Breakages increase geometrically as the square of the speed,' Lance told Jimmy as they bent their backs to a replacement spring while Mwanzo slid the pivot pin through the shackle.

Through the breaking light, Lance peered at the remains of the walls of what had once been Fort Archambaud and was now Sarh. Its citizens stood on the roofs of their houses, watching the huge convoy and its many armed men.

'Done, Master,' Mwanzo said. Lance and Jimmy and the row of Swahili bent their knees and elbows to let the spring down and crawled out from under the truck. Boo let down the hydraulic jack under the chassis.

'I think this is even better,' Pierre said. 'Now everyone can see we were trying to rush through Sarh before daylight and failed because of a breakdown.'

An utter silence hung over the people and the city until it was broken by sixty diesels starting up again. Then the people cheered.

'Strange,' Christine said. 'Hissein Habre who rules here is no better than Goukouni Queddei. Another brutal warlord.'

'They're Chaddi, we're taking food to hungry Chaddi,' Lance said. 'They're cheering you, Christine.'

Christine was amazed to find herself blushing. And then a hot flush of gratitude and acceptance spread through her.

Jimmy wondered: who among them is Qaddaffi's watcher? But, not to destroy Christine's moment, he kept his peace.

Lance led the convoy through Sarh at a crisp pace. Everywhere people were starting about their business but Lance kept his hand on the horn and none of the citizens showed any resentment at his unseemly haste.

'They all know who we are and what we are about,' Lance said.

'That's ominous, Mr Weber,' Nasheer said.

'The goodwill of the people may yet be our best weapon,' Lance said, feeling a little pompous and glad that Nasheer did not ask him *How?* because he did not know.

'There's something on the market stalls at least.' Esmeralda turned in her seat to study what was offered for sale as best she could from a speeding vehicle.

'The prices are excessive,' Nasheer said.

'They're near the divide between rain forests and the grain-growing regions here,' Lance said. 'There will always be *some* food for sale here even in the driest years. Further north, they're entirely dependent on the rain for their crops.'

'It's weird how suddenly the forests stop,' Esmeralda mused.

Beyond Sarh, travelling northeast to Am Timan, Lance kept the convoy to the fastest sensible speed the road would support. Now and again they would thunder up behind a single truck or two or three, which would draw off the road in response to Lance's Fiamm horns to let them pass. At that speed, no one overtook them and Jimmy reported only one car keeping up with them, a black S-class Mercedes that periodically appeared in his mirror and then fell back to stay out of the dust. When they stopped for brunch, the black

216

Mercedes drove past but, once they were on the road again, the black car soon reappeared behind them.

'It's them,' Jimmy told Lance on the radio.

'We'll know for sure at Am Timan, won't we.'

Esmeralda glanced at Lance. She could read from the map that they would reach Am Timan in broad daylight: would Lance really waste so many hours of travel by camping at the 'normal' time? Lance tapped the side of his nose and grinned boyishly at her.

At Am Timan, Lance turned northwest for Abou Deia and less than ten minutes later Jimmy activated the radio.

'Bingo!'

'How many?'

'Two, maybe three.'

'Communications?'

'They have a big whip aerial on the roof. You think they're listening to us?'

'Of course.' Lance searched the frequencies until he found a strong voice speaking rapidly in Arabic. He glanced over his shoulder at Nasheer.

'They're telling someone we know they're here,' Nasheer said. He listened to some more Arabic. 'They think we're trying to get around Abéché on the west side.' More Arabic, then a click. 'Their orders are to stay with us and keep reporting.'

Forty minutes out of Am Timan, Lance led the convoy off to the right of the main road onto a gravel track that had never seen a grader. Their speed was cut to thirty klicks an hour. The Arabs reported the change in direction, saying it now appeared the convoy would try to sneak around Abéché on the east side, using the tracks on the border with Sudan. 'They're Libyans, not Chaddi,' Esmeralda said. 'We could have stayed on the good roads for several hundred klicks more without giving away our intention so obviously. Chaddi would know that, wouldn't they?'

After ten minutes, Lance pulled off the side of the road and waved the trucks by. He turned the Range Rover in the dust; in his mirror he saw Jimmy turning his own Range Rover. He waited until Jimmy drove up level with him, then they accelerated side by side down that narrow track and around the curve.

The driver of the Mercedes lost his head. He saw the two Range Rovers looming huge out of the settling dust, their bull bars leading the charge; the Mercedes would have no chance. He flung the steering-wheel over, then let it go to cover his head with both forearms. One of his two passengers had a finger on the electric window button, the other merely smashed the window with the barrel of his pistol. He fired only one shot before the Mercedes crashed into a tree and immediately burst into flames. The driver and the front-seat passenger died instantly from concussion, the passenger in the back was directly in the path of the flames as they reached for oxygen through the window he had smashed; he breathed in flaming fuel and lived perhaps two seconds longer than the others.

Esmeralda's face was white and strained; Lance wondered if he should have left her behind, but there had not been time, the rhythm of forward motion and ambush imposing its own imperative. He touched her arm, then stopped the Range Rover and watched in the mirror as Jimmy swung the other one about to fetch the rest of the convoy; at least he could spare Esmeralda another sight of the burning wreck. 'We've no facilities for holding prisoners,' he said.

'I wouldn't ask you to risk the lives of our people to take men who'd shoot us like rabid dogs.' She laid her hand over his on the wheel. He turned his hand over and held hers tightly until, in the mirror, he saw the caterpillar of dust growing towards them and had to pull onto the road again.

At midnight they camped between Mongo and Ati and Lance announced grandly that they could sleep late the next morning. His fellow travellers, clutching weary backs and rubbing burning eyes, were not amused: they had been on the road for over eighteen hours.

The single-engined high-wing artillery command spotter had floated above them for the last hour, so the barrier across the road before Ati was not unexpected. Lance picked up the microphone, irritated at having to interrupt George Malcolm and the Stuttgart Chamber Orchestra under Karl Münchinger near the end of J. S. Bach's second harpsichord concerto. Today he was on a very tight schedule: if his convoy arrived at the front between the two warring Chaddi factions at any other time than just after sunset, it would all have been for nothing. 'Jimmy, bring Christine up here.' Lance stopped his Range Rover before the barrier and unsmilingly surveyed the fifty or sixty heavily armed soldiers manning it.

'Carefully arranged not to give offence but to put us in a crossfire all the same,' Nasheer said. 'It doesn't look like the government shares the people's enthusiasm for us to feed the northern Chaddi.'

Lance turned around in his seat. 'Never mind dragging up what I said yesterday. Can you buy them very quickly indeed?'

Nasheer seemed to count the soldiers. 'I don't think so, Mr Weber. A man who wants to be bought would not bring so many soldiers to share with.'

Lance stepped out just as Jimmy's Range Rover slid to a halt. Lance opened Christine's door. 'Stand by and keep your mouth closed until it's time for you to make like the director of a charitable institute, then make it good. Understand?'

Christine, not knowing what had angered Lance so,

nodded and climbed out. Behind Lance's back, she looked questioningly across the Range Rover at Jimmy, who winked at her. But his smile was in abeyance and she noticed his eyes turn and his head nod ever so slightly; she resisted the temptation to look around – behind them Pierre and Boo would be making their own dispositions.

Lance took ten paces, then stopped, nearer to his own vehicles than to the black Mercedes that stood ahead of the armoured personnel-carrier against which a major in battle-dress leaned negligently. Jimmy touched Christine's arm and she too stopped. After ten seconds, Lance folded his arms. After another ten, he made a motion to turn away and the major promptly detached himself from the armoured car and strode towards them.

'Mr Weber, I have long wanted to meet you. News of your exploits – '

'Why are you threatening me?'

'Threatening? I don't – '

'Then clear that roadblock.'

The major flushed and drew a deep breath. 'The Deputy Minister requests a meeting.'

'I'm here.'

'He is in the car. If you would just – '

'Bring him. And while we talk, clear the roadblock. You have five minutes.'

The major looked pointedly at Lance's empty hands. Then he turned on his heel and strode to the Mercedes. He opened the rear door and spoke to someone invisible behind the smoked glass.

'Lance, is this really necessary?' Christine demanded in a low voice.

'Watch and learn.'

'The limo's probably armoured too,' Jimmy said.

'Sure. And he'd lose face if he refused to leave it to talk to two unarmed men and a woman,' Lance said.

The man who came from the Mercedes wore the uniform of a colonel in the Army; he was the same age as the major, perhaps in his middle to late thirties but, whereas the major was lean and hawkish, the Deputy Minister was plump and sleekly sinister. He stopped in front of them but did not offer to shake hands.

'There is no need for intransigence, Mr Weber. We are on the same side.'

'I'm on the side of the hungry,' Lance said.

'We have our own hungry here.'

'Indeed. You yourselves made many of them hungry by burning granaries, crops and villages in the Christian south of your country. And now you can prove you care by releasing army trucks to carry food to them.'

Christine nodded enthusiastically. Lance had made a telling point. It was a bone of continual contention between relief workers and African governments that the food shipped in by relief agencies rotted because of the unwillingness of local governments to divert available transport from fighting their inevitable internal opposition to carrying grain for the hungry. Or, when they did release transport for famine relief, their deliberate policy of withholding the donated food from their political opponents.

'When we have disposed of the rebels, we will be in a position to feed everyone,' the Deputy Minister said smoothly. 'Until then it is my government's policy that all heavy transport entering our territory shall be at the disposal of the defence of democracy.'

'No,' Christine said. 'You won't take our trucks from us or the food from the hungry. I shall have you pilloried at the United Nations as thieves and pirates.'

The man had tiger-yellow eyes. He turned them on

221

Christine. 'Your grain will feed the hungry, Miss Rawls. Rest assured of that. There is no need for threats.'

'You've had your five minutes, Major,' Lance said over the Deputy Minister's shoulder.

'In any event, I have no discretion in this matter,' the Deputy Minister said, offering the major a cutting look, confirming Nasheer's guess. 'Besides, I have enough men to enforce my government's wishes, if it should unfortunately come to that.' His tone gloated that he would enjoy a show of force.

'Mwanzo!' Lance stuck out his right hand and a second later closed it around his rifle. With his left hand he grasped the Deputy Minister's lapels to detain the man, who was turning to scuttle back to his car. 'Before you do anything rash, Major,' Lance said calmly to the other officer, who had his holster unbuttoned and his pistol half out of it, 'you might care to look around you.' Lance raised his voice. 'Pierre, Boo!'

The major turned. Behind him and his men he saw two men rising from the cabbages in the market gardens on each side of the road.

'My lieutenants, each with twenty men,' Lance told the major whose mouth was hanging open. 'You didn't think irregulars would be able to think for themselves? Oh dear, Major.' The major's eyes flicked to the road behind Lance. 'Mpengo! Mbwato!' Two more men rose, one on each side of the road. The major studied his own men, who were now distinctly uneasy and fidgeting, turning this way and that . . .

'You will be cut down in the crossfire by your own men,' the major said, quite reasonably.

'But I would die in distinguished company,' Lance agreed expansively. 'Now, Major, clear the road.'

'Surely you don't think even you can get away with this outrage,' the major demanded.

'The colonel will be accompanying us.'

'We have strict laws against kidnapping.'

'Christine, tell him the facts of life.'

For a moment she was stumped, then she remembered Mobutu. 'I think, Major, when the Deputy Minister sees the favourable publicity he receives for helping our humanitarian mission even unto his enemies, he will suddenly find he accompanied us of his own free will. Enthusiastically, you might say.' God forgive me, she thought, I'm enjoying this.

'You'll never return,' the Deputy Minister grated.

'Oh, if your enemies are no more efficient than you, I think there is every chance we'll be passing this way again.' Lance had recovered his good cheer. 'The road, Major. Now!'

The major's lower lip quivered and for a moment Lance fancied the man would burst out crying. Then he spun around and shouted instructions at his men.

'Get the men back in the trucks,' Lance told Jimmy.

'Shall we disarm them?' Jimmy gestured at the Chaddi soldiers.

'They won't start shooting while we have the head honcho in our midst.'

'I hope you're right. Some of those boys sport parachute insignia. Others have sharpshooter badges.'

'We haven't time for fancy footwork, Jimmy.' Lance let go the Deputy Minister's lapels to switch his hold to the man's elbow. 'Mwanzo, Nasheer. Place him between you.'

'You will die for this,' the Deputy Minister said quietly.

'Join the queue, Colonel.' Lance pushed the man towards Mwanzo. 'If he speaks again, shoot him.'

'Yes, Master!'

The soldier-turned-politician studied Mwanzo's smiling face for a moment, looked meaningfully at the major, then turned and climbed into the back of the Range Rover. Mwanzo and Nasheer climbed in on either side of him.

Nasheer relieved the man of his sidearm and gave it to Esmeralda, who put it in the glovebox.

Eight minutes later Jimmy tooted his horn from the back of the convoy and Lance let the clutch in, threw an ironic salute to the major, standing stiff with anger beside his armoured car, and headed into the town.

While they ate their brunch beside the road, four trucks with mesh cages on the back passed, escorted by three jeeps overflowing with heavily armed men. The cages were crammed with people, mainly young women but also a good number of teenage boys. They all had two things in common: they were extraordinarily handsome and they were keening, thrusting their faces imploringly at the mesh, their fingers and hands clawing at the freedom just beyond it.

Christine's mouth twisted. 'Do those juvenile prisoners have water?' she demanded of the Deputy Minister, who was at table with them, wolfing his lamb chops.

The man stared at her, astonishment plain on his face. 'They're not my business,' he said after a long pause, then returned to his lamb chops, eyeing those left on the serving platter in the middle of the table.

'They're too well fed to be prisoners, Miss Rawls,' Nasheer said. 'They're slaves.'

Cutlery clattered as Christine rose abruptly to stare after the dustplume of the disappearing slave-trucks. 'Oh, my god!'

'This is the main slave route from the west to the eastern ports of Africa,' Nasheer added. 'Slavery is still a major industry of the Benin and big business elsewhere.'

Christine glared at those around the table. 'Well, do something! Somebody!'

'What?' Pierre asked.

'Take those poor people back!'

'And then do what with them?' Jimmy asked mildly.

'Why, give them their freedom!' How could they be so obtuse?

'To do what? To starve?' Jimmy asked.

'They can go back where they came from, can't they?'

'No,' Jimmy said firmly, 'they can't. Their own people will kill them or at least turn them out to starve. Their tribes value virginity highly in a woman and consider sodomy a crime punishable by death in a man. Do I make myself clear? At least now they are alive and will eat well. Now, if you don't mind, it serves no purpose to spoil our meal for something we are powerless to change.'

Christine saw she was wringing her napkin in her hand and flung it on the table before stalking to the edge of the road where she stood for ten minutes until the last mote of dust that so offended against justice and liberty settled. When she turned, she hoped the Deputy Minister, whose government allowed such a terrible traffic to pass unremarked, would speak out so that Mwanzo would shoot him. The urge did not shock or even sadden her. All, except the minister still wolfing his food, were looking thoughtfully at her; she was glad she had ruined their meal.

While Lance went about his usual thorough inspection of the site, Nasheer left the Deputy Minister in Mwanzo's care to join Christine beside the road. 'You *are* doing something about slavery, Miss Rawls,' he said.

'What?'

'You feed people. People who are not hungry have less reason to sell their children into slavery.'

'Oh god!' It had never occurred to her but yes, it was so logical. 'It happens?' But she already knew the answer.

'All the time. Prices on slave markets everywhere are depressed because of the famine.'

'How come you know so much about it?'

'No need to sound accusatory, Miss Rawls. My family gave

225

up slavery more than a century ago. And I'm not the only member of it now a little ashamed of the foundation on which the family fortune is built.'

She nodded. Nasheer was human after all. 'I'd consider it a signal honour if you would call me Christine,' she said.

'Christine.' Nasheer made a little bow. 'Perhaps when the famine is over, you will want to talk about slavery.'

Christine nodded thoughtfully.

'Mr Weber was deeply touched by the plight of those people, as was everyone except that fat slime in the fancy uniform.'

'Perhaps more obvious to you than to me,' Christine said tartly.

'Slavers,' Nasheer continued, pointedly ignoring her interruption, 'are signally violent people.'

Christine nodded again. 'And we stand amid the masters of violence, do we not?'

Nasheer smiled at her. 'If we return from Ellila, we can talk again.' He walked away to the Range Rover and climbed in.

Christine stood for a moment wondering how she had progressed from a do-gooder to one who stood casually planning bloody violence. She looked at the two Swahili assigned to guard her; they stood ten paces away, politely not staring at her, politely not listening but hearing all the same.

On impulse, she asked, 'Would you fight to free the slaves?'

They turned to look at her to acknowledge her remark, then looked at the ground again. 'Our people were slaves once. The Swahili is a cross between Arab and Bantu, Miss Christine. We freed ourselves.'

'Of course,' she agreed. 'But will you fight to free others?'

'Perhaps,' the other one replied. 'Who would lead us?'

It was as polite a way as any to tell her they would not follow her. 'Mr Weber, their Highnesses, Mr Habakuk?'

226

They smiled at her and nodded. 'If they ask us.'

That could be taken as humility, that they were not certain they had earned the right to be invited again. But it could also be a polite way of telling her she would first have to persuade the only men they would follow, and Christine knew damn well which it was. But she had learnt much on this journey so, instead of ticking them off as a couple of male chauvinist pigs, she merely said, 'First we have to return from the north.'

They considered this for several seconds and found it wise. In unison, they saluted her. 'Hau!' Then one of them held the Range Rover's door for her, a courtesy she had not warranted until now.

'Your woman is plotting something,' Lance said to Jimmy.

'Yes, but what?'

'Her next cause and campaign,' Esmeralda said behind them. 'The abolition of slavery.'

'Let's fill their stomachs before we worry about their freedom,' Lance said shortly. He felt vaguely embarrassed by the slaves he had seen and angry about his impotence to right the injustice done them. Instinctively, he accepted that they would be killed or cast out to starve if they returned to their tribes shamed and defiled; intellectually, he saw merit in the argument that it is preferable to eat in chains than to starve in freedom. But, emotionally, he felt a burning antipathy to the slavers. The solution to the slave trade, it seemed to him, was simple: if one shot enough slavers out of hand, the rest would be frightened off and the despicable trade would cease.

Late in the afternoon, when the shadows angled towards night, Lance led the convoy off the Ati-Ndjamena road onto a good gravel road that would connect at Moussoro to the Ndjamena-Largeau road. But Queddei's forces held the town of Moussoro itself and part of the connecting gravel road as well. The question was: which part? Lance did not want to run into the leading edge of an army at war. He had questioned the colonel but the man turned out to be more politician than soldier and all he could contribute was that the situation was fluid and that, while Moussoro was most definitely in rebel hands, the village of Tororo halfway along the gravel road to Moussoro might or might not be 'liberated'. Lance had sent Boo out to scout the situation; they had trucked a light cross-country motorcycle all the way from South Africa exactly for scouting missions like this. Lance had not been happy to send a single man into the desert on such a loud machine, but there was no way they could have brought a horse or a camel and a Range Rover was too difficult to hide when planes flew over.

Twenty-five minutes up the gravel road, the Deputy Minister said, 'You are coming very near, Mr Weber.'

Mwanzo promptly cocked his rifle. Lance held up his hand to stop him shooting the man. 'You're very brave,' he said sardonically.

'It might be a mercy to have your man shoot me. They will torture me to death. Please let me go. I can pay you – '

'I intend to free you anyway,' Lance cut him off. Earlier he had told Jimmy out of earshot of their hostage to tell the major he could follow, alone in the armoured car with his driver, but must send the rest of his soldiers back to Ati. Lance suspected the major had not yet informed his superiors at Ati or Ndjamena that he had lost control of his charge; he thought the man would attempt to recover the Deputy Minister before they found out. Otherwise there would by now have been planes overhead, perhaps helicopters with reinforcements. Telling the major to follow alone was a tacit commitment to a mutually beneficial arrangement. But Lance had not wanted the politician in the soldier's uniform aware of his intention to release him: he hoped fear would loosen the man's tongue. It did; pity he knew so little.

'You will not regret your decision,' the Deputy Minister said pompously.

Esmeralda turned in her seat to stare at the man. Could he not hear the contempt in Lance's voice?

'Shoot him if he talks again,' Lance told Mwanzo. He drew up beside the dusty figure sitting on the motorcycle at the edge of the road.

'Oh, my sainted piles,' Boo said in greeting, and spat. Lance offered him a water bottle and he rinsed his mouth, spat again, splashed his eyes, then drank deeply. 'Aargh, that sand grits everywhere.'

Lance waited patiently until Boo was ready to tell him.

'The government holds Tororo but the rebels are advancing on them,' Boo said. 'The front stretches to the east, as far as the village of Quérek.'

'Tch!' Lance said. He had planned to head cross-country from beyond Tororo or, if that was not possible, to cut between Tororo and Quérek, to rejoin the main road north of Moussoro.

'Can we go west around Tororo and cross the road into rebel country beyond Tororo?'

Boo shook his head wearily. 'I went behind the line. There's a lot of activity on the road between Tororo and Moussoro. We'll never get sixty vehicles across unseen.'

Lance looked down the road at his convoy; even with the trucks bumper to bumper, it was still nearly half a mile long.

'What I suggest,' Boo continued, 'is that we return to the good road and take that down to Ndjamena. From there we drive north until nearly at Moussoro. Then we cut cross-country around Moussoro. It's safe to join the main road to Largeau just beyond Moussoro. Their headquarters are at Moussoro, so the road is full of transport command trucks running back and forth. We'll disappear among that lot.'

'My god,' Lance exclaimed. He put a hand under Boo's

229

elbow. Boo had ridden that buzzbike over four hundred kilometres through the desert.

Boo removed Lance's hand. 'I'm just tired, not weak.'

'Sorry. We can't go to Ndjamena.' Lance gestured at his Range Rover. 'A Deputy Minister . . .'

'Ah,' Boo said neutrally. Then, disgustedly, 'Christ! Do you like cross-country travel?'

Lance shook his head. 'Two hundred klicks.'

'At least,' Boo said.

'We'd better get off this road. If there's a big battle up ahead, just about now some hustle and bustle could spread here as this side tries to bring up supplies and reinforcements. You catch up on your sleep. Leave the bike, I'll see it loaded.'

Lance walked with Boo to a canopied flatbed truck and boosted him up; the Swahili had strung a hammock for him in which he would be able to sleep undisturbed by whatever terrain they travelled over.

'My sainted piles,' Boo said again as he climbed into the hammock without taking off his boots. He put his forearm across his eyes and was instantly asleep.

Back in the Range Rover, Lance drew a line across his map with a wax pencil. He looked down at the large compass mounted to the drive tunnel. 'I hope that thing still works,' he said to no one in particular. He switched the maplight on and off again, after bending it over, to ascertain that it worked. Esmeralda turned to a fresh page in her notebook and noted the time and the odometer reading; she leaned over to press the button to zero the trip meter. Lance started the Range Rover and headed it off the road, into the wilderness. He was glad he had bought best-quality trucks new and looked after them well. His brother had believed it was not enough to be well organized, one had to be pure of spirit as well. He and his comrades were well organized and their intention of feeding the hungry was laudable. But those

230

ranged against them were ruthless. And Mobutu had come right out and said it. Sound organization, a pure heart and an indomitable will, Lance decided. The minimum without which one cannot triumph over evil. After darkness fell, he started questioning Nasheer, who turned out to be an expert about the slave trade, its origins, practice, politics, geographical range, economics; he switched off his emotions and merely filed the facts.

They were lucky that night. Only twice were trucks stuck in the sand and each time it required less than ten minutes to pull them clear, the tired Swahili swinging the PSPs into position with the smooth drill of long practice. At midnight they halted for an hour for food and rest and Boo said the going was better than it would have been north of the road. Lance told him to get all the sleep he could: tomorrow he would be scouting again. An hour before dawn they crossed the Ndjamena-Largeau road a couple of klicks north of Cheddra and almost immediately joined the dry bed of a river which provided good going. They had one more road to cross, the major one from Moussoro to Mao, and Lance decided to chance it in the first of the daylight. He deployed Pierre and twenty men to protect their flank from attack by Queddei's soldiers, who held the crossroads about four klicks east of where they ran the trucks across one by one at twenty-second intervals; the tension after a hard night was barely bearable but no one disturbed them. 'Better safe than sorry though,' Pierre said when all the trucks were across. He and Jimmy were both drenched in sweat and not from the heat; Lance never sweated from tension, though sometimes, when he was convinced fear would give him ulcers, he wished he did. Then they returned the soldier/politician to the major who had patiently followed them through the night; neither offered thanks or goodbyes before driving off southwards at high speed. In broad daylight, Lance's convoy camped in the Bahr el Ghazal a few klicks from the hamlet of Bemélé.

Everyone was too tired for a meal but Lance gave the Swahili a triple ration of cane spirit and Nasheer produced two bottles of champagne ready-chilled from his bribery reserve.

'What are we celebrating?' Christine asked.

Lance smiled tiredly at her. 'We're behind enemy lines and nobody knows we're here.'

At Ndjamena, the Deputy Minister soaked in his marble bath, being soaped by a luscious Senegalese boy he had bought from Rashomon not over a month ago. How could Westerners so stupid and so soft have come so far? How could a man like Weber, sickened by the sight of a few slaves, have achieved such a reputation? How could such scum have humiliated him? He hit the boy ringingly through the face with the back of his hand; the boy fell to the floor and promptly rose to continue washing his owner because shammed unconsciousness would be punished by whipping with the many-tailed lash. The Deputy Minister fondled the boy absently. 'Tonight,' he told him. 'Be bathed and scented for me.' He would have his revenge on Weber and the woman Rawls and their black familiars and those bronze-bodied warriors of theirs. The only question was how best to use his knowledge of their whereabouts for greatest possible benefit to himself, maximum discomfiture for Queddei's treacherous rebels, and ultimate destruction for Weber and his cohorts.

Then it came to him. So simple! Weber had offered his own head on a platter. He called out to his secretary in the next room. 'Call the journalists, especially the foreign ones, to a press conference in two hours. Do it now.'

* * *

232

At dusk, rested, even showered in only slightly tepid water pumped from a well Boo had found, they joined the main road to Largeau only twenty klicks north of Moussoro. At table, before they set off, Christine had asked, 'Doesn't it make you uneasy to be only four or five miles from the enemy?' but Lance laughed and quoted some poetry about hiding in plain sight; even so, he had not allowed any fires and they had eaten a cold meal.

At the main road a military policeman held up his hand and Lance stopped. He rolled his window down as the man parked his motorcycle and approached. 'Don't panic,' he admonished himself. Esmeralda chuckled. Mwanzo cocked his rifle and Nasheer shifted his weight onto his left side, all the quicker to get at the knife in his boot. The military policeman saluted smartly. Before he could speak, Lance said, in English, 'Special engineers. Which bloody way is north, mate? Oh, yes, you don't speak nothing but Frog.' In his most atrocious French, Lance explained they were a special engineering group on their way to Largeau but had become lost.

'They provide women for mercenaries?' the man asked, obviously astounded.

'Reel in your scummy mind,' Esmeralda told him sharply. 'Nurses. These men do very dangerous work. The trucks are full of explosives.'

'Never mind that,' Lance said to Esmeralda, adding to the military policeman, 'It's a secret that we're here at all, understand?' He hoped that would explain the absence of insignia to warn others they were supposedly carrying explosives. He waited for the man to nod. 'We're supposed to report at Largeau by dawn. Which way is it?'

'You'll never make it,' the military policeman said. 'It's at least twelve hours on the road and the refuelling stops are all crowded.'

'We have our own fuel tankers,' Lance said, pointing over his shoulder into the darkness, 'so we can stay clear of the rest of the chaps.'

'It's still too far. These aren't European roads and they're very busy right now. To be in Largeau at ten tomorrow would be more reasonable. You can radio in you'll be late.' He pointed to the radio installation on the drive tunnel, then stepped back and saluted again. He took a paddle from his motorcycle and stood in the middle of the road to hold up the line of distant but fast-approaching headlights as he waved Lance's column onto the road.

Minutes later, the transceiver came alive with the sound of Jimmy giggling convulsively. It only lasted three seconds before Jimmy cut transmission but Lance knew how he felt.

Through the night, Lance kept them moving as fast as the road would allow, slowing down only when they came up behind an Army convoy. They would not attempt to pass a slower convoy of any length even in daylight but at night on this road it was impossible as the road was in constant use in the other direction, with supplies and reinforcements being trucked to the erupting front. They would slow to the other convoy's speed and stay behind it until it pulled off the road for a rest break or to refuel from one of the tankers stationed at hundred-kilometre intervals. 'Queddei is making a big push,' Lance said after he counted a convoy of nearly a hundred trucks thundering south. 'We're lucky. This kind of military manoeuvre always creates chaos and we need only a little confusion plus a modicum of native wit to reach Ellila.'

In the rear Range Rover, Christine also counted the trucks. 'Those trucks should be heading the other way, towards Tripoli and Benghazi, to fetch Russian grain for the starving Chaddi.'

Jimmy merely shook his head in astonishment. She still believed the Russian grain would arrive and, having arrived, would be distributed. 'This road holds more than half of all army and civilian trucks in Queddei's part of Chad,' Jimmy said a hundred miles later. 'And the rest will be used to provision the soldiery at Abéché. If you want my opinion, he hasn't sent a single truck to fetch grain for famine relief.'

Christine sank despondently lower in her seat, curling up defensively against the door. 'We've risked so much, to arrive with food for only a few weeks and no hope beyond that. Damn these people and their petty internecine wars, damn them to hell!'

Later Jimmy switched on the late news from Paris on the shortwave receiver. The first report was an appeal by a United Nations Refugee Relief Agency spokesman for the Ethiopian government to release 700 trucks, which they were using to fight their internal opponents in Eritrea and the Tigré, to be used instead for carrying grain, piling up on the docks because of lack of transport, to the starving in their camps hundreds of miles away. The second item, neatly linked in the broadcast though temporally thousands of miles away, was the progress of Christine Rawls' relief column which had, with the assistance of Hissein Habre's Transitional Government of National Unity in the south, managed to fight their way behind the rebel front line and were even now heading for the refugee camps at Ellila with over three hundred tonnes of grain, medicines and two doctors rescued from another convoy whose men were killed and the women raped by pygmies in the CAR. Meanwhile the wheat Libya had obtained from the Russians for famine relief in Chad lay on the dock in Odessa but Russian sources said ships had been scheduled to transport it 'soon'.

'We should have killed that little bastard.' Christine meant the Deputy Minister.

'They're putting the Deputy Minister's story together with whatever your friend Mrs Exton bleated when she returned

235

to civilization,' Jimmy said clinically. 'You could almost hear that newsreader lick his chops about such a juicy story.' He picked up the mike. 'Listen to the comics on Auntie,' he said and put it back to cut transmission. Queddei's people, in the middle of a war, were no doubt monitoring the airwaves closely but such a brief transmission would never give them a fix or even the certainty that it came from within their midst – as if they required telling, with the international newscasts blaring out the presence of the relief column.

Lance listened to the last BBC World News bulletin and thought, We should've shot the slimy shit.

At the next refuelling stop, Christine asked Lance, 'What now?'

'We continue as before. We have no options left.'

'What when they find us?' We can't fight a whole army,' the black doctor added.

Lance shook his head. 'I'll face that when it arrives. My best guess is that in Largeau they'll discount the news from Ndjamena as nothing but opportunistic propaganda. They have plenty on their plate right now, what with a war on two fronts.' He glanced at the road as another convoy thundered by southwards.

None of them could know that Queddei's staff had in fact dismissed the news of Lance's entry behind their lines as Ndjamena's idea of a joke when, just after two the previous day, an AFP correspondent requested confirmation. It was not until Qaddaffi was apprised of the event through his second daily news digest, which he read after his evening prayers, that any real note was taken of the report. Qaddaffi, who in any event lives in a twilight world where the demarcation between reality and wishful thinking is at best fuzzy, believed wholeheartedly that this Weber person had led his convoy behind Queddei's lines. Not one of his staff could credit such a patent impossibility: one man might slip through the front between two warring nations, but not with a convoy of sixty trucks in tow. Not even Qaddaffi himself could manage such a thing. But no one mentioned doubts; Qaddaffi demanded and received unquestioning obedience. Ali, the Air Force pursuit pilot seconded to intelligence liaison, was summoned and given his order: proceed to Queddei's headquarters with all speed and shake them up about this undesirable Weber and his entourage of hired thugs. 'Mention to the General my undying admiration and friendship,' Qaddaffi told Ali without pausing to reflect on the irony of expressing in such words the terrible threat of withdrawing his support; a sense of humour is always the first casualty of fanaticism. Ali, with Qaddaffi's 'all speed' as his licence, commandeered a night fighter and flew himself to Largeau, where he delivered his message to a distracted, weary Queddei and his chief of staff, who shook their heads in disbelief, looked meaningfully at each other and told the visitor he could tell Qaddaffi they would see to it. Ali gently disillusioned them: his instructions directly from Qaddaffi were to stay, watch the destruction of the interlopers, and report every detail of their demise. Of course, if that was too much to ask in return for Qaddaffi's friendship and generous support . . . Queddei was starting to understand why such a skilled pilot had been detached to intelligence liaison. 'We shall be honoured to have such a close associate of our most munificent friend in Allah leading the search for these unwelcome visitors,' Queddei ruled, and yawned. It was an hour to dawn.

An hour before dawn, Lance led the convoy through Koro Toro at a crisp pace. The road turned northwest, away from Ellila, for sixty kilometres and Lance wanted to cover those and a few more before dawn. At ten minutes to dawn, they came to Kizimi, where the road turned north-north-east again. Ten minutes after dawn, Lance led the convoy off the road towards the low hills rising to the west. He prayed the soft sand would hold the trucks; if they were stuck so near the road, one of the passing convoys might stop and offer help, with unpleasant consequences.

He heaved a sigh as they drew up behind the first ridge high and long enough to hide the whole convoy. They were less than a thousand metres from the road but there was no point in driving any further. They would either be found during the day or they would not.

'Ellila is on the other side of the road,' Christine told Lance as they met at the wash-table.

'I can read a map. But that's exactly where they will look for us.'

'You changing your plan?' Pierre asked.

Lance splashed his eyes and dried his face on the towel Christine offered him. 'If they know we're behind their lines, they also know we arrived here only by travelling cross-country.'

'Logical,' Jimmy agreed. 'So you want to go as far north as possible before heading into the desert again?'

'Our best hiding-place is the chaos they've made of their own roads with this war. Out in the desert we'll be a sore thumb.'

Their horror would have been comical if he had not been so tired. He gave the towel to Pierre. Jimmy poured the dirty water into the bucket under the table to make space for fresh in the basin.

'Then what will you do?' Christine asked, not quite believing what she concluded from what he had already said.

Lance sighed. 'We will drive to Largeau and turn there for Ellila, keeping to the roads all the time.'

Though he knew he would get no more sleep until they reached Ellila, at five that afternoon Lance could sleep no longer. Esmeralda had gone from his side but in a few minutes she returned with a mug of unsweetened strong black coffee and a buttermilk rusk. Lance stretched. 'Aaah!' When he finished the coffee and the rusk, he pulled her towards him and started unbuttoning her shirt. It could be the last time they made love – they both knew it – and he could not bear to part from her until nearly seven o'clock. Before leaving the tent to shower, he checked his pistol. 'You and Christine should stay near the trucks and duck under the shelter if a plane flies over,' he said. The women were the most obvious recognition points about his convoy. He searched his mind for something memorable to say, should this be the last time they were to speak in private, but nothing came to mind. He didn't feel particularly heroic and was no keener to die than he had ever been, which was not at all. He blew her a kiss, which she caught out of the air and put in her mouth to fuel her inner smile.

There were two shower-heads rigged and Mpengo showered next to Lance. 'Honest sweat,' Lance said to him.

'The sweat of fear too,' the induna waiting his turn said soberly.

'This too is an honest thing on a man who is truly his father's son,' Lance said.

After a pause for thought, the Swahili nodded agreement.

As Lance dried himself, he said conversationally to Mbwato, who also waited his turn, 'I have always pitied men too stupid to be frightened by honest danger. The cunning courage of lion who must eat is one thing, the clumsy rush of a rhinoceros another.'

'Hau!'

'The rhinoceros charges blindly at any sound, merely to earn a place in the legends of the ancestors. I doubt the ancestors welcome those who try too hard for their approval.' It was a warning that, while he took their courage for granted, he wanted no bravado. Out of the corner of his eye he saw the induna look at each of the men in turn to ensure they grasped the wisdom.

Mbwato pushed a stool with his foot and Lance sat down on it to put on his socks and boots. He changed his tone. 'Have you heard the one about the rich Wabenzi?'

They crowded around, and the two pumping water for the showers from forty-four-gallon drums stopped, the better to hear the joke. This man not only had invincible juju and the wisdom of a six-times elder (most of these Swahili believed in reincarnation and none of the rest would dispute its possibility) but he also told the best Watusi jokes; the Watusi, who are so rich they seem to own every Mercedes in Kenya, meet the same need for psychic release of scorn in Africa as the Poles in America or the Irish in Britain. Lance waited until the water stopped. 'This Wabenzi was so rich, he could satisfy all his heart's desires.' They sighed for such good fortune. Lance waited patiently for silence. There is a ritual to telling the Swahili a story, whether a simple joke or the elaborate vistas of African history his brother used to paint, and breach of the ritual spoils the story for these large-hearted men. The point of the tale is not the punchline, but the manner of the telling and the audience response, formalized as High Mass. 'As many wives as his religion allowed, which I'm sure you know is only one.' Now they laughed at greed unfulfilled. 'So he became a Muslim, and could take four wives, three of them young and beautiful.' They groaned in envy, then grimaced at the duplicity of the Watusi. 'But the Watusi also had greed of another kind.' Lance paused significantly, allowing them half a minute to ponder the permutations. Some of the men seemed to stop breathing altogether. The induna's soap slipped through his fingers and Lance bent to return it to him. 'For food,' Lance said. 'This Wabenzi did not eat to stay alive, he lived to eat.' They

240

exclaimed at this marvel of apt phrasing; they cared naught for originality but their leader was one of the very few white men who could tell a story properly. 'He ate so much, he became of very little use to his three new, young, ardent wives.' Lance nodded at their widening eyes. 'I leave you to imagine the lovers they took, the plots they plotted to run away with them.' Now they were definitely holding their breath. A false trail, though enchanting, had run out and the tale was approaching its climax. 'Of course, this rich Wabenzi wore the finest Western suits rather than suitable local clothing, as a sensible man would.' Their expectant faces gleamed with anticipatory tension: the story was peaking and they were not fooled by his offhand tone. 'Every time he grew fatter still from his unbridled lust for food, he had a dozen new suits cut, with rows of buttons at the cuffs and flies.' Again he gave them time to imagine such sartorial splendour and wonder about the three young, ardent wives. 'In time, he grew so fat he could no longer reach past his belly to tie his shoelaces and he had to hire a piccaninny to do it for him. And still he grew fatter.'

'Like a pumpkin!' The induna could no longer contain the tension.

Lance nodded graciously. 'Like a pumpkin he grew, until his arms could no longer reach past his gross sides to perform even the most private functions and the piccaninny had to do that for him as well.' Here he looked between his laced boots as if in shame for what the Watusi had reduced himself to, while the Swahili shuddered at such indelicacy, even though only to be expected of a Wabenzi. 'Then,' said Lance ominously, 'came that horrible final day.' He paused briefly, looking from tense face to tense face. 'The fat Wabenzi had an urgent need to pass water and went into his water closet, taking the piccaninny along to be his arms and hands. The piccaninny unbuttoned him and held him while he passed water. Then the piccaninny shook the drops. Just then the rich, fat Wabenzi saw, through the little window' – Lance indicated its size with his hands – 'directly in front of him as he stood before the water closet, the lover of one of his new, unsatisfied wives crossing the street. He shouted threats at the man through the window and waved his arms excitedly. The piccaninny ducked and weaved and finally crouched fearfully in a corner so as not to be struck. Finally, the rich, fat Wabenzi calmed down and demanded to be put away and buttoned up. The piccaninny searched and searched in the rolls of fat and wailed, "But master, I can't find it!" and the rich, fat Wabenzi said, "You had better find it. *You had it last.*"' He left them rolling around in glee at the greedy Wabenzi who had disappeared into himself. The retelling of the story to the others would be prefaced by his earlier remarks about discretion under fire.

Lance found Pierre lying on the ridge, binoculars to his eyes. 'Anything useful?'

'There's a hawk hunting,' Pierre said, pointing.

For twenty minutes they watched the hawk soar and swoop until it dived for its kill and flew away with a large rodent in its claws. 'It has a nest with young,' Lance said.

Pierre answered Lance's earlier question. 'We'd better not leave before dark. They know we're here. Planes keep flying over the desert there. Pattern-flying. They're quarter-searching the whole shebang.'

Lance studied the glaring whiteness, rippled only by searing heat and the threat of the planes' sudden return, and felt sorry for the pilots. He listened to the rocks creaking in the sun; small rocks would blister carelessly placed hands or bare feet. But this was an oddly odourless place; Lance imagined Heaven would smell like this – it was not something to look forward to. 'Where's Boo?'

'He drove south along the road in Jimmy's Range Rover.

242

He took Nasheer. If they're stopped, they'll pretend to be mercenaries or Libyan military advisers.'

'Nasheer's shaping up very usefully.'

Pierre nodded. 'You know he and Christine are plotting something?'

'No, they're not. It turns out he's an expert on the slave trade. You want to be relieved here?'

'No thanks, Lance.'

Lance lay beside him and studied the trucks on the road below. After fifteen minutes, he said, 'These Chaddi have lousy security.'

'They don't need any. Who but us would be stupid enough to walk into the lion's den?'

'Boldness be my friend.'

'And saviour, I hope,' Pierre added dryly. 'There comes Boo. We can both go down and Mwanzo can take over here.'

Lance searched through the telescope of his rifle but could not find the Swahili. 'Where is he?'

Pierre pointed. 'Between those two clumps over there.'

Behind them, Mwanzo said, 'Here, Master.'

Pierre shivered. 'Now you know why I don't like sharpshooters,' he told Lance when they were out of earshot of Mwanzo. 'Always creeping up on people. Scouts are a bit like that too. Lot of people feel the same about Boo.'

Lance had felt the same unease about Kombi but said nothing of that; there was no point in speaking ill of the dead. 'I've noticed Mwanzo startles people sometimes but he's been with Esmeralda and me since he was little more than a boy, so we're used to him. And he's rock-solid.'

'I know. I think I've lived in the city too long.'

Lance thought Pierre was merely tired after their strenuous journey: in the forest or on the veld, Pierre was an immensely capable man.

Boo and Nasheer grinned hugely around dewed cans of

beer. Boo crumpled the empty can in one hand while with the other ripping the top from a fresh two-litre tube. When he had downed that as well, he drew a map in the sand with the toe of his foot. 'They've set a block here, at Koro Toro, which is where they reckon we'll cut cross-country to Ellila, and another here at Kizimi where the back road up the Bahr el Ghazal joins the main road to Largeau, presumably just in case we get smart.'

'When?'

'The one at Kizimi twenty minutes ago. We just made it before it closed,' Nasheer said.

Lance looked around his companions. It was triumphantly in their faces: they all thought the same as he did. But, just to be certain, he asked Pierre, 'When did the planes stop searching the desert?'

'About two hours ago.'

'Bingo!' Jimmy said from the flap of his tent. 'We're inside the cordon and they're facing the other way,' he added into the tent for Christine's benefit.

Lance opened a carton of the milky 'native' beer for which he had rather a taste and poured it into a pewter mug. 'Here's to another breathing-space,' he toasted them with it. 'We could be feeding the hungry at Ellila tomorrow this time.'

From the gathering darkness where the kitchen awning was spread, Esmeralda said, 'We *will* be feeding the hungry tomorrow.'

After less than an hour on the road, they were stopped and pulled off to let a very large southbound convoy thunder by. But the military policemen were more interested in catching up with their own convoy than in checking the papers of northbound empties; one of them merely waved Lance and his convoy to the side of the road and stood thirty metres away waving the other convoy south, then, with a gesture of thanks, mounted his motorcycle and roared into the night.

'Phew,' Lance said.

'That is a very dangerous machine to pass trucks on,' Mwanzo offered one of his rare remarks. 'I don't think I would care for motorcycle work.'

Lance astounded, looked into the back of the Range Rover but, as usual, there was no expression on Mwanzo's face except his huge grin which, according to circumstance, could be of enjoyment, deference, defiance or threat. 'What we do is dangerous, Mwanzo.'

'It is what we do, Master.'

To that there was no answer. Lance led the convoy on, towards Largeau.

At midnight, Esmeralda said, 'The map shows a track that cuts across the Bokalia and another from there that connects with the Largeau-Ellila road.' She measured on the map, looked at the trip meter and her watch. 'We're ten minutes from the turn-off.'

Lance considered. The congestion, relative but still almost unbelievable on this African road, was slowing them to between seventy and eighty klicks every hour whereas, on their own, they could easily manage a hundred klicks an hour. On the other hand, all the roads in these parts led to Largeau and none but them would be crossing the desert. Only one aeroplane had to fly over and see their lights . . .

'How long will we be exposed until we turn south for Ellila again?'

Esmeralda measured again. 'Sixty-five, seventy kilometres.'

That could take anything from seventy-five minutes to two hours, depending on the state of the road. But it could cut hours of delay driving into Largeau and out again in what seemed to be a permanent war-induced rush hour.

'That's the turning there,' Esmeralda said.

245

Lance peered ahead and into his mirrors to see who would witness their entry into the desert but for the moment the road was almost miraculously clear. 'Let's do it.'

He swung onto the track. It was not very good but it was better than travelling cross-country and it *was* good enough to cover almost as fast as the congested main road. After ten minutes, when he judged they were out of sight of the main road, he stopped. 'Please cover all but a small slit of the headlamps with Elastoplast,' he said to Esmeralda and then walked down the convoy, telling the drivers to switch off all their lights and follow his tail-lights. There was a good three-quarters moon, so he did not expect any difficulty. Halfway down the line he met Jimmy, coming from the rear of the convoy, giving the same instructions.

'Discretion is definitely the better part of valour,' Jimmy said approvingly.

'You think this less risky than staying on the road to Largeau?'

'Of course. Don't you?'

'Let's call it an honest difference of opinion. Wake Boo as you go by. I want to know what's on the Largeau-Ellila road before I get there.'

'Yes sir!' Jimmy made a smart salute. 'But for myself, I think the only way they'll catch us now is by paradrop.'

'Unless they're setting ambush for us at Ellila,' Lance said quietly.

'Don't even speak of such things!'

'It's what I would do, wait at the one place we *have* to go, rather than search millions of god-forgotten square miles.'

No, Jimmy thought, the Chaddi would not wait at Ellila – they would find it inconceivable that Lance could actually arrive. But there is no way to explain this to Lance Weber, who would in fact arrive at Ellila that very day unless stopped literally dead in his tracks by a vastly superior force and/or a commander luckier than any Jimmy had ever heard of. Boo once told him that the Webers had cornered the market in martial luck and Jimmy believed him; Mbwato had confided that many of the Swahili believed that to touch Lance Weber was to have some of his juju rub off on you. Jimmy was quite certain that, if, against all odds, there were Libyan-backed Chaddi lying in ambush for them at Ellila, their first reaction when Lance arrived would be incredulity.

'Are you all right?' Lance peered at Jimmy through the darkness.

'Sure. I'll wake Boo.'

Driving without proper lights slowed them down more than the condition of the road did and it took two and a quarter hours to reach the Largeau–Ellila road. Boo waited for them just out of sight of it. He wore the uniform of one of Queddei's military policemen.

'He demanded my papers,' Boo said, 'and then he refused to take Diner's and American Express.'

'Did you manage to question him?' Lance asked, still concerned about an ambush at Ellila.

'Sorry. It was too quick. He was drawing his pistol already. Maybe Pierre or your brother could merely have disabled him.'

'You did right, Boo.' Lance clapped him on the shoulder. 'The road's busy then?'

'Very. Too busy for it to be merely a reaction to our presence.'

'Maybe there's big fighting at Abéché as well,' Pierre suggested.

'The more the merrier,' Lance said, 'and the less attention and the fewer men they can spare to deal with us. Let's go. I want to reach Ellila before dawn if possible, right after if not.'

Almost as one man, Jimmy, Pierre and Boo looked a their watches.

247

'About a hundred and fifty kilometres,' Esmeralda said. 'Sunrise in two hours seventeen minutes.'

Robert Bruce Hilder was not quite what his name would suggest; he had been born on a farm in Alsace twenty-nine years ago, could speak German and French like a native – which he was – and English with a midatlantic accent understood by television viewers around the world; his Italian and Greek were adequate to the occasional broadcast. But his main claim to fame was not his easy way with languages – the commentary and questions were very often overdubbed in the voices of men on the payrolls of the networks which bought his freelance footage. No, Robert Bruce Hilder was famous as the one man who would stay in the trouble-spots of the world when even the BBC, always the last of the official mob to go, would pull its correspondents back because it feared for their lives. Robert Bruce Hilder had filmed Pol Pot entering Phnom Penh, had filmed the first Russian tanks rolling into Afghanistan after the Russians had warned they would shoot foreign journalists on sight, had lived on Beirut's Green Line when other reporters cowered in the George Hotel until they could be evacuated to Jerusalem or Nicosia (where they would continue to tape 'on the spot' commentaries to his footage). Robert Bruce Hilder had come to Africa from Beirut especially to cover the last stages of the Matthew Ellimore relief column, simply because the bravura tone of the attempt appealed to him. The networks who bought every foot he could shoot of the Shi'ite Amal attacks on the three Palestinian camps in Beirut shrilled that he was leaving them naked but Robert Bruce Hilder did not care; he was wealthy by dint of a smart agent and the fact that he never spent any money on himself – he continued working for the excitement and, when infrequently he thought of someday running the extensive family estates, shrivelled up inside at the boredom

248

of bourgeois life. He trusted his nose for news: Weber was news in the making, like surf on a rising tide. And the point where Weber had to arrive, if he succeeded, was Ellila, a place naturally difficult and dangerous to reach even in orderly times and now accessible only across two active fronts in a vicious civil war. Robert Bruce Hilder, with the shrewdness bequeathed him by a Scottish great-grandfather, judged the networks would not send their own men to Ellila but *would* sell their grandmothers for footage of the ultimate act of Weber forcing his way through the warlords to feed the hungry. He flew from Beirut to Athens and from there to Khartoum, where he rented a Mercedes G-Wagen against a thousand-dollar deposit in cash and then drove non-stop to Ellila, sleeping in the back among the jerry-cans when his cameraman and lover, the Greek known only a Demi, relieved him at the wheel. They crossed the Sudan/Chad border illegally by driving cross-country around the border post between Karnoi and Iriba, something the employees of the regular news agencies would never in a million years do because it would deprive them of even the minimum protection their consular officials could offer from retaliation by barbarian regimes.

Once at Ellila, Demi parked the G-Wagen in plain sight in the dusty, depressing town square and they took turns sleeping on the lilo in the back, waiting, waiting, waiting. At twenty-nine, Robert Bruce Hilder was at the top of a profession where all his competitors were dead or retired because he waited better than anyone else, and always in the right place. To him, as to Qaddaffi, it was inevitable that a man like Weber *would* arrive; it was in Robert Bruce Hilder's stars to film a man with grand dreams. It did not matter to him that Lance Weber's grand dream was feeding the starving. The starving were grist to his camera; he had not been born unfeeling, but he had seen so much suffering that he had himself become a moral vegetable. There was no other way to continue functioning. Always his lovers were his cameramen and none had ever left him; four in nine years had died violently while filming beside him. An officer came to their vehicle in the square and said that, if they wanted to film the starving in the camp, they could do so only under his supervision. Robert Bruce Hilder had already pointed out to Demi the significance of the two camps, one large and sprawling, one small and neat and separated from the other by barbed wire. The barbed wire was to keep those outside from getting in. Those inside were better fed, received some medical treatment, and there were only a few small bodies at the gate every morning whereas in the sprawling misery outside the barbed wire morning and evening there were huge heaps of new bodies. Yes, the Russians had filmed their good work in the 'official' refugee camp, the officer said. But Robert Bruce Hilder did not waste videotape on either camp, as he had shot no footage of the dying he passed in Sudan; starving children were no longer news. That African governments allowed people to starve for political reasons was not news either. That Lance Weber was doing something to change the situation was most definitely news. If Weber did not arrive, there would be no news but they would then proceed to the place where Weber and his convoy met their end and film the corpses; that too would be news. Either way, the trip would not be wasted. He and Demi did not talk as they waited: they were in each other's company twenty-four hours a day, seven days a week, and had long since said all they wanted to say to each other; idle chat could only irritate.

In the dawn, Demi shook Robert Bruce Hilder awake and pointed, waited for him to rub the sleep from his eyes, then handed him a camera with the light already glowing to show it was switched on. Robert Bruce Hilder did not even look in the direction Demi pointed until he had the rubber cup to his eye and his finger on the zoom button (in his kind of work, there was no time to change lenses and each camera had only the single 35-210mm wide-angle to tele-zoomlens). He saw a black man wearing the white armband of a military policeman, riding a motorcycle. He tilted the camera to the face of the gorgeous corn-fed corn-coloured hunk of giant muscle driving the leading Range Rover, panned to the statuesque woman glowing olive even in this light in the front passenger seat. He spoke into the microphone attached to the camera, laying his notes directly on the track in English, the lingua franca of journalism as of aviation. Later, if there was time before the tapes were dispatched, he would edit up his notes, if not, not. The main thing was the pictures, each frame telling its ten thousand words.

When Jimmy's Range Rover, at the rear of the convoy, passed, Robert Bruce Hilder jumped for the G-Wagen and was still closing his door when Demi spun the vehicle in its own length, connecting the rear quarters to something solid. They hardly noticed – there were other rental agencies if this one refused their custom next time round. Demi had his hands full passing the trucks, the last one still clearing the village.

'These mothers sure are moving,' Demi said in his careful but not quite successful copy of his employer's accent. They always spoke English together.

Robert Bruce Hilder did not look up from his work – fresh cassettes and batteries for both cameras – as he said, 'The black on the motorbike, he's one of the Baluba Butchers, not an official escort. For a moment I thought we came all this way for nothing – watch that donga! – that Weber'd made a deal and got an official escort. I want to be there when they arrive at the camp.'

'Flat out,' Demi replied. Visibility in the dust storm thrown up by the trucks was nil but he did not lift his foot and

251

suddenly they emerged from the duststorm next to the leading Range Rover and looking into Mwanzo's smiling face and his rifle barrel. But Robert Bruce Hilder had been here before and promptly held the camera sideways and in plain view in the window. He waited until the black man pulled the rifle back before turning the lens towards him and starting filming.

'How the hell does a journalist arrive here before us?' Lance asked.

Esmeralda misunderstood him. 'They were in the square of the village, darling.'

'Yes, I saw, but how did they get to Ellila?'

'Their car has Sudanese plates,' Nasheer said. 'That border is impossible to patrol perfectly.'

'Oh my god,' Esmeralda said as they drove onto the little rise, too low to be dignified even as a hillock but high enough to offer them a comprehensive view of the ramshackle accommodation spreading in three directions as far as the eye could see. The squalor, even in that uncertain breaking light, spoke of human misery greater than anything they had ever imagined possible. The piles of bodies were superfluous to the impact of that camp, mere punctuation marks to the horror of it. 'All our grain will feed these people only for a few days.'

Lance admired Esmeralda, who looked shocked and strained, for speaking of practicalities rather than abstractions they were powerless to change. He would do the same. There were in any event no words adequate to his rage. 'And our medicines won't last any longer,' he said in as level a voice as he could manage, adding, grateful for the distraction, 'I hope those idiot journalists don't get in the way.' He watched the G-Wagen sweep to a sliding halt at one side of two prefab buildings set at right-angles to each other. Two men jumped out, panned their cameras over the camp and the buildings to the approaching convoy and held it. The cameras pointing at him made Lance feel uneasy, quite as if they were rifles. But the journalists, he realized with surprise, were marking his target for him.

There were two guards in a tower, staring open-mouthed at the convoy, their rifles not visible, perhaps standing in a corner of their box. 'Mark the guards in the tower, Mwanzo, Nasheer.'

Lance stopped the Range Rover in the V of the building, climbed out with his rifle and circled his left hand in the air, instructing the drivers to encircle the building. The guards at last went for their rifles and Mwanzo and Nasheer fired two shots each. Both corpses fell out of the box and even from forty feet away Lance could see they were an old man and a boy who had not long had his first shave.

'They're not likely to detach crack troops to guard duty in the middle of a war,' Pierre said behind Lance. 'In a way, that's a pity. Experience tells a surrounded man to surrender. But the unblooded foolishly fight the odds.'

Lance nodded. He studied the Swahili, two groups of twelve, behind Pierre, and gestured at the left-hand group. He checked that Esmeralda was behind a truck and Mwanzo with her, then took several long paces to stand against the wall beside the single door in one wing of the building and waited for the Swahili, faces gleaming in anticipation of action, to line up on either side. Nasheer was first in line on the other side of the door. 'Kick it in, then stand clear. When I say.' He glanced at Pierre, before the door in the centre of the other building. Pierre nodded, he was ready. 'Now,' Lance said conversationally. Nasheer put his hand on the knob, turned it quickly and kicked the door open. Lance dived through the door and rolled, making space for the others to enter. Nasheer rolled upright beside him and Lance swung around so that they were back to back. His rifle pointed at the smooth face of another boy in his bunk, smiling

253

in erotic fancy in his dawn dream. Other men woke fuzzily. Their rifles were racked at each end of the barracks. Like the guards in the tower, they were unfit for front-line duty. They stared blearily, fearfully, at the Swahili entering in a disciplined rush, rifles pointing like porcupine spikes. A boy took one look and pulled his sheet over his head. An old man shook his head sadly. None attempted resistance.

Lance wondered if the Holocaust was like this, hundreds of thousands of Jews packed in to die by a few superannuated soldiers and weaklings weeded out even from conscript gunfodder . . . He put the thought from him: his not to judge but to help as much as he could.

The induna spat. The victory for which the Swahili had travelled so far was unimpressively easy: there would be no legends made here this day to be passed to grandchildren for all eternity.

Lance rose, and Nasheer and the Swahili with him. The rear wall, facing the camp, was blank, windowless, whitewashed; Lance wondered what had happened to the pin-ups or if they didn't have them in Muslim armies. Jimmy and Boo and more Swahili, round the back, were guarding nothing.

From next door they heard a single shot.

'Take over, Nasheer,' Lance said and strode out. He smiled at the rifles peeking over and under trucks at him and shook his head. He stopped beside the door into the other wing of the building. 'Anybody home?'

A smiling black face appeared around the doorjamb.

'Mpengo.'

'One cook him stupid. His Highness chop him once.'

Inside there was a mess hall, a kitchen, two small company offices with glass walls and a passage between them. The foolish cook lay in a puddle of his own blood on the floor; in the doorjamb quivered a meatcleaver of heroic proportions which, if it had struck flesh and bone rather than wood, would have split a man in half.

A plump naked man, his cupped hands covering his genitals, and a black woman, also naked but strutting her breasts defiantly in front of her skinny ribs, walked through the passage into the mess hall. Behind them, prodding the captives with their rifles, came Pierre and Mwendli.

'Guess what the commandant was doing instead of defending his camp,' Pierre said.

'Get them clothes,' Lance told Mwendli. He glanced at the meatcleaver in the doorjamb. 'Close call?'

Pierre shook his head. 'I was three metres away and he died for his stupidity before it struck. But it curdled my stomach. This is most definitely my last adventure.'

Lance nodded. When it was time to let go, it was time. Pierre would not see forty again and had earned the good life before him many times over. 'Lock them all up in the barracks after removing their arms.' One did not tell a man like Pierre, even right after a close call, to post guards.

He was almost at the door before they heard the clatter.

A fraction of a second later Lance and Pierre were ten feet apart and on their knees to offer smaller targets, their rifle barrels searching for the threat beyond the glass walls of the two small offices.

Lance nodded at the left-hand office. It was the only possibility. In the other one there was nowhere to hide, in the left-hand one the modesty panel on the desk reached the floor.

Lance rose, opened the door and stepped in. He held his rifle to one side of his body, then poked the business end over the desk; if whoever hid behind the desk was inclined to fight such impossible odds, if he was a fanatic, he would be firing at the wrong place. But two palms, forward-facing and empty if slightly grubby, appeared over the edge of the desk

255

and then the tear-streaked face of a young man with an unbuttoned uniform blouse which sported no battle ribbons on the breast but instead on each shoulder the lightning flashes of a communications technician. Behind the desk on the floor stood a mobile radio pack. Whoever was jabbering on the other side reached here as a metallic clatter because of the poor quality of the loudspeaker. Lance flicked the power off and escorted the victor of the battle of Ellila into the mess hall at gunpoint.

'This stripling beat us?' Pierre asked.

The hero of the day burst into audible sobs.

Lance nodded. 'And was betrayed by some ass of a staff officer bleating loudly for clarification. We have three hours to feed the starving and save our own lives before the Army descends on us.'

Boo glanced at the tears streaming unchecked down Lance's face, then away towards the almost regimented lines of knobbly, vacant-faced people shuffling with their makeshift containers towards where the heaps of grain had been tilted onto large tarpaulins.

'I would not stand in line,' Boo said. 'I would fight like a tiger for food for myself and my children.'

Lance nodded. He had thought the same and been ashamed of it. The difference between him and Boo was that Boo was not ashamed of the impulse; that did not necessarily make Boo a lesser man, only a different one. Lance suspected that, put to the test, he would have fought next to Boo – or against him – for the food. He had worried that the grain would be trampled into the ground before it could feed anyone, but these people were in the last apathetic stages of starvation: they lacked the energy to hurry to salvation. Even in the line before the food men and women and children would stagger and fall or sit down for a moment not to rise again, to be carried away to the heaps of dead by the Swahili.

Boo looked at the child Lance held on his arm. It stared listlessly at him.

Lance said, 'He's blind from Vitamin A deficiency. And he is in the last stage, where the body rejects even intravenous nutrition. The doctor says he'll die before the day is out.'

Boo leaned forward to sniff at the child's mouth. There was still a whiff of acetone and then it was gone on the air as Lance shifted his weight. 'It's dead, Lance.' His friend seemed not to understand and Boo took the wasted body of the child from him. 'Mpengo. Put this one with the dead.'

Beside the doctors, the stack of medicines that had filled two trucks had dwindled to half its original size in only two hours. Two truckloads of special nutrition for those who could no longer eat whole food were completely gone. Nearly four hundred tons of grain was dwindling fast and would feed the multitude for less than a fortnight. One of the doctors had told Lance the day before yesterday, 'Very few people actually die of starvation itself. It is not impossible under controlled conditions such as someone on a hunger strike under medical supervision, but in a famine people die of diseases that otherwise their bodies would shrug off with negligent ease. Pneumonia and diarrhoea are common. Those are the lucky ones . . . Byproducts of malnutrition like scurvy, pellagra and beri-beri actually turn into mass killers. I wake up in the night shivering at the thought of an influenza epidemic killing tens of millions of people too weak from hunger to resist the virus. If they can't be buried, plague follows and then . . .' But the doctor had let his sentence trail off and Lance questioned him no further: some horrors are better not expressed; there were no words to describe the actuality of the camp at Ellila. The two doctors applied

257

ruthless triage, saving their drugs and medicines for those who stood a chance, turning those who could not benefit away to die.

The induna walked towards them, several dead adders over his knobkerrie. 'The snakes kill many people every day,' he said to Lance, letting the adders slide to the ground. 'Bwana, the men enquire respectfully when you will kill the guards you have locked up.'

Lance pulled himself together sharply. This was the thin edge of a mutiny. 'I shall not punish them. When we leave here, we will take their weapons with us and give the key to the door to these people.'

The induna looked at the ground, then looked Lance straight in the eye, a rare thing to do, a challenge if not outright insolence.

'Bwana, we Swahili think these people have been abused too much. They are too weak, the guards too well fed.'

Lance sighed. 'Induna, we cannot stay to protect the hungry ones. If there is a massacre of the soldiers here, on whom do you think the government will pay retribution when they arrive in at most a few hours from now? We came to feed the hungry, not make their lot worse.'

Boo said, 'The Swahili are not just upset because they missed out on the fight they were spoiling for, they're genuinely angry at what has been done here.'

'I understand the anger of our men, Wise Elder,' Lance said. 'Tell them that. But tell them also that I command here and any man who discounts my anger when I am moved will surely by tonight have a wailing wife and orphaned children.'

The induna nodded at this terrible threat. 'Bwana, I shall not tell them that the hungry men will not avenge themselves on their keepers after we have gone.'

'Your tact and wisdom surpasses all.'

A woman approached them. She carried a baby at her hip, the thin trail from its bottom staining her leg. Despite this unbalancing force, she walked proudly upright, the small black cast-iron pot sitting still and unassisted on her head. Before Lance she kneeled.

'Thank you, Lord,' she said thickly.

Lance bent to help her up but she took his hand and kissed it. Lance was beyond embarrassment, deeply touched.

'What is your name?' she asked.

'Lance Weber.'

'You are the Lance of God,' she said and kissed his hand again.

Lance gently disengaged his hand and put it under her elbow to help her up. 'It is strange to hear English spoken in Chad.'

'We are from Sudan, sir.' She gestured slightly and Lance saw her husband and daughter standing to one side. He nodded a greeting. 'We will return there now you have freed us. We thank you.'

'What about the baby?'

'They all look like that. This one is healthier than most. It will survive. The other four are dead,' she added sadly.

Expressing his sorrow would not help. 'We lost our only child before we came here.' Lance gestured at Esmeralda, who was trying to feed a child too famished to salivate or swallow.

'God will reward you with more.'

'Wait near here,' Lance said to her. 'Perhaps I can provide transport. Can your husband drive a truck?'

'Yes sir.'

As she turned away, Lance saw her glance out of the corner of her eye at the dead adders.

He picked them up by their tails. 'Snakes are protein,' he said and held them out to the daughter, who ran forwards to take them with a sort of curtsey and then walked away backwards, her eyes never leaving Lance for a second.

'There is a legend of a good blond god in the making here,' Jimmy said beside Lance but he wasn't smiling. He had investigated the barbed-wire compound after letting out the people kept in it. 'They didn't want to leave. The Chaddi storehouse is right in the middle, unguarded but padlocked. I wasted a bullet shooting the padlock off. The shelf's bare.'

'What about our back?'

'Pierre has twenty Swahili all set to repel boarders but so far no one's shown any interest. Everything that moves just whizzes straight through and south. That's a smart plan, heading into Sudan. There's no shorter way out of Chad.'

'We're not,' Lance said. 'I'm sending most of the trucks into Sudan with as many of these people as they can carry. They'll never be able to walk home to sow in June for a harvest in November.'

'If the rains come.'

'Rain must fall again. Why not this year?'

'I hope so. What about us?'

'We're going to Largeau to free Tanner.'

'Just like that?'

'You're leading those who don't volunteer for Largeau into Sudan.'

'We'll see about that. How do you know Tanner is in Largeau?'

'That journalist told me. His name's Robert Bruce Hilder, full out like that. He says Tanner's arrival in Largeau and incarceration in the only maximum security prison there was television news a few days ago.'

'If the Chaddi treat refugees like this, how do you think Tanner's faring at their hands?'

'Exactly.'

'Tanner would come if it were me in choky.'

'Apparently they had him up before a drumhead court martial and condemned him to death. But they won't shoot him until tomorrow at dawn. Talk to the journalist, see what else you can learn about this place where they keep Tanner.'

'Pierre says it's about time to make tracks before the commando aces drop on us out of the sky.'

'They're probably too fully stretched fighting their civil war to bother about us.'

'Pierre also said that, no matter how widespread the war, even incompetent commanders always hold some shock troops in reserve for little surprises. I don't fancy fighting elite regular soldiers.'

'Me neither.'

Jimmy turned to the queues of human wrecks. His mouth twisted. 'All we brought them was a few weeks more of life. Somehow I don't feel we deserve their gratitude.'

'We've shown others the way,' Lance said. He nodded towards the journalists, busy with their cameras among the succoured famished. 'Their film is proof that it is possible. And we'll be back.'

But when it was time to leave, it was not so easy. The two doctors said mildly they were staying. Lance was not surprised: medicine was not food, deliver and run. His work was finished, theirs had hardly begun. Christine wanted to stay with them and would listen to no reason. In the end Jimmy had two Swahili pick her up and cart her bodily to his Range Rover. Lance sat next to her and waited until the torrent of recrimination and abuse ran down. Finally, when there were only racking sobs of pain and frustration, he said quietly, 'You're not Florence Nightingale. Your talent is awakening the conscience of the masses and raising millions to pay for more trucks and food.'

She did not reply but at least she was quiet, wiping at her eyes with the handkerchief he offered her.

'I'm sending most of our trucks into Sudan with as many of these people as want to go. Do you understand?'

'As a decoy while we escape?'

'You'll be travelling with them.' Even Christine would not think he'd maliciously send her into danger.

'And where will you go?'

'To Largeau to free Tanner.'

'I've always known you were quite mad, but this is certifiable.'

Lance smiled at her distinction. 'Sanatoria with hinged corners,' he said.

'What?'

'Occasionally we turn the walls around on their hinges and then the inmates become the citizens and the citizens the inmates. We can discuss the sanity of what you and I have done some other time. Right now I want you to get out of here and raise enough money to buy several hundred trucks and have them airlifted into any West African port that can take large bulk carriers. Then buy enough Argentinian grain to – '

'But you told poor Ollie Exton it is impossible to – '

'For him. Will you do it? Here you can ease the dying, there you can save lives. Which would you rather do?'

'Will you at least shoot the vultures before we go?' she asked inconsequentially, gesturing at the ponderous, repellent birds tearing at the sparse flesh of the dead, crunching the bones of children in their beaks to reach the marrow.

'No. They are part of Nature's balance. Sky burial. Without them, there will certainly be a plague here. About the trucks and the grain . . .?'

Christine nodded. Lance kissed her forehead and slipped out of the Range Rover. He could almost feel that planeload of commandos approaching . . . Pierre stood waiting for him.

'What's this about me leading the lame and the hungry to Sudan while you go to Largeau?' Pierre demanded.

Lance explained.

Pierre shook his head. 'You are talking about close-quarters fighting. Don't insult me.'

'But only this morning you said – '

'I like Tanner. It will be a glorious exit.'

'Then Jimmy has to lead the convoy to Sudan. As the older brother, you'd better explain to him.'

But Pierre had a better solution. 'Send Nasheer. He's done his part of the job.'

Lance told Nasheer he trusted him to defend Christine and Esmeralda with his life; Nasheer, who was as disappointed as the Swahili at the easy conquest of the camp soldiers, was not happy, but he was a disciplined young man and did not argue long. And it was the biggest command he had ever held.

All the Swahili volunteered for Largeau but Lance selected twelve by name and charged the rest with responsibility for his wife.

Rather than having to fight off applicants so as not to overload the trucks, Lance found that the famished were indifferent to the point of apathy about leaving this terrible place. Perhaps it was their fear that somewhere else might be worse but Lance could not imagine how. When the rains came (and Lance was convinced that this year they would come) and filled all the depressions dug to shelter fires from the cutting wind, this whole camp would turn into one very large diseased mudhole. He wanted to jerk them into life, into fighting for themselves, even as he realized his reaction was unfair. Christine spoke to the woman who had blessed Lance – neither of them knowing they had once before come within hours of meeting each other at a wrecked relief plane lying an hour from here in the desert – and the woman persuaded her husband to make a brief, urgent speech to the other refugees, after which he lifted her and the children into a truck to demonstrate his faith in a better future. The trucks filled slowly.

Esmeralda held tightly onto Lance. 'Come back to me, darling,' she said.

Lance helped her up into the truck, handed up a child who could still be saved by intravenous feeding in Sudan, and waved as the convoy rolled out of the camp and turned southwards. He shook hands with the two doctors. 'Are you sure you'll be all right?'

'I've survived camps like this before,' the Indonesian replied. 'The second time is easier.'

'You have my pharmaceuticals list?' the Mauritian asked.

'Miss Rawls has it.'

'Good. We won't tell them you went north.'

'Tell them anything they ask. There's no point in being beaten for it.'

The doctor nodded soberly. 'We must have food – six hundred grammes of wheat per person per day minimum – and medicine. It's not just the starvation, it's all the diseases that attend any mass migration.' He turned away to his charges. Neither he nor the Indonesian spared a single regretful glance for the convoy streaking south to freedom.

Lance stood for a moment looking southward at the dust plume that carried Esmeralda away from him. He wished he had thought to tell her he loved her, but they were words he always had difficulty uttering. She knew. He hoped she knew. He looked up to the distant but building drone of a heavy aeroplane, climbed into the Range Rover, put her in gear, let in the clutch and led his much-diminished convoy – two Range Rovers, a dropside truck with an awning and a single tanker – towards Largeau. On the main road they cut into the middle of a passing convoy racing north with wounded. Minutes later the transport flew over the horizon, circled over the camp, and decanted its string of human-stemmed blossoms.

Lance thought, Under the bell, as Esmeralda once said.

Major Ali had made nineteen jumps – five in training for his parachute rating, two ejections from accident-prone MiG-21s, a round dozen with the Libyan Air Force's jump club – and simply joined the queue of Libyan-trained Chaddi commandos to collect a parachute for himself. The strike commander glanced at Ali's badges and decided not to argue against an outsider jumping with his closeknit group, not with two staff colonels fawning on a mere major; this was a political rather than a martial matter and the way to survive was, as always, to execute his orders exactly. Once the aircraft was airborne, he shouted in Ali's ear, 'I jump with the first squad, my lieutenant with the second, then you come with the third. Understand?'

Ali understood perfectly: the commando captain didn't want his charge killed. He nodded. 'I won't get in the way.' Then he sat, as relaxed as possible in the cumbersome paragear, for the rest of the thirty-five minutes flying time from Largeau to Ellila. He'd had great difficulty persuading the Chaddi that the one place, *the only place* they could be certain of catching Weber and the Rawls woman was Ellila itself; the Chaddi simply would not believe the Weber convoy could make it. But now Weber was doomed: if he was not caught in the heavy dragnet the Chaddi had spread all the way up the Bahr al Ghazal, if he did not lose himself and die of thirst on the desert-crossing, they would be waiting for him at Ellila, the end of the line. Weber and his Belgian Congolese lieutenants were not quite a handful and even such men could not train a bunch of Swahili peasants to match elite commandos man for man. There were sixty-three men, plus the two officers, plus himself as an observer but he too could fight – Weber would be arming his kitchen staff before he disposed of sixty-six men. In a way, Ali looked forward to Weber trying to wiggle out of such a trap . . .

There was a bit of shuffling as men changed places next to him. The sergeant who now sat next to him tapped his watch and held up five fingers. Ali nodded. The man tapped his sergeant's chevrons and then Ali's chest. Ali smiled at him and nodded his head again. This was the sergeant of his squad. The man, perhaps thirty years old – in the commandos a grizzled veteran – pointed to other men and shouted the name of each in Ali's ear. Ali nodded to each man separately.

The red light over the door flashed on. The jumpmaster swung the door open. The captain of commandos pushed his men out hard on each other's heels, jumping himself in the middle of the string. The plane turned sharply and the lieutenant tapped the first of his men on the shoulder; he too jumped in the middle of his string. Beyond the jumpmaster's legs, Ali could see the road north through the hatch: two white Range Rovers, a truck and a fuel tanker, all with big red crosses on their roofs, had just swung into the middle of a northbound convoy. Weber's vehicles. He scrambled for the door and stared down at the camp. From eight hundred feet he could clearly see the orderly queues of refugees before the heaps of grain and before the tables of the doctors. The jumpmaster grabbed at his belt. Ali took his hand away gently. He shouted in the ear of the sergeant of 'his' squad, who stood behind him and looked perplexed, 'Don't jump! The people we were ambushing have come and gone. I'm going to speak to the pilot.'

He walked up the centre of the aircraft, staggering as the plane turned once more. He pushed open the door and entered the cockpit. The pilot took his earphones off and turned enquiringly in his seat. Ali bent to speak close to his ear. 'They got away.' He pointed through the windshield. 'The ones with the red crosses, that's a decoy Weber's sending north.'

'They could be our own ambulances,' the pilot argued.

'You haven't any Range Rover ambulances. And none of your fuel tankers have red crosses on top.'

'Uh-huh.'

'Then head south.'

'My orders are to make a drop here and return to Largeau.'

Nothing Ali said could persuade the pilot to fly south. Finally Ali asked to speak to Largeau and, after ten minutes more, instructions came for the pilot to take his orders from Ali, who told him to fly south along the road to Abéché. Weber, he thought, either had a very simple, straightforward mind despite all the contrary evidence, or he was in one hell of a hurry because he knew shock troops were hard on his heels – otherwise he would surely have taken more imaginative evasive action than sending three vehicles north as a decoy and then heading straight south with the rest. When they found the convoy, he knew why Weber needed all the trucks on his escape southwards: each of the grain skips was full of refugees. It was obvious Weber was taking as many as he could with him into the Sudan.

Nasheer, driving the lead truck himself with Esmeralda and Christine up front with him, tending to the dying child, and Mwanzo sitting on the back among the refugees returning home, saw in his mirror the plane circling high above the camp, the parachutes opening. He watched intently but saw no vehicles falling. But they could commandeer vehicles on the road if – when they found out the convoy had been and gone. The plane kept circling and Nasheer wondered if it was serving as a communications relay for the troops on the ground.

'They're dropping parachute-soldiers on the camp,' he told the women.

'I hope the doctors are all right,' Esmeralda said.

'They wouldn't dare harm them,' Christine said. 'Doctors are generally safer than anyone else, even in the most barbarian of states.'

'They still have the plane there,' Nasheer said. 'When they find out we've gone, it'll come along this road looking for us. It's our only escape route.'

Esmeralda shifted the comatose child on her lap. 'What do you intend doing, Nasheer? We can't fight while we have all these refugees with us.'

Privately, Nasheer would not be overly concerned if a few of the refugees died: after all, several of the Swahili had died or been seriously wounded while bringing the refugees succour and rescue from the Chaddi murderers, and all the rest of the convoy, including the women, had run the same risk – the least the refugees could offer was an equal willingness to sacrifice. 'The Oum Hawach is a valley of sand, the dry bed of a large long-gone river. Good going. It runs almost directly east. It peters out only a hundred and fifty klicks from the Sudanese border.'

'Cross-country?' Christine asked.

'Yes,' Nasheer admitted.

'You're not Lance Weber, Nasheer, and I don't think those refugees will be much help in the desert,' Christine said.

'I'm a quick study,' Nasheer replied cheerfully, though inside he was deeply afraid. But as a man he could not show fear before women, and as expedition leader it would be unwise to make them privy to his doubts. 'Mrs Weber?'

Esmeralda shook her head. 'A plane flying down the road will spot us immediately. Nobody else carries people in grain skips.' She hoped Nasheer was indeed a quick study: it was always easy travelling anywhere with Lance because he

268

prepared so meticulously and was so *certain* in everything he did. It had never, with Lance, occurred to her that she might die in a desert . . . 'They won't have to send a plane along the road, they could just alert the military police patrols. The desert is our only chance, as Nasheer says.'

Less than ten minutes later, Nasheer pointed to a gash in the earth across the road before them. 'That must be it.'

'It looks like a crossroads,' Christine said.

Nasheer put the indicators on, then stopped beside the road, jumped out quickly to stand behind the truck and point east and wave the trucks by into the Oum Hawach. He tried not to breathe in the dust storm that enveloped him but the job had to be done, someone had to count all the trucks in because it would be a disaster to lose one: Christine would probably want to come back and hunt for it! But the Swahili were all there, and the Zulu kitchen servants impressed as drivers to replace the Swahili Lance had taken to Largeau with him, thundering off the road with hardly a break in speed.

When the worst dust cleared, Nasheer looked into the muzzle of a machine pistol. He glanced at each of his empty hands and knew that he was not Lance Weber and would never be as good. In the same instant as it occurred to him to roll away into the shelter of the dust, the rest of the dust cleared as if blown away in a giant's puff and Nasheer saw the twenty-two men surrounding the truck. He threw his head back to look at the sun, as if for inspiration. It was not yet ten in the morning and, as days here went, relatively cool. He heard the desert singing and did not fear dying half as much as the shame of having failed Lance Weber so shortly after being entrusted with his wife.

A sergeant reached up and opened the truck door. He smiled up at Esmeralda and helped her down: Esmeralda brought the child with her. There was dead silence. Christine climbed down from the truck.

The sergeant, smiling, took the child from Esmeralda, looked down into its face, and reversed his hold to take it by the ankles. Swinging overarm, he crushed its head against the hub of the wheel.

Esmeralda was taken by surprise at this unexpected turn to the extent that she took a step backwards, away from the horror, rather than forwards to attempt saving the child. The head squashing against the wheel made a grisly sound; the child died without a cry. Still the sergeant smiled.

Beside Esmeralda, Christine stared big-eyed at the smiling sergeant as he raised his arm to bash the child's shattered head once more against the hub of the wheel. She was in a particularly nasty dream. She could not believe her eyes. She unbuttoned her holster, took out her pistol, thumbed the safety as she raised it, and shot the sergeant in the chest from three feet away. The pistol, at the full reach of her arm, was less than twelve inches from his chest. She could not miss.

The sergeant dropped the child's body – Esmeralda caught it before it touched ground but no one noticed, all eyes being on Christine and the sergeant – and clutched at his chest. He stared beseechingly at Christine. He no longer smiled.

Christine saw a plea in his eyes, *Why do you do this to me?* She saw blood oozing through his fingers, faster, faster, a driblet, then a continuous stream. She had never killed anyone in her life and never expected to; now she felt empty, detached. It was as Lance said: some people are bad and have to be killed – and someone must do the dirty work. This man had just murdered a defenceless child and then grinned broadly about it. Christine remembered something else: Lance telling Nasheer to use two shots, always two shots. Quite calmly, to make absolutely certain the thug died in retribution for murdering the child, she checked that her pistol was still aimed at his chest, and shot him once more in the heart.

Then the moment of stillness ended and all hell broke loose. From among the refugees frozen with fear on the back of the truck, Christine's two guardian Swahili rose shoulder to shoulder and shooting, while six feet away Mwanzo appeared, also firing. Christine stood rigid with shock at what she had done until Esmeralda carried her bodily to the earth and rolled under the truck's front axle with her. Nasheer seemed to have been hit but he was only bending over to grasp at his calf; when he rose, he kept rising until his hand touched the lower ribs of the commando into whose heart he drove his long thin knife. He pulled the knife free even as the man sagged to the ground; with his other hand he took the machine pistol from the commando's lifeless hands. Major Ali hit Nasheer at the joint of head and neck with the side of his hand, a blow that can kill or stun to choice if delivered by an expert. Major Ali was no expert but he was in a hurry to dive into the dust before he was shot by his own men. A refugee, trying to run to freedom, was cut down in the crossfire and fell across his head. Though the body smelt sour and dripped digestive fluids and blood onto his uniform, Major Ali made no attempt to move it except very slightly so that he could breathe. Under the truck, as he fell, he had seen the women reach shelter; there was an even chance the Arab would survive the blow; when this engagement was over, and there was only one way it could end, he would have transport to chase Weber with. If that was how even Weber's women reacted when faced with overwhelming force, no wonder the man had a reputation for invincibility. But, Major Ali thought, a certain Major Bashir Ali would this very day wreck that record; Weber could not but surrender once his wife and the Rawls woman, his employer, were captured.

The firing stopped. After a while, hearing single shots,

Major Ali flung the corpse from him and rose. His men were administering the coup de grâce to wounded refugees. Ali estimated there were thirty dead and wounded refugees. Perhaps ten were running away across the desert. Then Ali counted his own men and a ripple of pure terror climbed vertebra by vertebra down his spine. *There were only eight of them left standing.* He picked up the machine pistol from near Nasheer's hand and walked to where Esmeralda and Christine were crawling out from under the truck.

'Your pistols please, ladies. Take them out with two fingers and throw them well clear. Believe me, I *will* shoot you.' The bloody Rawls woman had, incredibly, holstered her pistol again and buttoned the flap! Nobody in the pilots' mess would believe any of what had happened here today.

'Of course,' Esmeralda said. She took her pistol out between thumb and forefinger and flung it from her. Christine just stared at Ali. 'She's in shock.'

'You do it then. Don't be foolish.' He felt diminished as a man for fearing this woman; it was as if he dreaded Weber by proxy. In all his life he had feared only Qaddaffi and no women.

Esmeralda took out Christine's pistol and threw it away. Then she turned smartly, ignoring Ali's machine pistol, and fetched the medical pack from the truck; Nasheer's FN was racked there but she did not touch it. She stepped over the body of the child with its crushed head, and over the body of his murderer. Christine's two Swahili were plainly dead, riddled with bullets: together they made too big a target. Mwanzo lay half over the tailboard of the truck. For a moment she thought the rictus of death was on his face but he was smiling at her though, from the sweat beading his face, she knew he was in great pain. One of the remaining commandos cocked his weapon and pointed it at Mwanzo's head. Esmeralda, without speaking, jabbed the disposable

272

syringe in her hand into the man's neck as deep as it would go. The man screamed and dropped his weapon to clutch at his neck. The truck's cab rang as the bullet entered it. Esmeralda calmly studied the strained faces over the circle of rifles pointing at her, then bent to give Mwanzo a shot of morphine. His right arm showed splinters of bone through the flesh, his left hand had the middle finger shot off between the knuckles, there was a flesh-wound high up on his left thigh, and his scalp was creased just above his right ear. Considering the firestorm he had been in, he was lucky to be alive at all. All round him refugees lay dead; in their panic, rising to escape, they had provided a shield for him.

Esmeralda looked up to find Ali staring at her. 'This one is my personal servant. Your man was murdering him.'

The man still clutching his neck bent to pick up his rifle and cocked it and pointed it at her. Ali put his hand on the barrel and forced it down. He jerked his hand away: the barrel was hot. 'Please, Madame. These men are in shock from the loss of so many comrades. Don't do anything to endanger your own life.'

Esmeralda saw that Ali was right: they were shaken, their faces as strained as Christine's – as she supposed her own was. They had finished killing the last of the wounded refugees and every rifle was pointed at her with a finger curled around the trigger. But there was a stillness in her . . . She nodded to Ali, then turned her back on them and again bent to Mwanzo.

'She's a witch. We should kill her before she puts a curse on us,' a man said behind Ali.

He turned to face the man. 'They're wanted in Largeau,' he said. 'If they don't arrive, we will all be executed. Is the radio operator alive?'

He was not and the radio was shot up. Ali yearned after the dustplume settling in the desert. But with one truck and

273

eight men, to take on Lance Weber and sixty of the Swahili whose mettle he had experienced at such uncomfortably close quarters – that would be suicide. But there was no need to fight. He would drive back to Ellila, use the radio facilities there to send a light plane to drop a message to the convoy, to Weber: We have your wife and employer and if you don't surrender, you can imagine what will happen to them.

But, at Ellila, he found the camp radio smashed by Weber, and the commandos too without long-range communications: theirs had been with the third squad and destroyed in his care. When they stopped a convoy on the road and used its radio, he was told to bring his prisoners to Largeau.

'And for Allah's sake, don't let the men rape the women,' the staff officer said. 'That didn't do us any good in the foreign press the last time.'

Major Ali was mortally offended by this slight on his leadership and honour. And he wondered, for the first time, why the hell Qaddaffi was supporting an army whose staff officers did not know that conscript scum would rape female prisoners almost routinely but elite regular troops almost never. Almost.

'I don't want to arrive in Largeau at three o'clock in the afternoon,' Lance told Pierre, in the leading Range Rover with him. Boo was in the truck, which had his bike on the back, Mbwato with the cool head had been chosen to drive the all-important tanker, and Jimmy brought up the rear in the other Range Rover.

'Cover of darkness?'

'Yes.'

'Why don't we lay up on that track through Bokalia? We could all do with a rest. You have a plan to spring Tanner?'

Lance shook his head. 'Play it by ear. Surprise. They won't be expecting anything. You have a plan?'

But Pierre too shook his head. 'We'd better wait until we see the lie of the land.'

When they stopped to wait for darkness, Lance sent Boo to watch the main road and then crawled into the shade under the truck to sleep as best he could; he expected to be kept awake with the imponderables of rescuing a man from a maximum-security prison or with the visions of hell he had witnessed at the refugee camp that morning, but when Boo returned from the road within twenty-five minutes, Lance was fast asleep.

Boo nudged Lance's head with his boot and, when Lance did not wake immediately, kicked him quite sharply. 'Wake up, dammit!'

Lance crawled from under the truck and sat up, rubbing his head with one hand and slapping at sandflies with the other. 'Stop dancing around and tell me,' he suggested.

'One of our trucks just went north at a rate of knots. The Chaddi have captured Esmeralda, Christine and Nasheer.' Boo, who had known a great many dangerous men in his time, and was himself reckoned one, recognized the sudden stillness that overcame Lance. It lasted only a second before Lance turned to take his rifle from Mtuku, appointed his bearer in Mwanzo's absence.

'Go on,' Lance said. Again, Boo noted approvingly that he used his normal speaking voice.

'They all seem okay. But the Chaddi also took Mwanzo and he's lying down, bandaged like an Egyptian mummy.'

'Any other Swahili captive? Any more of our trucks?'

'No and no. The refugees are either dead or they escaped. The guards are commando paratroops. There's a Libyan air force officer with them too.'

Lance glanced at Pierre and raised an eyebrow. But it was Jimmy who answered him. 'It looks like the Fates want us to arrive in Largeau in broad daylight. Unless they have two maximum-security prisons, this could be our chance.'

Lance turned to his friend. 'You mean, you drive through the gate behind their trucks as if we belong with them?'

'Unless you have a better plan.'

'No. But that one's reckless.'

'The last time they had Christine, they raped her.'

'I'll think of something,' Lance said. 'On the road. Let's move.' He touched his face: he had smeared ashes from a fire at the refugee camp on his hair and face to make him less easily recognizable as a blond white man but his pure size was a giveaway from distances at which his features would be only a blur. Damn! Broad daylight would halve or quarter their chances of reaching Largeau alive, never mind leaving again.

'There's another thing,' Boo said. 'That television reporter is parked just over the ridge there. I'd say he followed us and intends following us again when we leave here.'

'I hope he knows what he's doing,' Lance said. But when they drove by the G-Wagen, he had an idea and stopped, climbed down and walked to the passenger's window of the 4WD. 'They've captured my wife and servant and the treasurer of our expedition as well as Miss Rawls, the director of the Matthew Ellimore Foundation,' he said into the camera lens which Robert Bruce Hilder pointed at him without as much as a by-your-leave. Perhaps the man was shy and hid behind his camera; perhaps his world was defined by the viewfinder and whatever he saw outside it was not real for him. Lance was in too much of a hurry to comment on the man's rudeness and, in any event, he wanted a favour. 'They're probably taking them to the same prison where they hold the pilots. We'll attempt to rescue them all at once. Our plan is simply to follow the truck they're on to Largeau and to drive into the prison behind it. My scout tells me you are following us. Perhaps you'd care to join us, but in front, between us and them, so to speak?'

The whirring stopped and Robert Bruce Hilder lowered the camera two inches so that he could look over it at Lance.

'Did you actually have film rolling in that thing?' Lance demanded.

'Sure. The scoop of a lifetime, being invited on a prison-break.'

Lance blushed scarlet. 'Well, I wish you'd destroy – '

'What kind of truck are your wife and the others in?' Hilder interrupted him.

'One of our own flatbeds. White, red crosses on all surfaces.'

'Okay.'

Before Lance could again tell Hilder he wanted the bizarre record of his suicidal intention destroyed, Demi let in the clutch and spun the G-Wagen away, leaving Lance coughing in its dust. Lance jumped into his Range Rover and followed briskly. The main road was clear for the moment and to his left he could see the dustplume of the G-Wagen heading for a very big dustplume made by a longish convoy several miles up the road. Now Lance slowed down. As long as he could see the G-Wagen, he had a marker and would know where the prisoners were headed without exposing himself. Even if the prison-bound truck was the rearmost in the convoy, they would not be able to distinguish the details of his vehicles behind the dust the television reporter was throwing up.

'Clever,' said Pierre.

'But not enough,' Lance replied.

'There are a few things to be said for Jimmy's plan, you know.'

'Name one.'

'If there's shooting, either the prison guards or the

277

commandos will be in the middle. If we time it right, they'll be fighting each other while we go about our business.'

'Confusion be my friend?'

'Exactly. You had the right idea first off, to wait until dark. It's still our only alternative.'

The slant of the shadows thrown by the sparse scrub and the vehicle told Lance it was three in the afternoon but he glanced at the dash clock anyway. A couple of minutes after three. Sunset was six hours away, Largeau less than an hour. Too much could happen to Esmeralda and Christine in that time. He shook his head and drove on through a desert which seemed to have been taken on as a junior partner by Hell itself.

On the outskirts of Largeau, Lance closed on the G-Wagen: it was brilliant red but the road was busy. If he lost contact with the photographer, he would have to find the prison on his own and Pierre had just announced that they didn't have a street map of Largeau. Lance resisted the temptation to use the screenwashers to clear some of the road-muck off the screen; if he slowed down for even ten seconds while the resulting mud was washed clear, he would lose the G-Wagen.

'That journalist has his head and camera out of the window and is photographing away,' Pierre said. 'One of these kamikazes will take his head off. It's worse than Paris at the happy hour.' And indeed, in addition to the mess the constant stream of armed forces traffic in both directions made of the streets, there were three-wheeled scooters belonging to vendors of this and that darting everywhere; the populace of Largeau seemed neither to know nor care that there was a famine and a war.

Major Ali watched in the truck's outside mirror as the journalist photographed the prisoners on the back. Excellent! It would make all the major newscasts and Qaddaffi would

278

be immensely pleased. There was even a heavily bandaged Swahili warrior to prove that these people were by no means innocent do-gooders but had fought like tigers. He must remember to tell the journalist that thirteen Chaddi commandos had died under attack from Weber's convoy. Proof of what Qaddaffi had said all along: these people not only smuggled arms, they *used* them to flout the cause of freedom. There was no doubt that he had succeeded as instructed, even if Weber decided to abandon his wife to her fate. Qaddaffi would reward him: he would ask to be returned to active flying, with a wing-command of his own. A heady prospect. And here they were, the end of the line, where he would hand over responsibility to the Chaddi. The prison stood low and squat, a block square, only a single storey high; it was sinisterly windowless, the only entrance through big double wooden doors which were closed but had a smaller door inset. Two soldiers guarded this door, rifles over their shoulders. The commando captain stopped the truck in front of the doors and leaned out of the window to shout at the soldiers to open up. They reacted to the bars on his shoulders and the tone of his voice, swinging both doors open briskly, revealing a small courtyard with, beyond, the administrative offices of the prison; it was a standard French colonial design, secure rather than humane.

The red G-Wagen dashed past the truck and skidded to a halt on the turn on the cobblestones of the courtyard. Two men jumped out and pointed their cameras at the truck in the gate. The commando dropped his hand onto his machine pistol but Major Ali touched his wrist and said, 'Reporters. Those things really look like rocket launchers, don't they?'

The captain expelled his breath. 'Allah! They startled me.' Then he preened a little, straightened his beret, and drove the truck through the gate.

Esmeralda, sitting on the back of the truck with her back

to the cab, admired the journalists' tenacity and audacity. When she turned her head again as the truck lurched into the cobbled courtyard, she was hallucinating: she looked straight into Lance's face through the dusty windshield of his Range Rover, with Pierre in the front seat beside him and Mtuku and Mwendli in the back. They all smiled at her, Lance winked, Pierre put his finger to his lips. She rubbed her eyes. They were still there, driving into the courtyard after the captured truck. God, were the Chaddi commandos all blind? But they were too busy posing for the cameras to look behind them. Lance threw the soldier holding the gate for him a smart salute and Boo made a clenched fist – Uhuru! – out of the window as he drove through. Esmeralda turned to see if Christine shared her hallucination but she sat staring at her feet as she had for hours. But Mwanzo was conscious and on his face was not a grimace of pain but a grin of pure triumph.

'Massa Lance come for us,' he said softly. 'You lie down flat, Madame.'

Esmeralda shuffled down on her bottom, sliding her shoulderblades down the headboard of the flatbed. She pulled at Christine's elbow. 'Slide down, lie flat!' she whispered.

Christine looked up and straight into Jimmy's face as he turned inside the gate. He showed her thumbs up and a mischievous grin. Behind him the two soldiers closed the doors. Esmeralda tugged at her elbow again and Christine slid down to lie flat on the floor. The soldiers she and Esmeralda bumped in these manoeuvres cursed but kept trying to attract the cameraman's attention. Christine reached up to pull down Nasheer, on the other side of her from Esmeralda, but the Arab was already flat on his back.

Esmeralda turned her head to see where Lance was and so saw the commando captain swing down from the truck and

280

slam the door and turn briskly – to look straight into Lance's rifle framed in the window of the Range Rover. Esmeralda started screaming at the top of her voice, and elbowed Christine in the side; after a moment, Christine joined in, creating a distraction. The soldiers on the flatbed with them turned from their fascination with the television cameras to look down at the screaming women. Nasheer smiled up at them and circled his forefinger over his ear. '*La femme*,' he said in further explanation. A soldier reversed his rifle and raised the butt high over Esmeralda's face. Nasheer swept his arm out and connected behind the man's knees. The man screamed as he fell to the ground, landing on his head and breaking his neck.

At the same moment, Jimmy, Boo, Pierre and the Swahili opened fire on full automatic on the soldiers standing on the flatbed. They stood in an arc of sixty degrees and before that solid wall of bullets no man could live. Only two of the Chaddi fired their weapons: the first cut down one of his comrades in front of him in his hurry to squeeze the trigger and was himself cut down as the other man fell away in front of him. The other one shot one of the Swahili through the dimple at the base of his throat; the Swahili fell to his knees, his finger still on the trigger of the FN, and avenged himself even as he died, the rest of a full clip turning the commando into a sieve.

Christine reacted instinctively to the gore spraying her and sat up to wipe her face; Esmeralda and Nasheer reacted at the same time and their arms, simultaneously sweeping out to flatten her, drove the air from her lungs as she crashed back to the floor. Her mouth open, gasping for air, she swallowed some of the muck spraying on her face and, even when she could breathe again, gagged on the foul taste in her mouth. She would have suffocated in her own vomit but Esmeralda, comprehending the impending disaster, sat up to

281

flip her over on her face. A blow to her shoulder sent Esmeralda crashing to her own face; the pain was sudden, sharp, momentary, then a throbbing numbness set in. Trying not to raise herself high enough to be a target, she pushed her other arm under her and stuck her finger in the hole in her shoulder. But that would do no good. She felt the hole in the back of her shoulder: wet and slippery and ragged and much bigger than the one in front. She gritted her teeth not to cry out from the flaming pain of her own touch. She stuffed her handkerchief between the back of her shoulder and her shirt.

As suddenly as it had started, the firestorm stopped. The only sound in the courtyard was the dead Swahili toppling forwards from his knees to fall face-first in his own blood, his finger still clenched around the trigger of his empty FN.

Esmeralda could hear gastric juices burbling in the punctured intestines of the man who lay dead next to her. The smell was awful beyond description. Christine gasped for breath, once every ten seconds or so; she seemed to lack strength for greater effort.

The two photographers rose from the ground, their cameras still rolling, recording everything. My god, my holy Jesus, thought Hilder, who had not been to church since his twelfth birthday, my Mother Mary of God, this is what I have been waiting for all these years, the seven or eight or ten seconds of eternity when it actually happens, when men die or live for bad cause or good or by accident of geography.

What happened next was as inevitable as time. Later Lance would say he should have seen it coming but, at the moment it happened, in the awesome finality of that silent courtyard, with only the sound of life-fluids running away on the cobbles, no one could have expected further resistance against so crushing a victory. Lance could almost hear the jaw of one of the two soldiers at the gate drop open, only fractionally belated. Less than a minute had passed since the gates closed behind them. Lance had fired his own rifle only once, to cut the telephone wire from its pole, and then watched the two soldiers but neither reached for his slung rifle despite the fact that most of Lance's men had their backs to them, nor moved to the escape of the small door set in one of the big ones.

The near-silence and utter immobility lasted for perhaps half a second, then Jimmy and Pierre and Boo simultaneously ripped out empty clips, dropped them to the cobbles, slotted in full clips without having to look where they went, swivelling at the same time, their rifles covering the two soldiers at the gate. One fell in a faint, the other put his hands on his head and smiled uncertainly.

Major Ali rose from where he had sensibly fallen to the cobblestones the moment the firing started, dusted himself off, and walked around the truck. He pulled the commando captain, who had likewise fallen flat and throughout the engagement lain on the cobbles staring up into the barrel of Lance's rifle, to his feet. 'Mr Weber, I presume,' Major Ali said in English.

'Qaddaffi's Livingstone,' Lance said, smiling a little, reaching for the handle, pulling it, pushing the Range Rover door open, moving the rifle barrel to clear the windowframe.

Ali reached up to Esmeralda. 'Madame, you are hurt.' He held her middle and swung her down from the truck and – as Lance's rifle barrel swung to clear the Range Rover door – spun Esmeralda into the commando captain's arms. The man still had his own machine pistol in his hand and he promptly pushed the barrel into her temple as he clamped his other arm across her throat.

Lance climbed out of the Range Rover, his rifle loosely in his hand, pointing at forty-five degrees to the cobbles.

'But the battle is not the war, eh?' Major Ali said,

283

immensely pleased with himself. 'I would not turn if I were you,' he added to Jimmy, Pierre and Boo, frozen in the awkward attitudes of men on the attack, their backs to the real threat. 'We don't want any accidents do we?'

Lance did not take his eyes from Esmeralda. She was pale under her smooth olive skin and had taken a bullet in the shoulder – fresh blood was still spreading on her shirt – but she was smiling gamely, encouragingly. She no doubt remembered how he had freed the Exton woman from a similar predicament. But Mrs Exton had been short and her captor tall. The commando was the regulation five-ten, but so was Esmeralda; there was not enough of the man visible for the single killing shot that would instantly paralyse all his nerves. Lance did not want any chancy shot which could result in a muscular spasm on the man's trigger-finger that would kill Esmeralda. He could not imagine living without her; he would be able to bear neither the loneliness nor the guilt.

'Indeed not,' Lance said and bent to lay his rifle on the cobblestones. 'Lay down your arms,' he ordered his men. 'Nasheer, see if that Swahili is still alive.'

The commando captain's eyes opened wide at the tone of command Lance took even with empty hands.

Christine, remembering her earlier ordeal at the hands of the Chaddi, stifled a sob. In the end, even Lance Weber had failed her.

One of the Swahili spat. This was an act of cowardice that would cost them all their lives: he would gladly give his life in a fight for his leader's woman, but to *surrender* your life for a woman's was an entirely different matter. But his rifle boasted only an empty clip and he was the last man still with a rifle in his hand – he turned around to look at Jimmy, Boo and Pierre but they too had laid down their rifles – and even Nasheer the Baksheesh was staring at him from his haunches

284

beside the dead Swahili, so he laid the FN reverently on the cobblestones.

'Brains will always triumph over brawn,' Major Ali said to Lance and, to the rolling cameras, 'Note, I do not even have a firearm in my hands.' He turned to stare at Nasheer, who put the Swahili's head gently back on the cobblestones.

'He's dead,' Nasheer said.

'And,' Ali said to Lance, 'if you think you're getting this man an opportunity to reach the knife in his boot – '

'I used it earlier, when they ambushed us,' Nasheer interrupted Ali, 'and they took it from me. I'm sorry, Mr Weber.'

Lance hated himself for a gambler. A failed gambler. A loser. He could not look Esmeralda in the face.

'Hands on your heads,' Ali said crisply, all business now. 'Collect their arms,' he called to the soldier at the gate, who was busy unshouldering his rifle to share in the glory.

As they raised their hands towards their heads, Nasheer called out, 'Your shoelace is undone, Mrs Weber.' Ali – very quick on the uptake – turned towards the Arab, hand reaching for his sidearm, but in that moment Nasheer's hand flashed from the back of his shirtcollar, the sun glinted briefly on Toledo steel, and the knife sank to the hilt into the sole remaining commando's back under the collar, severing the central nervous column between the second and third vertebrae just as Esmeralda suddenly went limp at the knees and let her hundred and thirty pounds fall towards the earth without any resistance whatsoever, breaking the man's hold on her neck. The commando captain fired a single shot from the weight of the machine pistol falling against his dead finger on the trigger before two shots from Lance, firing as he rose with his rifle, entered his mouth and right eye, both passing through his brain and out of the back of his skull, before two shots from Jimmy, spinning as he picked up his

285

own rifle, passed through his head from temple to temple and through his heart from side to side. Pierre and Boo shot the young soldier, who was still cocking his rifle to be a hero, once each, both shots to the heart.

Major Ali was still lifting the flap of his holster when he found himself looking into too many rifle barrels to argue with. He smiled wryly. Weber would now shoot him but it had not been a bad life and the women he hadn't yet loved would simply have to remain frustrated. He glanced speculatively at Esmeralda but she lay on the cobblestones in a pool of blood and brains.

'Stand clear,' Lance ordered, striding towards Esmeralda. 'Kill him if he bats an eyelash,' he told Jimmy. He put his rifle down and raised Esmeralda's bloody head. 'Oh, my darling, there was nothing else – '

'Of course not.'

He had heard Esmeralda's voice clearly. 'Huh?' he said and immediately felt stupid.

'It's everybody else's blood and stuff on my head,' she said. 'It's my shoulder that hurts.'

Lance looked at her shoulder, both sides. The bleeding had stopped already. She screamed as he stuck his finger in the hole. 'It's not serious. No bone broken. Bullet out the back. We can attend to it after we rescue Tanner.'

'It feels serious.'

'You'll get used to it.' He reached for the back of her neck and knees.

'I can walk by myself.'

Lance looked past the nearly headless corpse of the commando captain to his men deploying to enter the double doors of the block across from the gates. 'Good work, Nasheer,' he called as he rose. 'Put the women in the Range Rovers. Settle Mwanzo in mine in the back near the gun rack.'

286

Nasheer sighed in relief. He had redeemed his earlier failure. He took the pistol from Ali's holster. 'Against the wall there, fingertips touching the wall one metre above the ground, toes at least a metre from the wall. If you move, I'll kill you.'

Lance walked up to the building just as Boo fired a short burst into the lock and Pierre and Mbwato crashed side by side through the double doors. There were shots inside, a machine pistol on automatic. Jimmy and the Swahili he had teamed with dived through the door side by side as Lance arrived, then Lance was at the head of the queue on one side of the door and rolled through with the Swahili from the other side. There was the crump of a grenade nearby and a big hand pressed Lance flat to the concrete floor as he tried to rise to defend himself. Out of the corner of his eyes he saw Pierre throw a grenade in the other direction and then fall flat on his face. Almost immediately the thing exploded. There were screams. The same hand held Lance flat for another second. Lance held his own arm firmly across the back of the Swahili next to him. When the hand let go, Lance rose to his knees, his rifle searching resistance. Boo was beside him: presumably it had been his ham-hand bruising Lance's kidneys.

'We took the grenades from the commandos,' Boo grinned. 'Meant for us.'

The place was in a mess, pieces of at least three or four people sprayed everywhere. At Lance's feet bullet-holes crept towards a target: he turned and found a Swahili lying behind him, perforated from crotch to chin. Mwendli the Cheerful.

'Find me someone who can tell us where Tanner and his co-pilot are,' Lance said. Pierre headed for the door. Before he reached it, Lance changed his mind. 'Wait, Pierre. That Libyan officer knows.' Lance gestured to the two Swahili nearest the door, who ran out and seconds later came back prodding Ali before them with their rifles.

'Where are the two pilots kept?' Lance asked.

'I don't know.' Ali jumped as Lance fired a shot into the floor close by his feet.

'Next, your ankle, then perhaps a knee, then my aim might become erratic.'

Major Ali thought of how an erratic aim could frustrate all the women he still wanted to love – he was now convinced Weber would not kill him out of hand. 'Perhaps we can come to an arrangement.'

Lance smiled thinly. 'You can tell me what you want after we free the pilots.'

'Through the door behind you, to the end of the corridor, down the stairs, down the next flight as well, to the old dungeons. Both in the same cell, third or fourth on the left.'

'How many warders?'

'They have only sticks, not firearms.'

Lance said to Pierre, who was already at the door, 'Go!'

Pierre jumped through and was promptly followed by Jimmy and two of the Swahili. When there was no firing from beyond the door, Lance told Boo, 'If we don't return, kill him for lying,' and walked through ahead of the other Swahili. At the end of the corridor, Jimmy and Pierre pointed their rifles at a gibbering warder on the other side of a barred gate who from pure funk kept dropping his ring of keys.

'Oh, shit, give me the keys,' Jimmy told the warder. The man held out the keys at arm's length and let go before Jimmy took hold of the ring. Then he walked backwards down the stairs, never once taking his fearful eyes from them. Jimmy pulled the keys towards him with his rifle barrel but there were too many on the ring and he could not pull it through the space between the bars. 'Must be keys on there from the Middle Ages. Stand clear.' He put a short burst into the lock and tried the handle. The door remained obstinately locked.

'Here, let me,' Lance said. He studied the hinges of the door, then fired a single shot into each, leaning over from as far away as possible to keep his feet clear. Jimmy tore the door out and they went through, Pierre scooping up the keys. The prisoners rattled their cell doors and called out piteously. The warders, brutal-looking men, cowered against walls with their nightsticks. Pierre unlocked the other two steel doors and they proceeded quickly, knowing now that they had nothing to fear. Down here at the lowest level the prisoners did not shake the bars in the little windows high up in the doors, did not even look through them. The smell here was abhorrent.

'Gangrene,' Pierre said. 'These are torture chambers.'

Lance looked through the bars of the third door along. In the corner of the cell huddled a bag of bones with chains around wrists and ankles. The prisoner had starved to death. Chilled to the marrow, Lance moved briskly to the next cell and pulled up the bar securing it by hooks in the door and the wall. He flung the door open and reeled back from the smell. He thought: At least the gastric juices outside were fresh, here they are long rotted. He steeled himself and walked into the cell. He did not know the man chained to the bunk before him: hollow eyes vague with madness, ankle-bones at odd angles that would never again control a plane's rudders. But the man was too small to be Tanner. He turned to the other bunk. This one was tall enough to be Tanner and he had Tanner's curled hair though it was no longer pitch black but shot with grey and the beard, washed, would be pure white. He had Tanner's cool grey eyes, though they were hot with fever. He had none of Tanner's muscle and too many of Tanner's bones in the sagging skin which showed burn marks on the chest near the nipples and on the genital-sac. But, most of all, he had Tanner's voice and Tanner's resilience.

'It took you a bloody long time,' the chained skeleton who was Tanner Chapman whispered hoarsely.

Behind him, Lance heard a camera whirring and turned furiously. But Tanner tugged at his sleeve with one hand and covered his genitals with the other. 'Let him,' he whispered. 'A picture. Ten thousand words. Water.'

There was water in the vehicles. They had to get the hell out of here. 'Soon,' Lance said. He watched Pierre unlock the ankle and wrist loops, then picked Tanner up tenderly. 'Him too,' Tanner whispered. 'Co-pilot.'

Pierre unlocked the other man, who seemed unaware of their presence, and Jimmy picked him up. They walked briskly up the stairs, Pierre unlocking some doors on the second floor and pulling the prisoners out so that he could lock the warders in. He gave the keys to the freed prisoners. 'Let everyone out. Lance Weber and the Knékwassés are liberating them. Death to Queddei. Death to Qaddaffi!'

As the tumult built behind them, they ran through the destroyed front office of the prison into the courtyard. Behind them, from deep inside the building, escaped the muffled sound of a shot. The armoury had been opened and distributed. 'They're slow,' Pierre said to Lance but all the same detailed two Swahili. 'Watch that door and shoot anyone who comes through it.'

As Lance laid Tanner into the back of his Range Rover next to Mwanzo, Ali said, 'We had an arrangement.'

'How the hell could they try people in this condition?' Lance demanded.

'Drugs will hold a man up quite as well as a backbrace,' Ali said. 'We had an agreement.'

'You'll be free when we leave here.'

'That's as good as a death sentence. Qaddafi's vindictive. I want to come with you.'

'You think we'll make it, do you?'

Ali nodded. 'Please.'

Though in no doubt that the Libyan was pleading for his life, Lance had to admire his dignified restraint. 'All right. On the truck with the Swahili!'

'Thank you. In return, I will give you this: there was a VHF transmitter in that office your man destroyed so effectively and time to use it before he arrived. So, even if you destroyed the telephone line . . .' Ali turned and jumped up on the truck among the Swahili.

Lance stood looking after the Libyan for a moment.

'Lance!' It was Jimmy, opening the gates, running to his Range Rover. 'Come on!'

But Lance stood still to listen to the approaching sound of racing engines. The Chaddi were responding with reinforcements and within no more than the fifteen minutes since the shooting started, which spoke eloquently of more elite troops, who would be forewarned and therefore all the more dangerous.

'Head for the airport,' Ali shouted at Lance.

'I don't know the way,' Lance shouted back. 'Get in my Range Rover to show us. Pierre, take my Rover, wait for me down the road. Jimmy, lead us out,' Lance shouted as he ran for the fuel tanker. Mbwato slid over the seat to let Lance in behind the wheel. Jimmy's Range Rover shot out of the gate, followed by the truck, followed by the journalists' G-Wagen, followed by Lance's own Range Rover with Nasheer hauling Ali in by his collar, the Libyan's heels alternately flying and dragging in the cobblestones. Iron protectors on the heels of his shoes struck sparks off the stone.

Lance, in the fuel tanker, followed the Range Rover out but made no attempt to turn the wheel; he just stopped the huge tanker squarely across the narrow road. Out of the corner of his eye he saw an armoured car approaching at speed, its heavy-calibre machine gun swivelling towards them.

'Run, Mbwato!' He pushed the Swahili, who was firing past him at the armoured car, backwards out of the truck and jumped over him. Lance paused only briefly to jerk the Swahili upright by his collar and shove him into a run before himself sprinting for the Range Rover stopped fifty metres away. Behind him some stupid sod kept his finger on the .50 machine gun's trigger. Soon that tanker would explode and he didn't want to be anywhere near it when it blew. His brother had died in the flames, a death on a par with the poison of the black treesnake, pain beyond comprehension. He shoved Mbwato again; the copper man was big and fast and fit but Lance had played at centre for the Springboks and could run a hundred yards under ten seconds carrying a fifty-pound sandbag in his arms. Lance and the Swahili reached the Range Rover before Esmeralda, who had been in the front passenger seat, could complete opening her door, running to the back, opening the hatch and climbing in. Lance shoved her in, closed the hatch on her, opened the rear door for Mbwato, and jumped into the front next to Pierre. The heavy machine gun stopped firing. Their pursuers had realized they didn't want to create a flaming barrier between themselves and the fugitives.

Pierre let the clutch in and the Range Rover fishtailed a little as the torque bit on the uneven road.

'Everybody duck!' Lance shouted. He turned in his seat. His first shot shattered the Range Rover's rear window. He clearly heard Esmeralda say something rude in Spanish as a piece of glass stung her. He could see fuel spurt out of the holes the heavy machine-gun bullets had punched right through the tanker. He himself fired low down on the curve

292

of the tanker, hoping to flatten the bullet and for the ricochet to strike sparks off the steel chassis. He could see the sparks flying but the diesel wouldn't burn. Damn!

'*Merde!*' Pierre exclaimed and flung the Range Rover into a violent evasive manoeuvre, throwing Lance against the door.

'Easy, Pierre. These aren't play-bullets.'

Pierre cursed again.

Then Lance noticed the grinning Swahili on the truck in front of them excitedly pointing backwards. He spun in his seat again just as Pierre said, 'They threw you a petrol drum.' Lance saw the drum. Thank god for the Range Rovers' petrol engines, for which they carried fuel in drums. He drove the rolling drum along with three shots and the third punctured it and simultaneously set the fuel alight from the spark it made. The drum was ten feet from the punctured tanker when Lance saw a man carrying a rocket-launcher climb up into the seat of the tanker. He fired at him and hit the rocket-launcher. A mushroom of flame and smoke blossomed as the exploding rocket compressed the diesel to combustion, just as cylinder pressure would inside a diesel engine. Lance looked left to check what caused the clang against the Range Rover and found himself face to face with Robert Bruce Hilder, who shook his head groggily and put his eye back to the viewfinder. Even at over four hundred metres the blast had been powerful enough to throw the two four-wheel-drives against each other. When Lance turned forward, Pierre was still fighting to right the Range Rover.

'See what I mean, Mr Weber?' Major Ali said behind him. 'That was a unit of the crack Eleventh Assault Brigade. The Chaddi have none finer. There is nothing between us and the airport now.'

'Except airport security,' Pierre said as he passed the truck. Lance saluted the cheering Swahili. It had indeed been a fine explosive display, their cheerful grins said louder than words. He was happy to please them: they had done well by him this day and would have to fight again at the airport. Security at an airport in wartime would be heavy.

He turned in his seat. 'Why did you suggest the airport . . . Major, isn't it?'

'Major Ali. Soon just Mr Ali. Perhaps sometime commercial pilot Ali. You have rescued two pilots, you fly yourself, so do some of your companions if our files are correct, and I too am a pilot.'

'That's a list of skills, not a reason.'

'You can't hope to escape by road after what you just did. These Chaddi will stop their war against their southern brothers while they find and kill you.'

Lance said nothing but merely stared at the man. If he misjudged the Libyan's sincerity or fear, they would all die in that miserable dungeon; the lucky ones would die fighting not to be captured.

'Granted, you have run around this country like it was your own backyard,' Ali continued. 'But now they know exactly where you are and probably how many men you have and precisely how good you are. Next they'll be sending ground-attack planes, whole regiments with mortars and other artillery.'

'You're overestimating our importance,' Lance said mildly

'Rubbish,' Pierre said distinctly. 'The man's right, Lance.'

'They can't afford to let you go,' Ali said. 'Qaddaffi has taken a personal dislike to you. He sent me with a message for Queddei: if the Chaddi don't stop you, he will cut off their military and financial aid. Since they're landlocked and otherwise surrounded by enemies, without Qaddaffi they're dead.'

Lance faced front. 'You believe a head of state will go to

294

such lengths because of a man he's never met?' he asked Pierre.

'Yes. Don't sell yourself short. You've wrecked a pet scheme of a man of unquestioned power. How could he let you live?'

'The man must be mad.'

'He is,' Ali said with utter certainty.

Lance blew his breath out slowly. 'Ali, give Pierre directions to the airport.' He reloaded his rifle and, when they were between directions, called, 'You okay in the back there?'

'Half my soul for a cushion,' Esmeralda replied.

'Yes, Massa! Thank you, Massa!'

'You send many to their ancestors, Mwanzo?'

'They pay dearly for wounding me, Master.'

'Your irregulars fought like tigers, Mr Weber,' Ali said. 'Thirteen paracommandos dead for only two Swahili dead and one wounded. I tell you, even in victory I was cold with trepidation.'

'What happened to the rest of the convoy, to the refugees?'

'They all got away,' Nasheer said. He explained how he had been taken by surprise as he counted the trucks onto a change of direction. When he told how Christine shot the sergeant who had murdered the child, Lance and Pierre whistled simultaneously.

Lance looked back at Esmeralda again, still overcome by the fear he had felt at losing her, still unable to believe his good fortune at not having lost her. She was cleaning the gore from her face with one of the foil-packed scented damp tissues she carried in her handbag. Her handbag? She had carried her handbag with her while people shot at them!

'Next time,' Lance told Esmeralda, 'leave your handbag behind, eh?'

She grinned impishly at him and flashed her mirror in his eyes.

'That's the airport, behind the row of armoured cars,' Ali said. 'Do you think I could have my pistol back please,' he added to Nasheer.

'Mr Weber?'

'Give it to him. And give him an FN as well and some clips.'

'What do you want to do, Lance?' Pierre asked, though he kept a steady, unsuspicious speed towards the armoured cars. 'They've seen us, I think.'

'Nothing for it but to drive right up,' Lance decided. 'Anything else would attract interest.' He turned to face the rear of the Range Rover. 'Major Ali, you and your colleague here' – Lance indicated Nasheer – 'are escorting me to the plane that will take me to Colonel Qaddaffi. Put your pistol to my head. Do it now.'

In the back of the car, Esmeralda stopped cleaning her face with a sharp intake of breath but, when Lance glanced at her, continued as if she were unconcerned. Beside her, Mwanzo took an FN from the rack with his bandaged hand and cocked it with his teeth.

'Exactly,' Lance said as he read in Ali's eyes that the Libyan too had heard. 'At the first shot, no matter who fires it, the faithful Mwanzo will shoot you through the seat. Probably in the kidneys.'

'I shall pray to be as lucky as you,' Ali said.

'I don't ever want to hear you refer to my luck,' Lance said evenly.

For the first time in his life, Ali understood it was possible to fear a man even while you held a pistol to his head.

'My husband used to be a gambler,' Esmeralda said courteously, in the same tone she would use to say, Do forgive the vicar for leaving so abruptly; the poor man is so utterly straitlaced about risqué jokes.

I'm dreaming all this, Ali thought. That desirable woman

296

is like her husband, ice right through, a black widow spider. She would eat me whole. He had never felt small before a woman; it was not an experience he would choose to repeat.

Pierre stopped the Range Rover before the barrier. 'The commander's in the rear on the other side,' Pierre told the sergeant who came to his window. 'I'd salute smartly if I were you.'

At Ali's window, the sergeant saluted smartly. Then he saw the pistol Ali held to Lance's head. His mouth gaped and he appeared as he was, an intelligent twenty-three-year-old bank clerk conscripted to an army in dire need of both youth and intelligence.

'Look upon the dangerous bandit Lance Weber and be grateful he's not pointing a rifle at you,' Ali said. 'And thank Allah your friend and protector Colonel Qaddaffi of Libya sent me to catch him rather than leaving it to your syphilitic generals.'

The sergeant snapped to attention. Anyone who could speak like this to strangers of generals must be a very powerful man indeed. He shouted at the men behind the barrier to raise it and let the convoy through.

Beyond the barrier, Ali sighed wearily. Lance laughed. Pierre chuckled.

'Perhaps you should go on stage, Major Ali,' Esmeralda suggested.

'Left here, then right at the end there,' Ali said. 'We still have to pass the security gate.' He opened his window and put his head out as they came to the gatehouse but the man inside, hugging the machine pistol in one hand while taking a clip for it out of a drawer with the other and cradling the telephone between ear and shoulder, had his back to them.

'Drive through!'

'Why?' Lance asked. 'That gives the game away.'

'Why is he holding that firearm in his hands instead of slung over his shoulder as is normal?'

'Go, Pierre!' Lance twisted in his seat just as the man on the phone turned on the swivel of his office chair to look him straight in the face. The man jumped to his feet with a shout, the phone dropped to the floor of the hut and the outside glass shattered as he opened fire. The Range Rover rang as two shots hit the roof. Lance shot the guard twice. 'Somebody should've told him to hold the barrel down to allow for torque-climb,' he said to no one in particular. The two shots from the back seat had been one from Ali's pistol and one from Nasheer's rifle. Lance had seen both hit. 'Where to now?'

'That Hercules, and let's pray it's fuelled.' Ali looked away from the big transport towards the hangar where his night pursuit fighter rested. A pity not to be leaving in that: there was nothing in Chad to catch it, while every jet they had could catch the lumbering Hercules long before it reached either Sudan or Niger, respectively five and four hundred klicks away. And fighters would scramble in minutes if they got the Hercules airborne, in itself a doubtful proposition as there was shooting behind them and already an alarm clanged angrily.

'I'll need Mr Weber in the cockpit as co-pilot,' Ali said. 'Can someone else keep that bunch at a distance meanwhile?'

He pointed at the jeep-load of soldiers racing towards them.

Lance put his rifle to his shoulder and his thumb on the telezoom button and blew both the jeep's front tyres. The jeep reared up and fell over on the soldiers.

'Fifteen hundred metres, a moving target from a moving vehicle,' Ali said incredulously. He craned around to be quite certain in his own mind the jeep was upside down. It was.

'I'll handle the rearguard,' Pierre said to Lance. 'Don't let

298

him leave without me.' He jerked his thumb over his shoulder at Ali. He drove up the ramp and brought the Range Rover to a stop inside the Hercules.

'Thanks, Pierre. I won't.'

Pierre grabbed his rifle from Lance's footwell, patted his pockets to count clips and ran down the ramp just as the truck stopped below it and Jimmy drove his Range Rover up it. The red G-Wagen slid to a spectacular halt fifty metres away and to one side, out of the direct line of fire between the soldiers and the fugitives; both reporters jumped out and started their cameras rolling before it actually stopped.

Lance told Nasheer. 'Get the wounded out of the vehicles and someplace where they can hold on to something.' After Jimmy, already running down the ramp with his rifle in his hand, he shouted, 'We need ten minutes. Tell Pierre.' Then he ran forwards after Ali and up the companionway and forwards again to the flight deck.

'My licence only stretches to light twins,' he told Ali, already in the command pilot's seat.

'Fully fuelled,' Ali said, ignoring Lance's doubts. 'Now, if the batteries are charged . . .' He flicked switches.

Christ, Lance thought, this bugger's not making the pre-flight checks. He's just going to fly this plane away.

'Okay,' Ali said, 'there's a battery charger connected under the port wing. Remove it please.' Lance ran out again. As he passed Esmeralda, he said, 'Go up to the flight deck with your pistol in your hand where Ali can see it. Stay there until I return.'

He didn't hear what she replied because he was already halfway down the ramp. He didn't look back to see if she obeyed; it was never necessary to paint pictures for Esmeralda.

Jimmy stood behind the truck bed, using the cant rail as an elbow rest to shoot at soldiers setting up a mortar near where the jeep had overturned. 'In five minutes, when those morons get the idea of sheltering behind the jeep and just mortaring the runway all round us . . .' Jimmy said as Lance passed.

He found Pierre under the wing, with Boo and two Swahili, using scoped rifles to return fire from soldiers on the visitor's viewing gallery on the roof of the main reception terminal. None of the soldiers' shots came near but Lance saw several soldiers fall. 'There's one assembling a sniperscope in the shadow of the doorway,' Lance said to Pierre, who grunted and shifted his aim and killed the sniper with three shots. Lance studied the battery charger and its cable and fitting, not looking up as the first mortar shell crunched somewhere beyond the plane. The cable was thick and screwed onto the female end in the plane with a bright round knurled fitting. Lance screwed it anti-clockwise until it rotated freely, then pulled at the cable. It took considerable force to dislodge it; as he suspected, it was a large DIN plug. He threw the cable onto the trolley. The trolley itself was in front of the wheels. Lance leaned into the driving compartment to put the handbrake off and then put his shoulder to its frame but the thing was too heavy to push. He would have to drive it. He climbed into the seat, quickly familiarized himself with the controls and started it up. As he pushed the lever into forward drive, a shot clanged off the screen frame. 'Sniper!' Lance called to Pierre.

'Lucky shot,' Pierre said, unconcerned, as he pushed a fresh clip into his rifle.

Any more lucky shots, Lance thought, and this fully fuelled plane will be our funeral pyre.

As the battery cart emerged from under the wing, several more shots rang off various parts of it. Lance jumped for the ground. He had his rifle in his hand but he didn't try for a shot: the sniper knew where he was, he would have to search for the sniper. Instead he ran for the shelter of the wing, bent

300

double so as to offer as small a target as possible and also so that Pierre and Boo and the Swahili could fire over him at the sniper. A bullet struck the tarmac a metre to his left. The firing stopped as he rolled under the plane's fat belly.

'You call all those lucky shots?' he shouted pointedly to Pierre.

'His luck ran out,' Pierre said drily, lowering his rifle. There were no more shots from the terminal.

Lance watched the battery cart putter wearily towards the overturned jeep behind which the mortar squad had now taken shelter.

'Pierre!' Jimmy shouted. 'Can you see the mortarmen? They're zeroing in.'

Lance saw Pierre swivel and heard his shout, 'No. We'll have to winkle them out.'

Lance checked that nothing was attached to the other wing and nothing obstructed the wheels or propellers there, then rolled out from under the plane as a mortar charge exploded only the length of a rugger field diagonally in front of the plane. He ran to the rear and found Pierre climbing into the truck and Swahili clambering onto the back: Pierre had left Boo under the wing to cope with possible reinforcements in the terminal and was on his way to deal with the mortar.

By the time Lance returned to the flight deck, the whole plane was vibrating: Ali had the engines running. Esmeralda stood against the rear bulkhead with the pistol in her hand resting against her thigh and Tanner sat in the co-pilot's seat. 'Wheels and props all clear.'

Ali looked over his shoulder. He held up two fingers. 'Two minutes to circulate the oil in the engines, then we leave. There's a phone beside the hatch: let me know the moment it is closed.'

Lance looked doubtfully at Tanner but Ali shook his head, then nodded. Tanner, half-dead or not, was the best pilot aboard. Lance ran down the companionway again, becoming a little breathless. He found the phone beside the hatch and picked it up. 'Testing. Hatch to captain. Testing.'

'It works,' Ali said.

The truck made a wide, sweeping turn around the jeep, the Swahili on the back firing a mad-minute. The soldiers had abandoned the mortar – actually there were two mortars, Lance now saw – to shoot at the truck. Suddenly the truck swerved violently and two of the Swahili fell to the grass to roll over and continue firing. One of the soldiers had hit a tyre. The truck turned on its flat tyre and roared back, slowing between the soldiers and the two Swahili on the ground. The Swahili ran for the truck and scrambled aboard. And then the truck just puttered on quite slowly, idling along. Lance saw Jimmy, on the back of the truck with the Swahili, clamber over the headboard and onto the runningboard and fling the door open and push the driver aside to take the wheel. The truck picked up speed and headed straight for the plane. It skidded to a halt at the bottom of the ramp in the backwash from the huge props. The Swahili scrambled from the back, fired a few shots towards where the mortar was starting up again, this time distinctly a single mortar, crump crump crumping closer closer closer still. Lance ran down the ramp and jerked the truck door open. Pierre fell out against him. His eyes were open and he was breathing but the head-wound didn't look good. 'Come on!' Lance shouted at Jimmy, who was firing his rifle out of the truck window at another jeepful of soldiers charging the plane. Lance ran up the ramp. Nasheer had his finger on the button to raise the ramp. The Swahili from the truck and Boo and the Swahili from under the wing all ran up the ramp into the plane and Lance nodded to Nasheer, who pressed the button. Pressing Pierre against the bulkhead to free one hand, Lance lifted the phone just as Jimmy ran around the rear of the

302

truck, moving backwards, firing his rifle. Then Jimmy jerked as he was hit, staggered and fell. Lance gave Pierre to Mpengo, ran across the elevating ramp and jumped over Robert Bruce Hilder and Demi, who were scrambling aboard with their cameras, just as the plane began to roll. He grabbed Jimmy, who, even flat on his back on the ground, was still firing his rifle at the jeep speeding towards them, under the arms and flung him forward to catch him at the waist and fling him over his shoulder in the classic fireman's hold. The plane was twenty metres away and accelerating! Lance ran for it but Jimmy weighed 230 pounds. He could almost touch the rim of the ramp, now elevated nearly chest high, when the plane put on a sudden spurt and accelerated out of reach. Lance stopped and turned to the closing jeep. He would die fighting.

'Sorry, we didn't make it,' he said to Jimmy.

'Plane's stopped,' Jimmy said mildly. 'Run, Lance, run.'

'Bless Esmeralda,' Lance said as he turned. The ramp fell again, the plane stood dead still, the props threw up a great wash – it was like running repeatedly up the steep hill behind Coetzenburg with Dr Danie Craven standing at the bottom, shouting sadistic orders through his megaphone until you dropped in your own vomit from utter exhaustion. Nothing worthwhile is ever easy, Lance thought irrelevantly, and then he reached the ramp, now hip-high, just as the bullet tugged at his leg and he stumbled and flung Jimmy onto the ramp but Jimmy had his wrist and Nasheer pushed the button again and Boo and Mtuku rushed onto the ramp to pull him in. Behind them, Lance saw Demi take a bullet to the chest and slide gracefully to the floor, the camera still to his eye and still running.

Pierre, sitting up against the bulkhead beneath the phone, said clearly, 'In the event, it was you who were almost left behind,' and closed his eyes.

* * *

On the flight deck, Esmeralda heard Nasheer say on the intercom, 'All aboard. Please leave quickly.' She pulled her pistol away from Major Ali's temple and said, 'Now we can go.'

'That was really not necessary.' His eyes followed the pistol. 'An honest misunderstanding.'

'People are still shooting at us,' Esmeralda said drily as a mortar explosion sprayed grass and earth onto the screen, 'and we'll be misunderstood by that red fire-engine if we don't leave sharpish.'

Major Ali shook his head to rid himself of his instinctive fear of this spider-woman with her unnatural calm. The fire-engine was indeed heading for them, straight down the runway. Tanner flicked the brakes off and Ali opened the four throttles simultaneously.

'Ever play chicken?' Tanner asked Esmeralda conversationally. 'No, I don't suppose Spanish convent girls do. Remind me to explain some time. Most instructive.'

'Chickens?' asked Major Ali, touching the throttles to reassure himself they were indeed against their stops and glancing down to check that Tanner had indeed set the flaps as instructed.

'Whose nerve breaks first,' Tanner explained without shifting his eyes from the fire-engine, now only four hundred metres from them. He gently removed Major Ali's hand from the throttles and placed his own over their handles. 'I'm not going back down the dungeon.'

'We'll never make it into the air,' Major Ali said calmly. Then, more urgently, to the driver of the fire-engine hidden behind the reflection of his windshield, 'Chickens, you son of a whore!'

Esmeralda noted that Tanner had his eyes on the dials in front of him, four of which showed needles in the red segments. She looked up and saw the fire-engine looming huge even from the great height of the Hercules cockpit. The driver was a fanatic: he would commit suicide to kill them.

'Now,' Tanner breathed just as Major Ali hauled back and lifted the lumbering Hercules into the air almost as if by the strength of his own muscles.

'Too late,' said Major Ali. 'It was a privilege flying with the great Chapman.'

The huge fire-engine rushed at the screen. Esmeralda could see dirt in the slots of the screws fixing the windscreen wipers to their spindles. There was no hope for those in the cockpit but she hoped Lance and the others, far back in the plane, nearer the earth, would survive.

Then the fire-engine turned left and Major Ali with a small sigh tilted the Hercules ever so slightly. There was a crash under the wing and Tanner twisted the other way in his seat to see how much space there was between the runway and the tip of the other wing and said, 'No more!' and Major Ali levelled her with a lurch totally unlike the smooth emergency manoeuvre he had performed only a second before and said, 'Madame, if you could manage to wipe the sweat from my eyes.' Esmeralda, who had used her handkerchief at the prison to stem the flow of blood from her shoulder until she could put a steripad on it, wasted a moment looking for a clean part of her shirtsleeve –

'Quickly, Esmeralda,' Tanner said. He was himself wrapped in the tarp that had been used to cover the firearms racked in the back of the Range Rover.

– and then pulled her shirttails out of her trousers and wiped Ali's forehead and eyes with that, holding onto the back of his seat with her other hand as the Hercules climbed at maximum rate, juddering as it clawed at the air. The moment she finished, Ali levelled the plane off only two hundred feet above the ground.

'Don't want to give the jets room to manoeuvre.' Ali looked towards Tanner, who nodded approvingly.

On the load-deck, the hatch clanged shut and Lance shouted, 'Get everyone the hell out of the way of those Range Rovers.' He dragged himself along on his knees briskly against the acceleration to where Mpengo stood, bracing himself as best as he could while holding Pierre in his arms.

Nasheer put his hand on Lance's shoulder. 'It's all right, Mr Weber. I chained them down.' He pointed to the chains that led from under the Range Rovers to the hooks in the floor. He helped Lance up. 'Is your wound serious?'

Lance felt behind him, then laughed loudly enough to drown the racing engines, causing Christine to look sharply at him. 'By god no, I got shot in the arse. A flesh-wound. Quick thinking that, Nasheer.'

Just then the plane's tail dipped sharply as the pilot flung her into the air and a second later, while Nasheer and Lance and all the others staggered, rolled, even flew towards the now closed rear hatch, the plane tilted on its longitudinal axis and they all fell in a heap in one corner. Demi's camera crashed into the side of Lance's head and for a moment he saw stars with, looming in the galaxy, a huge Range Rover straining to break its chains to devour them. Then Swahili curses, more curses in the click-clack sounds that had once been Jimmy's native tongue, and a scream from Christine brought him to his senses and he rolled Nasheer from him towards the unoccupied corner at the other side of the plane just as it was jerkily righted. Nasheer took off as if jet-propelled and crashed head-first into the plane's skin, denting it with his head. He sat up a moment later to stare groggily at Lance trying to sort out the tangle of bodies, then crawled forward to help.

'You're not on a rugger-field now,' Christine told Lance

as he grabbed her arm and jerked her clear of the tangle of bodies.

'Help me get everybody off the wounded,' Lance gasped. He could still not see quite straight from the blow to the head and there was blood running down his leg from the flesh wound on his buttock. Then the plane levelled off and it was possible to attend to the wounded. Christine came running with the medicine chest to where Lance and Jimmy kneeled on either side of Pierre.

Lance held Pierre's wrist. 'His heart's beating.'

Jimmy ripped his own trousers and slapped a dressing on his wound. 'Eeeoww! You bastards had to fall on my broken leg.' With his other hand, he gave Lance a dressing. 'Put that on, you're making a mess. We'll see to Pierre, Christine. You deal with the others.'

Lance stuck the dressing into his underpants and pressed it home. He expectorated a few drops from the tip of the needle and plunged it home in Pierre's arm and slowly injected the morphine. Jimmy poured surgical spirit over his hands and washed them in it, then poured the rest of the bottle over the side of Pierre's head and swabbed away the blood. He held the flaps of skin apart and picked out a splinter of bone.

'Skull's broken,' Lance said. He looked into the wound. The brain was visible but the sac protecting it was intact and none of the fluid that cushions the brain had leaked. 'Don't bugger around in there. Boo, make Pierre comfortable while I set Jimmy's leg.'

'If you don't mind, old chap,' Jimmy said in his plummiest British public school accent, 'I'd rather Esmeralda did it. It hurts like bloody hell already and I don't fancy your tender touch.'

Lance rose to count his men. He had come with twelve Swahili and he had rescued Mwanzo, thirteen in all. Two

307

had died at the prison. Later he would sorrow for them; now he had to attend to the living. He counted ten Swahili. 'Where's Mbwato?' he asked aloud.

'Here, Master,' a voice said from under a Range Rover. 'Checking chain.'

Jimmy was wounded, Pierre was seriously wounded, Lance himself had a somewhat embarrassing wound. Esmeralda was wounded and the back of her shoulder would carry a disfiguring scar.

Christine, Boo and Nasheer had escaped physically unharmed, though god knew what psychic damage they had sustained.

The hungry had been fed. Doctors had, serendipitously, been brought to the ill.

Tanner and his co-pilot had been rescued from death by torture or starvation.

Robert Bruce Hilder sat on the floor of the plane and rocked Demi's head in his lap. Lance bent to hold the Greek's wrist even though the bullet-hole was directly over the heart; there was no pulse. The journalist sang a lullaby in French to a tune Lance recognized: Esmeralda had often sung it to Emmy, though with Spanish words. Lance decided not to take the body from the grieving man yet: later would be time enough.

He picked up his rifle from the floor and, calling to Jimmy, 'I'll send Esmeralda to set your leg,' hobbled away to the stairs, wondering how long it would be before the fighter jets caught up with them.

The whole plane shivered with speed and, when Lance stepped into the cockpit, he instantly knew why: the two pilots were running the engines in the red.

Tanner saw Lance's glance. 'They won't seize up before we cross the border.'

Lance told Esmeralda, 'Thanks. Jimmy insists only you can

set his leg. Then clean and dress your own wound properly.'
When Esmeralda had gone, he looked out of the windshield.
'Eastwards? I thought the other border – with Niger – was
closer.'

'They'd hand us straight over to Qaddaffi,' Tanner said.
'It's Sudan or nothing.'

'Forty minutes to the border,' Major Ali announced.

Tanner tapped the radar screen. 'If we make it.'

Lance saw two dots closing fast with the centre of the
screen. 'Jets?'

'Fighters,' Major Ali said. 'Three minutes to contact.'

Lance looked at the back of the Libyan's neck. The man
did not sound particularly frightened about jets shooting his
lumbering transport from the air with rockets, but then,
Lance supposed, he himself, however he might cringe inside,
did not sound particularly frightened when dealing with the
dangers of his own work. He raised an eyebrow at Tanner,
who said, 'He'll do.'

'Thirty-seven minutes is an eternity,' Major Ali said. 'And
there's no guarantee *they* won't cross the border.'

Major Ali punched buttons on the communications con-
sole. A jabber of Arabic filled the cabin. He jerked his thumb
over his shoulder, indicating that the voices belonged to the
jet pilots. 'They have radar-contact with us and expect visual
contact very shortly.'

'That means,' Tanner said to Lance, 'they won't come in
shooting. First, they'll try forcing us back or down. They
probably don't want to destroy a valuable plane. That gives
us a few minutes while we play games.'

'But not enough,' Major Ali said. 'Sooner rather than later
they *will* fire their rockets and then we're finished.'

'We'll cross that bridge when we come to it,' Lance said,
'and hope it's not the one over the Styx.'

Major Ali held up his hand for silence while Arabic filled

309

the cabin. When it stopped, he said, 'They've sighted us and reported back. Their orders are confirmed, to bring this plane "home" intact.'

More Arabic. Commands.

'Don't answer,' Lance said.

More urgent Arabic.

'They're Libyan pilots,' Major Ali said. 'The Chaddi are not very good.'

English: 'Stolen Hercules. Return Largeau. Repeat, return Largeau. We are armed and have you in our sights.'

This message was repeated several times in tones of rising exasperation.

Then the Hercules rocked as the jets cut close over its nose from above and behind.

'Nearly four minutes gained,' Ali said with satisfaction

On the radio, the two Libyan pilots could be heard giggling obsessively as they flung their jets into steeply banked turns.

'I've met these two before,' Tanner said through clenched teeth. Then he sighed and smiled the old Tanner smile. 'I shall take over now, Major. With your permission of course.'

Major Ali shrugged. 'All right. I too know those two. They're fanatics. Qaddaffi decorated them for shooting down your "gun-running" plane.'

Lance smiled at the irony of this. 'Let's give them another gong, eh? Major, may I speak on the phone to the loading bay?' When Ali handed him the phone, Lance told Boo, who answered it, 'Run up the engines of both Range Rovers and keep them running. I want them good and hot.' He held his hand over the mouthpiece. 'Will you be flinging the plane around much, Tanner?' Tanner shook his head. 'And undog all but a single chain on each so we can free them quickly.'

'We can't land in the rough,' Major Ali told Lance as he took the phone back from him. 'We lost a landing-wheel to a fire-engine during take-off.' He pointed out of the window beside him. 'What will you do?'

'We can't hold them off another – ' Lance looked at the stainless-steel Rolex which had survived the fire his brother died in ' – thirty-two minutes. So let's deal with them right here and now before they catch on that we're serious.'

'This is an unarmed transport, Mr Weber.'

'But I'm not.'

Major Ali looked doubtfully at Lance's rifle and winced when Lance reversed it and smashed the butt into one of the side windows, which promptly popped out of its surround and disappeared into the slipstream.

'Here they come,' Tanner said.

The two pilots giggled loudly enough to be heard over the wind rushing through the frame even before Ali turned up the volume. They flew side by side, straight at the nose of the Hercules.

Lance put his rifle out of the side window. Major Ali turned in his seat, away from the growing pinheads in the sky rushing towards them, to look doubtfully upon this procedure. Even Weber, he thought, could not be serious about taking on two jet fighters with a semi-automatic rifle. And the man didn't even have a sightline to their attackers, having to hold the rifle outside the window at an awkward angle beside his body.

The giggling intensified.

'We're closing at a combined speed of over twelve hundred miles an hour,' Tanner warned Lance. 'About two thousand feet a second.'

'Just hold her steady as she goes,' Lance said. The jets would be in range of his rifle for only three-quarters of a second. Then, suddenly, they could see the fighter pilots, their blankfaced helmets and masks serious and forbidding, contradicting the giggling which Lance thought decidedly deranged. He remembered that Teddy Bruun had always giggled when he tortured or killed. He steeled himself against the shudder of revulsion.

Lance squeezed the trigger three times, then moved the barrel and started squeezing the trigger again but he fired only once at the second plane before the Hercules bucked and was flung almost onto its back as the first jet exploded. Lance hung onto his rifle and gritted his teeth as his wrists were cut against the window-frame. Huge pieces of fragmented jet flew across the sky. Out of the corner of his eye he saw the remaining jet cartwheeling *upwards* across the sky. He cursed aloud. Now the remaining pilot would call for reinforcements. But he could hardly have expected to down two modern jets in less than a second.

'What'd you do?!' Major Ali shouted at Lance as Tanner fought to right the plane.

'I fired into his air intake,' Lance said. 'A piece of red-hot rotor must've been shot off and sliced through his fuel tank.'

'Allah protect me!'

'What's the other one saying?'

The remaining fighter pilot screamed in Arabic while his base tried to cut in, obviously to calm him down.

'He wants them to send the rest of the squadron. He says you shot down his wingman. They don't believe him. They say this plane is unarmed. They tell him to bring us back. He insists.'

More Arabic.

Lance picked up the phone. 'Nasheer. Drop the hatch and undog both Range Rovers.'

'They already swing round dangerously every time – '

'Do it!'

'Yes sir.'

'I'll be there immediately.'

Still Arabic crackled in the cabin.

'They tell him to destroy us,' Ali said.

'How many rockets does he have?'

'Four. He fires two at a time. But he also carries machine guns.'

'Correct for the open hatch, then hold her steady,' Lance told Tanner and ducked through the door.

When he reached the load bay, the hatch was down and he could see, past Robert Bruce Hilder, who stood squarely in it with his camera to his shoulder, the jet lining them up from at least three miles away. He grinned wryly: that was one Libyan pilot who was not likely to venture near enough to be able to use his machine guns.

But rockets were another problem altogether.

The air was hazy with the exhaust fumes of the two Range Rovers. As Lance leaned into the rearmost one to release the handbrake, he saw that the water temperature gauge was already into the red. Excellent. He put his shoulder to the doorjamb and pushed it to the lip of the hatch, then held up his hand to the Swahili who had jumped to help. 'When I say, all together,' he told them. 'Boo, bring the other Rover too.'

Lance slammed the Range Rover's door – he did not want it to sweep him with it when it went.

The jet lined up and two puffs appeared under its wings. Rockets. They seemed to move very lethargically and Lance wondered if they would run wide. But, with that thought still in his mind, the rockets were almost upon them. Lance consciously restrained himself from giving the order: too soon and the rockets would not be diverted by the Range Rover's hot engine but would instead seek the greater heat sources of the plane's engines.

Then he could read Cyrillic script on the rockets and shouted 'Now!' and heaved at the Range Rover and saw it fall and the rockets turn almost sixty degrees in midair and hit the Range Rover less than a hundred feet under the plane. The next moment Lance found himself lying across the bonnet of the other Range Rover twenty feet into the plane. Boo, who was wheeling the second Range Rover into position to try the same thing again, pulled Lance off by his ankle. Lance picked up his rifle, checked it, slotted in his last clip. He saw Jimmy inspecting the end of a Range Rover radius arm sticking from outside through the metal of the plane at head-height.

'You're cutting it fine,' Jimmy shouted at him.

Lance pumped his ears as he walked briskly beside the Range Rover. Esmeralda touched him fleetingly as he walked past her and he smiled lopsidedly. His teeth had been jarred and his head rang. He stopped on the lip and teetered. Nasheer caught his arm.

'Ready, Lance?' Boo asked beside him.

Lance nodded. The fighter lined up again. Surely the Libyan would not fall for the same trick twice?

'Mr Weber!' Nasheer shouted from the bulkhead with the phone. 'Mr Chapman says there's a valley he can hide us in.'

'But quickly!' Lance replied. 'Brace yourselves,' he shouted at the Swahili. He caught a grabhandle beside the phone as the plane dropped sickeningly. Through the open hatch he saw the trails of two more rockets. Oh, Christ! The rockets would reach them before they were low enough to hide but when they were already too low to throw the Range Rover decoy out without the explosion knocking them too out of the sky. Lance watched the rockets grow frighteningly and, behind them, the jet following the rockets instead of peeling away as before. The Libyan pilot was coming in to finish the job! Lance had to admire his tenacity, if not his good sense. They were still two hundred feet above the lip of the dried-up riverbed when the rockets closed. 'Heave!' Lance shouted but he did not help push the Range Rover out. He stood to one side with his rifle at the ready, waiting for the plane, without much hope against heavy machine guns but unwilling to go down without a fight. One rocket followed the Range Rover down *but the other one kept coming at the plane, straight for him.* Lance's first shot missed but then he gauged the speed of the thing and his second shot struck the orange nose-cone and exploded it a hundred metres from the plane and slightly above it. Once more Lance picked himself from the floor of the plane, found his rifle, checked that it seemed all right, hoped that his eardrums were not burst, and ran to the rear lip of the plane. Robert Bruce Hilder was already there, camera to shoulder.

The plane was diving on them from perhaps two miles away and two thousand feet. When the pilot pulled the stick back, he would be lined up and aimed and it would all be over.

Lance hooked his arm through the handhold and steadied himself against it as he put his rifle to his shoulder. Out of the corner of his eye, he saw Jimmy hobble up to the other side of the door and brace himself similarly before bringing a scoped FN with a sniper barrel to his shoulder. The journalist, realizing there was no handhold for him, walked backwards into the plane.

'A rifle isn't much against a jet,' Jimmy shouted.

'Shoot into the air intake at the nose,' Lance shouted back without taking his eye from the scope. The moment he could see squarely into the air intake, that would be when the pilot had the Hercules lined up in his sights and could squeeze the trigger. Seconds later the curtain would fall on the final fiery act.

The heavy machine guns would be set for a range of about a thousand metres, Lance guessed. But a pilot who had already seen a comrade destroyed by an unarmed plane would open fire well before that. And fifteen hundred metres was the effective range of Lance's special custom rifle; Jimmy's FN was hopeless at that range even with the sniper barrel.

The air intake in Lance's scope turned ever so slightly more round than oval. The pilot was flattening out.

'Bullets striking the sand below us,' Esmeralda said behind Lance's shoulder. 'Hundred metres behind. Creeping closer.'

The pilot already had his finger on the firing button. But he was still fifteen hundred metres distant and Lance did not want to waste a bullet; he was on his last clip.

'Keep calling the range,' he told Esmeralda.

'Ninety metres. Eighty. Seventy. Moving faster. Fifty.'

The jet was twelve hundred metres away. Lance fired two shots into the air intake.

'Thirty.'

The jet was a thousand metres distant. Lance heard Jimmy fire two shots. Lance shifted his field to see the pilot. He wondered if the man sat behind armoured glass. It wasn't likely – they didn't have dogfights in the skies any more, just impersonal battles from opposing horizons with long-range rockets; the machine guns were for strafing ground troops or aircraft caught parked on airfields.

'Fifteen metres.'

How wonderfully calm Esmeralda was! Lance put two shots into the dining-plate area of the canopy in front of the pilot's face. At nine hundred metres he could not miss. Still the jet roared inexorably towards them; he could even hear the machine guns stutter over its airscream.

'Almost here,' Esmeralda said.

Lance fired the rest of his clip into the full frontal view he now had of the air intake. Jimmy, he could hear, was also emptying his clip. A heavy *clang*! near him convinced him that it was too late: the jet was lined up and –

'Here,' said Esmeralda.

316

Lance turned to push Esmeralda back out of the line of the bullets: he would never pull his arm out of the tight handhold in time. He was flung against her by the monstrous force slamming him back and, when she swung him around by her weight on his free arm, over her shoulder he saw the jet mushrooming at the bottom of the dry river bed: between them, he and Jimmy must have hit a control. Whatever, instead of pulling out of his dive to line up the fleeing transport inescapably in his sights, the pilot had flown his jet nose-first into the desert.

Esmeralda was hugging and kissing him. Lance disengaged only long enough to pick up the phone and say, 'Home, James.'

As a result of the enormous publicity the Robert Bruce Hilder film received, General Goukouni Queddei opened the border between his part of Chad and Sudan to the international relief agencies and allowed them to repatriate the Sudanese refugees to their homeland and feed and tend to the Chaddi remaining in the camp. Christine raised very substantial funds for this major relief operation and Lance opened the road from West Africa before the rainy season started, making it safe for the other relief agencies and freeing the already overloaded Sudanese road and rail system to deal with their own famished; neither Christine nor Lance thought it prudent to return in person to Chad. *Time* magazine featured Christine and Lance on their cover and, inside, speculated that it was high time the international relief agencies got tough with the brutal governments reigning in many of the hunger-stricken areas to force them to stop their petty wars and release their trucks for famine relief.

A single paragraph in the London *Telegraph* reported that thirty thousand tons of grain in granaries at Odessa, thought to be earmarked for famine relief in northern Chad, had been railed inland to feed the Soviet Republics.

The families of the Swahili who perished on the expedition grieved for a son or husband and father forever lost. Mwanzo, Jimmy and Lance (he had broken his arm in the handhold while trying to push Esmeralda clear of the machine-gun bullets) mended quickly but Pierre had to bear six months of physiotherapy before he recovered the use of his left leg and arm: he would not fight again. Jimmy saw Christine fleetingly in London and was shocked by the new lines at the corners of her mouth; already she was planning her next big campaign, against slavery, to be initiated as soon as the Hunger was beaten. Nasheer persuaded his family to let him open a London branch of their bank and saw Christine often: Jimmy thought him as obsessed with the slave trade as she was. Tanner, reunited with Ruby, was given a new Hercules by public subscription organized by Christine; he recovered his old self (though the grey hairs were permanent) but young Paul Hasluck, his co-pilot, hanged himself three days after being discharged from hospital. Major Ali found a job with a charter airline operating out of Fort Lauderdale.

In July of that year, rain fell for the first time in three years, and in November the first harvest was taken from the seedcorn brought in over roads Lance had made safe. The Hunger, if not vanquished, was in retreat. But the spectre of Famine will remain even when the present Hunger is beaten, unless radical political and agricultural reforms are undertaken – and of these there is no sign.

Nine months, almost to the day, after they flew out of Chad, Esmeralda gave birth to twins, a boy and a girl, on the game reserve Lance had bought in Kenya.